ANGELS *of* MUD

BOOKS BY VANESSA NICOLSON

The Sculpture of Maurice Lambert

Have You Been Good?

The Truth Game

ANGELS *of* MUD

A Novel

VANESSA NICOLSON

HARBOUR

First published as paperback original by Harbour in 2021
Harbour Books (East) Ltd, PO Box 10594
Chelmsford, Essex CM1 9PB
info@harbourbooks.co.uk

The drawing, *Daniel in the Lion's Den* by Parmigianino,
on page 319 is reproduced by kind permission of Christie's Ltd

A CIP record for this book is available from the British Library

ISBN 9781905128341

Typeset by Tetragon, London
Printed and bound in the UK by TJ Books Ltd, Padstow, Cornwall

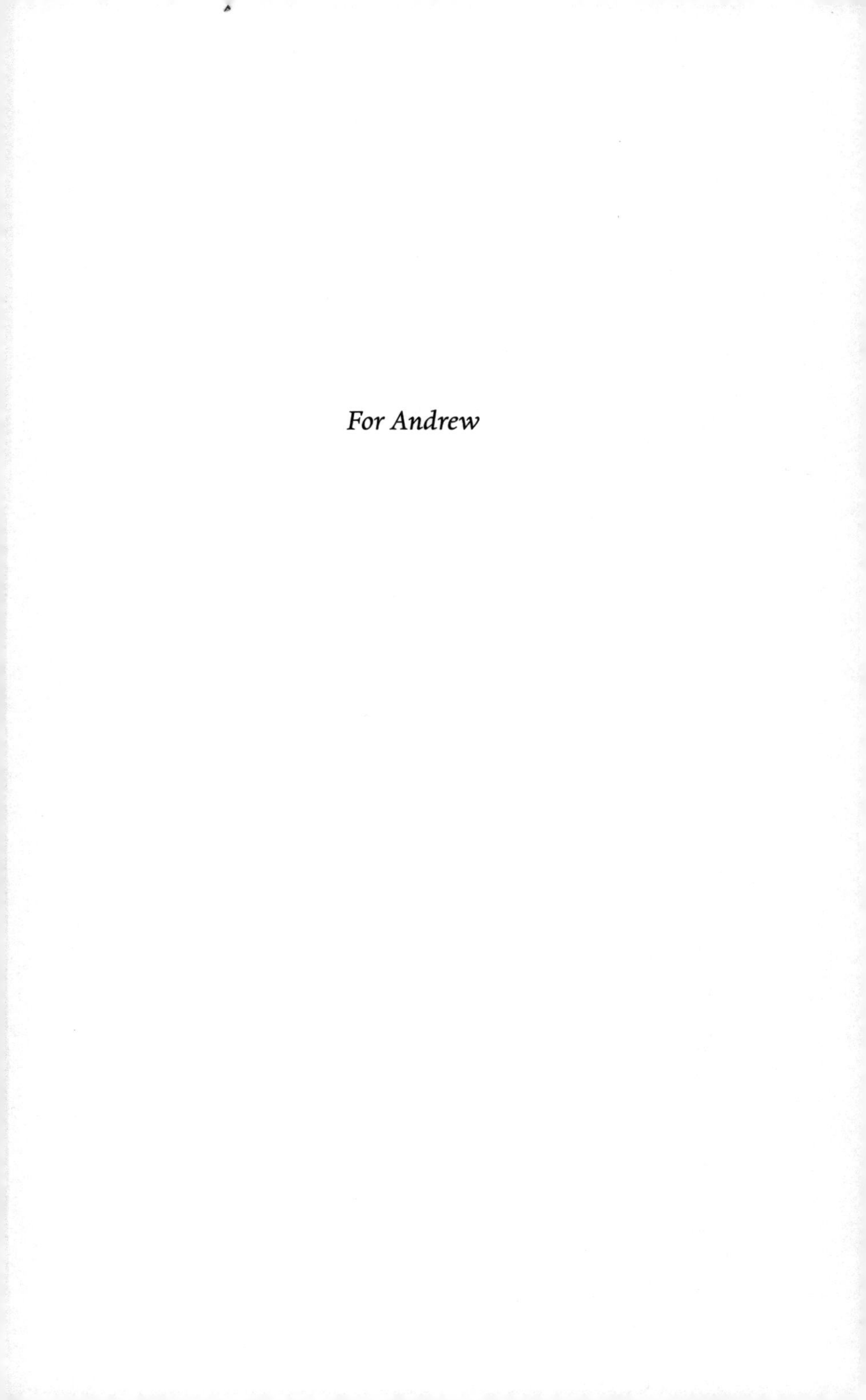

For Andrew

'Tu sei l'angelo che mi proteggerà
nella fossa dei Leoni'

(You are the angel who will protect
me in the lions' den)

1

Clerkenwell, London

OCTOBER 1959

The boy's fair appearance set him apart from the small, dark Italian children. This one was blond, good-looking and tall for a youngster of eleven. Cara watched him out of the corner of her eye whenever she had the chance, which wasn't often as the genders were separated, with the Boys' Department on the top floor and the Girls' Department in the middle.

He wasn't rough and loud like some of the others. He didn't fight or encourage the ones who did. His voice revealed no sign of an accent or the mix of Irish, Italian and Cockney common to the rest. But despite these differences, he remained popular. He larked around and made the other children laugh. These were Cara's first impressions of the new boy she had heard was called Tony Herrin.

One afternoon, as she was making her way home with her friend Paola, she heard his voice behind them. 'Hey, I need to ask you something.' He was breathless from the effort of catching up. Cara and Paola gave each other a look. Boys never usually bothered to speak to them.

'Is it true that your Miss MacMahon takes her teeth out and puts them on her desk when she wants to eat her elevenses?'

Cara and Paola giggled.

Tony turned from one to the other. 'Well?'

'Yes, she sends two of us to get her tea and a roll and then she takes her teeth out,' Paola tittered.

'And when she's got the roll, she crunches it up.' Cara made the gesture with her fist. 'And sometimes she dips it in the tea ...'

'Yeah, and sometimes it falls in,' interjected Paola.

Tony looked fascinated. 'And when she's finished she puts the teeth back in?'

'Yes!' The girls sniggered.

'You going down The Hill?' Tony said, with a grin.

As the three walked together he told them about the teachers' eccentricities in the boys' department: Mr Lewis who was about to retire and was said to be still affected by the shell shock he had suffered as a young man forty years before; Mr Matthews who liked a swig and a pinch of snuff when he thought the boys weren't looking; Mr Lynch who kept a cane behind his desk but seemed to like Tony, who, so far, had avoided feeling its sting.

Paola arrived at her house first, and Cara was tempted to walk straight past her own in order to extend the time in Tony's company. She wanted to listen to him forever. He was funny and playful and in those fifteen minutes he had brought out those same qualities in her.

That night she went over everything he had said, smiling once more at the jokes he had made, erasing Paola's presence from the memory of the short time they had spent together. Boys treated girls as if they were an alien species, but Tony didn't seem to care about that. Then the doubts arrived: tomorrow he'd pretend not to know her, he wouldn't want to be seen with her, he would be horrible to her in front of the other boys.

Her fears proved unfounded. The opposite in fact, he began seeking her out. When he walked past her house to get to school, he knocked on the door so they could walk up The Hill together in the morning, and he found her after school so that they could walk back down. Paola sulked and gave her the cold shoulder for a while, but Cara pretended not to notice. And some of the boys teased Tony and tried to pick fights – 'You a girl, Blondie?' But he shut them up by sending himself up before they could go further. 'Yes, I'm saving my dress for Christmas ...'

Rumour had it that Tony's father had been a well-off businessman, although Tony could never explain exactly what he did, and rarely saw him. The truth was that Mr Herrin had developed a taste for gambling at backgammon in private clubs, although Cara only learnt this later. His losses rapidly exceeded his winnings, money had got tight, and the family – much to Mrs Herrin's shame – had been forced to move from Hampstead to a small house in Clerkenwell.

Cara loved their house. From the outside it looked much the same as her own, but inside! The first time she entered the Herrins' sitting room (Cara's mother still referred to theirs as 'the parlour') she looked wide-eyed at the brightly patterned curtains, the teak G-plan furniture, the shiny television, the cocktail cabinet in the corner, and thought it all wonderfully modern and glamorous, if not particularly comfortable. Mrs Herrin was the same as the furniture – fashionable and hard-edged. She was distant but polite, and not unkind to Cara, who at first had been shy.

Conversely, Tony told Cara how much he liked coming to her house. He lapped up the homely teas set on patterned tablecloths, the comfortable old armchairs covered in fading tartan, the collection of books in piles on the floor. In the Herrin household, he told her, there was nothing to read apart from the *Encyclopedia Britannica* and his mother's magazines.

Their respective parents became so used to them being inseparable that they didn't worry about leaving them on their own. At school, the teasing eventually stopped, and everyone accepted the friendship. They were a unit: they bantered and joked, they finished each other's sentences, fell out and made up, just like a brother and sister would. When she was with him Cara knew she could say anything, be anything. He was on her side, and even when they didn't agree, he gave her the benefit of the doubt.

Naturally, the way they expressed physical affection as children – nudging, pushing, joshing – was going to evolve once they got older. It was the mid-1960s now. As teenagers, at the pictures, or walking along the street together, Tony's arm would come around Cara's shoulders in the way other boys' arms went around other young girls' shoulders. She would lean in, resting her head on him, loving the familiarity of his smell and the safeness she felt having him beside her.

But she became perplexed by one thing. He never attempted a kiss. Tony's jokey commentary about everything was fun but increasingly she found the tomfoolery exhausting. He was clever with words and always had a witty *bon mot* to divert her attention when the mood shifted into seriousness. Bemused, she would give way to him, but it bothered her.

He repeatedly told her she was pretty, he took an interest in her clothes, he laughed at her jokes; he was flirtatious and they embraced whenever they met and they parted, so what could be wrong? Perhaps, she wondered, she wasn't beautiful enough, and he didn't dare say.

It was far too humiliating to ask. If she and Paola had still been close, she might have sought advice, or at least shared this anxiety. But Paola went around with other girls now, and her new friend Bethan was an innocent – definitely not the type to have this kind of conversation with. On the other end of the scale there was Nancy, a girl so confident with the boys that questions of this kind would only lead to endless teasing.

Nancy would probably have suggested Cara initiate a kiss herself. But if she made the first move, wouldn't Tony perceive her as 'fast'?

In teen magazines she consulted the advice columns. 'Get with a swish hairdo and a snazzy dress, slosh on lots of perfume.' One reader had written to *Jackie* magazine worried over her date 'getting fresh' and was advised: 'If you don't want to kiss, just say no – don't duck.' But Cara was desperate for Tony to kiss her. Could she consider them boyfriend and girlfriend even if they hadn't kissed? Everyone else seemed to think they were. Mrs Herrin, much to Cara's mortification, had once called them lovebirds. She had said it tightly behind the lipsticked smile, and Tony had laughed it off. Perhaps that was it, Cara thought later, Mrs Herrin might have a better girlfriend in mind for her son. This was something she might check with him. But she never seemed to find the right moment.

The summer of 1966 was in full swing. It was a good time to be young, with London bright and full of possibilities. Even if Tony and Cara didn't go walking down the King's Road and Carnaby Street, they sensed the buzz. The Kinks and the Rolling Stones were on the radio, and everyone was talking about the World Cup – it looked like England would actually win. Neither Cara nor Tony had shown any interest in football before this, but the sense of national optimism put them in a cheerful frame of mind.

One particularly balmy evening, Cara took great care in getting ready. The cinema auditorium would be dark but she'd at least make sure she looked as good as possible when Tony came to collect her. She washed and styled her hair, carefully applied some new make-up, and dressed up in the mini shift dress that had horrified her parents.

Tony arrived, funny and attentive as usual, and both were in high spirits. Overall, the film was dull, and they made faces at each other during the more plodding parts. Later, they linked arms, laughing about the imperfections of the plot and the actors. She was drunk with the joy of being in tune with him, and when he paused outside her front door, she knew that now was the moment, and the moment must be grasped. He was lingering as if he intended to say or do something important, something of consequence.

She leant forward, tilted her head up and closed her eyes, waiting for his embrace and the softness of his lips on hers, and it was in that instant that she had no doubt she had fallen in love with him. 'Fallen' was the right word, a stumbling, tumbling, precipitous descent into something unknown, something deeper and less controllable than the affection she had felt for him up until then. This was uncharted territory. All she knew was that in that fall she had lost any power she might have held over him previously.

Tony did and said nothing, and slowly Cara opened her eyes. He was hunching his shoulders and passing his hand through his hair in that way he did when he was nervous and her heart lurched because he looked so beautiful, almost like a girl. And then the humiliation for presuming he felt about her the same way, the embarrassment in revealing that she had expected a kiss. They met up a few days later and a new distance had crept in between them. Tony was preoccupied, remote, and she was too unsure of herself to refer to the awkwardness. She simply could not address it directly, to ask him what was happening, why had the mood so changed?

The thought of what she had lost made her desperate. They had spent much of their time together leafing through Mrs Herrin's fashion magazines or looking at Cara's art books and dreaming about visiting the galleries of Europe. He was the only boy she had ever met who was interested in painting and travel and expanding his horizons beyond Clerkenwell. He stimulated her with his ideas and curiosity. He respected her. Best of all, he made her laugh.

Now she cried, punched her pillow, stared blankly at the wall. Ma had told her that you can get over these things, but what did she know.

From the safety of her bedroom, Cara could hear her mother calling. 'Come down, love, tea's ready!'

A pause.

'And I've made cake!'

Cara remained lying on her bed, gazing at the ceiling. She had been studying a mark she had never noticed before, much larger than a blemish but not as big as a face, in the expanse of yellowing cream paint. It had probably taken form during the past wet winter. For now, it was dry and fixed in its amoeba-like shape. It appeared a small island, set apart, waiting either to be covered up or joined by other stains.

The curtains were half closed, and the room was stuffy with trapped summer heat. It was unbearably claustrophobic; she should get up and let in some air. As she made to move towards the window, the sketchbook beside her slid off on to the floor, coloured pencils scattering like a broken rainbow.

'Cara!' The shout came, louder this time. Then, more cajoling: 'It's your favourite.'

Cake in the Williams household indicated a special day: a birthday, Christmas or the arrival of a visitor. That none of those factors were in place puzzled Cara. What was her mother up to? Her father was at his bookshop, so they were the only people in the house, and as far as she was aware, no one else was expected that day.

She pulled the doorknob hard after herself, to make sure the bedroom door was properly closed, wanting to keep her private space hidden. Still wearing her crumpled pyjamas despite it being late afternoon, she shuffled into the parlour, pulling at her unwashed hair.

Her dishevelled appearance matched her mood. She didn't care any more, why should she? At the table she rested her chin forlornly in her hands, a habit she had fallen into as a small child when bored or upset. 'You've got a long face on you,' her mother Mary would have said then, with affection. Today Mary was ignoring the sour face, while she busily put the finishing touches to the table.

Cara, registering that the partly laid tea-set was the posh one, wondered out loud what had happened to the usual chipped brown teapot. 'Why is the special china out? And why cake?'

'We have something to celebrate,' Mary answered brightly. 'I think you will find it exciting ...'

No I won't, Cara thought. Nothing could relieve the despondency that had snaked into the core of her being. Her mother meant well, she knew that, but the false jollity jarred, as did the deliberate avoidance of ever mentioning the momentous 'thing' her parents never acknowledged: her broken, eighteen-year-old heart. How could they expect her to act as she had before? How could they possibly understand this all-consuming pain? They had been married for years. It was beyond their experience.

'Well, as you know, I had to go to the doctor this morning to get my pills.' Mary said. She brushed some imaginary crumbs off her apron and sat down on the opposite chair.

Cara's sigh was stuck halfway down her throat.

'I had to wait for ages for my turn because the place was full of pregnant women. Mrs Patterson was there, you know, from number 42.' As she spoke, Mary poured the tea and cut a large slice of cake. It wobbled slightly before coming to rest on its side, slightly too close to the edge of the plate. With her cake fork, Cara began dissecting the layers of sponge and filling. Strawberry jam and cream oozed over the plate. She had no interest in Mrs Patterson. And the gossipy tone was irritating. It made her mother sound fussy and interfering, traits she didn't even possess.

' ... I must say she didn't look happy. She was surrounded by whining little ones; she's always shouting at one or other of them.'

Cara's nod was half-hearted, but she smiled for the first time that day. 'That woman is cross all the time, pregnant or not.'

'Yes, not surprising, with that useless husband. But she was quite chatty today.'

Through a mouthful of cake Cara mumbled, 'Is this the "exciting news" you wanted to tell me?'

'No, of course it isn't. Just listen. Mrs Patterson was called in to see Dr Gould and I picked up one of those magazines left on the table, you know one of those posh ones.'

'*Punch*?'

'No, it's called *The Lady.*'

Cara rolled her eyes.

Mary glared. 'Let me finish. So, I got to the classified advertisements at the back and something caught my eye ... this ... oh, I've left it in my handbag. Wait a minute.' She rushed out of the room and reappeared with a crumpled piece of paper that she handed over as if it were a precious gift.

'What's this?' Cara read out a list of provisions: eggs, bread, ham, tea, potatoes, flour.

'No, no, the *other* side.' Mary sighed impatiently. 'I wanted to tear the page out of the magazine, but I was worried that one of those other women in the waiting room would spot me. So I copied out the announcement on the back of my shopping list.'

Cara turned the paper over and read:

Accommodation and a small remuneration offered in exchange for part-time administrative assistance and English conversation in Florence. Age and experience less important than a responsible outlook. September–December. For further information contact …

There followed an Italian name and address.

'Are you suggesting …'

Mary interlocked her fingers and grinned. 'It's such an opportunity, I told you it was exciting!'

'But, Ma …'

'Try it! I'm not suggesting going to Australia. You've often said you'd like to see Italy. After all, you've been surrounded by Italians all your life, you probably wouldn't even notice the difference!'

Cara was unconvinced. Florence seemed a world away from Clerkenwell's Little Italy. Her mother's eagerness made her feel even more listless. Why did she have to interfere? Why couldn't she leave her be?

'I don't know, Ma.'

'You can speak a little of the language. And you love Italian painting. You've got Italy in your blood.' She paused for a few seconds. 'Come on, don't you think it's a great idea? At least write to the woman to find out more.'

'I'm not sure it's the right time …'

'It is *exactly* the right time. You're unhappy because that stupid boy has gone and ditched you. You need a change, that's all.'

A frisson went through Cara, hearing a reference to *him*. 'Tony is not stupid,' she snapped back. 'And anyway, he didn't "ditch" me.'

'You've said worse about him yourself,' Mary observed.

'That's because I was upset …'

'Well, he *was* stupid to let you down. To lead you to believe that his intentions were more serious than …'

'"His intentions?" Cara snorted. 'Tony didn't lead me on to believe anything. I just misunderstood, that's all.' She was hurt, but she felt pleasure in saying his name out loud. It brought him into the room. 'Anyway, he's probably got a girlfriend by now. I've hardly seen him around since …' Under the table she pinched herself hard. Physical pain was more bearable.

'Oh, love,' Mary said more gently, noticing Cara's expression. 'You know I always liked Tony. He's a nice lad. But the thing you will learn when you're older is that boys and men can let you down. You can't rely on them … you have to make your own way in life …' She reached across the kitchen table and squeezed her daughter's hand.

'Geoffrey hasn't let you down though, has he?'

Mary pulled herself up, withdrawing her hand rather too quickly. 'No, you're right, he has always been a good husband.' For a second the familiar look of resignation crept across her face. 'But look … you're a clever, talented girl. You've got your whole life ahead of you. You can't let a boy ditching you ruin everything …'

'I told you, I wasn't ditched!'

'Well, he's an idiot for not wanting to marry you.'

'Marry me? Who said anything about marriage? Can't you understand, I never wanted to marry him!' Funny, maverick Tony would laugh at the idea of doing anything as conventional as getting married.

'Whatever his reasons for the disappearing act, you have to put it behind you and get on with something. You're not a little girl any more. There are so many more possibilities open to you than I had as a young woman. When I was your age and the Blitz was going on, London …'

Here we go, the war. Ma and her interminable anecdotes about working on the buses – Cara couldn't face hearing it all again. Even if there was some comfort to be had from the familiarity of those stories, the suffocating sensation was happening again. She picked up her teacup and gulped down the dregs.

The dark parlour with its wooden table and the small kitchen and smaller spaces beyond had been Cara's home all her life. During that time nothing had been altered or substituted for a newer model, down to the linen tea towel, fraying at the edges, which would not be replaced until it fell apart. The 'best' tea-set that this afternoon was laid out before her, the storage jars and weighing scales, the jelly moulds, the long rolling pin and other wooden bits of equipment in the scullery: these objects had been inherited from Mary's in-laws when she'd married at the end of the war, twenty-one years before. Even the apron Mary had put on to start the baking was the one Cara had leaned into as a little girl, the one that was now straining over her mother's thickening waist.

The sweetness of the cake had made her feel slightly bilious. Perhaps she had grown out of liking it so much. The sugar was filling her with energy she couldn't release, and her nerves were frayed. Mary's voice in the background was trailing off. Now she was saying, 'You'll think about it, I hope. What an opportunity, to go to Italy! And it's landed in your lap.'

'Landed in my lap? If anything, it's landed in *your* lap.' A volcanic anger was rising up in Cara that was hard to contain. 'What is this obsession you have with everything Italian? I know our neighbours are Italian but we're not, are we? Why aren't you obsessed by everything Irish instead? Is it because you didn't like your drunken Irish father?'

Mary looked crushed, and Cara knew she should stop there, but the venom kept coming out. '*I've* got a good suggestion. Why don't *you* go to Florence? You're the one who likes those Italian things you've been pushing down my throat all my life!' Sweat gathered along her hairline. She was hot then ice cold, as if she was getting the flu. Never before had she spoken to her mother like this. And at the same time as wanting to hurt her and lash out, she longed to be taken into those arms, to absorb Mary's warmth, to be stroked and soothed like a child. *Make it better. Make him come back. Please make him come back.*

'Ma ... look ... I'm sorry. I didn't mean it. You know I love learning all the things you teach me. I'm ... I'm not feeling myself, that's all.'

She had to get away from this claustrophobic familiarity. The walls were closing in. She picked up the discarded scrap of paper from the table and waved it in the air. 'Thank you for this. I'll think about it, all right?'

Then she ran up the stairs, back to her sanctuary.

Mary had wanted everything to be perfect, for the tea to be a success. They all needed it to be. For weeks Cara had been infecting the atmosphere with her gloom, and the previous evening as they were getting ready for bed Geoffrey had muttered, 'Can't you find something – anything – to distract her? She won't even come and help in the bookshop and she isn't making any use of those secretarial skills.' It was he who had insisted on the secretarial training as something to fall back on in case Cara's artistic aspirations came to nothing.

'I'll think of something,' she had told him.

Mary knew that being a secretary held little appeal for Cara, who liked – and had a talent for – drawing and painting. But Geoffrey had made it clear that, in his view, going to art school was an admission of academic failure. It was all very well, he said, but unless you were going to be a brilliant artist – unlikely, he thought, in his daughter's case – what was the point? Typing skills led to a steady job.

That first evening, when Cara had come home tearfully upset,

Mary had felt nothing but empathy for her daughter's suffering. She understood, of course she understood, and she had tried her best to comfort and console. But as the days turned into weeks and Cara continued to be unresponsive and withdrawn, she no longer knew how to help. She was beginning to agree with her husband for once. A bit of stoicism wouldn't go amiss.

So she'd adopted a different approach: ignore the moodiness, carry on as if nothing was wrong. This didn't work either. She hated the pretence, and in any case it seemed to make matters worse. Her daughter, usually so curious and engaged with life, had become unrecognisable. In fact, they were all acting out of character. Mary knew she had begun to sound fractious, and Geoffrey was more distant than ever. At least before, the three of them had been able to rub along well enough. But now the damn boy had snapped this delicate equilibrium and infected Cara with a misery that contaminated them all. Something had to be done, and as soon as she had stumbled across the advertisement in *The Lady* she knew that, however much she would miss her, the only solution was for Cara to be removed for a while. If that meant her leaving them to live elsewhere and recover, so be it.

Mary's lip quivered as she glanced at the rejected, half-eaten slice of cake abandoned on Cara's plate. She replayed her daughter's earlier outburst, and then her own anger began to rise. How could Cara say those cruel, accusatory things? Why be so unkind? She felt wronged. From the moment Cara was born she had done everything in her power to expand her child's education and horizons. If there was one advantage to being married to a bookshop owner, it was to be able to learn, to escape into other worlds. All those stories she had read out loud to her child; the illustrated art books she had brought home; the encouragement she had given her when she showed a talent for drawing.

Frustration turned to envy. *My God, if only I had been given such a chance*. Long-held resentments began taking shape. *For Mary O'Neill to travel to Italy now! I should be so lucky. But even if it were possible, I can't just jump ship, abandoning home and marriage. But Cara, as an unshackled young woman, especially one with knowledge of the language and interested in art to boot. And …* (here she couldn't help smiling to herself) *also trained in secretarial skills*.

Regret, sadness and disappointment segued into determination that her daughter would not suffer the same fate as she had. Why wouldn't the girl let herself be guided? Especially since Tony had turned out to be a bad bet. Why remain in Clerkenwell?

The table needed clearing. She gathered the cups and saucers, the two plates, the two little forks and the hardly eaten cake. The delicate tongs that balanced over the bowl full of sugar cubes were put away for another occasion, the china washed with extra care.

'I just want her to do things better than I did.' Mary said this out loud, knowing no one would hear.

2

Florence

SEPTEMBER 1966

The first thing that struck Cara was the intensity of the heat. Never had she experienced such a swelter, not even during those unusually hot days in an English summer when everyone says they've 'never known anything like it'. The stagnant air made Florence feel even more stifling than Milan, where she had changed trains and bought a *panino* from a man wheeling his cart along the platform.

The morning before, at London's Victoria Station, her heart had squeezed as she had watched her parents diminishing in size until they were tiny dots on a grey platform. Their goodbyes had been sober, touched with resignation, as if there was no alternative to her departure, as if it were inevitable. Her change of heart, her decision to go, had seemed as natural as a shift in the weather.

The ferry at Dover had been difficult to find, and after the crossing there was another train to catch. In Paris, a *croque monsieur* and *café au lait* lifted her spirits before she boarded the sleeper, lugging the suitcase along narrow corridors and checking her ticket to locate the right couchette. It had been hard to sleep, what with the snores of the other passengers, the border-control announcements, and then the excitement of hearing foreign voices outside.

With the new morning she had staggered along the swaying train to a messy version of a lavatory with a wet, slimy floor and a broken tap. On her way back down the corridor the young soldier smoking by the window hardly shifted to make way for her, intentionally forcing contact. She sensed his body as she passed, and his eyes tracked her as she looked for her compartment. When she found it, she took her place by the window opposite a nun and stared mournfully out at the passing landscape. Her thoughts about Tony had taken root. She couldn't seem to shift them, they were always there, needling and invading. During the long train journey that was taking her farther away from him they kept revolving around in her head until the other passengers in the carriage wondered at the pretty girl who every so often squeezed her eyes shut as if cringing in an agony of shame and remorse.

The porter guided her out of Santa Maria Novella station and to the taxi rank, manhandling her suitcase while politely but firmly preventing a bustling, middle-aged woman from jumping the queue. Cara wondered how much to tip him, not yet clear about the currency: the lire notes seemed to be for thousands. In the end she passed on her change from the *panino* purchase and the porter seemed satisfied enough, grinning as he thanked her.

The taxi driver was jolly. 'This is heavy! You come for long holiday?' he asked in uncertain English as he hoisted the large suitcase into the back of his yellow taxi.

'No, I am here to work,' she answered warily, not wishing to encourage conversation.

'Ah, you are au pair?' Suitcase dealt with, the driver indicated the door to the passenger seat but she deliberately opened the back door instead. The car smelt vaguely of tobacco and plastic.

'No, not au pair.' She removed a crumpled piece of paper from her bag to check the address. '*Via Laura, angolo Via Gino Capponi.*'

She could communicate in basic Italian but felt strangely self-conscious doing so, especially as he had already spoken to her in English. '*Numero Settanta.*'

'*Si, subito.*'

The driver was pretending to look at the traffic in the rear-view mirror, but he was clearly checking her out. Foreign, in her late teens, with dark hair cut into a bob that brushed her shoulders. Pretty face. Clear skin. Doe-like brown eyes. Sweaty. Cara hoped she didn't resemble the occasional tourists walking along the pavement, big boned and red faced, clutching guidebooks or maps, looking lost and rumpled and too hot. Unusually for a British visitor, she wanted to pass for an Italian.

She looked out of the taxi window, grateful that the driver had understood she wasn't up for talking. She wanted to take everything in as the car weaved through streets and past monuments she had seen only in photographs, or depicted in the backgrounds of Renaissance paintings. The wonder of it resonated inside her – it was as if she had moved from a world of dull monochrome into one of colour; it excited her. Shutters in green, houses in red and ochre, the geometrically patterned Cathedral with its terracotta dome – bigger than she had imagined – the pinks and white of marble, the gold doors of the Baptistry.

They began driving down a long road flanked by palatial houses with a tiny pavement on either side. At the far end the street opened into a broad square edged on two sides by buildings fronted by arched colonnades punctuated with glazed blue roundels. Turning past a church and right up a side street, the driver came to a stop. '*Eccoci*, here we are!' He removed the suitcase from the boot and Cara followed him for a few yards, past a bar on the corner and into the street to their right. He deposited the suitcase on the step of a tall, old building marked number seventy.

She fumbled in her purse to get another note out.

'*Grazie signorina, arrivederci!*' He made a little bow.

'*Arrivederci!*'

Next to the large front door was a brass plaque with the tenants' surnames. Once more the crumpled letter came out of her bag. Ah, Nomellini, right at the top. She pressed the bell and a minute later a woman's voice came through. '*Si?*'

'Hello, it's Cara Williams, from Lon–'

A buzz and clicking noise interrupted her. She grabbed the handle of the suitcase and pushed the heavy door with her shoulder. The dark vestibule she came into smelt strongly of drains. As the door closed behind her and her eyes adjusted to the cool gloom, she made out another door, much smaller, in front of her, possibly leading to a cellar. Otherwise there was nothing, apart from a row of wooden post boxes identified by the tenants' names that hung on the wall.

Somewhere above her she heard a noise. Suddenly an electric light came on to reveal wide stone steps ahead. There was no lift, so no alternative but to lug the suitcase up the stairs, stopping at each landing to breathe deeply. So many steps! Above her a door abruptly slammed.

At the fourth floor, after over ninety steps, the stairs ended. Standing in an open doorway right in front of her was a slim, attractive woman in her forties wearing a light-blue, sleeveless linen dress and offering Cara her hand.

'Hello, I am Nicoletta. I am sorry about all the stairs.' The smile was practised, the English accent almost perfect. She was about the same age yet could not have been more unlike Cara's mother. Groomed rather than homely, polite but without real warmth, as if she were holding herself back. Nicoletta's world was clearly different from that of the Italian housewives Cara had come across at home.

Taking the outstretched hand, Cara noticed well-manicured nails. The handshake was soft.

'Come in, come in. You will be tired. It is hot, yes?' She stepped back to let Cara in.

'Oh yes, so very hot!' Cara's throat was parched, and she felt the beginning of a headache.

A large chest opposite the front door was covered with a piece of damask on top of which sat a beautiful bowl of orange Murano glass. The wallpaper in the narrow hall was decorated with delicate sprigs of flowers. To one side was a door with a long mirror. She quickly registered her own reflection with a critical eye before looking away, not wishing to appear vain. Her slacks looked cheap and her blouse was stained. Hair was escaping from the wide red band she wore to keep it in place, and her flat English shoes were scuffed and dusty on the polished parquet floor. She cut a sorry figure set against this woman's natural elegance.

'Could I wash my hands?'

'But of course! Here is the guest bathroom.' Nicoletta pushed open the door with the mirror to reveal an exquisite little cloakroom with marble basin, toilet and a window overlooking an internal courtyard. Still smiling at the idea of a bathroom that was only for guests, Cara looked around. The walls were covered with exotic birds and foliage, an English William Morris pattern. The smile froze on her lips. It was identical to the one Tony's parents had had in their hall before Mrs Herrin had changed it to a more modern design in geometric brown.

The excitement generated in the taxi had gone. Cara longed to be alone, to take stock, to lie in a lukewarm bath, to relax, to sleep. She wanted to hear Mary's reassuring voice telling her that coming to Italy was a great opportunity, that it would be an adventure.

At least the cold water was a relief as she splashed it on her face. She took a deep breath and whispered earnestly at her reflection, *Pull yourself together.*

Across from the cloakroom, double doors led into a sitting room, but Nicoletta's voice – 'Cara, in here!' – was calling her to another door, this one ajar. It seemed there were doors everywhere, like in a strange dream. She followed the clattering sounds and found herself in a kitchen, where, placed at one end of the wooden table, was an oval dish of sliced tomatoes and mozzarella strewn with shredded basil. Next to it was a plate with a variety of salamis and cured hams. There was a large bowl containing salad and two much smaller ones, filled with olives and anchovies. A basket of bread, jug of water and carafe of wine completed the still life.

Cara looked at the beauty of this feast with wonder.

'Do sit.' Nicoletta indicated one of the chairs.

'Please, could I have some water?'

'Of course, pour yourself some.' Nicoletta smiled. 'You have a beautiful name. Did you know Cara means "beloved" in Italian?'

'Yes, I do know. My mother told me that when I was a child. I come from that part of London known as Little Italy. We have an Italian family living next door – well, the children are grown up now but Signora Baldoni is still there. When I was little, she would hold my face in her hands and say, "Cara, Cara, Carissima." I think it embarrassed my mother! It's also an Irish name, my mother's parents were originally from Ireland ...' She stopped abruptly, afraid that she was talking too much.

'Ah, it is interesting,' Nicoletta said in a withering way, as if it wasn't at all interesting. 'Well, I hope you will pick up many more Italian words whilst you are here.' She gestured at the food. 'Please, you must eat.'

'Thank you ...' Cara took the salad servers in her hand. She didn't add that she already had a rudimentary knowledge of Italian, picked up from attending the Italian School in Clerkenwell. She felt she had said enough for now.

Nicoletta waited for her to fill her plate until she spoke again. 'I received several responses to my advertisement. But I chose you, even though your application arrived late and my husband thought you inexperienced.'

Cara looked up anxiously. Was Nicoletta regretting her choice?

'Do not look so worried. I liked your letter. You sounded like the one who wanted to visit Italy the most. That it was something you needed to do.'

'Oh yes, it was. I mean I did,' she answered quickly, with relief.

'Good. And your decorations were lovely. I mean the pictures of Italian things ...'

'I live in the Italian quarter so ...'

'Yes, you have told me this already. But really, I thought your drawings displayed a freshness ... you have a talent for design.'

'Oh, thank you. I'm looking forward to visiting the museums here.' What she said was true, so why did it sound as if she was only trying to please?

'Yes, you will have that opportunity. So, as I explained in my letter offering you the job, your main task is to list the books and objects in the apartment. Just an approximate inventory will do. I do not expect you to be an art historian. My aunt was one, and made files with photographs and information on the works of art. Just make sure everything is here and add anything that you can't find in the files. And then I would like you to come to lunch twice a week on Tuesdays and Thursdays so that my boys can practise English – and me too, of course.'

'But you already speak so well,' Cara interjected politely. She was doing it again, trying to say the right thing.

'Thank you. I studied in London just after the war. I stayed in Tite Street, where Oscar Wilde once lived. It was a boarding house for young ladies, with an old landlady. Ah, the food … it was so terrible!' She said 'terrible' with a long 'e', *teeeerible*. 'There was still … how you call it?'

Cara had no idea. 'Um …'

'Rationing.'

'Oh, yes!'

'What was I saying? Ah yes, lunch with the boys and myself. And in the mornings, beginning on Monday, you can work on the inventory here. You can type, yes?'

Cara grimaced. 'So-so.' She had not excelled in the secretarial skills course.

'Well, no matter, my husband's secretary can do that. You can write in longhand but make sure you keep a carbon copy. My aunt has left behind so much that we are not sure where to start. She never threw anything away and she never had children. My brother lives in Switzerland with his family and my husband is so often away on business that I am left with everything to sort out.'

Cara thought of asking whether Nicoletta had other living relatives but decided to stick to the task in hand. 'When you say, "an approximate inventory", how approximate do you mean?'

'The library is going to the city of Florence. We need a general inventory, it does not have to be too detailed, just the number of books, grouped by subject. You said in your letter your father is a bookseller, no? Most of the books here are about art, but there is also literature, philosophy, history, archaeology, religion. Then there are my aunt's papers and letters. When we finish eating, I shall show you around.'

The meal was rounded off with a juicy white peach followed by a shot of black coffee in a tiny cup. Cara had never tasted anything as strong. It was like swallowing burnt tar, even with a spoonful of sugar in it. Within seconds she felt the caffeine coursing through her veins, pushing out the tiredness but adding an edge of jumpy anxiety.

The meal was over, and the tour of the apartment began. Books, papers, journals were stacked on every bit of furniture and floor space and the walls were lined with shelves. 'There are more books here than in Geoffrey's bookshop,' Cara observed.

'Geoffrey?'

'My father. I've always called him by his name, since I was a little girl. I copied my mother, who always said "Geoffrey".'

'Ah.' Nicoletta paused, looking thoughtful. 'Well, books grow like mushrooms. Now, come and see the bedrooms.'

Down a long corridor there was a light-filled room with a single bed pushed against the wall. On the chest of drawers was a plaster bust of a beautiful young woman. 'This was my aunt aged twenty,' Nicoletta said, noticing Cara admiring it. 'She was engaged to a sculptor, but he never returned from the First World War to cast the portrait in bronze. That is why it is unfinished. And these ...'

Cara really wanted to know more about the aunt's engagement and the tragedy of her sweetheart's death, but Nicoletta's eyes had moved towards two austere portraits framed by heavy gilt. 'These are my grandparents.' A haughty looking man with thick moustache and sideburns stared down at Cara disapprovingly. Next to him, his wife looked pale and frightened.

'Here,' Nicoletta said, opening another door, 'is the second bedroom.' Two single beds with a small bedside table between them and a still life on the wall above, showing a delicately painted vase of anemones. This was the quieter room at the back, overlooking the deep, internal courtyard.

'Choose whichever bedroom you prefer. The linen is in there.' She pointed at a chest in the corner. 'Now come with me.' Up another flight of stairs they reached a small terrace and steep steps leading to a flat roof.

'Go on,' Nicoletta encouraged, as Cara hesitated at the foot of the iron ladder.

She climbed up to the roof and gasped. Against a bright blue sky, the panorama unfolded before her, revealing buildings she would soon be able to identify: the Churches of San Miniato and Santa Croce, the tower of Palazzo Vecchio, the green domed roof of the synagogue, the hills of Fiesole on the other side. Most impressive of all was the Cathedral – the Duomo – directly in her line of vision. Puncturing the Florentine skyline, its famous cupola looked like a large terracotta umbrella standing at the centre of the city. It gave a focus, like the point of a painting from which the eye can move around but to which it constantly returns.

And Cara's eyes did move around. Far below to her right was the large square she had passed in the taxi, framed by colonnades and a lofty church; to her left, many feet below, lay a formal garden where stately evergreen trees towered over intricate paved paths.

But to look down made her feel dizzy. Behind her was a low shed that held a water tank and an area that jutted out from the wall like a wide seat, the perfect place to rest. She knew immediately that this spot would become her place of escape. She would be able to climb those iron steps whenever she needed to feel air and space, away from all those dusty books and papers. On balmy early autumn evenings, leaning against the wall for stability, she would be able to catch the last rays of golden sun and admire the city surrounding her. And from the first time she took it all in, she was conscious that the view would remain in her memory for a long time.

Her thoughts were hard to articulate. At a visceral level she understood that this moment – the initial discovery of such beauty, face to face, combined with an awareness of its future loss – was imbued with significance, even as it was happening. The desire to photograph or sketch the view as soon as possible in order to fix it was replaced by the pleasure of simply enjoying it as an experience, like observing a beautiful sunset, or birds in flight.

Pulling back her shoulders, she breathed in the sultry air.

Tony would love this, she thought. She wanted to linger for a while, but Nicoletta might wonder what was taking her so long.

*

In Clerkenwell, Mary woke to the gentle sound of late summer rain against the windowpanes and Signora Baldoni next door, going about her business. Facing away from her Geoffrey slept, lightly snoring. Heavily framed glasses and a folded white handkerchief lay carefully placed on the bedside table. Tartan slippers were coupled neatly on the mat by the bed, positioned in the best place to be stepped into. The back of her husband's neck was pale, the mottled hairline shaved above the collar of his striped pyjamas. The wavy hair was thinning, and there were streaks of grey that Mary hadn't noticed before.

She thought about her Cara far away, feeling the conflicted emotions of longing to have her close by and relief that she had gone to forge new experiences. She knew that eventually her daughter would come round to the idea of Florence and sure enough, within a few days of the unsuccessful afternoon tea, Cara was decorating the margins of her letter to the lady in Italy with illustrations of spaghetti, ice-cream cones and bulbous, raffia-covered wine bottles. At the top of the page she had sketched an elegant frame around a convincing copy of the *Birth of Venus*. Mary worried that this might be considered childish, or at best frivolous. She did not voice this for fear of seeming critical, of sounding like her own mother.

Strangely, the evening before Cara's departure, there was a moment when she wondered whether she might discourage her from leaving. She would miss her. And there was the envy, unresolved. However much she tried to hold it down, it was there, serpent-like, whispering in her ear. Why should Cara be able to escape to enjoy opportunities she had never had? Apart from the honeymoon in St Leonards-on-Sea during the summer of 1945 and a few other trips to the coast, Mary had hardly set foot outside London, let alone been to the Continent. She had often wondered what it would be like to experience the real Italy, not the version of it found in their neighbourhood. Her friend Elsie used to say that by living in the Italian quarter they may as well be living in 'ruddy Italy' so why bother to go there? But it would be different, surely?

Geoffrey hadn't shown much enthusiasm once Cara announced she was going to Florence and staying there until Christmas. 'Three months away!' he had exclaimed. 'Is it even safe? And what do we know about the woman who placed this advertisement?' Mainly, like Elsie, he couldn't see the point of the trip. 'What can you learn about living in Italy that you haven't experienced here already?'

'There are no Botticellis in Clerkenwell,' Cara had answered cheekily, and Mary had suppressed a smile.

Geoffrey was stirring. In a moment, Mary knew, he would reach for the handkerchief and blow his nose, loudly. This was her cue to lift the eiderdown off her body, pull her nightdress down and swing her legs round to step on to the wooden floorboards. After opening the curtains, peering outside and commenting on the unseasonable weather, she knew she would say, 'I'll get the kettle on.'

In the kitchen, Mary looked at the kettle as if it were an alien object, feeling horribly lonely. She left the room and climbed the stairs to the top of the house to sit on Cara's bed. Next to it, on the floor, was a stack of *I Maestri,* a series of illustrated books on Italian artists. She picked up *Bronzino* from the top of the pile, feeling the ache of her daughter's absence but by association with this room and its objects, sensing her presence.

The reproductions were large and clear. One study of a Medici princess reminded Mary of how her beloved child used to look. The artist had managed to catch something curious and intelligent in the girl's expression, but there was wariness there too, as if she were on her guard. Another portrait, of a young man, recalled Mary's Italian neighbour's son Pippo, as he had looked twenty years ago – dark, virile, confident. Perhaps she was seeing resemblances where none existed, like discerning a landscape in a stain, or a face within the moon. Neither Cara nor Pippo were likely to have been as perfect as these sitters. Memory tends to tweak the truth. But nevertheless, Mary would have liked to frame these reproductions and hang them on the wall, to keep them fixed in her mind.

The distant sound of a whistling kettle broke the reverie, calling her back to reality. Anxiously she rushed downstairs, anticipating a kitchen full of steam. And Geoffrey would be expecting his breakfast.

3

Clerkenwell

MAY 1945

It was VE Day when Geoffrey Williams had made his proposal.

'It's so romantic,' sighed Elsie when she heard the news.

'Well, I'm not so sure about that …'

'Don't be such a misery! The war has ended, and a man wants to marry you … you should be over the moon.'

'But Geoffrey …' Mary made a face. 'He's kind and everything, but … he's not exactly Gary Cooper, is he? *And* he's ten years older than I am. That's not very romantic. And the limp …'

Elsie laughed. 'Gary Cooper is at least *twenty* years older than you. And it's not Geoffrey's fault he had polio as a child. At least it got him out of getting killed … Anyway, you're courting. That *is* romantic.' She nudged Mary in the ribs. 'And about time, I'd say.'

'It's not *really* courting though, is it?'

But Mary couldn't deny she had encouraged the attention received between the dusty bookcases at the back of Geoffrey's bookshop. For a while she had taken to lingering by his side as, together, they turned the pages of something he had picked out to show her. There was a reassuring warmth to be had in sensing him close, a welcome relief from the tension she felt when her father was at home in one of his moods, casting darkness over everything.

On top of that, the war had seemed never-ending, the bombs, the destruction, the food shortages. At last it was over.

If it hadn't been for Elsie, Mary would have stayed at home to keep her mother company. Liam O'Neill was in the pub, using the VE celebrations as an excuse to get plastered – not that he needed an excuse. But by late afternoon her friend was banging on the front door. Mary spotted her from the parlour window and shouted up the stairs. 'Ma! Elsie is here, I'm off!' Despite the warm weather, she grabbed the jacket hanging by the door – just in case – and shoved a pair of cotton gloves into her handbag.

'Hurry up, everyone's celebrating!' Elsie stood waiting on the doorstep, beaming, infecting Mary with her good humour.

Oh, to be more like Elsie. Shiny, auburn waves of hair framed her open, freckly face, and her irrepressible, vivacious laugh drew people to her. Mary was attractive, but in a less obvious way. Darker, shorter, less obviously pretty, more hesitant in expression and speech. Her best features were her green eyes and her flawless creamy skin, a cliché of Irish beauty. She had always relied on Elsie to do the talking, to get things going, to introduce some fun into their lives, even when they were little girls. It was Elsie who had instigated the games of skipping or hopscotch after school and now it was Elsie who dragged her out to the pub or the pictures or the dance halls where austerity might be forgotten, at least for an evening.

Linking arms, the friends walked along streets decorated with Union Jacks and fluttering streamers, passing groups of celebrating soldiers, sailors and civilians. Men with tricolour rosettes in buttonholes, giggling girls with red, white and blue ribbons in their hair or in crazy paper hats, confetti, banners, trestle tables covered with flowers, children with eager faces waiting to tuck in to jelly and sandwiches, small toddlers sitting up in prams gazing in wonder at the festivities, matronly women standing by to replenish cups with tea. In one street, a stage of crates outside one of the houses had been knocked up so that some older children could sing to the locals.

The two girls must have walked for hours, swept up in the excitement. Along the way they stopped and chatted to acquaintances and strangers, helping themselves from piles of small sandwiches, staying for a while with one group then moving on, walking past pubs alive with celebration. A man came out of one of the saloon bars and as the door opened they heard a blast of delirious singing from the rejoicing crowd inside. *It's a long way to Tipperary, it's a long way to go!*

Families were packing up by the time they reached a street in the East End mostly reduced to rubble. The architecture of destruction was a familiar sight all over that part of London. The remains of a row of houses framed a large bombsite where a bonfire had been lit by the revellers and was beginning to blaze.

Mary touched Elsie's arm. 'Look, over there ... I think that's Geoffrey.'

'You sure?' Elsie peered at the man standing slightly apart from the group that had gathered around the fire. She had been taken into Geoffrey's shop a couple of times by Mary but, unlike her friend, had no interest in books, nor in Geoffrey. A quietly spoken bookshop owner crippled in one leg by childhood polio, useless for war service; to Elsie he was just a man working locally who had been left behind.

Mary called out. 'Geoffrey, is that you?' For a second, he did not recognise her, and she wondered whether she had made a mistake. But then a flame illuminated their faces.

'Hello! I'm sorry, I didn't realise ...' His spectacles glinted in the firelight.

'You remember Elsie?'

He nodded distractedly.

'Can we join you?'

'Of course.'

Old mattresses were scattered amongst the debris and they set about sitting themselves down next to a small group of people also trying to make themselves comfortable around the bonfire. Two lads in uniform gestured to Elsie to sit between them. 'Come here, sweetheart! Here you are ...' they said as they passed her some beer. Elsie giggled. Someone began singing.

'Are you all right?' Mary was aware of Geoffrey next to her, motionless and silent. He looked older than his thirty-three years, hunched, with the beginning of lines at the corners of his eyes. He stared glumly into the fire without answering.

Then, 'Do you know where we are sitting?' he asked abruptly, turning towards her with watery eyes.

She returned a questioning look.

'This was my sister and her husband's house.'

'This? You mean ... right here?'

Mary had heard the news five years before, but they had hardly ever spoken of it.

'Yes, this pile of rubble was their house.'

'I ... Right here? Oh, I'm so sorry.'

'Rubble. That's what it comes down to, doesn't it? Maybe we are sitting on their bedroom wall. Or part of the nursery ...' He cleared his throat. 'You know, if I hadn't been delayed but had gone with my parents as I was supposed to that night, I would have been killed along with them. Perhaps that would have been better.'

Mary shrank with horror. 'No ... don't say that.'

'All of them dead. Mother, Father, my sister, baby Nicholas ... By the time I got to the house at lunchtime there was no sign of them, just the shell of their wrecked house. It was like a stage set with nothing in front or behind other than shattered glass and detritus. The only movement was a burst water main spraying over the mountain of rubble. And in the air the ominous smell of escaping gas.'

Instinctively, Mary put her hand over his.

'And look at it now, four years later and it's still the same.' His breath shuddered as he let it go. 'Well, I suppose if the bombing hadn't got them that night, it would have got them another time. Better maybe to be bombed at home in one's own bed,' he said with an air of resignation.

Mary wondered out loud what on earth would bring him back here, the site of so much pain. Geoffrey shrugged. 'I don't know. I suppose it's like visiting a cemetery.'

'Yes, I see. But ... What I don't understand ... that night ...' She wasn't sure whether to continue.

'Hmm?'

'Why didn't they get out when they heard the air-raid siren? They would have got to the shelter in time, wouldn't they?'

He didn't answer, as if she had posed a rhetorical question.

'I'm ... sorry,' she stammered, 'it's none of my business.'

'No, please, I've wondered the same many times. I think because there had been false alarms, and my sister was not well, and there was little Nicholas who perhaps had only just settled. I don't know. Possibly they were all too tired to move. I reckon they didn't really believe it was going to happen, thought they'd risk it. I mean, those sirens sounding off night after night ... it had got to the stage that the noise had become normal.'

'It had,' Mary agreed.

They both stared into the bonfire in silence, side by side.

'You know, when I got back to the shop, the parcels of books that had been delivered were still wrapped in brown paper. It took me weeks to find the strength to open them.'

'What were the books about?' As soon as she had asked this, she regretted it, berating herself for being insensitive.

'In any case,' he continued, taking no notice of the question, 'going to the shelters was no guarantee of survival.'

'True,' she interjected quickly, relieved that they were back on track. Then silence. She thought of the families crushed on the entrance steps of Bethnal Green station. 'Like …'

'Bethnal Green?'

'Yes. The air-raid warning was a test. They didn't need to be there at all.'

'Exactly.'

'Or the school in Canning Town …' She was getting into her stride. 'Ma's friend Vera lost her young brother Billy there. It's horrible. But it's all over now, Geoffrey. No more bombs. You've got to be thankful for that.'

'You're right …'

'Life goes on.' Now she sounded like her mother. 'Just look at Elsie,' she said, wanting to change the subject. Elsie was dancing around the bonfires with the two boys in uniform. 'Such a flirt!' Mary laughed affectionately then retracted. 'She doesn't mean anything by it though …' She didn't want Geoffrey to think her friend was a tart.

Once again, he appeared not to be listening. He started speaking to the fire. 'You're a grand girl, Mary. You're kind. And have a lovely voice.'

'Ha! Cockney–Irish?'

'It's soft and warm.'

She flushed in the dark. 'Yours is more like a schoolteacher's …'

'I was going to become a teacher if I hadn't ended up working for Father and then having to take the bookshop over.'

'What would you have taught?'

'Maths, or history.'

'Ooh, I could never do maths … I would have liked a teacher like you though. Mrs Danieli was always so strict and …'

'I hope you don't think of me as old. My sister used to tell me I could appear quite severe.'

'Oh no, you're like a schoolteacher … that is, a kindly young one …' She was beginning to feel flustered again. 'What I mean is, you – and your father – you both taught me so much, you were very generous. The day your father let me into the shop changed my life. Do you remember *The Girls' Empire*?'

'Of course I remember.' He turned towards her and smiled to encourage her to say more.

'I wanted that book more than anything.'

'We should have just given it to you.'

'I was so shy when your father opened the door to invite me in. I could hear Ma's voice in my head, telling me that a bookshop wasn't for the likes of us. She had the same view about the public library. "Waste of time, if you ask me."' Mary mimicked Nora's strong Irish accent. '"How's books going to put food on the table?"'

Geoffrey chuckled. 'Well I'm glad Father *did* open the door to you. It was about time. You'd been peering through the window long enough.'

'The wonderful smell of wood and old paper that hit me when I came in! Do you remember how you offered me a crate to turn upside down and sit on?'

He nodded. It seemed an evening for reminiscing, as well as looking ahead. 'Yes, and once you got your hands on *The Girls' Empire* you were so engrossed, it was touching …'

'I'll never forget leafing through the pages that first time. I wanted to be the girl on the cover with the long hair, outlined within a halo of gold. And all those articles with advice like *How to be Strong*! And then the stories ... If your father hadn't told me it was time to leave, I would have stayed all day.'

'He was worried that your parents would be concerned about your whereabouts.'

'That's an understatement! I'd completely forgotten the time. I ran all the way home. Da was so angry, he'd arrived back from the pub to find Ma hysterical because she didn't know where I was.'

'You kept coming, though didn't you? Even after Father died.'

'Well, you were generous, because when I hardly had any spare money to spend you would tell me to use the shop like a library, taking home secondhand books.'

'I liked suggesting what you might read. And you were only borrowing them. Did your parents mind?'

'They got used to it. I would smuggle books in but then they would find me absorbed in them. Pa ended up calling me his little bookworm.'

Those were the days when Liam O'Neill showed kindness and affection, when the drink didn't cloud his mood. But what Mary didn't disclose were the times she had made sure her father did not find her reading, for he could fly into a rage in an instant. Increasingly he found books a threat, as if his daughter's expanding education emphasised the lack of his. Once, in a temper, he tore the pages as he pulled the book away from her and she had shamefully to pretend to Geoffrey's father that it had been lost.

Mary and Geoffrey continued to stare into the fire, talking of the past, an edited past, punctuated by long silences. The flames of the bonfire were beginning to flatten into glowing embers and people were leaving for home. Elsie had disappeared along with the lad with whom she had been dancing and Mary wondered why she hadn't said goodbye.

Geoffrey had seemed preoccupied for a while, deep in thought. He cleared his throat again. 'Mary?'

'Yes?'

'This is hard to say … But … what I'd like to ask you … well … Hmm … this is a very big question.'

'What is it?'

'It's difficult to ask. Impossible really. But what I'm trying to come out with …'

'Yes?'

'I hope you don't think I'm being forward …'

'Say what's on your mind.'

'The thing is … All right, here we go. Would you consider marrying me?'

Mary gasped. 'Oh …' She hadn't expected this at all. She pulled slightly away from him and nervously pushed back her hair.

'I mean it. I've been trying to ask you for years. I'm completely, utterly serious.'

'I'm flattered Geoffrey. But really, I can't … You don't know what you're saying. You're upset about your family and tonight we're all relieved the war is over and … goodness knows how many marriage proposals have been made!'

'I know *exactly* what I'm saying.'

'No, I … I mean … Look, I'd better get back, my folks will wonder where I am.'

'Just promise me you'll give it some serious consideration.'

'I don't know, you must give me time.'

'Fair enough, I can give you time, but I shall be a sleepless man until I have your answer.' He smoothed down his trousers. 'Come on then,' he said quickly, standing up and helping her to her feet. 'I'll walk you home.'

———

It was Wednesday, the day after the proposal. Nora O'Neill was getting through the pile of ironing she had taken in, when Mary told her what Geoffrey had asked the evening before.

Nora let go of the iron and almost burnt the linen by forgetting to put it back on the stand. 'Holy Mother of God! Why didn't you tell me this last night?'

'Well, it was late and anyway … I'm not sure …'

'You're not sure?' Nora's expression was incredulous. 'My goodness, you should count yourself lucky,' she said, recomposing her features and beginning to move the iron along the length of cloth once more. 'You're no spring chicken, my girl.'

'Ma, I'm twenty-three!'

'Well none of us are getting any younger, are we? And have you noticed there aren't many men going spare? You're lucky, I tell you. He's one of the decent ones.' She briskly folded the ironed tablecloth and pulled it by the corners. 'So, what did you answer him?'

'That I had to think about it.'

'"Think about it?" What's wrong with you? Now what's stopping him going and asking another girl?'

'Not by Friday! I asked him to give me more time, but he said he wouldn't sleep until he had an answer. It's only in a couple of days. I told him I'd give him my answer by then.'

'Look at it this way, he may be a bit older, but he's got the shop … and the house is all ready for you to move into. It's in a good street – a few Eyetalians for neighbours, but it's decent people they are. And his leg doesn't slow him down much. What more could a girl wish for?'

Mary grimaced. Yes, Geoffrey offered security, but she didn't want to step into his mother's dead shoes. Cleaning, washing, ironing, cooking, like her ma did for the women who paid her because they were too rich or too lazy to do it themselves. And who knew what state Geoffrey's house was in? His parents had been dead almost five years.

As if reading her thoughts Nora said, 'And what's wrong with keeping house? It's what I do for your da.'

'Yes, and you know Da doesn't deserve it.'

'Never mind about what he deserves or not.'

'And … I'm not sure I love Geoffrey enough, you know … in that kind of way, as a husband.'

'Oh my, "in that kind of way"?' Nora snorted. 'You've been going to the pictures too much, my girl. Who are you waiting for? A handsome prince to carry you off on his white charger?'

'Well, no, but there's got to be someone more exciting than …'

'You think your father was exciting? Or come to that, any of the husbands in this street? – those that are still here at any rate, bless their souls …' Nora made a quick sign of the cross. 'What you need is someone honest you can care for, and you do care about Geoffrey, don't you? You've spent enough time in his shop.'

'Yes, I do care about him.'

'Good, because you'll have to put up with him even when he's a bloody nuisance and, mark my words, most husbands do become a bloody nuisance once they stop making an effort …'

'So why would I want to marry him if he's going to become a nuisance?'

'They all become a nuisance. But do you want to stay here the rest of your life? Turning slowly into a bitter old spinster? And you'll have to graft, you know, if you stay here. I can't keep supporting the three of us until I die.'

A few hours later there was a knock on the door, a knock that would be seared into Mary's mind forever. There was the knocking, then Nora muttering, 'Who can that be?' whilst she lightly touched the kerchief that hid the curlers beneath. Mary went to the window, trying to peer through the net curtains without being noticed, in order to see who was standing outside.

Meanwhile Nora wiped her hands on her apron and opened the front door on to a street still hung with faded victory decorations. Shreds of soiled streamers and bunting lay scattered at regular intervals along the pavement. No one had yet wanted to sweep away the party spirit.

'Oh, do come in,' Nora was saying in the voice she put on for those she deemed her 'betters'. It made Mary cringe. A man thanked her. And then Geoffrey appeared, hat in hand, stammering slightly. 'Hel-lo, Mary, it was ...' he coughed, '... Mr O'Neill I was hoping to speak to.'

Mary's heart sank a little.

Nora began calling up the stairs, 'Liam! Someone to see you!' She came back into the parlour, her smile set stiff at the lack of Liam's response, then muttered, 'Just a moment,' before going up to find him.

Mary hissed at Geoffrey, 'Why are you here?'

He looked sheepish and she realised, panic rising, why he had come.

'But I told you I'd give you an answer on Friday.'

They could hear Liam yelling, 'What does *he* want?' as he crashed down the stairs, bursting into the parlour wearing smeared long johns and a dirty vest. Nora was waving from behind him, signalling at Mary that they should leave the room.

'Sir, I ...' mumbled Geoffrey. Mary darted him a look – a mix of sympathy, embarrassment and warning – and left to join her mother on the other side of the door. The swearing and shouting they could hear lasted no longer than a minute, until the door opened, and Geoffrey strode – as much as his limp would allow – out of the house with a slam. Liam O'Neill, still perhaps a little drunk from the night before, called out behind him, 'Thinks he's so clever working in a feckin' bookshop, he's a feckin' nancy boy if ya ask me. Ya, run away, go on … Run, nancy boy …'

Nora bowed her head. The way her mother absorbed the shame enraged Mary, but they both knew that to challenge Liam would lead to a slap around the face, or worse. All Mary could do was rush out into the street, catch up with the stooped figure walking away from her, and breathlessly splutter, 'I'm so sorry, he doesn't know what he's saying when he's in one of these moods …' She hated herself for doing exactly like her mother did, make excuses to absolve Liam from his bad behaviour.

Geoffrey, tight lipped, kept limping on. Mary, skipping alongside, clutched at his jacket. 'Stop, please, listen to me …'

Finally, he came to a standstill. Regarding her intently he whispered, 'I only wanted to ask him for your hand in marriage. I couldn't wait until Friday. I have to know. You *have* to put me out of my misery.'

A decision made in an instant, a chance to escape. Her father had gone too far. She had to leave that miserable house.

'I *will* marry you,' she said abruptly, with a note of defiance.

'Oh Mary …' He gasped, as if he couldn't quite believe what he was hearing. Slowly, a grin spread across his face. 'You've made me so happy. The thought of you slipping away was unbearable.'

As he bent to kiss her, she felt calmed, made safe. But in that embrace, she was unable to dismiss an uneasy thought that over the years would keep coming back, like an echo.

You smell of dust.

*

Back in 1922, Liam O'Neill had been overjoyed by Mary's birth. 'The next one will be a boy, you can bet yer life on it,' he said as his mates slapped him on the back while he bought another round of drinks. But there was never to be a 'next one'. In time the pregnancies were no longer celebrated because within a month or so they would end in a mess of blood and tears. The doctors could never give a reason why.

The miscarriages that marked the following years took their toll on both parents. Nora turned to her faith for the answer – 'It's the will of God' – whilst her husband turned to drink. Drink alleviated the pain Liam felt he should not feel, let alone show. He had been a social drinker but became a bitter boozer, at best maudlin and sentimental, at worst angry and confrontational.

As a young man fresh from Ireland he had been a good worker and had aspired to becoming a foreman. The work was hard, but he made a decent wage. He managed to scrape together enough money to buy their tiny house and in his spare time mended the broken floorboards and patched the roof. He even taught himself enough to fix the plumbing and with the help of a friend got the electrics sorted. The neighbourhood was poor – in reality, it was more of a slum – but he was proud that his wife wasn't stuck in a damp boarding house like so many of his Irish compatriots.

The alcoholism – although he would not have called it that – crept up on him slowly. The occasional drink became a daily habit, taken earlier and earlier. He began arriving late for work and when the labouring jobs ended and he had to go back to waiting with the other men to be recruited, he got selected less, as if the foremen knew he was unreliable. For a while, his friends tried to cover for him, but in the end they no longer bothered. They had their own problems, and in any case why should they help a man who was quick to pick fights, throwing punches and insults? He regularly came home with a bloody nose, waking his wife and daughter as he crashed into the house. As a child and then a young woman listening to him retching and swearing and spitting, all Mary longed for was silence.

Liam's belly had become distended and his features rougher. When he was sober, he would be contrite and promise he would mend his ways. But Nora and Mary knew they were meaningless words.

Nora, despite her carping and her absurd snobberies, looked out for her small family. But why was she so impressed by some of the women she cleaned and sewed for? To Mary they sounded intolerable. What was there to admire in their airs and graces, their condescending gifts of hand-me-downs and good works? But for Nora they represented a world of cleanliness and security, of crisp clothes and home decorating. Of happy, efficient, smiling wives with trim waists. Even the ration-filled years of making-do did not seem to diminish the comfort of their homes. Nora loved the ladies' magazines discarded by her employers, even if, by the time they were passed on to her, they were long out of date. She brought them home to savour every page, avidly reading articles with headlines like 'Let the Guest Room Play a Dual Role!' And she could indulge in the fantasy of a genteel visitor coming to stay, at least for the time it took to drink her cup of tea.

This was the world she wanted for Mary and she imagined Geoffrey would provide it.

Mary and Geoffrey Williams were married in the Italian Church, Clerkenwell, a few weeks after VJ day. Mary had received First Communion there. She loved everything about St Peter's, in the heart of 'Little Italy': the holy water at the entrance, the individual chapels illustrated with stories from the Bible, the Neapolitan crib set up in December and the banners and statue of the Virgin brought out for the summer procession in July.

As a small child she had been awed by the richness of the materials that had gone into the decoration of the church. The high altar had a canopy supported by opulent black and gold marble columns, the wooden angels were gilded, the stained glass glowed with translucence. Every element combined to offer comfort and delight. It was theatre really; the environment a stage set, the priests and altar boys the actors, dressed in bright costumes. She was fascinated by the Italian families who gathered for Sunday Mass and to celebrate Easter and Christmas, everyone out in their best clothes, the old ladies muttering as they fingered their rosaries, the younger women chattering in dialects she could not understand. Mary absorbed the foreignness and colour of the Italian community, transported into a world beyond the wet lanes and sooty bricks of Clerkenwell. But despite having made friends with Italian girls at the Catholic school nearby, she always felt peripheral to that community. The Italian boys were friendly but kept their distance, even if some of them had married Irish girls. It was as if they were wary of trusting too much.

In the summer of 1945, the Italian clergy were still interned, so a group of Irish priests had come to serve the congregation's needs. Nora, convinced that by washing and mending the altar linen she would counteract the damage to her family's reputation caused by her husband's drunkenness, was happy about this. 'Father Kelly will see you all right,' she said on the morning of the wedding. Even her husband had come round to the idea of the marriage and managed to postpone getting drunk until after Mary and Geoffrey had left for their honeymoon.

As Mary stood in the parlour that morning while Nora checked the hem and folds of the dress they had made from material acquired with their coupons, her eyes fell on the photograph of her parents' wedding day taken twenty-five years earlier. It showed a young and smiling couple, Nora with hair cut into a newly fashionable bob,

Liam in a suit that didn't quite fit, passed down by an older brother, one of several who had remained in Ireland.

The photograph came back into her mind for a brief moment, a fraction of time in that long interminable day, when Father Kelly asked her to promise to love, cherish and obey. Glancing sideways at the gathering of friends and family, she saw her mother, head held high, looking proud because in her eyes her daughter was marrying well. Liam O'Neill was sober for once and Elsie was smiling, looking pretty next to her young man, the one she had met on VE day. They were all there to celebrate hope for the future. How could she let them down? How could she humiliate Geoffrey, kind Geoffrey who had no one left?

She felt a ringing in her ears and pulled herself together.

... till death us do part, according to God's holy ordinance.

It was just the beginning, but it felt like the end.

At the seaside hotel they followed the landlady up to their room. 'The best room of the house,' the woman had said in a way that seemed practised and insincere. The room had pretentions to be something grander than it was. Twisted rope ties held the swept-back curtains in place. A screen was covered in similar material but here the floral pattern was brighter, less faded by the sun. The carpet was threadbare and the counterpane slightly grubby, giving an overall impression of dreary dinginess. As soon as the landlady had left them alone Mary glanced at the bed and tried not to think too much about the other honeymooners who had occupied the room before them.

She clicked open her case and pulled out a new satin nightdress, draping it over the bed like a maid might for a lady, unpacking the rest of her clothes and placing them tidily in the old chest of drawers. Later, after a supper of ham and potatoes in the dining room, they came back upstairs and as she picked up her nightie she thought with both relief and sadness, *this is the first night in my life that I have been away from home*. She went behind the screen to undress, even though Geoffrey was washing in the bathroom along the passage – unnecessary considering there was a washstand in the corner.

'You are lovely,' he said when he came in, wearing his pyjamas.

She was standing by the screen, waiting for her husband as if to be checked for suitability. Her satin nightdress skimmed her knees, its delicate straps slack over her bony shoulders. She glanced at her distant reflection in the mirror hanging on a chain on the wall behind him. Her face was perhaps a little thin from the deprivations of war, and the ivory of the nightdress emphasised her pallor, but she could see from his face that in that moment Geoffrey found her beautiful, and that was gratifying.

They both climbed under the pink eiderdown, lying side by side like a medieval couple stretched out on a sepulchral tomb.

'I haven't done this before,' said Geoffrey.

'Done this?'

'You know.'

'Oh! Neither have I,' she said.

He began caressing her as he would the cover of a rare book, savouring the moment before opening it to see what was inside. Gently admiring, respectful. She let herself be stroked, feeling more akin to a pet than a new wife. Should she stroke him back?

He had removed his round wire-rimmed glasses and placed them carefully on the bedside table, as he was to do every night for the rest of their married life. Without them his eyes took a different form: small, squinting. He looked like a stranger. Not turning but reaching towards him, she touched the short, crinkly hair, slicked back with pomade that morning in preparation for his wedding day.

As he climbed on top of her and her nightdress rode up, she could see the mix of fear and desire in his eyes. All they had shared during their short engagement – in the physical sense – were a few kisses instigated by him. She liked being treated gently. He was, in every sense, a gentleman. But why now, on her wedding night, did she feel nothing but duty and a vague disquiet about the whole business?

Geoffrey's exertions were soon over, and he rolled away from her. Turning towards the wall, she felt loneliness wash over her like a wave.

Count your blessings, Nora had said.

Perhaps Nora was right. Geoffrey was a better bet than most of the someday-to-be-husbands she had grown up with, those local lads who scrounged cigarettes off each other and chased her and her friends. With some she had flirted even, or given in to the odd cuddle on the way home from a dance or the pub or the pictures; had let them lean her against a lamp-post or a wall and do their fumbling. So many of them had left though, in those long, grey war years, and were still gone. Gone in the widest sense: either had not yet come back or never would, or had returned as older, damaged versions of their younger selves – physically and mentally changed, broken in some fundamental way.

Her eyes closed. Finally, she felt tiredness overwhelm her, an exhaustion born of thinking too many sad thoughts. Before she fell asleep, she tried to dismiss the lingering unease and discontent she felt in her heart. It had been a long day, after all.

'I'm sure you will learn to love me,' Geoffrey was saying as Mary played with her breakfast in the cheap seaside hotel. How unappetising the food looked, just one slice of undercooked bacon sitting uncomfortably next to a poached egg, withered inside its white, vinegary sack. She could taste the greasy, tart combination even before she had lifted the fork to her mouth.

'I trust you don't feel it was a mistake?' He looked at her earnestly, before tucking into his kippers. Was he referring to the wedding? Or the wedding night?

She reached for a triangle of white toast and smiled weakly. 'Darling, everything is perfectly fine.'

Darling! Why had she called him darling? *Getting above yourself.* Ma's words were in her head again. Wasn't *darling* what married women said, the ones in motion pictures, anyway?

He seemed reassured by her answer and changed the subject. 'What do you think we should do today?'

'I don't mind,' she said, turning to look out of the window. The advertisement for the hotel had promised 'Hot and Cold Water. Tea. Breakfast. Sea Views.' All present, but Mary noticed only drabness in the furnishings and the weather on this breezy September day.

'Don't you think those screeching seagulls would drive you crazy after a while?' She said it quietly, as if to herself.

'Hmm? A walk perhaps? We could stroll along the seafront. Or explore the streets nearby.'

'That sounds nice,' she answered unenthusiastically, 'if you can manage it.'

'What do you mean, manage it?'

'You know, with your limp ...'

'The limp isn't painful, it doesn't really affect me at all,' he snapped, adding in a kinder tone, 'but thank you for your concern. Yes, a walk is a splendid idea. You never know, we might even find a bookshop!'

She nodded before realising this was his attempt at a joke and forced herself to smile. 'Yes, we can compare it to yours,' she answered, trying hard to look amused.

'Don't forget, the bookshop is yours too now.'

Mary looked at her pale, earnest, well-spoken husband. Geoffrey, who loved her. A man so different from her dark, swarthy, unpredictable, father.

She glanced at the others in the dining room. Couples mostly, some middle aged and silent, others youthful and amorous. Her eyes lingered on a pair who had forgotten their food and were holding hands across the table. She wondered whether they were lovers on an illicit weekend and felt a pang of envy for the young woman, flushed, animated, wrapped up in the attention of her companion.

Geoffrey interrupted her musing. 'Well, I suggest we get our mackintoshes before we go out. Looks like rain.' Napkin in hand, he brushed some crumbs away from the edge of the tablecloth before turning to her with a smile. 'All finished? Shall we go back upstairs?'

Mary answered flatly. 'Yes, of course.'

Elsie and Mary stood in a shop on Farringdon Road behind a portly middle-aged woman asking for groceries in Italian. Every time they thought she had finished, she pointed at something else. She was taking forever.

'No, we couldn't have been any more unlucky, what with the weather!' Mary was answering a torrent of questions from Elsie about the honeymoon. 'Solid rain for days.'

'So, you and Geoffrey had to stay in your bedroom most of the time then?' Elsie made her naughty crinkled-nose expression.

'Well, I don't know about that ...'

'Oh, come on now, don't be boring! Spill the beans ...'

'No beans to spill. St Leonards-on-Sea in the rain isn't exactly St Moritz is it?'

'I ain't talking about the weather, am I?' Elsie grinned.

'We played cards, mostly.'

'Cards? You joking? Why in heaven's name would you bring a pack of cards on your honeymoon?'

'They were there. At the hotel, in the drawing room. Geoffrey taught me whist. And patience.'

'Ha! "Patience". You'll be needing some o' that! Couldn't he think of anything better to do? Something a bit more … fun?'

'Fun?'

'I dunno, like going dancing or something.'

'Can you picture Geoffrey dancing?' The comment came out more harshly than she'd intended.

Elsie smirked, not unkindly. 'I suppose not. Well, what else did you do with yourselves then?'

'There was a woman telling fortunes on the seafront, but Geoffrey thinks fortune tellers are a waste of money. Anyway, as I said, it rained so much we mostly stayed indoors.'

'You're impossible! Come on, tell me something more interesting,' she lowered her voice. 'What was it like … you know, with Geoffrey?'

Mary stuck her nose in the air with mock haughtiness. 'I don't know what you're talking about, I'm sure!'

'*Grazie, signora*,' the Italian shopkeeper was saying, as he took some change from the woman in front of them.

'Good morning,' said Mary politely, recognising the profile of her neighbour, Nanella Baldoni.

'It eez Mrs Williams, Geoffrey's new wife, is right?' Mrs Baldoni turned her head in Mary's direction as she clipped her purse shut.

'Yes, I'm Mary, and this is my friend Elsie …' But Elsie had already started asking the shopkeeper for her bacon ration and didn't hear. 'How are you, Mrs Baldoni?'

'I very 'appy.' Her accent was strong, with the sing-song Italian cadence common in the district. She was short and squat, with a round, open face and a warm smile. 'My boy, Filippo, he arrive to see his mamma. His cousin got him building job so he stay. He be with his little brother and sister. They need him …' She put her hands together in a prayer position, a caricature – Mary thought – of a pious woman. 'Now that his poor father has been taken from us, God rest his soul …'

'Yes, I'm so sorry,' mumbled Mary. 'Geoffrey told me …'

'All yours!' said Elsie brightly, turning away from the counter.

'Elsie, this is Mrs Baldoni, our neighbour.'

'How do you do?' Elsie nodded.

'You no worry, I go home now.' Nanella Baldoni smiled at both the young women, but particularly, Mary noticed, at Elsie. 'You come meet Filippo? He like company of beautiful woman!'

Yes, thought Mary with an envious twinge. Because Elsie is more desirable, and I am spoken for, no longer free.

'*Arrivederci e grazie*!' Mrs Baldoni called out to the shopkeeper on her way out of the shop. With her hand on the doorknob she looked back and repeated, 'You come and meet my Filippo, eh?'

Walking home with their provisions, Mary was quiet. It was left to Elsie to break the silence. 'What was that about? I caught something the lady was saying to you about her husband. Was he one of the men that went down in that ship?'

'What?'

'You know, the one torpedoed by the Germans five years ago?'

'Yes, yes he was. I was just thinking about that. Drowned with his brother and his father-in-law. All those men … There were almost five hundred on that ship.'

'They were mostly Eyeties, though, weren't they?'

Mary scowled at Elsie's brutishness. 'Does that mean it is less tragic?'

''Course not! My, you're touchy today.'

'Sorry. It's just that Geoffrey told me that Mrs Baldoni's husband, her brother-in-law and her father weren't at all dangerous, his parents knew them as good neighbours. They weren't "undesirables", they were anti-fascists. Why would they leave wives and children? It makes me so upset to think ...'

'That's what I'm saying, they were probably forced to go ...'

'You're right.' Mary shook her head. 'Such a tragedy. It wasn't long after that when Geoffrey's sister's house got that direct hit.' She paused. 'Bloody Germans.'

'Bloody Germans,' repeated Elsie. 'The ship had lots of Germans in it too, didn't it? Internees, prisoners of war. So basically, it was Germans killing Germans ...'

'... and Italians who were supposed to be on the same side! Lucky for Mrs Baldoni her son stayed in Italy during the war. At least she didn't lose him too.'

'He's been away five years? Why isn't *she* going back to Italy? She must have other family there.'

'I suppose she's made a life here with her younger children. Poor woman,' said Mary. 'Now he's coming to London so no wonder she's happy.'

''Ere,' Elsie nudged her friend, in a change of mood. 'D'you think he's good looking? They're quite handsome, ain't they, these Eyeties?'

'Yes, if you like that sort of thing,' Mary answered as they turned into her street.

Mary got her chance to check him over on Elsie's behalf a few days later as she was picking up milk bottles from the doorstep.

'*Signora*,' she heard behind her.

A man in his late twenties was standing by her neighbour's door. He was dressed in baggy trousers held up by braces and a beige shirt with the sleeves rolled up well above his elbows.

Thick black hair, eyes deep brown.

He put one hand on his chest. 'I am Filippo Baldoni. My mother told me you and your friend are very nice.' He pronounced it *naice*, with a long 'a'.

'How do you do?'

'How do you do?' Filippo mimicked. 'I like the English! Very … how you say? Polite.'

'Well, I'm Irish actually …'

'I beg your pardon,' Filippo said, as if reciting lines, and bowed with a flourish. Was he mocking her?

'Not that it matters,' she said, less stiffly. 'Anyhow, I must get back to my jobs.' She had left the front door ajar and now kicked it open with one foot, slamming it shut with the other once she had got inside. She rested the milk bottles down on the little table in the entrance hall feeling unsettled, not knowing why. He wasn't that good looking. Rather short. Stocky. Ears a bit large. Muscular. Eyebrows too thick.

So dark, so earthy, so hairy. So male.

She shivered, pulling herself together, and looked at her list of chores, written as a reminder of the tasks that needed doing. Her mother had suggested this practice, inspired by the lists the ladies left out for her when she went to clean their homes. Clearly Geoffrey's house, despite having two bedrooms, a parlour, a dining room, a kitchen and a yard with a privy, was not as large, but the basics were the same. Sweep porch and steps. Lay fires. Mop surrounds and dust. Look over larder, check provisions.

Mop and dust, mop and dust. She put the food away but would leave the rest until later.

Mary wasn't sure where she was going, but needed to walk for the sake of walking, without the goal of doing errands. She passed rows of houses with their façades still covered with soot, and open craters created by bombing raids. Children played in the debris of rubble and clay, mothers passed, wheeling prams.

She strolled aimlessly on through the streets she knew so well, made less familiar by the battering they had suffered. A city reduced by the upheavals of war. Although she was ashamed to think it, the destruction that had caused so much suffering now created space. She could breathe more easily. It wasn't logical and she would never have been able to explain it to Geoffrey, but this exposure of streets previously hidden made her feel less hemmed in. It was as if the city had shed its old skin and was in waiting for a new one, and that felt exciting.

And then there was nature, reasserting herself, glorious in her resilience, determined to impose her mark on this bare, skeleton city. The optimism of growth and renewal: a butterfly emerging from a pile of fallen stone, clumps of wild flowers flourishing amongst the wrecks of houses, pushing through crevices and railings and cracks in the pavements. Flashes of colour relieving the grey, the mud and the clay. Mary stopped and looked and took it all in. But soon her sense of purpose and responsibility took over and she found herself turning back. She had to get those chores done.

It didn't take long for Mary to get to know her new home, and the life that was expected of her, now that she was Mrs Williams. Geoffrey had carried on sleeping in his own room after the bomb had destroyed his sister's house and family. When he brought Mary back from their honeymoon, their first night was spent in there, as if he could not sully his parents' bedroom by bringing into it a bride.

After an uncomfortable night, Mary tentatively suggested they should move to the larger matrimonial bed. This they did, but when she went to fill the heavy brown wardrobe with her clothes, she found her dead in-laws' outfits still hanging there. She swallowed her repulsion and moved the suits and dresses to one side, and without sorting through the contents of the chest of drawers she stuffed everything together in the bottom drawer, freeing up some space for her things. Geoffrey continued to keep his own clothes – and those he wore of his father's – in his room.

It was this habit of wearing some of his father's clothes that gave Geoffrey an old-fashioned air. A cardigan or scarf appropriated from Mr Williams senior lent a certain gravitas to the younger man but made him appear older than his years. In the early stage of marriage this offered Mary some comfort – she had found a father figure who had paternal attributes very different from those of her own father. She didn't miss Da's moods, unreliability, his harsh words and inebriated behaviour, or having to be on constant alert to know when to make herself scarce. Geoffrey was polite, considerate and attentive. She would look at him buttering his toast in the morning, or putting on his pyjamas at night, and be reminded of her mother's words, 'He is a decent man.'

A year had passed, and it wasn't happening. *Maybe I'm like Ma,* thought Mary.

Barren.

Could there be a worse description of a woman?

Like a bleak landscape devoid of trees, bare and desolate, incapable of nurturing new life. Empty.

'I'm only just twenty-four years old and already dried up and withered,' she wanted to say to Elsie when they bumped into each other in the street. 'What can I do?'

But she couldn't say this. It would be disloyal to Geoffrey. In any case the two women were seeing less of each other since Elsie had got a job in one of the Italian cafés on the main road.

Elsie loved flirting with the workmen who came into the café and was picking up more Italian from the family who ran it. 'The regulars call out *bambola* to get my attention. Do you know what it means?'

Yes, Mary had heard that word before. Italian boys in the neighbourhood had sometimes called her that too. 'But Elsie, why would you want to be called a "doll"?'

'Yeah, the first time one of the boys said that, I thought it was cheeky. I wanted to bust his chops, but then I thought it was sweet. They all call me that now.'

'What happened to Jack?' Jack was the young man Elsie had met around the bonfire on VE day.

'Oh, he's history. Plenty more fish as they say.'

Mary nodded sagely, feeling priggish and disapproving.

'You're looking sad, Mary.'

She lied. 'No, I'm not sad.'

'You'll be having a baby one of these days, and …'

'Doesn't look like it. Much as I want it to happen.'

'Oh, Mary! There's me scared about getting myself up the duff, and you wanting it to 'appen. Sorry, shouldn't say that should I?' She chirruped on in her well-meaning, tactless way. 'I wouldn't worry. It could take ages. Enjoy it being just the two of you, think of all that bawling and nappy-washing to come …' She scrunched up her pretty face and grinned. 'The good thing is you can have lots of fun trying! I know you'll have a beautiful baby in the end.'

Mary trembled inside at the thought of the months ahead, being subjected to Geoffrey's mechanical attempts at love-making, Saturday nights mostly, after an evening of listening to the wireless. Months, stretching into years. She was already sick of her life as a housewife: the food shortages, the restrictions, the coupons and rations, the domestic responsibilities of keeping house efficiently.

Mostly she was tired of pretending that everything was running smoothly, being careful never to divulge any frustration or dissatisfaction, not to her parents, not to Geoffrey, not even to Elsie.

Months passed and still no baby. People stopped making enquiries as to whether she had any good news to tell. But she could read the question in their faces, and her longing increased. Was she the problem, or could it be Geoffrey? Given her mother's difficulties in conceiving, she decided it must be her fault. But she would not give up, ever hopeful. Once a week Geoffrey would perform his marital duty. They pretended the unsatisfactory ritual was not happening, and it was never referred to. Mary's regret was that this man who was essentially decent could not make her happy, and surely Geoffrey's sadness was that he was only too aware of her feelings. Perhaps he hoped that if he persevered, things would improve.

4

Florence

SEPTEMBER 1966

Cara's first morning began, as every morning in the apartment was to begin, with the peal of bells from the church next door. The travel alarm clock by her bedside that Geoffrey had given her said 7 a.m. Her initial sensation was relief that the glass-shelved bookcase screwed to the wall directly above her had not dislodged overnight, releasing all those hardbacks on to her head. The night before she had hesitated when deciding on which bedroom to choose, but the forbidding-looking couple in the family portraits – the Victorian gent with handlebar moustache paired with a dour woman overdressed in black and lace – put her off the smaller bedroom. In any case, it overlooked a street noisy with the revving of motor scooters and men shouting, a cacophony of sounds she would for evermore associate with Italy. The other room with the two single beds was quieter. An occasional shout from the harassed mother in the apartment below calling her children – 'Massimo! Michele!' – otherwise silence.

That is, apart from the bells. Cara hadn't taken account of the nearby church waking her so early. In a state of half sleep, half wakefulness, with the bells ringing in the background, her thoughts, yet again, turned to Tony. They always did. She had left London quietly. Part of her longed for Tony to walk past her house at the precise moment she was leaving and beg her to stay. She felt broken, fragmented, and part of her wanted him to suffer too, even just a fraction of what she was suffering. When she decided to leave for Italy, she didn't seek him out to tell him, despite desperately wanting to do so. Her feeling was to let him find out and be sorry.

With the shutters closed, the room was dark. The smell of burning incense lingered from the coil Nicoletta had given her to ward off mosquitoes. It made her headache worse. She untangled herself from the linen sheet, damp with sweat, and sighed as the bells started up again, only fifteen minutes after they last stopped ringing.

She hoped she would get used to the bells. Ma used to tell her, with information gleaned from Italian neighbours, that death knells in Italy commonly tolled nine times for men and six times for women. According to Mary this was another example of women's subordination: from what she had seen in 'Little Italy', men had it easy. 'If you ask me, the women work twice as hard but get half the respect,' she'd concluded. 'Lazy scoundrels most of them,' repeating her own mother's favourite words.

Cara smiled sadly to herself remembering Ma's comments and Grandma Nora's mutterings, boring to hear at the time but now tinged with the melancholy of missing home. She turned over in the bed with eyes still shut. But when the bells started again at 7.30 a.m. she decided to give up on a return to sleep. In any case, the usual thoughts, those she needed to keep at bay, kept intruding.

Let him find out that I have gone. Let him miss me. Let him regret not loving me back.

She wandered sleepily towards the kitchen to make coffee the way Nicoletta had demonstrated yesterday. The cool of the marble floor underfoot felt good.

There was no kettle, just a coffee percolator and basic provisions: sugar, honey, olive oil, spaghetti and bread that seemed to lack salt and taste a bit stale. She had also been left eggs and a pulpy tomato sauce to be heated up later with the spaghetti.

She had clear instructions. Today was Friday and she had the weekend to orient herself and settle in. On Monday, she would begin compiling the inventory. On Tuesday, she was to walk across Florence for lunch as agreed and make English conversation with Nicoletta and her boys.

'Just work through it room by room, perhaps two hours in the morning and a couple in the afternoon, and bring me what you have done on Tuesday when you come over,' Nicoletta had said.

Between these commitments she planned to explore the city. Nicoletta had suggested some courses on Renaissance Art at the British Institute, but these were expensive. *That's what rich girls do,* Cara thought – *take Italian and art-history classes, before going back to England and forgetting it all.* She would not be like that. Her intention was to discover the art treasures herself, face to face. And erase Tony from her mind. As she sipped her coffee, she felt stronger.

After breakfast she unpacked. She had been too tired to do so after Nicoletta left. In her bedroom of choice was a huge armoire, lightly decorated with a floral motif. The two central doors revealed six drawers, like a hidden chest. Inset into the inner sides of the doors were mirrors, so if she positioned herself in a certain way, she could see her back and front simultaneously. She looked better than yesterday. In fresh clothes, her hair washed, she was ready for anything.

But as she opened one of the drawers and looked inside, she felt unsettled by seeing the limp paw of an animal. Out of a bag emerged not only a whole leg but also a tail and the head of what appeared to be a fox – the full pelt – made into a stole. How horrible!

She frowned. How could women wear those things around their shoulders? Next to it in a larger drawstring bag was a cape of soft brown fur that was slightly more appealing, but the sweet odour of camphor mixed with lavender was sickly. It was overwhelmingly redolent of the past.

She closed the drawer and opened the one above. Envelopes made of satin contained clips and fastenings, suspenders, seamed stockings and corsets. Everything was a light shade of pink. Nicoletta hadn't mentioned making an inventory of the clothes. She would have to ask about that. But meanwhile where could she store her own clothes? Every drawer was overflowing with stuff. In the hanging section of the wardrobe were drop-waist dresses, little sequined boleros and beaded evening dresses that might have been worn in the 1920s. A beautiful Chinese robe of blue and yellow satin looked as if it should hang in a museum. Then there were the tailored suits and coats of more recent times. On the shelf above, hats of every shape and size – large straw ones and small cloche and pillbox ones; on the floor of the wardrobe were boxes of shoes stacked high.

She pulled everything over to one side of the wardrobe and hung up a few summer dresses and blouses of her own on the other. The winter things could remain in her suitcase until needed. With a kick, she pushed the suitcase under the bed. She must get out now and start exploring before the day was gone.

Halfway down the communal staircase she met a middle-aged man with a little moustache who was coming up towards her. He touched his hat in greeting.

'*Buongiorno!*'

'*Buongiorno,*' she echoed.

'*Lei é la signorina inglese che è venuta a lavorare per la nipote della signora Nomellini?*' He spoke very quickly.

Cara understood the gist of the sentence from *signorina inglese* to Nomellini – that was the surname on the bell, Nicoletta's aunt.

She gestured up the stairs. 'Signora Nomellini?'

The man nodded.

'*Signorina inglese, si!*' pointing at herself.

The man smiled and offered his hand. 'Fernando Lotti, *piacere*.' With his other hand he pointed to the door on the second floor. '*Il mio apartamento*.'

'Cara Williams,' she said, shaking his hand. '*Piacere*.'

Leaving the house and walking around the corner, she found herself in the piazza with the church. Cara knew that she should probably go and familiarise herself with the neighbourhood and buy some food. The day before Nicoletta had explained that the road leading from the piazza to the Cathedral had everything she would need and that until recently the old vegetable seller delivered to the apartment.

'He carried all the heavy things up to my aunt's door,' Nicoletta had told her.

'Up all those stairs?'

'Yes, of course up the stairs,' Nicoletta had answered. 'But he's gone now, and his son Beppe runs the shop. If you don't want to go there, there is a cheaper market at St Ambrogio. I shall show you where it is on the map. If you go at lunchtime the *contadini*, how you say … the peasants, they come from around Florence and sell everything cheaply so as not to carry it all back.'

'Peasants?' Did she mean farmers? Maybe in Italian it didn't sound so patronising.

In any case, Cara decided to leave the shopping until later. There was something she wanted to see first. Something she had grown up with, something that had hung on her bedroom wall.

Her bedroom in Clerkenwell, like the rest of the house, had barely changed since her childhood. The pretty rose-patterned eiderdown and matching curtains remained the same, although now Teddy stood guard on a bed that had been stripped of sheets. The books in the small bookcase ranged from an illustrated volume of fairy stories to Dickens and the Brontë sisters. A collage of pop idols and actors on a cork board above a desk – fresh, boyish faces torn out of magazines – and some monographs on artists piled on the floor by the bed were the more recent concessions to her teenage years and interests. In the corner sat the portable gramophone and a small stack of records: mainly the Beatles and the Rolling Stones, although Tony had told her that most people preferred one or the other and had tried to persuade her that the American Bob Dylan was better than both put together.

Hanging alongside the bed was a reproduction in a cheap wooden frame of the Annunciation that had been there as long as she could remember. It represented the Virgin Mary sitting on a plain wooden stool in a vaulted loggia receiving the news of her miraculous pregnancy. Geoffrey had brought it home for 'the baby's room' to celebrate their own 'little miracle' just before Cara was born, and she grew up seeing the picture every time she raised her eyes from saying her goodnight prayers.

Her devout grandmother had often repeated Geoffrey's story about Cara being a 'little miracle' for it had taken a while for the couple – in Nora's words – to be 'blessed with a child'. As a little girl Cara absorbed this information and believed that expecting a baby was something decided on by God. The story of the Annunciation had been explained to her and because in her mind she associated it with her own mother's miraculous conception, she imbued the picture with an aura of magic.

Years later she came across her picture reproduced in one of her books on Renaissance artists. She had gasped with recognition, as if she was the owner of the original. From the caption she learnt that it was painted by a monk commonly known as 'Fra Angelico' (the 'Angelic Friar') and that it hung in the Museum of San Marco, originally a convent occupied by Dominican monks in fifteenth-century Florence. When yesterday she checked in her new guide-book where the museum was situated, she realised it was only five minutes' walk from the apartment she was staying in. This would be the first place she would visit.

The door of the erstwhile monastery led into a simple cloister; its dark corners decorated with frescoes. Cara would save those for later, for she was in a hurry to locate what she had come to see. She began climbing the stairs leading to the monastic cells which were organised in rows on the floor above, beneath a huge wooden roof. And suddenly, there it was, majestically displayed in front of her. For a moment she felt as if she were the only visitor, alone in ascending a heavenly stairway towards this monumental image of divine revelation. It was of course so much bigger and the colours more luminous than in the reproduction at home.

She studied the painting carefully. The soft light within it created a restful stillness. There was no clutter to distract, nothing to indicate what the Virgin Mary was doing before the Annunciating angel arrived. No book on her lap, no basket of sewing beside her. At first, Cara tried to suppress a brief disappointment. She would have preferred her prettier, she wanted to tweak her into being as beautiful as Botticelli's Venus. The Virgin here looked like any girl you might walk past in the street without a second glance. But perhaps, Cara went on to think, this was intentional on the part of the artist, for this Virgin Mary was supposed to be an ordinary young woman, chosen to be extraordinary.

She continued looking, her observations tumbling one into the other. The kneeling angel resembled the Virgin, like a younger sister, mirroring her gesture, hands humbly crossed. Behind the angel and the columns of the cloister (which echoed the real one downstairs) lay a verdant garden dotted with spring flowers and divided by a humble fence: more ordinariness present within the divine. But the budding artist in Cara began to notice how the blocks of colour across the painting worked both separately and in unison: the green of foliage and the ochre of pavement, the pink of the angel's robe and deep blue of the Virgin's cape; the beautifully layered bands on the angel's wing, rolling from darkest purple to luminous gold, patterned with a design you might see stamped on leather or on the wings of birds.

There was excitement in the seeing. She was looking through the prism of art, not religion. Ideas were coming into her head, and she longed to call Tony over and have him stand next to her to examine it with her, to sense his concentration and ask him what he thought. She would make him be attentive and serious but also enjoy his inevitable droll remarks.

A young couple holding hands walked past and reality struck. She was on her own now. Not being able to work out what Tony's funny comment would have been consumed her with a deep melancholy.

On Sunday the pealing of the church bells seemed incessant. Cara stretched in bed, happily ignoring their call to prayer. She felt liberated by the realisation that, other than to look at the art and architecture, she needn't step into a church ever again. At least not while she was in Italy. Her mother and grandmother would never find out. But when, a few hours later, she went out for a walk and saw groups of locals pouring into the Basilica of the Santissima Annunziata in the nearby piazza, curiosity overcame her, and she considered having a look inside.

'*Signorina!*' A middle-aged man, wearing a heavy coat despite the warm day and accompanied by a woman and four boys of varying shapes and sizes, had noticed her hovering and was grinning from ear to ear.

'Viene alla messa?'

Cara recognised the neighbour she had met on the stairs, now with family in tow. He was asking her whether she was coming to Mass. 'Ah, *si* ... no ...' she answered, contradicting herself. But Mr Lotti was already introducing her to his family, taking her by the arm and guiding her into the church.

The interior was centuries older than the Italian church in Clerkenwell where Cara's parents and grandparents had married and where festivities had been celebrated throughout her childhood. Its age and size lent it a gravitas that the London church lacked. And yet there were similarities: that combination of sombre and ornate, from the grey angels to the flourishes of gold.

She sat with the Lotti family close to a tabernacle covered in ex-votos, candles and lamps that gave off a textured light. A bouquet of flowers had been left in front of the tabernacle, possibly by a recent bride as a gift to the Madonna to ensure a healthy marriage and children.

The service began, the Latin chanting adding to the sensory overload. Cara absorbed it all, and as the singing gathered momentum, this encounter with the vast interior, the soft candlelight, the shadowy paintings and the smell of incense increased in her a melancholic longing for home. She was missing everything and everybody she had thought she wanted to get away from.

Silently she began to cry, before scolding herself in frustration. Her sentimentality arrived at the most awkward moments, at times when she craved more than anything to be strong and in control. She wanted to be curious, mature, engaged with her new experiences, but her bid for independence was clearly failing if she kept thinking about what she had left behind.

Aware of a gentle nudge, she realised that Mrs Lotti was pressing a handkerchief into her hand. Cara took it gratefully and dabbed her eyes. When the service ended Mrs Lotti insisted on taking her arm and, after many greetings and introductions to others from the neighbourhood, the whole Lotti clan persuaded her, with encouraging smiles, to join them for Sunday lunch in a local trattoria.

The meal was long and lasted several hours. Everyone was talking at once and eating with gusto. Thanks to the flowing wine and despite some stumbling over words in a hybrid of English and Italian, Cara was beginning to feel better. The Lotti children were sweet, their parents friendly, the food good and the sun was shining outside. Towards the end of the meal Fernando Lotti raised his glass of red wine.

'Mangia bene. Ridi spesso. Ama molto!'

She understood. 'Eat well, laugh often, love a lot!'

Flushed with wine, she raised her glass in response, determined to try and follow these three suggestions, however hard that might be.

The first time Cara arrived at Nicoletta's house overlooking the River Arno she was apprehensive. The building was imposing in a classical Florentine fashion, and it made her feel small. There was a confidence within the beauty of this city that Cara admired, but sometimes she sensed arrogance too, born of privilege and affluence. She was a shrunken Alice in a land of wonders, always looking upwards at palaces and churches and looked down upon by monuments and sculptures. Bronze men of consequence on horseback and beautiful marble goddesses were awe-inspiring reminders of her shortcomings. Would she ever know enough to trust her own opinions, to judge art and history? At that moment, she wasn't sure she ever would.

She hesitated, but finally rang the bell. After a few minutes the door was opened by a small Italian woman in a knee-length black dress, a half apron, white collar and cap. It took Cara aback. She had never known anyone with a maid. A charlady, yes (or, as Tony's mother would say, 'a daily'); Grandma Nora was one. But a maid in uniform? Here was another thing to make her feel out of her league.

The anteroom was bigger than that of Signora Nomellini's apartment in Via Laura, but gloomier. The high ceiling and dark wood panelling gave the space a solemn air, a pair of delicately painted *cassoni* providing the only decoration. Above another wooden chest, this one undecorated, hung a few summer jackets and a straw hat. The maid pointed at Cara's cotton jacket, offering to take it. 'No, no, *grazie*,' she stammered. She would keep it on for now, even though it was a warm day. It gave her a sense of security.

'Ah, Cara, welcome!" Nicoletta swept in with both arms outstretched and took her by the hands. She was wearing well-cut slacks zipped at the hip, flat shoes in soft leather and a creamy silk blouse. A string of pink-red coral around her neck completed the look. '*Va bene, Teresa, grazie*,' she said, dismissing the maid.

Cara hesitated. '*Buona – Buonasera.*'

Nicoletta laughed prettily. '*Ma no bounasera! Buongiorno per favore*. It is not yet siesta hour. But, my dear girl, we must always speak in English, not Italian, on Tuesdays and Thursdays or we shall never improve. Come in …'

Inwardly, Cara berated herself. It was just past one o'clock and she had presumed *buonasera* to be the correct greeting. Wrong again. So far, she felt constantly wrong footed with her employer, as if there was nothing she could get right. The sense of unease continued as she was shown into a large *salone* where there seemed to be nowhere obvious to sit. The walls had a few pieces of furniture placed against them but the pair of stiff-backed chairs looked hard and uncomfortable. The principal feature of the room was a large stone hearth with an enormous hood covering the grate. Cara thought wistfully of the little coal fireplace and the comfortable old armchairs covered in fraying cloth that occupied the parlour at home in Clerkenwell.

Nicoletta pointed to one of the window seats, also in grey stone. 'Wait here, I shall check whether lunch is ready.'

What would Ma make of all of this? The decor was dignified, it shouted nobility and rank, but was austere. The painting hanging on the wall opposite her was so sooty you could hardly make out the shadowy figure from the background. She got up from the window seat to peer at it more closely. There seemed to be a half-naked old man with a long beard sitting at a desk covered in velum-covered books. Next to him was a skull.

What a depressing picture, she thought, *why would you choose to hang that on your wall?*

'Ah, I see you are admiring our St Jerome!' Nicoletta was standing right beside her.

Cara jumped. 'I'm sorry, I didn't see you ...'

'No matter. Lunch is ready, come with me.'

Nicoletta led the way past a kitchen where Teresa was preparing some food, and into a dining room with a round table laid for four. The table was wide, with the place settings far apart.

'Make yourself comfortable, Raffaele and Sandro will be here shortly.' As if on cue, a clatter of footsteps was coming closer and a moment later two boys, aged about twelve and fourteen, burst into the room.

'*Calma, ragazzi*. Say hello to our new friend Cara.'

'*Piacere*,' said the older one, proffering his hand.

'English please,' Nicoletta interjected severely.

'Pleased to meet you,' Cara said as they shook hands.

'I am Raffaele, this is my brother Sandro.'

After the hand-shaking, they sat down, and Teresa came through the door with a steaming bowl of pasta covered in a meat sauce. She brought it round to Cara's side. No one spoke.

'Do you always have lunch at home?' Cara asked the boys, as she began filling her plate with a mound of unruly *tagliatelle*. She smiled up at Teresa, who didn't respond.

'Yes, we come home from school for lunch. It is our custom,' Raffaele answered, choosing his words carefully, as he took his turn at the pasta bowl.

These two boys were only a few years younger than herself and yet – Raffaele at least – seemed so much more composed than Cara felt. She thought how beautiful he was, with olive skin, deep brown eyes, an aquiline nose. This angularity might have reduced his striking beauty but only increased it. It gave him character. Sandro, spotty and with heavier features, was less good looking. Perhaps, Cara thought, he took after his father.

As they ate, Cara asked various questions about their school, whether it was nearby, what they liked studying. 'Your English is good!' she said to Raffaele, and then realised she had made this same observation to his mother, a few days earlier. But Nicoletta looked pleased, and Cara relaxed slightly, turning to the younger boy. 'And, Sandro, how is your English?'

Sandro remained sullenly silent. He would be more difficult to involve. And how could she get on with eating such delicious food and make conversation at the same time?

Nicoletta came to her rescue. 'Sandro, show Cara what we do when we eat pasta …' He looked blank. Nicoletta picked up her napkin and gestured at his chest.

'Ah!' he smiled shyly and tied the large linen napkin around his neck. Raffaele followed suit.

'Oh!' Cara laughed and did the same.

'Now we must eat, or Teresa will be offended!'

They all tucked in, apart from Nicoletta, who held her napkin delicately over her chest with one hand rather than tying it around her neck. Her portion was half the size of the others'.

Cara's nerves were giving her slight indigestion. But she managed to finish and place her fork down just before Teresa arrived to clear the plates.

'*Grazie*,' Cara said. '*Molto buono*.' She began wondering what sort of pudding would follow.

There was no pudding, yet. A few minutes later Teresa reappeared with a platter of sliced beef and small roast potatoes, accompanied by a bowl of steaming green beans. 'But I can't ... I mean ...' and Nicoletta's boys laughed at Cara's widening eyes as she patted her stomach.

She helped herself anyway, and the ice was broken. By the time Teresa was bringing in the fresh fruit even Sandro had managed to join the general conversation.

When Cara wasn't lunching at Nicoletta's house, she had established a routine. In the mornings she worked on the inventory in the flat, and afternoons were spent visiting churches and museums or simply walking the streets of the city, stopping for coffee to rest and watch people go by. She bought a sketchbook and pencils to record the buildings, piazzas and works of art she wanted to imprint on her mind, but she also liked drawing the people she observed from café tables. The sketching made her feel actively connected to the city and less of a tourist. She was discovering the rougher areas, the artisan quarter around Santo Spirito, the framers, gilders and restorers of via Romana, the humble region around the food and junk markets of Sant'Ambrogio, the poor district north of Santa

Croce and the narrower, darker streets away from the refined residences and smart antique shops around the river.

But occasionally she would treat herself to a hot chocolate at Rivoire, the elegant café in the very centre. The weather was still mild, and she liked sitting at one of the outside tables across from the Town Hall and the copy of Michelangelo's David. Unfortunately, this presented a problem: the men.

There was a medieval maleness to the city at street level which she had not anticipated, whether it be the workers relieving themselves openly at street-corner urinals or the *mutilati di guerra* – the war veterans with missing limbs – begging outside shops. Even the robust fortifications of so many *palazzi* seemed much more aggressive than the Victorian streets she was used to in London. And here in Florence, it was unusual for a young woman to be unaccompanied, so for some she was seen as easy prey. She discovered that a respectable Italian girl – unless doing errands – would not be out and about without mother, brother, cousin or at least a friend. Cara may have looked Italian but what Florentine girl would brazenly sit outside Rivoire wearing sunglasses, sketching or reading a book on her own?

At first, not wishing to seem rude, she would vaguely acknowledge the boys and men circling her table like nonchalant vultures. But she soon realised that if they perceived any encouragement it became impossible to get rid of them. The worst were the young ones who roamed in packs – hair shaved, wearing the uniform of the *Servizio Militare*, or National Service. She came to dread the '*Eh, bella signorina*, you ees Engleeeish?' The moment she looked up from her sketchbook they sat down uninvited, trying to peer at her drawing, pointing at themselves and asking her to make their portraits. All the preening and smirking was unbearable, and it often meant she would pack up and leave before she wanted to, with the boys snaking down the Via Calzaiuoli after her, making comments she could only half understand. She was beginning to experience the negative aspect of having a young body and a pretty face.

It wasn't just the young lads. Men old enough to be her father – even her grandfather – would lean against the stone walls as she walked by, watching her, not moving out of the way as she passed them. She was troubled by the directness of their stares and the blatant way they undressed her with their eyes.

Just once she was tempted to respond. She was peering into a café on the Via dei Servi, the road that led from the Duomo towards her apartment. It was one of those cafés that displayed rows of pastries and Cara was considering a purchase when her eyes caught sight of a young man sitting at a corner table and waving at her. She immediately pulled her head back, but for a few seconds she lingered. From what she had seen he was good looking in a boyish way, scruffy but attractive, with his brown hair kept a bit longer than most. He looked vaguely familiar; someone she might feel comfortable with.

He continued beckoning. She looked about her and made a questioning gesture. He nodded. And then, despite being enticed by both him and the pastries, she decided no, best to leave both alone and go on her way.

The following week a particularly insistent older man pestered her while she was attempting to write a letter to her mother. This required concentration because Ma had sounded a bit strange during their last telephone call, and Cara had been worrying about it all week. She was trying to combine her news with accounts of what she was seeing in Florence but all she wanted to ask was, 'Why were you distant with me, as though you were hiding something?' She longed to make another call home, to ask her directly. But it was expensive and time consuming to go to the central post office and request calls to London, and Nicoletta didn't want her making calls from the apartment. During their last conversation mother and daughter had agreed only to telephone in an emergency.

'Hello, are you Engleeeeish?' A voice was interrupting her train of thought. She glanced up at the looming figure silhouetted against the sun, heart sinking.

'*No, sono Fiorentina,*' she replied wearily in Italian. This made the man laugh.

'*Ma che Fiorentina*! You are not Florentine, you have Engleeeish accent!'

Cara kept her eyes fixed on her letter. '*Per favore, lasciatemi stare* … leave me alone …'

'But a beautiful lady should never be alone.' He pulled the chair out to sit down.

'I want to be left alone!' Cara said this more forcefully, but the man continued to wheedle. 'I show you the Uffizi, you come with me?'

'I have been to the Uffizi many times.'

'Palazzo Pitti then?'

'No!' She had had enough. 'I told you I want to be left alone! Do you not understand? Go away! *BASTA!*' Her voice was loud enough for customers at other tables to turn around.

A younger man who was walking past had stopped in his tracks to watch the scene. When she shouted, '*BASTA!*' once more, he walked straight up to the table. 'Can I help you? It is Cara, *vero*? And the *signore,* you no want his company?'

Taken aback by hearing her name, she took in a face that looked familiar. She could not place him. Where had they met? He was like one of those youths who stand in the corner of Renaissance frescos, just on the edge of the action, piercing the spectator with their stare.

'I … But how do you know my name?'

The younger man turned to the older one who had been sitting at the table, watching cautiously. *'Questa signorina e amica di famiglia. Per favore lasciatela stare. Vada …'*

Grumpily the older man, admitting defeat, picked up his cigarettes and slouched off.

Cara smiled gratefully at being described as a friend of the family. '*Grazie!* But how do I know you?'

The young man's hands were on the back of the café chair. 'May I sit down?'

She gestured for him to take the chair.

'I know your neighbour, Fernando Lotti. Well, he know my cousin Stefano who works in the bar at the corner of Via Laura. I work there too sometime. But I be student.' His sentences came out fitfully, but she found his rhythmic Italian cadence and linguistic mistakes appealing. 'I saw you talking to Fernando in the piazza,' he continued. He paused before adding sheepishly, 'I saw you standing outside the bar also. And so, I ask Lotti your name.'

'Yes, you were the one waving at me in the café!' Her face flushed at admitting she had remembered him. 'Fernando Lotti has been very kind to me. They are a nice family,' she added, happy to change the direction of their conversation.

'Yes, *sono simpatici.*'

'So, can I buy you a coffee to thank you for being my knight in shining armour?'

'A "night" you say?' He looked confused. 'But coffee, yes.'

She laughed. 'It's just an expression.'

'I try to speak English, but no understand very much.'

'You are very good.' *Why do I keep saying that*, she thought?

He beckoned a passing waiter. '*Un espresso, grazie.*' Turning back to Cara he grinned and extended his hand. 'My name is Gianni Magnelli. I pleased to meet you.'

'Cara. But you know that already.'

'Beautiful name. In Italian Cara means ... how you say ...'

'"Beloved!" Yes, my parents called me that because ...' And she told him about living in the Italian quarter of London, and about their neighbour Nanella Baldoni, and the Italian school, and Paola, her little schoolfriend, and St Peter's Italian Church. Tony came into her mind, but she pushed him away.

She ought to be suspicious, guarded. She should put this young man off. Test him. She knew that. But she hadn't wanted to. An hour and a few more pastries later she had been persuaded by Gianni to show him her sketchbook and agreed to go for an ice cream with him the following day. 'I come to the house after your supper tomorrow and take you to Vivoli,' he said on the doorstep of Via Laura after he had walked her home.

'After supper?' That seemed a long time to wait. Cara couldn't hide her disappointment.

'You no like ice cream?' Gianni asked, misunderstanding her expression.

'I love it.'

'Then you will love Vivoli. They make the best gelato in Florence.'

In those last warm late September days, Cara ate a lot of ice cream. Gianni's assessment of the quality was accurate, Vivoli's ice cream was delicious and there were many flavours to choose from, from those made with fruits and nuts, to varying types of cream puddings and cake. 'I shall go back to London very large,' she joked.

'You will be beautiful even if you be very large,' he replied gallantly.

Gianni's English began improving with practice, but Cara also insisted on trying out her Italian. Chats with her neighbours or to Beppe in the vegetable shop were becoming freer as she gained confidence with the language. Gradually she ventured into the other shops around the apartment. Mario, the *pollaiolo,* sold only chicken and eggs, while his butcher friend – Ernesto, the *macellaio* – hung tender cuts of veal and beef in the window of his establishment on the other side of the street. They would conduct conversations across the traffic until a customer turned up and need serving, whereupon they'd go back into their shop looking slightly saddened by the interruption. The *panificio*, next to Beppe's vegetables, sold warm bread in the mornings as well as home-made tarts and biscuits. Within two weeks the shopkeepers knew Cara's name and greeted her like an old friend, as did some of the regular customers. As in Clerkenwell, the daily chats were as important as the buying of provisions.

Nicoletta seemed pleased with her inventory and the English conversations with her, Raffaelle and Sandro were going well. Teresa continued to provide delicious food and gave her leftovers to take home. Neighbours were friendly. The art she was slowly discovering in the museums, galleries and churches was more than stimulating. She had Gianni to show her around.

But still, when Cara woke in the mornings to the sound of the bells, her first sensation was one of melancholy. She couldn't talk with Gianni the way she had with Tony. It wasn't just a language problem. They had no shared history and their cultural references were dissimilar. Gianni never understood her jokes and asides, nor she his, and it was tedious to have to explain everything.

She was also disturbed by Gianni's underlying suspicion of anyone too different from himself. One evening he made a disparaging remark about 'negroes invading London'.

'They are not "invading" London! What about Italians "invading" London?' she retorted. 'I live in the Italian Quarter, it is – obviously – full of Italians!'

'They are English Italians, not real Italians.'

'But their grandparents were Italian Italians.'

'You always have an answer!' he laughed, and because she did not want to spoil the evening, she laughed too.

The next time they met he referred to an effeminate-looking man walking past as a *finocchio*, or 'fennel' – an offensive term for a homosexual. When Cara asked him what that meant, he made a limp-wristed gesture as he pirouetted on the spot, laughing all the while. She did not laugh and took him to task, and he sulked. But after moments like these he had a way of coming out of his moodiness and winning her over with charm, and she would end up forgiving him.

At times, when they were together, she felt he was holding back, as if there were some thoughts he was not expressing. She had not divulged anything about Tony, except that one of the reasons she had left London was to get away from 'bad people'. She knew Tony wasn't bad. But she needed to make him so, to soften the hurt, to lay the blame on him.

During those first weeks as they went for their evening strolls, ice cream in hand, she learnt that Gianni was an architecture student, and the faculty was near the apartment in Via Laura. As his cousin Stefano ran the café on the corner of that street, he sometimes worked shifts there. He lived with his widowed and partially disabled mother Marcella, whom he didn't seem keen for Cara to meet. His sister was married with a child and lived in a suburb of Florence.

He was handsome and flirtatious, and happy to show Cara around his city. But why, she wondered, had he not yet tried to turn the relationship into one of girlfriend and boyfriend? Would he treat her like Tony had? Was it something about her that put men off? Did she seem untouchable? She could not face going through the humiliation of rejection again.

One early evening he took her on the back of his *motorino* to the Piazzale Michelangelo. As they admired the view of Florence, she plucked up courage.

'Gianni, can I ask you something? It is personal.'

'*Cara mia*, of course you ask me!'

'Do you have a girlfriend? A *fidanzata?*'

His expression clouded over. '... *È difficile.*'

'Difficult? *Ah capisco*. I see.'

So, he did have someone. She was just an easy foreign girl to amuse himself with, on the side. These Italian boys were all the same, taking advantage, leading girls on to believe there may be something more. And she had thought he might be different. She felt a lump lodging in her throat.

'But it is only Ilaria,' Gianni muttered.

'*Ilaria?*' Cara repeated, slowly moving away from the balustrade that overlooked the city. She had arrived at this place clinging tightly to Gianni on the back of his Vespa. Now she wanted to be alone. Would it be too far to walk down into Florence?

'*Aspetta*. Wait!'

She had spotted a couple of tourists getting out of a taxi and jumped in, with Gianni behind her, still calling out, '*Aspetta!*'

'Via Laura. *Presto*,' she said to the driver, slamming the door. The taxi almost ran Gianni over as it turned around in order to go back in the direction it had come.

The heat of summer ended abruptly with prolonged bad weather. As Cara ducked into the shops in the Via dei Servi to shelter from the rain, she heard the same question on everyone's lips: when will we get the sun back?

'*Sei sfortunata*,' said Beppe in the vegetable shop, as did Luigi the baker. 'You are unlucky. Here in Florence, it can be warm through the whole of October. You have brought us your British weather!'

And she felt she had. 'It is like this in London at this time of year, it is no surprise.'

Cara didn't mind. She wanted to get on with the inventory in the apartment, and the rain made it less tempting to go out and explore. Her newly discovered organisational skills had surprised her, and she found she was quite enjoying the task. Rather than work methodically from room to room, she began dividing everything by generic category such as books, sale catalogues, papers, works of art, furniture, clothes, jewellery, general objects. Within each group there were further divisions to be made. This system allowed her to jump from category to category according to her mood: to the lists of books and papers when she had more intellectual energy, to the drawings and works of art when she was visually alert. Hours passed, quite pleasantly. She was an only child. She was used to organising her time and working on her own.

But how, she wondered, was it possible for one person to have accumulated so much stuff during one life, and all contained in one apartment? Much of Signora Nomellini's archive was boring, administrative paperwork or boxes of photographs of unknowns. But there were treasures.

A row of Old Master drawings on rusting picture hooks lined a dark corridor, protected from the sun. The most beautiful – unframed – was in a chest, under a clutch of unused folders. Cara had come close to placing the hard-backed brown envelope on the pile to be discarded with all the other bits of old stationery but on checking inside she noticed the edge of a page sandwiched between two bits of cardboard, and so she carefully pulled it out towards her.

The drawing was small but exquisite. It showed a naked young man in profile, lightly sketched in red chalk. He was young and muscular, with arms clasped around a large, contented animal at his side: a pet dog perhaps. Then she noticed that by his feet lay another docile animal, and realised they were lions, resting on either side of him. She checked the folder that Signora Nomellini had compiled with notes and photographs of all the works of art but there was nothing there that described it. Yet even her inexperienced eye could tell there was draughtsmanship here more skilful than in all the other drawings in the apartment. Why would Signora Nomellini not have included it?

She put her hand back in the envelope and felt a little card.

Tu sei l'angelo che mi proteggerà nella fossa dei leoni, she read. 'You are the angel who will protect me in the …' She looked up *'fossa'* in her dictionary: 'pit or den'. The lions' den?

Underneath it was signed Daniele. Who was Daniele? She decided to ask Nicoletta about it the next time she saw her.

Sometimes it felt wrong, rummaging through the property of a woman she had never met, even if this was what she had been employed to do. She hardly knew her first name – 'Giovanna' she had read on a document or letter – but was party to her most intimate possessions. The plaster bust Nicoletta had told her was by the hand of the lover lost in the Great War showed a striking version of feminine beauty, timeless in its essence. Swept-back hair, an elongated neck, clearly defined cheekbones and a high forehead. Back in London Cara had a book with a picture of the Egyptian queen Nefertiti looking just so.

Giovanna Nomellini had also been a lady of fashion. When in more frivolous moods, Cara enjoyed rifling through the large wardrobes, dressing up in clothes and jewellery. After all, there was no one to stop her, and being relatively small she was even the same dress and shoe size. It seemed meant to be.

Cara's style began to change as a result. Being alone in the apartment gave her the freedom to dress up and experiment, mixing clothes and accessories. She would pose theatrically in front of the long wardrobe mirrors as if her own reflection were a friend with whom she could play-act. A box of lace cuffs and collars; a 1920s' sequined bolero partnered with a long string of pearls; a fur cape and muffler from the 1930s; a 1940s' dress and jaunty hat; a 1950s' bright, patterned scarf: all these offered her the chance to investigate what suited her. But there was more to it than that. The afternoons became time to play, to restore and to regenerate. Slowly she was beginning to feel repaired.

She didn't miss Gianni particularly, or the post-supper excursions for gelato, now that the weather had turned cooler and the rain had set in. But her anger towards him simmered beneath the surface, unresolved. Partly this was frustration that still hung over from Tony's rejection; whatever it was, it made her irritable and impatient. In the week that had passed since she had left him standing in the Piazzale Michelangelo, she had not heard from him. He knew where she lived. The university department where he studied was in the same street. If he cared about her, why had he not come to find her?

It was lunchtime, a couple of weeks into October, and she was on her way back to the flat after buying provisions. She was beginning to tire of the constant rain. At the front door she closed her umbrella and fumbled in her bag for the keys. Inside, she glanced over at the mailboxes. One of her jobs was to collect any letters that arrived in the name of Signora Nomellini and pass them on to Nicoletta.

There were some official looking envelopes with Italian stamps and a leaflet about local church services. Hidden between them was a letter that made her heart sing – the stamp was British, the origin

London. Her mother's familiar handwriting loped across the light-blue Basildon Bond envelope. Englishness encapsulated in stationery.

She couldn't wait. Leaning the dripping umbrella against the wall, she carefully lowered her bag of shopping to the floor and tore it open.

My dear Cara

It was wonderful to receive your letter today and to hear that things are going well. Nicoletta and her sons sound nice. Do you think you will ever meet her husband? I'm glad also that you are seeing all the beautiful things that Florence can offer. You didn't say whether you are sketching again? I hope so.

As you can imagine, everything is pretty much the same here. Life continues in its usual way and sometimes it feels as if it's only the seasons that change. The weather is getting autumnal, there was definitely a nip in the air this morning and the leaves are slowly turning.

Well I had better get to the point, hadn't I? I'm not sure whether to mention it in case it upsets you. Yesterday I saw Tony.

Tony. An intake of breath. Her eyes darted from the letter to the door as if he were about to come in. With beating heart, she looked down and resumed her reading.

He said he had only just found out that you had gone to Italy. I did point out that he hadn't been seen or heard from for a while. But he seemed terribly upset and said that he needed to speak to you urgently. I wouldn't give him your telephone number in Florence, but I did pass on your address (eventually) as he kept banging on the door even after I'd closed it in his face. He insisted he needed to write to you.

I hope I haven't done the wrong thing. Especially as he may not write after all and then you will be wondering what he had to say. But if I didn't tell you and then he did write, it would give you more of a surprise, and I thought you might like some warning. Whatever happens or does not happen, I hope this hasn't unsettled you too much.

Do write more letters when you have the time. I love receiving them. Your loving Ma

'I hope this hasn't unsettled you too much.' How could it not unsettle her? She walked slowly up the stairs to the apartment and unpacked the groceries in the kitchen, without removing her coat. She didn't want to be in the apartment on her own. She needed some distraction.

The café on the corner of Via Laura was busy. At the side of the building was a hatch overlooking the street where large pizzas on trays were cut into equal squares and passed to hungry students for a few coins. Some youths huddled close, sharing umbrellas and chatting while waiting for their turn. She scanned their faces before walking past them and through the door.

'*Ciao, bella!*' Gianni's cousin Stefano looked up from the other end of the bar. Two tiny white cups sat waiting on the counter for the coffees he was preparing. '*Come stai?*'

'*Bene, grazie. Sto cercando Gianni.*' She wanted to sound unconcerned but was hoping Stefano would know where he was.

'*Viene domani, e a casa con sua madre,*' Stefano answered, carefully pouring the coffee.

Of course, he was with his mother Marcella, the most important woman in his life. She would have to wait until tomorrow afternoon after one of her lunches at Nicoletta's house.

Teresa had excelled herself. 'You are lucky,' Cara remarked to the boys as she tucked into a plate of *pappardelle* covered with wild-boar *ragù*. 'Is there anything Teresa can't cook?'

'*Trippa* …' said Sandro, making a face.

Nicoletta gave him one of her looks. 'Yes, Sandro is not fond of it. I think you call it tripe. It is considered a delicacy in Florence, boiled with a tomato sauce …'

'Boiled tripe?' Cara made a face and the boys laughed.

'It is good if it is cooked *al dente*, like spaghetti,' said Nicoletta.

'What is your favourite food, boys?' Cara was learning to ask the right questions to get them to practise their English. Nicoletta looked pleased. But soon conversation stalled, and they were still only at the second course.

'Nicoletta, I wanted to ask you about your aunt …'

'Yes, Zia Giovanna …'

'I found a drawing that was given to her by someone called Daniele.'

'Ah, that must have been Daniele Ferrero. He was a young art student from Piedmont who wanted to become a sculptor. You know, I showed you that plaster bust he made of her.'

'Yes, it is beautiful.'

'He never had the chance to cast it in bronze …' Nicoletta sighed. 'They met before the First World War, while holidaying with their families in the Alps. By the end of the summer they were engaged.'

'Oh, they were to be married?'

'Yes, but their engagement was interrupted by the war. Daniele was killed – shot dead by an Austrian officer he was in the process of arresting. He was only twenty-one years old.'

'That is tragic.' Cara put her fork down. She felt shaken by this story.

'Yes, my mother – Giovanna's sister – always told me that she carried his ghost with her for many years. But in the end, she married a much older man …'

'Signore Nomellini?'

'Yes, but he also died after a few years of marriage.'

'Oh, but that is so sad!'

'You are sweet, Cara. But I think really she was quite happy with her academic work and her interests ...'

'There was a note with the drawing. I copied it out ...' She reached for the bag by her feet and read the phrase out in Italian. 'A "*fossa di leoni*" means a "lions' den", I think?'

'Yes, the young man was called Daniele. *Daniele nella Fossa dei Leoni*. Daniel in the Lions' Den.'

'Of course! He is saying that Giovanna is the angel who will protect him from the lions. But he wasn't protected ...'

'Was Zia Giovanna very beautiful when she was young?' Sandro interrupted. He looked incredulous at talk of this romantic story. 'I remember her, she had many ...' He pointed to his neck.

'Chins?' suggested Cara.

'She was fat!'

'Yes, Sandro, by the end of her life she was no longer thin. But we are all beautiful when we are young.'

Cara felt herself blush at Nicoletta's words, not knowing why.

A few days later another letter was waiting in the wooden mailbox addressed to Miss Cara Williams and postmarked London. She opened it and sat on the stairs to read, heart pounding as she held the paper in her hands.

Dear Car – his nickname for her –

My writing this letter to you is probably an exercise in futility, a kind of self-immolation (my new phrase, as I feel like I'm constantly stepping on burning coals). But you have been so much in my mind today. I have just come back from Piccadilly on the bus; it's evening and the weather is beginning to get cold but it's fresh and clear. On the walk from the bus stop to my house I couldn't help thinking about this time last year when we'd been out on a crisp autumnal evening and I was carrying you through the streets on my back because your new shoes were pinching. Do you remember?

'Of course …' she thought wistfully.

London is not the same without you. It's less fun being here on my own, even though I have made a good friend where I'm working.

Anyway, you're in Italy! That is exciting so forgive me for sounding melancholic. You must tell me everything. Life for you must be radically different – no pubs, for a start. Are you overwhelmed by immaculately dressed, smarmy pint-sized Lotharios? I should come straight over there with my sword to protect you from dangerous amorous entanglements. Sorry, that was insensitive.

You probably hate me. Please don't hate me. It is very hard to explain why I haven't been in touch until now. One day, if you give me the chance, I will be able to explain a lot of things. I need to do this face to face as it's too difficult for me to write it down.

Another phrase Cara struggled to read was crossed out.

~~*You are lovely and the perfect friend, but I realise*~~

Her heart sank. He must be in love with someone else. He owed it to her to identify this rival. Was it a girl they had been at school with perhaps? Paola, who liked him, and whom he pretended not to be interested in? How could she not have known?

Can we still be friends? I miss you so much.

Yours truly, Tony

P.S. I wish I could be with you in Florence. Give Botticelli and Michelangelo my love.

Cara walked slowly up the stairs, ruminating. She felt shaken, but there was also relief at hearing his voice through his written words. It connected her to him again. By the time she had opened the door of the apartment the longing to see him, or at least hear him, overrode everything else. She sat down and read his letter again and again. He hadn't specifically said there was anyone else. There was still hope. But what did 'you are the perfect friend, but I realise …' mean? What was he concealing?

If she thought about it too much, she wouldn't do it. She walked straight to the central post-office and booked a call to the Herrin household in London. The young woman at the counter said she would make the connection and pointed at a booth. Cara stood there, smelling cheap wood and plastic, waiting for the telephone to ring, and when it did, she grabbed it quickly, only to hear the slow, familiar British tone. She could imagine the shiny black telephone in the chilly hall of Mr and Mrs Herrin's house, demanding attention.

Dring, dring … dring, dring. It rang and rang. Cara's palms were beginning to sweat. The next unanswered ring and she would put the receiver down.

A woman's voice said, 'Hello, Herrin household.'

'Hello, Mrs Herrin? It's Cara Williams here …' She hoped the disappointment wouldn't come through in her voice.

'Cara! What a surprise. How nice to hear from you, we haven't seen you for so long. Tony said you were in Italy. How marvellous!'

'Yes, I'm in Florence … I was wondering if Tony was at home?'

'No, he's working, but he will be back later.'

Damn. She squeezed her eyes shut. Idiot.

'Of course, yes he must be working.' She answered quickly, wanting to cut the conversation short. 'Could you ask him, if he doesn't mind, to telephone me as soon as he can? I mean if *you* don't mind. I know international calls are expensive. But I need to speak with him. I've got the number here, in my pocket diary …' She still had her eyes clamped shut, as if this prevented Tony's mother from seeing how embarrassed she felt.

Cara waited impatiently as Mrs Herrin slowly repeated the number.

'Thank you, yes, that's it. I'm sorry, I have to go now, goodbye …'

Later, back home, she opened her eyes and saw that it was getting dark. Momentarily confused, she looked at her watch and realised it was late afternoon. She must have fallen asleep fully clothed when she lay down to read after coming in from making the telephone call. Feeling groggy, she got up to make herself coffee – she had given up tea in her attempt to divest herself of too many English habits. But she craved one of Ma's special scones with homemade jam.

As if on cue, the telephone rang as she passed the hall table on her way to the kitchen. Taken aback, she stared at the machine for a second before grabbing the receiver.

'Hello?' Not waiting for the English operator to connect them, she breathlessly blurted his name out. 'Tony?'

'Tony, eh? Who this Tony?'

'Oh, Gianni …'

'Stefano tell me you come to see me. But who is this Tony?'

'Yes, stupid of me, I thought he might call. He is a friend of my family.' She answered quickly. 'But where have you been? Where are you now?'

'I call from Stefano's bar. I am here now. You come down to see me?'

'No, you come here if you want to.' She was annoyed that everything with Gianni was reduced to a power game, a negotiation.

'I will come. So, you tell me who this Tony is …'

Two minutes later Cara was buzzing him in. She waited for him to climb the stairs, leaving her front door open, not quite sure how she would receive him. But when his figure appeared on the landing, panting from the exertion of the ninety-five steps, she felt pleased he had come. As he passed through the door, she went to kiss him on both cheeks, but he deliberately caught the kiss on his lips. Instinctively she jerked her head away, but when he pulled her back towards him, she was happy to relax into his embrace and let him find her lips again.

She began kissing him back, tentatively at first. Tony's letter flashed into her mind. What had he written? *Smarmy, pint-sized Lotharios*. Well, this one wasn't smarmy or pint-sized. With that thought she went back to kissing Gianni more enthusiastically. There was an element of revenge, but most of all she wanted reassurance that she was a desired, appealing young woman. The softness of Gianni's kiss had become passionate and insistent. She drew back and closed the front door behind them before taking his hand and leading him into the kitchen.

'I hoped you going to bedroom, not kitchen,' Gianni laughed. 'I do not want to stop!'

'No, I need coffee. I fell asleep this afternoon.'

'A siesta?'

'Yes, a siesta. Come to the kitchen.' Cara felt in control. 'Now, tell me – why have you not come to see me before?'

Gianni's face clouded over. 'It was *you* who leave me in Piazzale Michelangelo, remember? But that is not a problem.'

'What is the problem, do you think?'

'My mother is not happy.'

'I'm sorry. Why is she unhappy?' Cara busied herself spooning coffee into the percolator as Gianni sat down at the table behind her.

'Ah, it is difficult.' He looked at his hands. 'You think I have a *fidanzata*, yes?'

She turned around to face him with a sense of foreboding. 'I don't know. You tell me. You mentioned someone called ...' She pretended momentarily to forget her name. 'Ilaria, I think?'

'Sit down.'

Forgetting the coffee, Cara pulled up the other chair and settled in front of him.

'OK, I tell you everything,' said Gianni. 'You want to know everything, yes?'

'Well, I am beginning to feel I'm the last person ever to hear about anything ...'

'Eh?'

'Don't worry, carry on, you tell me.'

'It is that my mother, Marcella – she want me to marry Ilaria.'

'Hmm. *Eeee-laria*,' she repeated, giving the name emphasis.

'Ilaria is the daughter of Mamma's good friend, Rosella.'

'And Ilaria wants to marry you?'

'Yes, we have been close for long time.'

'Close?'

'You know, as friends. Since we were children.'

'Ah yes.' She said this thinking of Tony. 'But you don't want to marry her?'

'No. She is lovely girl but very shy. I love her like friend, not *fidanzata*. I tell my mother that I no want to marry but she no like this.'

'I see.'

'Everything was bad. You were angry with me, Marcella was angry with me, Rosella, my sister, was angry. What do I do? When I try to explain to Ilaria she cry.'

Cara wasn't sure how to respond. Strangely she felt sorry for, rather than envious of, the girl. 'Gianni, listen. I'm glad you told me this. Look, I'm happy we met and that we like each other.'

'Ah, this is good. I like you very much …' He grinned.

'I like you too,' she said, trying not to feel anything. 'But I'm only here until just before Christmas. Then, as you know, I have to go back to London. I want to try to get into art school. We probably won't ever see each other after that. Maybe you should try and make Ilaria and your mother, and everyone else – happy.'

'No no! That is not good.'

'No, not really good, but that is the way it is.'

'I know what we do. I take you to meet Mamma Marcella and she will love you, and then …'

'I don't think so!'

'But Cara …'

'Now, I was making that coffee …' She turned quickly and looked around as if forgetting where she had left everything. 'There it is …'

She looked to the illustration on the side of the coffee percolator, a little man with a long moustache, his body appearing submerged because the bottom of the image had faded. His arm was raised, as if in a plea for help. She pointed this out to Gianni.

'It's me,' he said, 'the drowning man!'

She laughed. 'You Italians are so dramatic. Everything is opera!'

They finished their coffee, leaving their empty cups and moving into the sitting room, where they sat side by side on the sofa and spooned. *He will go back to her*, Cara thought, imagining Gianni with Ilaria, *but for now it feels good to be with him*. Twilight turned to darkness as he muttered exaggerated compliments and endearments and she giggled and intermittently pushed him away.

'We go to bedroom now …' he murmured, burying his face in her neck.

'No, I …'

She needed to explain that she wasn't ready. 'I need more time.'

She felt guarded, unsure.

He tried a few more times until her shoving him off became less playful and more insistent. He looked affronted as he pulled away from her. 'You no like me!'

'I do like you, very much. But I don't want you to rush me and then leave me here to go back to your mother …'

'Ok–aay,' he drawled. 'I understand. But I come back, yes?'

'Yes, you can come back.'

'And you come to meet Marcella?'

'No, not yet.'

He was crestfallen but acquiescent, and when she closed the door behind him, she felt pleasure in having made her feelings clear. It was too easy to slip into saying and doing what others expected of her. The last thing she needed was to become like her mother, who so often appeared to be swallowing what she really wanted to say. But when he was gone, the apartment seemed empty and silent. She almost regretted not allowing him to stay.

She was alone, on her way to the bedroom, when the telephone rang. She paused before picking it up, composing herself, knowing exactly who it was going to be this time.

A woman's voice, a London accent. 'Cara Williams? I have a call for you.'

'Yes, yes,' she said impatiently. 'Hello? Hello? Tony?'

'Car! I'm so glad you telephoned earlier. Sorry I wasn't here. You got my letter?'

'Of course, why else would I have telephoned?'

'Don't be cross with me …'

'Sorry. I'm not.' Part of her wanted to punish him for hurting her, but she couldn't contain the excitement of speaking with him.

It was strange hearing his voice for the first time in months. 'It just feels like a lot has happened today, your letter arriving, then other things. Anyway, how are you? I mean, I know how you are, I just wanted to say I'm glad you wrote to me, but I don't understand ...'

Tony mumbled something she couldn't hear.

'What's that?'

He coughed and called out, away from the receiver. 'Yes, Mother, I won't be long!'

'I see you've got your mother listening?'

'Something like that. I wasn't thinking, but it's supper time.' He lowered his voice and whispered urgently, 'I wish I could see you.'

The thrill of this! Then she heard a female voice calling shrilly in the background.

'Yes, I'm coming,' he shouted back. 'Car, you have to tell me all about Florence! Have you made any friends? Is your Italian getting better?'

'Yes, it is. And yes, I have made a few friends. One or two.' It wasn't the moment to tell him about Gianni but she wanted him to know she was enjoying herself, and not pining for him. 'And how is the apprenticeship at the restoration place?'

'It's good. Mr Lengyel is demanding but I'm learning a lot. He's Hungarian. It's shocking you know. His brother was shot in front of him ten years ago ...'

'Oh no ...' She would have liked to hear more of Mr Lengyel's story but now didn't seem the time. She could hear some background noise at Tony's end and, as if on cue, he whispered, 'Must go now. But I'm so happy we have spoken. Maybe I'll try and get to Florence before you come back. You can show me around. I could stay in a youth hostel or something.'

'I would love that.' And she meant it, despite wondering how she would explain him to Gianni. 'Goodbye. Write to me again!'

'I will.' He paused before saying, 'I'm glad we're still friends.'

Tony did write again. Letters full of information about art restoration and what he was learning, but nothing personal. Cara answered, describing her life in Florence, including Gianni, thinking this would encourage him to share something about his private life. She wanted to tell him that she was in love, and that if he was in a similar situation she understood because she was in the same boat.

The only problem was that she wasn't. She was not in love with Gianni, however much she wanted to be. He attracted her and she enjoyed his company, but he didn't make her heart beat faster. It was Tony she had imaginary conversations with; Tony with whom she wanted to share jokes and observations; Tony who filled her thoughts. He stretched ideas in all directions and made her see and think differently. He made her the more interesting, curious, funnier person she wanted to be.

But it was Gianni who desired her, and in the following weeks she began seeing more of him. The constant rain meant they tended to stay indoors, either in Stefano's café or in the apartment, before he went back to his mother. But every time he attempted to get Cara off the uncomfortable old sofa and into the bedroom, she resisted.

'I want you,' he would repeat, again and again.

At this point she wanted him too, but not as a quick interlude in his day.

'And then, once you have me, what will you do? Run back to Mamma?'

'You know I have to help her. Why you not understand? She is in a wheelchair. And she worry if I no come home.'

'Yes, I'm sorry. But you said that she can still get out of her wheelchair and into her bed?'

His jaw tensed and the corners of his mouth pulled downwards with displeasure. 'Yes ... but I cannot say to her, "I stay with my English girlfriend for the night."'

'You do not need to say it,' she answered pragmatically. 'You know, you don't *always* have to tell the truth.'

'*Solo a te?*'

'That's right, only to me!' And they both laughed in agreement.

5

Clerkenwell

DECEMBER 1946

That winter promised to be harsh. The wind and rain were relentless, and by mid-December the snow began. Just before Christmas there was a short thaw before the temperatures plummeted again. Some said it was the coldest winter Britain had seen for three centuries. Icy easterly winds and repeated snowstorms marked the beginning of the New Year and continued for months. It was a challenging time for those like Mary, who relied on coal-fired boilers for hot water when coal was still being rationed. Stockpiles were running dangerously low. Rivers froze into icy conduits, roads and railways were blocked by drifts of snow. This made it increasingly hard to get the fuel to the power stations. Factories and businesses closed. Vegetables withered in the frosty earth. Livestock either froze or starved to death and rations were reduced even further.

Mary tried to make decent meals out of imported whalemeat and snoek, a tinned fish from South Africa. She commiserated with Nanella Baldoni who would ply her with reminiscences of the plentiful figs and tomatoes of her childhood. Even the local Italian shops were struggling to re-stock because of the bad weather conditions and roadblocks.

The housewives in the locality were fed up with counting points and coupons, with queues and empty shelves. 'It's worse than the war,' they grumbled. Beef, pork, poultry, butter, bacon, sugar, eggs, tea, milk – all the basics – were still being restricted. 'And now bread too!' wailed Nanella, clasping her hands together in the way she did, and raising her eyes to the sky as if levelling her reproach directly at God.

The tasteless snoek remained a staple, for a while at least. It was oily and bony and its dark colour and lumpiness steeped in brine made it extremely unappetising. Mary's mother had taught her to heat it up, smothered in cheese or tomato. In the morning Geoffrey was sent off to the bookshop with mustard-and-cress snoek sandwiches. He never complained.

Apart from the hunger, there was the cold. No one could keep warm. Families shivered in their beds under useless eiderdowns. Ice formed on the inside of bedroom windows. Hot-water bottles were not enough to cut the damp of old mattresses, and Mary and Geoffrey, like many others, wore layers of clothes, and even woolly scarves around their heads to keep their ears protected from the nighttime chill.

It was not only the basic necessities that were in short supply. Radio broadcasts were limited, and newspapers were reduced in size. Geoffrey continued to bring Mary books that he thought might amuse or interest her. She thanked him for his thoughtfulness as she opened the packages. Her visits to his bookshop had become less frequent since their marriage. Somehow there was an unspoken agreement between them that her job now was in the home, and that shopping meant finding food, not browsing Clerkenwell's scruffy bookstalls or the shelves of bookshops, even one owned by her husband.

But still, at any opportunity she would read. Once the household chores had been done and she'd trudged back up The Hill with enough food for a couple of days, she would sit with a blanket draped around her shoulders and escape into the classics and the popular fiction that Geoffrey brought home. She also loved the guidebooks to foreign places: Paris, Rome, Florence, Barcelona and some farther afield. The illustrations on the covers led her to imagine herself as the slim young woman looking through binoculars at a Norwegian fjord or as one of the handsome couple driving a shiny red automobile under captions like 'Touring in Southern Rhodesia' or 'Down to Mexico in Your Own Car'. She knew that she and Geoffrey would never get as far as Scotland, let alone Mexico or Southern Rhodesia, but she liked to dream.

Mid-March brought warmer air. The snow thawed. It was then that Mary got ill. It started one morning as nothing but a cold, but by the evening her forehead was burning. When she tried to get out of bed the following day she could not move, all her muscles ached and her head was pounding.

'You stay in bed,' said Geoffrey, depositing a jug of water on the bedside table. 'I'll try and come back early this evening.'

She spent the day worrying about the washing and cleaning waiting to be done. She wasn't hungry but she was cold and almost thankful for the waves of fever that took over as she began sweating and burning up. Finally, she slept, only to be woken in late afternoon by Geoffrey standing at the foot of the bed. He looked concerned. 'You are awfully flushed … Wait …'

'What do you mean, "wait"? Where do you expect me to go?' Downstairs, she heard the front door close.

The door was opening again, and she could hear voices and a clattering coming from the back of the house. There was talking, an exclamation, some laughter. Fifteen minutes later, two pairs of feet were coming up the stairs. Geoffrey was entering the bedroom again. 'I've brought you someone who can help …' Behind him appeared the dark figure of Nanella Baldoni carrying a tray with a teapot, a glass and an old jar of honey that had been removed from her larder.

'You no look good, I bring you my *medicina*. It make you well.'

Nanella looked around for somewhere to deposit the tray for there was no room by the bedside. She swept the hairbrushes on the dressing table to one side and placed the tray next to a small bowl that had been there since Geoffrey's mother had filled it ten years ago with *pot pourri*.

'Sit up, sit up.' Nanella plumped up the pillow, then felt Mary's forehead. She made a shaking gesture as she took the hand away, 'Ah, eeze very hot!'

Back to the tray, she poured some clear liquid into the glass and added a spoonful of honey. 'This good, good,' she said encouragingly, bringing the glass to Mary's lips. It tasted of lemon, of honey, but with an additional pungent taste Mary could not identify.

Nanella stood back, looking pleased. 'My mother, she give to me when I have cold. Two lemon in hot water, on the stove …'

'You boiled water on the stove? Here?' She wasn't sure she liked the idea of this woman coming into her house, taking over.

'Yes, your stove. I bring the lemons and *l'aglio*. For my *medicina* you put the *aglio* … how you say,' she hesitated before remembering, '*si!* the garlic in the water and you boil, yes? For ten minutes. You …' she made a fist and began smashing it into the palm of her other hand, '… before the garlic go in the water. Is good, yes?'

'Yes, very good. You are kind, thank you.' Mary didn't understand why Nanella had chosen to bring her a glass rather than a teacup, but she didn't wish to seem ungrateful. She continued sipping. The glass felt hot against her lip.

'I come tomorrow, I make for you *brodo*, it good for influenza.'

'There's no need …'

'I make soup from the chicken, is no trouble.'

Geoffrey had remained in the doorway. Mary darted him a wary glare. Did she really want this woman thinking she could come over every day, exploiting her weak and vulnerable state to nose around her house, however kind her intentions?

He ignored the look and guided Nanella out of the room. 'It's so kind of you to help, she has no energy to cook, I can leave the door on the latch ...'

'Of course, Mr Geoffrey! I make sure I bring you some food too. *Pover'uomo*! What can a husband do if his wife is ill, how will he eat?' She grimaced as if this was the most unimaginable thing.

In the end Mary was grateful for Nanella Baldoni's benevolent interfering. Nutritious soups, first a simple bone broth, then a chicken one with tortellini, then more substantial ones were delivered: a thick minestrone, one of lentil and beans, a *stracciatella* of meat broth and small shreds of an egg-based mixture. 'This is good!' Mary beamed when a soup made of tomato and bread arrived on her tray. As she started to feel better, she began tasting the food she was given, before leaving the rest for Geoffrey. She pretended she still felt ill long after her high temperature had subsided.

'This is really delicious,' she said tucking into layers of *lasagna* thick with meat and cheesy sauce. 'How do you get hold of all these good things?'

'I know where to go. The shopkeepers, who get the best supplies from Italy ... they are my friends!' Nanella grinned. 'You look much better. The colour is back in your cheeks. *Sei di nuovo bella*.'

'I wish I could cook like this. I shall miss these treats.' Mary was beginning to like Nanella and look forward to her visits.

It was Geoffrey who began getting annoyed, finding their neighbour in the house whenever he came back from work.

'Why does she always stay so long? She's constantly wandering around downstairs.'

'You were the one who invited her in the first place. You should be grateful. She brings you supper.'

'I know, but can't she just leave it and go away? If she's not pottering around the kitchen making a mess, she's spending hours with you in the bedroom, chatting about nothing.'

'How do you know what we are chatting about? Anyway, she doesn't stay that long, she has to get back to look after the children.'

'Not after her good-for-nothing son comes back from work to take charge!'

'I like her company as much as the food. It makes me feel better. As for Filippo, he's not a good-for-nothing. Nanella says he's very helpful.'

She had heard Filippo in the mornings, leaving for work on building sites often hours before Geoffrey left for the bookshop. She found herself listening out for him, wondering what he was saying when she heard him talking loudly and fast to his mother, his voice muffled, but clearly Italian.

'Well, if you've got enough energy to argue about this, you'll have enough energy to get up tomorrow,' said Geoffrey, going downstairs.

She had never seen him so severe. But if he thought she was going to give up her friendship he was wrong. She would just have to go to Nanella Baldoni's house instead.

At first, all Mary wanted was the food. She was weak following her illness and had little taste for her own small repertoire. And Geoffrey, being essentially a reasonable man, would not impede her convalescence by preventing her from going over to their neighbour to improve her culinary skills, especially as he benefited from them. His meals had, up to then, been tasteless and mediocre by comparison. This hadn't been entirely Mary's fault, given the rationing, but he admitted he was impressed by Mrs Baldoni's ability to find interesting ways to use the ingredients available in the local Italian shops. He was, however, appreciative only up to a point. It was, he felt, all relentlessly foreign. When presented with another *lasagne* he would talk wistfully of the steak and kidney pies, the stews and oxtail soups his mother used to make. And he could not abide garlic.

'Hasn't she taught you enough by now?' he said one evening as he was finishing a meat casserole cooked with olives and tomatoes.

'Didn't you enjoy it?'

'Yes, it was very nice, but don't you think you are spending too much time over there? Are you sure Mrs Baldoni is happy about the arrangement?'

'She loves teaching me the recipes her own mother taught her. And all the Italian shopkeepers know her. We get good ingredients for a reasonable price ...'

'What about her family, she must have other things to do than teach you her childhood recipes? And how is she paying for the extra food for us?'

'Well obviously I contribute with some of my housekeeping money,' she answered irritably.

Geoffrey frowned.

'Anyway, she likes preparing food for her family, and I help to distract the children when they are around. And we keep each other company.'

'Hmm, I suppose, yes, company ...' But Geoffrey didn't really know what to suppose. He had no need for such a thing as 'company', and so found that notion incomprehensible. Mary knew that books were his company; in his eyes they were more interesting, more constant and reliable. They might disappoint at times, but they didn't die or let you down.

Mary cleared the plates and replaced them with a small bowl of semolina.

Geoffrey looked pleased. 'Ah, thank goodness, something British!'

To change the subject, Mary asked him about the bookshop.

'Well, business is slow, but ticking over.' Then he told her a young mother had entered the shop that afternoon holding a little boy by the hand. After looking around the boy had chosen a secondhand copy of the *Boy's Own Annual* and left the shop with an expression of eager anticipation on his face.

'How nice,' Mary said.

'Yes, very nice.'

What he did not disclose was that seeing the mother and her young son that afternoon had dissolved his usual control. Reminded of his little nephew, he had felt a visceral ache deep in his chest. By now Nicholas would have been about the same age as the boy. When Geoffrey's family had died, customers at the bookshop had said, 'At least they will always be together.' But they wouldn't be, would they? They were nothing but ashes mixed with the rubble that was being cleared to make way for new dwellings. Geoffrey had been unable to say that, it would have been churlish when people were only trying to offer some comfort in difficult times. He had even mumbled the same platitudes himself to others in similar circumstances. But occasionally, at moments like that afternoon in the shop, the knot of pain he kept well hidden would loosen and rise up regardless, and sometimes it felt impossibly hard to push it back down. Geoffrey had waited for the mother and child to leave. He had walked over to the entrance and calmly turned the sign hanging on the door from 'Open' to 'Closed'. And then, winded by grief, in the darkness at the back of the shop he had broken down and sobbed.

Mary had noticed that he was particularly remote and out of sorts that evening. As if guessing the reason for his mood she said, 'You know, if nothing else, cooking for us takes Mrs Baldoni's mind off her husband. She misses him so much.'

For a second, Geoffrey looked deeply troubled. 'Yes, I can imagine …' But then he shrugged. 'Well, we all have our crosses to bear.' He said it quickly before getting up to switch on the wireless.

Mary understood. But what she could not endure was this constant shutting down of conversation. Every time they got close to discussing anything real, any true human emotion, her husband would distance himself further from her and put on what she came to name his 'headmaster's face'. Disapproving, controlled, patrician. Only that one time, when he had spoken of the Blitz on the evening he proposed, had Mary seen a chink in his iron reserve.

He was not insensible. Mary did not realise how much he struggled with feelings he perceived as 'unmanly.' What was he to do with them? He felt compelled to lock them away, keep them concealed. And because he rarely gave in to his vulnerability, Mary understood that her role was to keep her true feelings hidden too. The underlying message was clear: their mutual misery must not to be mentioned.

So, Mary did not tell Geoffrey that the true reason for continuing to go over to Nanella Baldoni's house was not so much for the food but because that loud, chaotic household made her feel alive. She liked the noisy children, the mess and the unpredictability, the shouting and the laughter. It injected her with an energy that was missing in the tidy, silent, grey-brick house that was her marital home. Two London houses that looked identical from the outside but were so different on the inside. In one, all was hushed and ordered – even the furniture looked prim, with antimacassars crocheted by Geoffrey's mother still draped on the backs and arms of the chairs. In the other, framed family photographs jostled with Catholic trinkets and Italian souvenirs that Geoffrey – should he have seen them – would have called 'vulgar'. The chaos of family life in the Baldoni household infused everything with a warm glow. And at the centre of it all was Nanella Baldoni: motherly, affectionate, tactile.

Tactility was something missing at home too. In contrast, it was heart-warming to see Filippo playing in such a physical way with his little brother and sister, spinning them around, ruffling their hair, chasing them up the stairs or into different rooms. Mary couldn't imagine Geoffrey acting like that, should they ever have their own children. And she loved the way Nanella welcomed her into her home with a kiss on each cheek every time she opened the door. Her own mother would never have done that, and since they had married, neither would Geoffrey. Kisses were clumsy gestures made in the dark as a required precursor to lovemaking. So awkward were they that they often involved a clash of noses, followed by Geoffrey's apology – 'So sorry!' – before he continued with the matter in hand.

She began spending more and more time next door. As soon as Geoffrey had left for the bookshop, she would be over there, offering to help Nanella with the shopping or asking about special Easter recipes, for it was now the beginning of spring. Being able to escape was her lifeline. But what she wasn't admitting to either Geoffrey or – as yet – to herself, was that it wasn't just the cooking or the warm family life that interested her.

It was Filippo.

Years later when she thought of him, she knew that the wariness she had at first experienced in his company was simply due to fear. The physical attraction alarmed her. It had been unsettling and, also, felt dangerous. She tried to shut it down, to pretend she didn't feel it. Why would she, she reasoned, be interested in a short, dark, not particularly handsome man with a dirty, manual job, who spoke English badly, when she had an educated bookseller as a husband?

Filippo's work on London's many building sites was erratic. Sometimes he laboured long hours, some days just a morning. Mary could never be sure quite when he would be home, so if Nanella told her that Filippo would be out for a while, she honed her excuses. She would remember that there was washing to hang out, some bed-making to complete, a forgotten bit of darning that needed doing before Geoffrey's return. 'I shall pop in later,' she would say and spend the afternoon catching up on chores, at the same time straining to hear the sound of him through the walls of their terrace. The best days were those when she was already in Nanella's house, knowing that his arrival was imminent. She would hear him coming through the door, shouting, '*Sono io …!*'

He often remained in the kitchen, watching the women prepare the food. At first, he teased Mary about her lack of cooking skills, then he turned to flattery. 'You learn fast,' he said one day as she was rolling some minced beef into small, round meatballs.

'Not really, Filippo, your mother is a good teacher.'

'Why you still call me Filippo? Pippo, please, I tell you many times.'

Mary knew this was the nickname given to him by his mother and young siblings. He hadn't ever asked her to call him that before.

'But you only stopped calling me Mrs Williams quite recently!' She flushed at the realisation that they were flirting. 'But all right, Pippo it is,' she said. It felt like an honour bestowed, like being accepted into the inner circle.

'Put in a handful of grated *parmigiano*!' Nanella called out. There were no scales in this kitchen, only references to a 'handful', a 'bunch', a 'splash', as if precise measurement would repress the artistry of the cook.

By now Mary felt so at home in their kitchen that she walked over to check the pot and without hesitation picked up a wooden spoon and plunged it into the pan, then lifted the spoon to her mouth.

'And what is this sauce, eh?' Filippo said, coming closer, pointing at the contents bubbling on the stove.

'Oh yes, and you must stir it, Mary,' Nanella said from the sink.

She could feel his breath behind her.

'You let me taste too?'

As she turned to offer him the spoon, she realised he was standing closer than she had expected. His chest jostled her arm and the sauce fell on to his shirt.

'Oh no, I'm so sorry … I …'

'No, don't worry,' Pippo took the fold of stained material on his chest and lifted it to his mouth to lick off the excess, keeping his eyes on hers all the while.

'I, I'm sorry, I …' She knew she was blushing, mortified that he should see her so flustered.

'It is no problem!' he said, without a trace of embarrassment. 'You no worry, *bella signora*! I go and change my clothes.'

Bella signora, bella signora. She absorbed those words like a healing balm.

From a young age Mary had learnt there are words you must never say, thoughts you must not think, feelings you should not feel. But there was excitement to be had in the forbidden. Once in the early hours of the morning she left the marital bed and, sitting in the dim light of the bathroom, she whispered to the empty room, 'I want him.'

There. She had said it and the room had received the forbidden feeling. There had been no thunderclap, no bolt out of the blue.

But it must remain a secret. She would not even tell Elsie, because she knew that if she did, the sweetness of the feeling would be corrupted, reduced. She knew that Elsie would spoil it by turning it into something else. For now, it could remain innocent, precious.

The Sunday before Easter Mary woke wishing there was something to look forward to. She had practised the sentence over and over in her mind, hoping she would sound as if the thought had only just occurred to her. 'I wonder if we should invite Mrs Baldoni and her son to supper?'

Geoffrey lowered his newspaper to reveal an expression of complete bewilderment. 'Whatever for?'

'Well, she has been so kind, and it would be nice to cook her a meal for a change.'

He gave her a searching look. 'Are you suggesting a dinner party? We have never even had your parents here for a meal. Or Elsie.' His look seemed to be indicating that she had lost her mind. 'Are you feeling unwell again? You do look rather pale.'

'Well, they live next door after all and …'

'And why on earth would you invite her son? What about the younger children? That noisy little boy and the girl? I suppose you want them to come … Why not invite the whole street?'

'I just thought …' Her plan suddenly seemed ridiculous. As she began clearing the plates, her hand shook and she knocked over a cup, spilling tea. A knife fell, staining the floor with jam. Geoffrey glanced up and a flicker of annoyance crossed his face. Then he went back to reading the newspaper.

It is this, she thought, *this is the worst thing. It would be better if he were angry: if he acknowledged my clumsiness. But he thinks it best to keep silent. He knows I will clear it up, and that the table and the floor will be clean again. That I shall do it quietly and with no fuss because we are civilised human beings and silence is what we aim for.*

And in that moment, she wanted to make a great deal of noise. She was sick of remaining mute, controlled, well behaved. She had an overwhelming urge to sweep the rest of the crockery from the table in one stroke and hear it clatter to the floor, then in rebellious rage rip the newspaper out of his hands and pour the jug of milk over his smug head. Why did he always have to be so calm and composed?

He had folded the newspaper into a neat rectangle and was looking at his watch. 'Are you intending to meet your mother at St Peter's? If you don't hurry, you'll miss the service.'

Mary took a deep breath that juddered shakily as she exhaled. 'Yes, of course. I must dash …'

'You can do the dishes later.'

Nora O'Neill was waving in her direction as Mary walked into St Peter's. The church was alive with chatter as the large congregation, dressed in their best clothes, gathered together.

'I thought we were meeting outside,' her mother hissed as Mary slipped into the pew beside her.

'Yes, sorry Ma, I got held up.'

'Are you looking for someone? Your eyes keep darting around all over the place …'

'No … shush, it's starting …'

Where was he? Mary looked about her and recognised many of the local shopkeepers she had got to know better when shopping with Nanella, along with the stallholders from nearby Leather Lane. There was Neldo from the Italian café and Salvatore from the delicatessen next door. She suddenly spotted Nanella and her younger children sitting in a pew at the front. But where was Pippo?

The service seemed interminable. The sermon was about the betrayal in the Garden of Gethsemane and the Crucifixion. As a child Mary had loved Sunday Mass, especially around Christmas and

Easter, but this day she found herself criticising everything about it. What was the priest saying? That Christ died for us – for Ma and Da and Nanella Baldoni, and Salvatore and Ernesto and the rest of the congregation – so that we could rise out of our sinfulness with repentance? All the praise, the supplication, and particularly the repentance – what relevance did it have to her?

Nora had instilled in her the notion of gratitude, sacrifice and endurance. Well, the fact that at this moment Liam O'Neill was spending the last of his meagre wages in the Coach and Horses instead of sitting here next to his wife in church was typical. Liam didn't practise self-denial, did he? Even though it was Lent. And Nora, married to such a drunk, had always pretended that life was going smoothly, that they were a respectable family. It infuriated Mary. Her angry thoughts churned with her frustration unleashed. The memory of the cramps she had experienced a few days ago was painful proof that another month had passed without her falling pregnant. There was ambivalence in this discovery: part of her craved motherhood, but she knew that this would tie her further to enforced domesticity. Perhaps she would never bear a child, and then what? But according to Nora, whatever happened was the will of God.

Finally, the service came to an end. Families were getting up and making their way slowly out of the church, the women stopping to chat before rushing home with their children to get lunch on the table, the men lingering on the street for a smoke.

'Ma, I have to catch up with someone, I'll see you next week.'

'Oh, is that the person you were looking around for?'

'No, but I must go.' She was trying to keep Nanella in sight, but it was hard to keep track of all the dark female heads. Mary had almost given up but once out of the church she saw her walking ahead with the two young children and ran to catch them up. The eight-year-old saw her first.

'Mamma, é la signora Mary!'

'Hello, Rosa, that's a nice dress. Can I walk home with you?'

The little girl smiled broadly.

'So where is your big brother?'

'I'm here,' said ten-year-old Carlino proudly.

'Oh, yes,' Mary laughed. 'But I meant your big, big brother …'

'He go yesterday to Broadstairs,' interrupted Nanella. 'He take delivery to Fausto.'

'Fausto?'

'Yes, he my husband's cousin, he and wife have café there. Salvatore get big delivery to his shop, and Pippo take food for Fausto in, eh, you say, van?'

'But Pippo does not have a van. What is he taking?'

'It is Salvatore's van. He take tins tomatoes, olives, cheese, salami. Fausto pay Salvatore, and Salvatore pay Pippo and me with cheap food. Why you think we get good bargains?' she grinned.

'But is that allowed?'

Nanella laughed. 'We Italians help each other!'

They had almost reached their street. Mary felt dizzy. She must get herself indoors.

Stopping by her doorstep, Nanella let the children in first before placing her hand on Mary's cheek. 'You are pale, *tesoro*. Come, next week and we will make liver. *Con spinaci*.'

Mary nodded. 'Yes, thank you … goodbye,' she whispered, and pushed open her own front door.

'Is that you, Mary?'

Who else would it be, she thought. 'Sorry, Geoffrey, I'm not feeling very well, I'm just going to lie down for a minute!'

'What's the matter?'

'Women's problems!' Mary shouted down the stairs.

'Women's problems …' Geoffrey repeated, shaking his head.

Monday was washing day and Mary didn't feel like doing anything but lie in bed. But her mother had drummed into her, 'The chores won't do themselves,' so she forced herself to get up and put the bacon on for breakfast. She longed to get under the eiderdown again. Her cramps were over, but a sort of torpor had set in, an empty listlessness. What was the point in doing the washing? Next week it would need to be done again. And again, and again. And there was the spring-cleaning to begin, the curtains to be washed, the mirrors to be wiped, the upholstery to be brushed, the drawers to be emptied and cleaned. Perhaps Geoffrey wouldn't notice if the sheets remained grubby for a while longer.

'What do you have planned today?' Geoffrey was getting ready to go to the bookshop and seemed to be in a good mood. Business was beginning to pick up a bit thanks to buyers from outside the locality. Word of mouth, he supposed.

'Planned?' The word came out more ferociously than she intended. Geoffrey looked at her in surprise.

She pulled herself together. 'I'll go out to the butcher's later. I don't think there's quite enough left over from the Sunday joint to make shepherd's pie.'

'Jolly good.' He turned towards her and gave her a peck on the cheek. And with that, he left.

The day stretched ahead in a haze of greyness. She needed to clear her head. Perhaps after the butcher she would go and have a cup of tea in the café where Elsie worked. That would cheer her up. Then she would come back home to get the washing done and prepare the supper well in advance.

She tied a wide piece of cotton fabric around her head to keep her hair off her face, fastening it on the crown like a turban. She fixed a curl, applied a stain of lipstick and walked into the spring sunshine. Basket on one arm, list in hand – to her neighbours she wanted to appear purposeful, as if on a housewifely mission to buy groceries, but all she longed to do was sit down with Elsie over a brew and moan about her dull, monotonous life. It seemed to be dimming, all colour removed.

As she walked eastwards towards Leather Lane and the café where Elsie worked, she knew that a quiet, intimate chat was unlikely to be possible. The old days, when they would take every opportunity to spend time together, were gone. She remembered the fuss Elsie had made once when they were given a break from their shifts on the buses that did not coincide. 'The bus routes aren't organised for you to spend time with your friend,' their supervisor had said.

Mary had loved working on the buses with Elsie. Later she would say, 'We weren't flying Spitfires or decoding messages or anything like that, but the war years were some of the happiest of my life. Even girls like us had opportunities.' She liked that word, *opportunities*. Being a 'clippie' had provided her with a sense of purpose. Naturally shy and reserved, at first, she found it hard to engage with her passengers, but she gradually gained in confidence and soon she would look forward to going to work, despite the long hours. It had given her independence and that felt good.

She also missed the nights out with Elsie: jitterbugging together in the dance halls when there weren't enough boys or sitting in the shadows of the picture house, weeping over sentimental films. Now that she was married it would be proper for her husband to accompany her, but Geoffrey had no interest in either dancing or films.

Ahead, a stout woman was rapidly approaching. She slowed down as they came close and Mary recognised her as Mrs Turner, an acquaintance of Geoffrey's parents from before the war. She looked like a sheep trussed up in tweed and a little hat. Mary's heart sank as she stopped, poised for a gossip.

They exchanged pleasantries. 'Good morning, lovely day.'

'How are you Mrs Williams? And dear Geoffrey?'

'Very well, thank …'

'I should warn you, if you're on your way to Wards, there's a sign up in the window that says, "No more meat today". They've sold out yet again. But I went into the shop anyway to see Mr Ward – known him for years – and he told me young Charlie is round the back preparing some rabbits.'

'Thank you, I'll be sure to pass that way later.'

'You seem in a hurry?' There was a malicious undercurrent to Mrs Turner's voice, as if she was digging for information.

'No, not really. But you know how it is, so many things to do … It's very kind of you to tell me about the butcher. Well, must get on my way now, goodbye …' Her forced smile vanished the second Mrs Turner was out of sight. Nosey old woman.

Half an hour later she had reached the café. Two men hanging around outside were chewing tobacco and spitting, but they stopped as she came close and gave her sidelong glances as she pushed open the door.

It was a simple, welcoming place, with a dozen tables arranged in three neat rows, set regularly apart. Different accents filled the air, reflecting the clientele. Neldo the owner was Italian, but as well as his regular compatriots who came to chat and play cards there, people from across the whole community used the café, drinking mugs of tea and eating large English breakfasts. It was smoky and overwhelmingly male.

Weaving her way through them all was Elsie.

For a moment Mary stood to one side of the doorway, unnoticed, observing her friend.

She's so pretty, she thought. *So confident.*

With a plate in each hand Elsie had come to a halt at one of the tables. The two men looked up and grinned. Mary wondered if it were through appreciation of Elsie or the food? Probably both. She watched their bantering exchanges before Elsie made her way back to the counter to pick up a couple of mugs of tea. Her auburn hair was swept up, her apron pulled tight across a slim figure, strings nipping in a tiny waist.

In comparison Mary felt drab, old before her time. And the one thing that made her feel alive – going to the Baldoni house – had lost its allure with Pippo away.

It was Neldo's wife who spotted her. Anna was standing on the other side of the counter, her back to the kitchen, sandwiched between two large, framed photographs of Neldo's parents that hung on the wood-panelled wall.

'*Signora?*'

Hearing Anna, Elsie turned. 'Oh, Mary, hello! What you doing, hiding in the corner? Sit yourself down and I'll bring you a cuppa.'

There was nowhere to sit, unless she chose to share a table with one of the groups of men. 'Don't worry, Elsie,' she said. 'I was just passing, but I've got a lot to do, I'll come another time …'

'Don't you dare run away! Look, I'm sure Paddy won't mind you squeezing in.' She walked over to a man sitting on his own. 'You don't mind, do you?' Paddy shook his head and lightly touched his cap towards Mary.

'You've finished anyway, haven't you?' Elsie spoke to him a bit too loudly, as if he was a child, or a very old man. 'Let me clear your plate away so you'll have more room. You hungry, Mary?'

'No … no thanks. Just a cup of tea would be nice. A strong one. Perhaps some toast?'

'Coming up.'

Mary felt large and cumbersome, as if the wicker basket she was unhooking from her arm was an extension of herself, occupying too much space. She slowly lowered it on to the floor by the chair, worrying that it would be in the way. She removed her purse from the inside and sat herself down.

Paddy nodded and she smiled stiffly back. He reminded her of a younger version of her father, and a distant memory from early childhood flashed into her mind of a man in overalls coming in from work, hungry but happy to be home, kissing his wife on the cheek, and ruffling her hair. Not drunk and bitter and angry …

'You all right?' Paddy spoke with a soft Irish accent.

She wondered how she appeared to this man. Respectable married woman about to begin her errands for the day? And what was he: a working man, a good man, possibly with wife and children at home, stopping off at the café to get food between shifts? Had he left behind many relatives in Ireland? Did he miss them and hanker after home? Should she tell him she was of Irish descent too? Why would he care?

'Yes, I'm all right, thank you.'

Questions kept coming into her head. Did this man ever wonder, she mused, what the point of his existence was? Of course not, everyone was just surviving. What else could you do? Meanwhile, Paddy was watching her cautiously before standing up suddenly and pushing the chair backwards away from the table. 'I'd best be going,' he said, touching his cap again.

Elsie was arriving with the tea and toast. 'If you wait till it gets quieter, I can join you.' She placed plate and cup on the table.

Mary looked at her friend with a sense of hollowness. She knew that what she had hoped for, what she had originally anticipated – a heart to heart, some comforting reassurance – was never going to happen. She also believed she could not possibly confide in Elsie because, once revealed, the secret could not be pulled back. It wasn't so much about trust or Elsie's teasing, more that if she uttered the words out loud – 'I love another man' – they would be heard and take a form in the world. She could not risk them becoming real. Unsaid, they remained a fantasy. She would simply have to keep it all locked in, and in that realisation, she felt a depth of loneliness close to despair.

'Are you all right?' Elsie's words, an echo of Paddy's earlier, brought her back.

She shook her head, as if throwing something off. 'I'm sorry, I've only just remembered I've got to collect the rabbit from Mr Ward.'

'Rabbit?'

'Yes, there's no other meat left.'

'But you haven't touched your tea.'

Mary opened her purse and threw some coins on the table, clipped it shut and put it in her jacket pocket. 'I quite forgot about the meat … I'll see you soon.' She picked up the basket and rushed out of the café.

'Mary!' Elsie shouted after her, but the door had already closed.

Head down, she went back towards Clerkenwell, passing a group of condemned buildings waiting to be demolished. They were still occupied by families with nowhere else to go. It was terrible how people had to live. She wondered how she would bear it, sleeping in a dangerous wreck of a tenement building or a damp, rat-infested slum with six children to feed. Mary was fortunate, she knew that. Count your blessings. Be thankful. Her mother's sayings didn't soothe, however often she repeated them. The phrases only made her feel guilty for being unhappy.

By the time she arrived at Ward's, she knew she could not possibly go in, her tearful state would be too visible. How hopeless she was at controlling her emotions. But she needed to buy something for supper. She resolved to get home, have a rest and then set out again.

Just beyond Ward's she began to feel dizzy. If only she had eaten the toast Elsie had made for her after all. She stopped walking and leant against a brick wall, her basket still hooked over her left arm, empty like her stomach. Feeling waves of faintness, she crouched down and lowered her head to her knees.

I'm almost home. I must get home …

The noise of an engine. Brakes. A car or truck was coming to a halt alongside the pavement where she crouched. She could hear a door opening and slamming shut, but why bother to look?

Then a familiar voice very close by.

'It is Mary?'

She opened her eyes and started up in bewildered recognition.

'Pippo! What are you doing here?'

'I coming home with the …' He pointed to the truck, badly parked, with a wheel halfway up on the pavement. 'Are you ill? You look not well.'

She tried to pull herself up as elegantly as she could, but as soon as she managed to stand, she sank back against the wall and slipped back down to her hunched position.

'Wait, I get water.' He strode off and reappeared with a small jerry can of water he held to her lips. The metal was cold, and the liquid tasted faintly of petrol.

'And food … I have food too, come.'

'No, I have to get rabbit …'

'Rabbit?'

'Yes rabbit, for supper.'

'Ah, we will get rabbit later. Right now, you come into the truck.'

Gently he helped her up. Heart racing, she leaned into him as he walked her a few yards and opened the door of the vehicle, waiting patiently for her to settle into the passenger seat. It was an old Bedford van, manufactured before the war and battered inside as well as out, but she felt as if she was climbing into a Rolls Royce.

He took something out of a paper bag at her feet and offered it to her. 'Eat, eat, it is good for you.'

It was bread, roughly pulled from a loaf and torn in half, with some sort of salty ham sandwiched in the centre. It tasted good. He watched her with satisfaction. She glanced at him gratefully. 'Thank you.'

'And now more water.' He passed her the metal container. 'You feel better, yes?'

He looked eager and concerned. She wanted to sink into those eyes.

'But, Mary, what is this? Why do you cry?'

It was only as he said this that she became aware that her cheeks were wet. 'No, I … it's just you are so thoughtful …'

'It is nothing. Why are you sad?'

Neither her father nor Geoffrey – the two men she knew best – would have ever asked such a question. They would have wanted her to suppress any misery and pull herself together as quickly as possible. She put her hands over her eyes and began weeping.

'It does not matter why you are sad. You must not worry, come …' Pippo put his arm around her and pulled her towards him so that her head rested on his shoulder. It was only when her sobs subsided that she became acutely aware of him – his smell, his touch, the warmth of him. She breathed him in like a tonic. All this time he had not spoken but simply held her, and when she tried to compose herself and raised her hand to her face, he stopped her. He pulled her hand down and replaced it with his, wiping away the remaining tears.

Suddenly she felt naked, exposed. Reality swept over her. 'Please, I must go home.' Abruptly, she pulled away, the spell broken.

'Yes, yes. I will take you.' He coughed as he put his hand on the steering wheel.

When he came to a stop in their road, she waited for him to open the door on her side. She dreaded him leaving her to face that grey, lonely house. That was the overriding motivation, she decided later, when she was trying to justify to herself what had happened after they stepped over the threshold. That was why she had let him follow her in. She just wanted not to be alone.

The atmosphere over breakfast the following morning was chilly. 'Do you think Mr Ward might have a bit more on offer today?' asked Geoffrey. Their supper had been meagre and now he was craving sausages.

Mary buttered her toast with increased vigour. 'I told you, even the rabbit had run out by the time I got back to his shop.'

How easy it was to lie. She hadn't been back to Mr Ward at all. When she had let Pippo take her home, he had opened the passenger door and, even though she no longer felt dizzy, she had taken the arm he offered her. As she took her purse out of her pocket to remove her key, she noticed Pippo looking up and down the empty road as if checking whether anyone had seen them. Without saying anything, she pushed open the door and he followed her in.

She had turned towards him as the right words formed themselves in her mind. *It was very kind of you to see me home. Thank you, Pippo. I am quite well now …* but the phrases seemed empty and stuck in her throat. She couldn't let them – or him – go.

'It was very kind …' she managed, but the sentence stalled.

Standing in the tiny hall, Geoffrey's parents' hall, she had felt Pippo's hands catch her as if she had swayed, as if she were about to fall. He was so close she could feel the heat of his body. How could she pretend to herself there was nothing unusual in their proximity? She sensed his physicality with a pang of longing. The urge to touch him and feel his skin next to hers felt like a raging thirst.

As if understanding this, he lunged forward, and his mouth was on hers. She was in a vertiginous spin and, afraid she really was losing her balance, she stepped back, flailing her arms around to find the small table behind her. Her hands clutched the edge to steady herself, leaving her body open, unprotected, like an offering.

Pippo paused and looked at her, as if asking for permission to go further. His action remained suspended as she waited to see what he would do next. She held his gaze – defiant, lustful – willing him to continue. He took her by the shoulders again and pulled her towards him, continuing to kiss her. She felt his arms encircling her, embracing her tightly, and enjoyed the strange, exciting sensation of her breasts pressed against an unfamiliar body, a body so much stronger and muscular than Geoffrey's.

The release of energy was intense. The quiet, well-behaved young woman who followed rules had disappeared, or at least temporarily receded from view. She had tried to be the person she was supposed to be, but in that moment she could no longer manage it. She did not care. The agonies of doubt would come later, but in that moment the good wife had ceased to be.

Years of repressed feelings were unleashed as she returned his kiss. They clung to each other and began staggering around the tiny hall, bumping into everything that stood in their way; the key that Mary had rested on the nearest surface was knocked on to the floor as the two of them fell again against the table. At one point she banged her head against the wall, but the momentary pain was heightened into gratification. Every sensation was elevated into something extraordinary. It was a release from the mundane, the ordinary, and she savoured every second. She was tearing at his clothes, hungry to possess him, to get at his skin.

Never had she imagined she could be so impatient and voracious. After a whirlwind, she was lying on the stairs underneath him, pulling him to her, into her. A small part of her brain was telling her this was wrong, but in that moment she didn't care, so at one with Pippo did she feel, so liberated from the constraints of pretence and respectability and moderation. She was tired of being good. For a while she needed to forget self-denial and abandon herself to pleasure.

Afterwards she began feeling uncomfortably squashed beneath him. She stirred, and he pulled himself off her. Slowly, silently, separately, they stood up and began adjusting their clothes, brushing themselves down. She tidied her hair and picked up the cotton fabric that – seemingly a lifetime ago – she had tied around her head. It was only when dressed that she felt a shred of shame and remorse. She looked at him almost reproachfully. It had been his fault, leading her astray.

'You must not worry,' he said, as if reading her thoughts. They were the first words he had uttered since they had come through the front door. She smiled in response. 'You said that before.'

'Your mouth always smiles, but your eyes are sad,' he answered.

Yes, and what now? What about tomorrow? Would he be disgusted by the ease with which he had possessed her, by her unrestrained response? Would it make him think less of her? How could she possibly claim any commitment? She wanted more of him but how could she, with Geoffrey and Pippo living as neighbours? How would they keep this secret? Geoffrey was safely at the bookshop until evening, but he might well have decided to come home unexpectedly. The idea of him finding them on the stairs together as he walked through that front door made her feel sick. What had come over her?

But she said nothing.

'I must go now, but we will see each other.' His voice was tender, which was a relief. She nodded. He moved away from her, briefly ran his hand along her cheek and opened the front door. She remained standing, still as a statue, and watched him leave.

Later, in bed with Geoffrey, while she savoured the enormity of what she had done, another worry snaked in. What had happened to her shopping basket? Had she left it where Pippo had found her, dizzy and faint, on the street? How would she explain its disappearance? Not that Geoffrey would necessarily notice. But it felt imperative to find it. Her dead mother-in-law's basket encapsulated everything that was safe and secure. It was a container of respectability, and the loss of it seemed symbolic. She would look for it more thoroughly in the morning, it had to be somewhere in the house. This reasoning calmed her down as if in the finding of the basket she would be able to restore the propriety she had lost that afternoon.

Breakfast was finished. Mary was waiting for the moment Geoffrey would leave for the bookshop – if only he would hurry up and go, so that she might replay the afternoon with Pippo without being observed. If she hadn't been aware of the soreness between her legs, she might have convinced herself that it had never happened, but the feeling was there, and she liked it. It meant she could still sense the mark Pippo had made on her body.

Geoffrey frowned. 'You seem distracted. Are you feeling unwell again?'

She sniffed. 'No, not at all, I'm quite well. I'm just thinking about what I need to do this morning. I'll get back to Ward's and see what he has in today. I'm sure if I get there early ...'

'Yes, that's a good idea. Well, I must be off. Another delivery of books is arriving. Sales are picking up, and John from the Charing Cross Road has been kindly sending customers my way when he can't get hold of what they are looking for.'

'Good.'

'Yes, and the browsers at the barrows and bookstalls in the Farringdon Road end up coming into the shop. Some of them have become regular customers ...'

Mary wasn't listening. It was a monotonous drone and all she wanted was for him to go. But he was peering at her more closely.

'Are you sure you don't feel unwell?'

'Oh, I'm quite well,' she repeated blankly. 'Thank you.' At least he sounded concerned. 'You must not worry,' she added, echoing her Pippo's words.

With Geoffrey finally gone to the bookshop and the remnants of breakfast cleared away, Mary prepared to go out. Today she would be a good wife, and make sure her husband had a hearty supper that evening.

The purse was still in her jacket pocket and the front door key had been put back on the small table in the hall. But she was anxious about the disappearance of the shopping basket. She looked around, checking under the table she had almost knocked over during the passionate tumbles of the afternoon before, but no, it wasn't there.

She must focus and remember. She replayed the scene: opening the front door, Pippo following her in, and then ... no, she wasn't holding the basket then. It must still be in the road, at the spot where Pippo had found her when she had felt faint. Perhaps, if she went back as quickly as possible, it might still be there.

She stepped on to the street, darting a glance at Pippo's house as she passed. He must be taking the truck back to his cousin, she decided, as it was no longer parked in the street. There was loneliness in the realisation that he was probably getting on with his daily tasks without giving her a second thought, whereas she felt incapable of concentrating on anything but what had taken place yesterday. What would happen when they next bumped into each other, how would he be with her? The possibility of his coldness, his indifference, was horrible. She would have to harden herself to this dreaded probability.

'Mary!' A woman's voice behind made her stop in her tracks. She turned and saw Nanella gesticulating from the doorstep. 'Come here!' she was shouting. There was urgency in her voice.

'Yes, what is it?' A wave of guilt shot through her.

'I have something, you come.'

When Mary reached the open door, she found Nanella had disappeared into the back of the house. She stood outside until she heard her friend call out to her from inside, 'Why you not come in?'

Nervously Mary stepped inside, and as she did so Nanella reappeared, basket in hand.

'Oh, the basket, thank goodness!'

Nanella was beaming. 'Yes, Pippo he say he was going to bring this to you later, he go now to take truck back. He say he saw you yesterday, you were not well, you sat in truck?'

'So I left it in the truck?'

Nanella nodded.

'Yes, he was very kind, he found me, I was feeling dizzy ... He saw me home.' A chill went through her, recalling the times she had heard Nanella's children playing next door. The walls were so thin.

'Yes, you dizzy, he told me. Please, Mary, come sit down. You do not look well again.'

'But I must go shopping ...'

'No, no, you come sit down.'

'Perhaps now,' Nanella said conspiratorially once they were settled with their cups of tea, 'you are waiting for a baby?'

'What? Oh … no.' She giggled awkwardly. 'I'm definitely not. At least I don't think so!'

'I felt dizzy when I was pregnant. Not so much with Rosa, but with the two boys, yes.'

Nanella's face was so open, so amiable. Mary longed to confide in her. Instead she said, 'I do not think it will ever happen. It has been over a year and a half since I married. Dr Gould told me there was no reason for concern but …'

'A year or two is nothing! It is not a long time to wait.'

'Hmm. You know, my mother lost several babies. I mean, before they were born. Miscarriages. So, you see, perhaps I will be the same. Perhaps it is best not to get pregnant at all. I could not bear to have one and then lose it … I may never have one, not even one. Sometimes it is not meant to be.'

'But you are still young! I tell you not to worry. If you worry, you will never have one.'

'That's good advice. I will not worry.' Mary grinned, thinking of Pippo's words once more. The warm tea and the chat had made her feel better. 'You are kind, Nanella. But I must get off to Mr Ward now.'

As she queued at Ward's, she thought about Nanella Baldoni. Was her warmth and good-natured openness attributable to her being Italian? There was none of that pursed-lip bitterness so entrenched in her own mother's face. Despite becoming a widow under tragic circumstances, Nanella brought joy into the way she spoke, cooked and cared for her family. She could not be well off, even taking into account what Pippo might be bringing in, but at least the Baldoni household was free of Nora's repressed disapproval and the stoic unhappiness Mary had grown up with and replicated in her own marriage. It was tragic that Mr Baldoni had died but perhaps, in the long run, it was easier to get on with life without a husband interfering, or dragging you down? She wondered whether her mother had ever wished for deliverance from her husband. Of course, she must have done. Mary shivered. That was a dreadful thing to think.

A loud voice interrupted her musing. 'How are you, Mrs Williams?'

'Oh, yes, good morning, Mr Ward ... very well, thank you.'

She admonished herself constantly in the following few days. Agonies of guilt were building up inside her. She should have controlled herself, or at least not have succumbed so quickly. Men did not respect women like her. She was a hussy, she had sinned.

During the war, Elsie had teased Mary about being prudish, a stick-in-the-mud. She would say, 'You don't know who is going to live and who is going to die, with the bombs going off and all, so you may as well enjoy yourself, act as if each day was your last.' There was no excuse now. No one was dying. But in more dramatic moments she felt that she would truly die if she could not have Pippo.

Was he avoiding her? Every passing hour increased her apprehension. She crept out of the house on tenterhooks, nerves jangling, in case she should bump into him or any of his family. How could she look them in the eye, especially the younger children, after doing those things with their big brother? She dreaded yet craved another meeting in equal measure.

She must pretend that it meant nothing. When they next met, and surely they would soon, she would greet him politely and retain her dignity, then forget all about him and return to her housewifely routine. She must set aside the encounter as an exciting memory, to be brought out and examined when it could be enjoyed undisturbed. It had been a moment of insanity, an aberration. And yet the yearning would not stop. How could she block this craving for more, imagining how it would be?

The torture was hearing him through the walls, playing with the children, calling out to his mother, going up and down their stairs. To have him so close was tantalising, it was a constant reminder of the unattainable.

A week passed like a decade. She tried to distract herself with intense bouts of spring-cleaning. Curtains came down, floors were mopped, surfaces wiped, upholstery cleaned. The doorstep was scrubbed. Far corners of cupboards were dusted, mattresses turned over, carpets beaten, woollens washed and carefully put away, layered with sprigs of lavender. Even the odd bits of hardly used silver belonging to Geoffrey's parents were polished until they gleaned. In a frivolous moment she wondered whether Geoffrey might value good housekeeping over sexual fidelity, but decided, probably not. It was a joke she could have once made with Elsie, but of course she could not do that now.

Geoffrey had noticed her newly found enthusiasm for housework and mentioned it one morning as he was preparing to leave. 'I must say, the house is looking very clean,' he said. 'And I've never seen so much fresh washing hanging up outside.'

'Well, the sunny weather helps.'

'Don't overdo it though, will you? You must watch your health. After your illness this winter, you don't want a relapse. You still look very pale.'

'I'm fine, I promise you. And, as you always say, it's good to get on top of things. Now I must make your sandwiches.'

He glanced at his watch. 'Oh dear, yes, I am rather late. Would you mind bringing them over when you go to the shops?'

It was midday and she had dropped off the brown-paper package of ham sandwiches for Geoffrey at the bookshop. Making her way back she saw Pippo walking purposefully uphill towards her. She instinctively put her hand to her face, as if this would hide her from view. Torn between wanting to remain invisible and wanting him to see her, her mind raced through what she might do. On her left was the brick arch opening into the stairwell that ran up to Rosebery Avenue, to her right, the warren of streets that led to Clerkenwell Road. Either choice might offer an escape. Or she could turn around and hide in the shadows formed by the viaduct bridge above her until he had passed by.

It was too late. He had spotted her. 'Mary!' he called out.

She stood still, frozen, as he caught up.

'Are you going shopping?'

'No, I have just dropped off my husband's sandwiches,' she said coldly, with the emphasis on the word 'husband', deliberately not referring to Geoffrey by name.

He glanced around the street, and following his gaze, she saw a couple of men coming from the direction of the Coach and Horses walking up towards them.

Pippo reached out his hand to touch her shoulder.

'Are you crazy? Don't touch me!' she whispered, longing for him to touch her.

'But why?'

'What do you mean, why? It could be someone we know, coming up behind us! God forbid it might even be my father!'

With a swift movement Pippo grabbed her shoulder and pushed her off the street and under the arch.

'What are you doing ...' she began. She was flustered, she could hear male voices right above her and footsteps coming down the stone stairs.

He pushed her gently against the wall of the stairwell. As the voices of two lads came closer, he pressed himself on to her body, his arms on either side, his head concealing her face, and kissed her.

The boys passed by, whistling and directing lewd comments at Pippo. As soon as their voices faded, he released her. Instinctively she went to slap him, but his hand caught her wrist and brought it to his face. He clearly felt she had responded to his kiss, that she had been happy to yield.

'Come, we will walk home.' He briefly took her hand, letting it go as they came out of the stairwell, but giving her a knowing look. We are together, he seemed to be saying; we are conjoined. It was from that moment that she understood with rising excitement that they were lovers now.

6

Florence

NOVEMBER 1966

Cara hurried through the dark city, eager to get back to the apartment. October had been a wet month and during the first three days of November the rain continued to fall. It was the kind of rain that showed no sign of letting up – little point in sheltering in doorways to wait for the downpour to stop. The citizens of Florence pulled up their collars and made a dash, hats down and overcoats tightened to keep out the damp. A scattering of umbrellas danced about in the cobbled streets, busy with workers going home and women buying last-minute provisions for their families. Green, white and red bunting had been put up around the city to mark the Giorno della Forze Armate, celebrating Italy's victory over Austria in 1918. Tomorrow was *festa* and the shops would be closed.

Cara's kerchief, knotted under her chin, was already sodden under the ineffectual umbrella she had brought with her. Limp strands of hair stuck to her forehead. As she turned into Via dei Servi she spotted that the metal shutters of the vegetable shop were halfway down. Beppe was closing early and bringing in the produce on display.

'Aspetta!' she shouted.

She wanted potatoes, carrots and something green to serve with roast chicken – Gianni would be arriving in two hours. Beside the shutters, Beppe paused, allowing her to reach his shop and stoop under the half-closed metal grill, holding the dripping umbrella in front of her like a shield. She chose a few vegetables and Beppe added a large bunch of parsley to her shopping bag for free. He had been like a kindly father figure since her arrival, and thanks to their chats her Italian had greatly improved.

'*Tremendo, vero?*' He nodded towards the rain outside.

'I walked past the river earlier. Has it ever been so high?'

Beppe shrugged. 'It is not surprising. This rain has been going for so long! "*Piove sempre sul bagnato!*" It always rains where it's already wet. But it has to stop soon, surely?'

They both agreed it was awful. But really, why worry?

'*Veramente, me ne infischia.* To be honest, I don't care!' Beppe grinned. Tomorrow was a holiday, and nothing could dampen his good mood. Cara felt the same. Back on the street with the bag of shopping in her hand, she laughed off the spray from a car speeding through a deep puddle outside. There would be plenty of time for a hot bath while the chicken cooked.

This was to be a special evening, in fact a momentous evening. She had finally agreed to let Gianni spend the night with her. As she had repeatedly made clear, if he wanted to sleep with her, as he clearly did, she was not going to be slotted in before his mother wondered where he was. At first, she had used this as an excuse to stop him 'going all the way', but she had got to the point of wanting him to (and wanting him too).

So, a plan was hatched. He would tell his mother, Marcella, that he was staying with cousin Stefano over the *festa*. Stefano could be trusted. All was sorted out.

All, of course, apart from the fluttering anxiety, mixed with the excited anticipation, that had taken hold in her chest. She wasn't so naïve as to think there were no risks involved but Gianni had said he would be 'careful', and she had explained to him that women in her family had low fertility.

'My grandmother and my mother are always calling me "a miracle",' she had told him. 'We are all "only girls" ...'

'*Solo ragazze!*' he said. 'No, it is good, I understand. *Siete figlie uniche*. No brothers. No sisters.'

It was early evening, and the chicken was in the oven, when Gianni arrived at Cara's door carrying a cardboard tray of *bomboloni* – large doughnuts filled with cream – wrapped in several layers of grease-proof paper as protection against the rain. He opened the package in the hall, looking sheepish. 'I hate lying,' he grimaced. 'Mamma make these especially for Stefano, he love them. She was so happy they came out well ...'

'Stefano does know you are here, doesn't he?'

'Yes, he does ...'

'Well then, you must tell him to thank Marcella for them. She will never know any different.'

'I will, I speak to him tomorrow.' A mischievous smile spread across his face, which warmed Cara's heart and diminished her initial irritation. He looked boyishly handsome when his eyes widened in that playful way. She didn't feel the same depth of affection she had for Tony, but he was fun and there was something about his faltering Italian-accented English that was quite seductive. She smiled back, more to herself than at him.

'Come into the kitchen,' she said. 'I am cooking my favourite meal. Before I left London, my mother taught me how to make her special roast potatoes ...'

He followed her and placed the *bomboloni* on the kitchen table, then said, 'you have red cheeks from the …' pointing at the oven Cara had crouched beside to check the chicken.

Her hands went up to her face to cover her flushing cheeks. 'Oh yes, it is very hot!'

Gianni grinned and looked around the kitchen. 'Where is the …?' His fist made the gesture of uncorking wine. She liked the way he used his hands instead of words to finish sentences.

The meal she produced turned out even better than anticipated. The chicken was succulent, the potatoes crispy, the carrots sweet. Pastries consumed and the bottle of wine finished, Gianni rose from the table and walked to Cara's side, taking her by the hand. She knew what was going to happen next, and although they had not slept together before, they had grown close. It felt like the right time.

Together they walked silently down the corridor towards the bedroom. They stopped by the bed and he pulled her to him. '*Sei cosi bella,*' he said, and began unbuttoning her blouse. Cara relaxed.

Although her need to be desired was perhaps even stronger than her desire for him, she did not feel coerced. By putting him off until this moment, she had taken some control. She was his equal partner in orchestrating this evening. When he pushed her gently on to the bed, she was ready.

She knew that he knew he was her first lover. She had told him so when they had planned this night together. 'I have not yet had a proper lover,' she had said, as if she had had boyfriends but not one of consequence.

He noted these words. His lovemaking was gentle and considerate, and he took his time. At first Cara responded hesitantly, but as she gained confidence, she allowed her body to behave instinctively, and surrendered to moving at her own rhythm. Her increasing ardour surprised and delighted them both. She felt safe with him, unhurried, considered. When she experienced a moment of pain and cried out, he comforted her with reassuring murmurings until she relaxed again. It was good to feel the warmth of his body, the comfort of his being there. She had been alone too long.

Afterwards, sitting up in bed, he smoked a cigarette and listened as she told him, in her mix of English and Italian, about life in London. She described the streets near her home; the sounds of milk floats on cobbles, rag-and-bone men shouting, metal dustbins clanging; the rows of terraced houses and the backyards and gardens, the coal sheds and the thick days of fog referred to as 'pea-soupers'.

'*Nebbia come "minestra di piselli". Stupendo.*' He laughed and repeated her phrase, 'pea-soupers', trying to mimic her English vowels. Then he added more seriously, 'I will come, one day, to London.'

'You will feel at home in Clerkenwell, it is full of Italian shopkeepers,' she answered brightly.

Abruptly, his tone changed. 'Why do you say that? I do not want to be a shopkeeper.' He sounded annoyed, insulted. 'One day I shall be a successful architect! You English girls think Italians can only be shopkeepers or waiters ...'

'But, Gianni, I didn't mean that at all ...' her voice trailed off, and for a moment she felt the sadness of disconnection. So often they spoke at cross-purposes. The mood when they were together could alter from carefree to distrustful in seconds. 'Anyway, what is wrong with being a shopkeeper? My father runs a bookshop. He's a shopkeeper ...'

'That is not the same thing. Books are literature, culture. Not tomatoes. Your father is, how you say, intellectual.'

'Not really ...' Cara thought of Geoffrey and his limited enthusiasm for her interest in art.

Gianni flicked ash into the small saucer Cara had provided on the bedside table. 'You think I will come to London and have no work and be poor … Well, *Cara mia*, if I am to be poor, I would rather stay in Italy. At least in Italy the sun shines!'

And then to her relief, as they heard the rain drumming outside, he laughed. 'Come on, it is OK. I'm sorry. Come here.' He stubbed his cigarette out and pulled her towards him and she let herself be kissed. At least when he was kissing her she could forget the frustration and unease she sometimes felt in his company.

Much later, after more talking and love-making, they settled down in the single bed. The loss of her virginity did not feel to her like a loss, but more of a gain. She was proud, as if she had achieved something. Proud and, as they curled into one another, content. They slowly drifted into a fitful sleep to the sound of the sheeting rain lashing the stone of the inner courtyard below them. Tomorrow they would be able to enjoy a lie-in. There was nothing to get up for.

The bells that woke Cara were slower but more relentless than ever. Dong … dong … dong, they went, with longer pauses in between. Less of a joyful peal, more ponderous somehow. She wished she could turn them off so that she could catch up on her sleep. The single bed felt smaller than it had done the night before when she had enjoyed their tangle of limbs. She wanted to stretch unhindered and pick up the blankets that had fallen on to the floor without disturbing Gianni, whose arm was limply draped across her. Gingerly she lifted it and moved it away. He grunted as he turned his body towards the wall.

The bedroom windows had internal as well as external shutters and they made the room very dark. So dark in fact that at times, when she had first arrived in Florence and was lying very still, missing Tony and waiting for sleep, she had to fight the sensation that she had been buried in a tomb. It had been warm then, but there was a smell of plaster and stone that caught in the back of her throat and never quite went away.

So much had changed in the last two months. She had matured to the point that she was contemptuous of her previously sentimental tendency to see herself in the role of tragic heroine. She wore her new-found independence with pride. And now, she thought, as she glanced at Gianni beside her, she even had a lover. Would she tell Nicoletta about this? And when would she mention this romantic adventure to her mother? Or even to Tony, she wondered. Probably not until he admitted to his own.

As she climbed out of bed she felt a surge of energy, a feeling of exhilaration about the immediate future. *I shall clear up the kitchen before he wakes*, she thought, *and we will have the morning together before he has to leave*. Not wishing to disturb him by putting on the bedside light, she stepped gingerly over the clothes hastily discarded the night before and groped her way to the window to open the internal shutters. A slither of grey light filtering through the slats of the shutters on the outside was enough to help her find her way to the bedroom door.

She fastened the towelling dressing-gown around herself before pressing down the door handle as quietly as possible. In the corridor the light switch didn't work and neither did those in the bathroom and kitchen. Had the whole electrical circuit of the building gone down?

The window in the kitchen made its familiar creaking noise as she opened it before folding back the shutters and looking up at the overcast sky. It was another dull day and still raining. Would it ever cease? It was unusually quiet out there – but of course it was *festa*. Noise would come later, as revellers returned home. Florentines were never much concerned with the volume of noise they made in the streets, whatever the time of day or night. She heard a woman farther up the street shouting out of a window but couldn't make out the meaning of the words.

The kitchen was chilly and damp. Placing her hand to the radiator she found it was cold. A hot drink would warm her up, she decided. When she turned on the tap at the sink, water came out fitfully, yielding only enough to fill the small pan she used to make her tea. She picked up the matches to light the gas, striking several without success.

And then Gianni was walking into the kitchen, wearing only his underwear, looking rumpled and sleepy.

'It's cold! I must put more clothes on. But I wanted to see where you had gone.' He came up to her and circled his arms around her waist from behind.

'It *is* cold. I don't know why the heating has not come on. Even these are damp,' she said, matches still in hand.

'Why is it dark? Have the lights gone in here as well? They are not working in the bedroom.'

'Yes, no light. And the radiator is icy ...'

'Make some coffee. I'll check the other rooms.'

Cara picked up the small percolator, opened it, and poured in the water she had intended for her tea. She looked at one of the flagons that Nicoletta had indicated under the sink – 'always keep spare water' she had said. That would have to do for their next drink, she thought, hoping it wasn't too old.

But the gas rings on the cooker would not light, even when she had managed to ignite one of the old matches. Turning the dials up higher, she leant down to sniff. No smell of gas. Another half-dozen matchsticks were wasted before she called out, 'Gianni, nothing is working. *Niente!*'

He came back into the kitchen in the clothes he had been wearing the evening before, looking more awake. Strands of his hair were damp from some drops of water he had managed to squeeze out of the bathroom tap and wipe across his face. The shadow of stubble on his chin made Cara wonder whether he had brought a razor with him – his mother would be suspicious if he returned home unshaven. She was about to question him about this when he pointed at the box of matches Cara was holding and said brusquely, 'Give to me.'

She passed the box to him with a wave of irritation. 'I do know how to light the cooker,' she said.

Ignoring her, Gianni tried unsuccessfully a few times. 'The stove won't light.'

'Yes, I know that! I told you, nothing is working.'

'There must be something wrong with the whole house. We must ask Fernando. Wait here.'

'Don't disturb them now, it might be too early.'

Gianni glanced at the little clock on the kitchen shelf. 9.32 a.m. 'It is not very early. He will probably be out by now. But I will telephone his wife.'

'The number is on the table,' Cara said, following him into the hall.

Gianni stood, holding the receiver away from his ear. 'Silence. There is nothing.' The two of them looked at each other blankly.

The church bells began ringing again. 'The bells!' They said this simultaneously and laughed. But Cara felt uneasy, why would the bells ring now, at well past nine?

When the bells stopped suddenly, they could make out some shouting in the distance, but they could not understand the words.

'I think we should go and knock on the Lottis' door after all,' Cara said. 'We shall see if they have the same problem. Wait. I'll get dressed.'

'I will go down now, come when you are ready.'

Cara was pulling her jumper over her head when she heard raised voices coming from the stairwell. She rushed to the hall and saw that

Gianni had left the door of the apartment ajar, so she stepped out and leant over the banisters. Fernando Lotti and Gianni were both shouting at the same time, not in anger, but in distress. She could see the tops of their heads, and their arms were gesticulating wildly.

'*Ma come? Cosa é successo?*' Gianni was asking, so Cara called out the same, from above them, 'What is happening?'

Gianni lifted his eyes towards her. 'Look out of the window! The street has turned into a river!'

She ran back inside the apartment and opened the kitchen window. How could she have missed what met her eyes? She had probably been too busy scanning the sky. There, way below her, the street was a mass of dark, swirling water, carrying with it large logs and branches as well as a number of unidentifiable objects: an array of debris ranging from clothes to furniture was being thrown around by its angry swell. Something resembling a chair was bobbing along but it was hard to be sure what it was from so high above. The only sign of human life was a man slowly wading through it with a little girl clinging to his back, her arms tightly linked around his neck. The water had reached the man's waist, but he struggled on.

She rushed out on to the landing again. Each landing beneath her was filling with the occupants of the apartments, who had opened their doors to find out what was going on or to put forward their own views; some of them she had never met.

'At least no one in this building lives on the ground floor – there is only the cellar ...'

'Yes, and there are steps up to the front door ...'

'But have you seen the force of the water?'

'It looks so dirty ...'

'Brown, almost.'

'I have no electricity, have you?'

'No, nor gas ...'

'Me neither.'

'What can we do?'

'...and only a trickle of water ... how will we wash? Cook? What can we drink?'

'There's lots of water outside,' one of Fernando Lotti's children piped up, before being shushed by his mother.

'Gianni?' Cara called from above, not seeing him any more.

Fernando looked up and began climbing the flight of stairs towards her. *'E terribile, terribile,'* he kept repeating over and over again as he reached her side.

'But where is Gianni? Why didn't he tell me he was going?'

'He has gone to Santa Croce to see about his mother. He will be back as soon as he can.'

'But how will he get there if the water is so high?'

'He will wade, or swim.'

'The bells ... I thought the bells sounded different this morning.'

'Yes, they are rung differently when disaster comes. *Campana a festa e una a morte.*'

She translated the phrase in her head. One bell for celebration, one for death. 'And today was supposed to be a *festa*,' she said out loud.

Fernando nodded his head solemnly.

Cara excused herself and went back inside to look out of the kitchen window, hoping to catch sight of Gianni struggling down the long stretch of Via Laura. She wondered if Lotti was now asking himself why Gianni had been here at all, unshaven, rapidly dressed, shortly after nine in the morning. But right now, that was the least of anyone's worries.

She leaned right out, craning her neck to look farther up. But she could see nothing. Even the wading man and his little girl had disappeared.

For the rest of the day and the following morning, Cara didn't leave the building. Before going back downstairs Fernando had called out that he would get more information, but she had heard nothing from him since. What was preventing her walking down to the next floor and ringing their bell? Since she had met them, the Lotti family had been so generous, offering her meals and stopping to chat whenever they bumped into each other. She knew it wouldn't seem strange if she asked them for news. But a sort of torpor had come over her, replacing the excitement she had felt only hours before. She was more acutely aware than ever that the family downstairs was a unit and that she would always remain the outsider. In times of trouble it was natural for them to hunker down. She did not blame them, but she felt overwhelmingly alone.

It was not just about being a foreigner and a newcomer. It went deeper, to a feeling she had experienced before. At school she had never understood the need for some of the girls to be part of a close-knit group, a tribe. Perhaps it was because her classmates mostly came from big Catholic families, whereas she was an only child, happiest in her own company, or with one good friend. That friend had been Tony, and for a moment – forgetting about Gianni – her heart ached with the missing of him.

The pile of plates left unwashed from the night before sat congealing in the sink. Cara looked at them disconsolately, wondering how she would get the dishes done now the taps had run dry. Fortunately, there was spare bottled water under the sink to drink, and the leftovers were plentiful.

For several hours she repeatedly opened the kitchen window and looked out at the river that had replaced the street below, and at the relentless rain, willing it to stop. By late afternoon it was dark, and she still felt cold, despite wearing layers of her warmest clothes. Rummaging around in one of the kitchen drawers, she found some candles and lit one, carrying it down the corridor in its holder like a woman from a previous century. Placing it on the bedside table, she rearranged the bedding, rumpled from the night before, and climbed into the bed. She leaned over to blow the candle out and noticed the cigarette stub Gianni had left in the saucer. She should have tried to follow him out of the house, perhaps. But now there was nothing else to do but rest and wait.

When, by lunchtime the next day, Cara had consumed the last bit of chicken – cold, as she still could not warm anything up – she experienced more pangs of sadness. She had seen from the window that the water had receded but there was no sign of Gianni. Less than two days ago they had been sitting in this room eating together. It seemed a century ago.

She stood up to remove the dirty plates to the sink, adding them to the pile. Tomorrow, Cara decided – even if it was Sunday and not the day she would normally be expected – she would walk over to Nicoletta to see how they were managing and ask for advice. How might she get a message to Ma? A telegram perhaps? The telephone exchange at the Post Office, would that be working? A letter to England would take so long.

And what of Gianni? She couldn't simply appear at his mother's house; that would make him angry. She resented not being allowed to be part of his life, instead being kept in the shadows as a 'foreign' girlfriend. It diminished her. Had she slept with him too soon? Had he taken advantage of her? Was all the attention and the promises he had lavished on her simply a ruse to get her into bed? She was pondering these thoughts, feeling lonely and forgotten, when she heard a knock on the door.

'*Permesso?*' It was Fernando Lotti, asking to come in. Cara had been so distracted that she hadn't locked the door behind her the day before.

'*Si, si, venga*, come in,' she called back, relief in her voice.

Fernando appeared, offering her a package. 'Here are some biscuits from my wife. I always tell her she stores too much food but this time it is lucky, there is no bread to be had out there. Most of the shops are closed. And here is the newspaper,' he added, waving a copy of *La Nazione* with his other hand.

'*Grazie, molto gentile. Venga, venga.*' She led the way into the sitting room, like a hostess. It occurred to her that the place had begun to feel like home after all. At least, she was treating it as such.

'I hope there has not been too much damage in the city,' she said, indicating the sofa for him to sit on.

'Much damage, I'm afraid. You have not been outside yet?' Fernando lowered himself on to the sofa, throwing the newspaper down beside him.

'No, but I was planning to go out soon. Now that the rain seems to have stopped for a while.' Cara glanced at the newspaper headline. '*L'Arno Straripa Firenze*' it shouted in huge letters.

Straripa. A word she had not heard before but understood the meaning of. Floods, overflows, invades, overcomes. Poor Florence.

'Yes,' muttered Fernando, 'the sun, *finalmente*, has reappeared. Thank heavens many people were out of the city because of the holiday.'

Cara thought of Gianni's cousin Stefano, Beppe and all the other shopkeepers she had got to know locally during the last two months.

'But what happened?'

'It was during the night and in the early hours of yesterday that the river grew and grew to a dangerous height and the Mugnone ...' Fernando made a sweeping gesture with his hands as if he could not bear to say the words.

The Mugnone, Cara knew, was a tributary flowing into the River Arno near the Cascine, the biggest park of Florence.

'Went on to the land?' she prompted. She didn't know the Italian phrase for 'burst its banks' but Fernando understood.

'Yes. You know there are stables at the Cascine?'

Cara nodded.

'Some horses were saved, but many were drowned, trapped in the stables. I was told that the noise of their desperate neighing could be heard from far away.'

'Oh no! Poor horses … they must have been terrified …'

'And by the time the water had reached the parapets of the Lungarno …' continued Fernando.

'The Lungarno?' Cara thought of Nicoletta's building along the Lungarno, overlooking the river. At least they didn't live on the ground floor.

'Yes, the Lungarno. By the time the water came up that high, it was too late to contain it. It was so fast, you know. It came crashing over the parapets and within a short time it was racing through the streets, right into the interior of the city. I tried to go out yesterday, but I did not get far. The water was too high.'

'But how are people moving around?'

'The police have used boats and rafts to reach the stranded. Most have stayed inside or climbed to higher levels – even their roofs! But it is not just Florence to have this problem. There are storms all over Italy. In Tuscany, many other parts are flooded. Pisa is bad. But what can we do? We are cut off. The roads are blocked. No trains, no buses, nothing can get through.' He paused. 'No help can reach us.'

Cara's fear was rising but she didn't want to voice the question she was desperate to ask. She did not want to sound as if her only concern was for Gianni.

'But has anyone managed to get out of their buildings?' she asked. Had Gianni not walked out of the building straight into that raging torrent?

'The *carabinieri* have been getting around in dinghies, trying to reach those trapped in their homes. Many managed to go up to the higher floors, from which they are being rescued. Army helicopters have been brought in to save people stuck on the rooftops. Can you imagine, clinging to the ridges in the dark, in the cold and rain, thinking about the water rising?'

'Yes, it sounds terrifying ... But what about Gianni?' She couldn't contain herself any longer. 'Have you heard from him? What do you think has happened to him?'

Fernando lowered his gaze. He looked older, weighed down, as if he was keeping a bad secret. For two months, every conversation Cara had had with him had been marked by cheery optimism: the contrast in his manner was striking. He looked flattened.

'To tell you the truth,' he said, 'I am worried. The Santa Croce district where he lives has been the worst hit. And his mother is disabled. Marcella cannot move around easily in her wheelchair without help.'

'That's true, she needs help ...'

Fernando lifted his head and said, 'He was here with you when the flood was at its height, but she ...' and Cara wondered again whether it had occurred to him to question the reason Gianni had been with her in the apartment that morning. Not that respectability mattered any more.

'I have heard,' Fernando continued, 'that in that area the water was over six metres high.'

'Six metres! How is that possible?' Cara put her hand to her mouth, quickly making the calculation. That was about twenty feet. 'Their apartment is on the ground floor,' she said. 'And Marcella's windows have those iron bars over them.' Cara remembered, with a sinking dread, how she had admired the old wrought-iron metalwork that protected ground-level windows in the historic centre. 'How would she have got out?'

Fernando made another gesture with his hands. '*Chissá*. Who knows? I am going to try and walk over there to see what is happening. Yesterday Gianni promised to come back as soon as he had checked on Marcella, but I have not seen him. I don't know where Stefano is either, but before all this happened, I think he was planning to be away for the *festa*. Did Gianni mention what he was doing?'

Cara shook her head.

'The bar on the corner still has the metal shutters pulled down. But look, I'm sorry, I do not want to worry you. Can I get you any …'

'Please, can I go with you to Santa Croce? I *shall* go with you,' she said decisively before Fernando had time to answer. She didn't care if Gianni refused to allow her near Marcella. These were unnatural circumstances and she needed to see for herself how things stood.

'Let's go,' Fernando said.

*

Mary had finished with the carpet sweeper and was about to tackle some darning when she heard the front door opening.

'Did you forget something? You've only been gone an hour,' she said to Geoffrey as he stumbled into the parlour. 'What on earth is the matter? You look very agitated.'

Geoffrey, who had never looked agitated over anything, answered forcefully. 'Put the wireless on, now …'

'Why?'

He strode across to the table and turned it on himself, then began fiddling with the knob as it made loud crackling noises.

'Damn thing!'

'What's wrong?'

'One of my customers was asking if I had heard the news … Apparently the wireless has been broadcasting something about a flood in Florence that has destroyed the city. It sounded serious, there have been fatalities …'

'What?' Mary jumped up, a wave of nausea sweeping over her. 'What do you mean, fatalities?'

'That's what I'm trying to find out.'

'I must get the operator and put in a telephone call immediately,' she said hurrying to the hall.

'I think the phone lines there will be dead,' Geoffrey called after her. 'Blasted wireless, I can't get the news.'

She ran back into the room, not knowing what to do, imagining Cara swept away by an uncontrollable mass of water. 'How do we find out what's going on?'

'Perhaps you could ask Mrs Baldoni if she's has heard anything from Italy?'

'You know I don't see her much any more. But … yes perhaps …' she felt flustered. 'I'll try … um … I can buy a newspaper. I'll see if there is something in *The Times*. You keep trying the wireless.'

Mary was tired. The day before she had left Geoffrey tuning the radio and wandered around, trying to gather information. She had found nothing in the newspaper, and the few Italian shopkeepers she had spoken to had told her only that the whole of Italy had been suffering violent rainstorms. Pasquale was concerned about the gales in Naples. As he cut some ham, he told her, 'My wife heard that the liners – the *Queen Mary* and the *Leonardo da Vinci* – could not approach the port and are tossing on the high seas. Even the lighthouse at Mergellina is leaning over in the wind!'

Geoffrey had returned from the bookshop early, disappointed that he too had not obtained any news. 'You would think, being right at the centre of the Italian community, that someone would know something, wouldn't you?' he said, breaking the silence as they ate an early supper. 'What about Mrs Baldoni, did you ask her, has she heard anything?'

'No, she hasn't,' Mary lied. In the end she hadn't felt like knocking on her neighbour's door and so had not seen her. 'Let's go to bed early,' she said. But she spent the night awake, thoughts churning, worrying about Cara, berating herself for encouraging her to go to Italy in the first place. Although the disaster was unforeseen, she felt personally responsible for putting her daughter's life at risk.

The next morning, Geoffrey was up early and as Mary prepared breakfast, he called out, 'I'm going to get the newspaper!'

'There was nothing in it yesterday!' Mary shouted back, but the door had already been slammed.

Ten minutes later he was back. Mary was sitting at the breakfast table, staring into space. He sat opposite and passed her *The Times*. A large photograph showed a flooded urban landscape. *An aerial view taken yesterday of the town of Grosseto, Tuscany, flooded after several days of violent rainstorms,* said the caption.

'But this isn't Florence, is it?'

'Read it,' he answered.

'So, this was written yesterday?'

'Yes, read it.'

FROM OUR OWN CORRESPONDENT, ROME

Cloudbursts and gales which struck Italy today from Sicily to the Brenner Pass caused thirteen deaths, the Ministry of the Interior announced tonight. Some 50,000 men are deployed in rescue operations.

Florence is flooded and all its communications cut off except by radio in the worst natural calamity to have struck the city for centuries. Eyewitnesses said about two-thirds of the city was under water. It is nearly seven hundred years since it was struck by an inundation on this scale. By early this afternoon all the streets of Florence were torrents of rushing water as the River Arno broke its banks. Cars were lifted bodily and buried beneath water and mud. Dr. Bargellini, the mayor, was trapped in his offices at the Palazzo Vecchio. According to radio reports the centre is a desolate sight. Several square miles are under mud and water, in places up to six feet deep. Main roads from north and south are cut either because they are flooded or have collapsed. Railway lines are out of action. Appeals have gone out from the Prefect to conserve drinking water. Food is short, and the bakers of Fiesole, a town overlooking Florence, are working all night to help supply the population.

Mary paused her reading and looked up at Geoffrey. 'But this is awful,' she whispered.

Geoffrey nodded, gravely.

The railway line through the Brenner Pass was cut. Severe flooding is reported from many parts of the Alto Adige (S. Tirol) and many roads are impassable. In Venice high seas and winds have flooded the lower floor of many houses, rising to levels untouched for some two centuries. Immense waves have battered and seriously damaged the Lido. In Rome the fire brigade received more than a hundred requests for help by midday after a morning of tremendous rain and wind at times reaching 70 m.p.h. Most of the calls were for help with flooded cellars and shops. Heavy damage is reported from Palermo, Sicily, which has suffered the effects of gales.

'What should we do?' Mary said, pushing the newspaper away.

'Well there isn't much we can do, is there?'

'But what if …'

'What if what?'

'What if … you know … she's hurt?'

'Oh, don't be silly, there is no mention of any injured citizens, is there?'

'But you said yesterday that there had been fatalities?'

'We would have heard.'

'All right, but what if … what if she hasn't enough food? Or drinking water? The article mentions food shortages …'

'That's a typical worry for a mother!' He chortled. 'Don't be silly. She'll be able to get food. Honestly, she will be all right.'

'It's not funny, Geoffrey. Remember what it was like during the war?'

*

An eerie silence had descended in Via Laura and the surrounding streets, normally so noisy with motorcycles, car horns and people. The water had subsided but been replaced by a shallow river of oily slime. Despite her sturdy shoes, Cara felt the cold mush between her ankles and her knees and remembered the Wellington boots she had left behind in Clerkenwell. Never would she have expected to need them here.

The weather had improved, but the grey streets seemed devoid of light, the colour drained out of them. Warm sun hitting houses painted red and ochre, clean washing hanging out to dry in an instant was a distant memory. Cara remembered strolling along the banks of the Arno when she had first arrived, enjoying the September sunshine, looking at the curve of river stretching under the sequence of bridges in front of her. Now the only people around were preoccupied with more important things.

They passed an open doorway where a woman was trying to sweep a thick, muddy liquid out of her house. Fernando stopped to greet her. '*Signora*, how are things going with you?'

'What does it look like? I've lost everything I had in the cellar. My mother is eighty-eight years old and fell over in the dark. We have put her to bed, but she has badly sprained her ankle and I cannot get hold of the doctor ...'

'I'm sorry,' said Fernando. 'Can I do anything to help?'

'Why, are *you* a doctor?' The woman spluttered, bitterly.

'Well, no ...'

'It does not matter. We shall wait. We are all alive! It could be worse. The house has taken a beating but at least we still have a roof over our heads.'

'That is true! *Arrivederci, signora.*'

The pavement underfoot was a mix of brown and black. The force of the flood had ruptured domestic fuel tanks, and left a sticky, grimy mess of mud, oil and water. Normally it would have taken less than fifteen minutes to walk to Santa Croce from Via Laura but Cara and Fernando had to pick their way past tree branches, oil drums, barrels, flagons, splintered furniture, fridges, all matter of flotsam and battered detritus. Vehicles had been lifted and thrown upside down as if by an angry giant. Trees were uprooted, bicycles lay in tangled heaps; doors pulled off their hinges. Cara was struck by the speed with which the river had invaded these streets, causing so much damage, and then, almost as quickly, disappeared.

The few people who had come out of their houses wore expressions of stoic desperation as they tried to salvage what they could. One woman was crying out in tears as she threw household objects and ruined linen from her first-floor window, items that had become unrecognisable sculptures bearing little resemblance to their original form.

But mostly there was a lot of sweeping. The women swept the muddy water out of doorways and off front doorsteps; the men used shovels to clear paths in the roads. Others stood silently by their shops and businesses, looking forlornly at their damaged livelihood. One man had taken an old wooden chair and sat outside his grocery shop as if it were an ordinary day. Cara could see through the open door that the shelves had been smashed and the contents overturned, taken prisoner by layers of mud and oil.

The pervasive reek of sewage and gas filled the air. Cara removed the scarf from her head and wrapped it around her mouth and nose, like a mask. A young woman of a similar age to her, standing close to her mother, stood watching as they walked past, and it struck Cara that in a different set of circumstances that could have been her with Mary. A few doors along, a bedraggled pink bow hung lifelessly around the knocker of a front door, indicating that a baby girl had recently been born there.

Fernando walked beside her, but they did not speak, both preoccupied with their own thoughts, taking it all in.

At every corner there were memories and associations for Cara: a *trattoria* she had been taken to by Gianni, with windows reduced to shattered glass; a shoe shop she had stopped in front of only the week before, to covet some boots she had wished she could afford, now occupied by a desperate owner throwing out sodden boxes containing the ruined merchandise.

Cara thought of all the churches that she had stepped inside to admire a painting or fresco. How would they survive the ravages of water and oil? This city, famous for its beauty, filled with treasures, had been ambushed and defiled by all the rubbish left behind. She was sickened, as if the city was her own and the flood had violated it like an invading army. Two months ago, she would have felt like an intruder. It was not her homeland, she knew that, but she sensed a wound within her, as if she had been personally attacked. Perhaps this was what her mother had meant when she spoke of the devastated plight of London after the Blitz, of walking through a wasteland of bombsites and rubble. Mary had described the starkness, the greyness, the smell of gas and mould. In that moment Cara realised how deeply one could identify with a place and feel its pain.

Aware that she was experiencing this despite her vicarious claim on the city, she wondered how Fernando must feel – as a Florentine – to witness these cataclysmic scenes? As they entered Piazza Santa Croce she glanced sideways at the figure beside her – hunched, hands in pockets – but could not read Fernando's expression under the rim of his hat.

They had both stopped to take in the scene. Some of the cars were still in line, abandoned where they had been parked two days earlier. Others were upturned, resembling giant cockroaches that had fallen on their backs. A street sign impaled another car that had been swept up in the torrent. Jumbles of metal were dotted around the square. Between them, people picked their way. Beside the buildings that ran along the perimeter of the square, some joined in conversation, others stood alone with expressions of passive resignation. Most were busy trying to establish some form of order: moving, cleaning, sorting things into piles. On a stone bench a mound of odd shoes had been placed in a neat row, as if each shoe was waiting to be reunited with its pair. A woman on her knees wearing rubber gloves to her elbows had laid out a selection of ironwork and was attempting to polish a large unidentifiable object.

At first the entrance to the street where Gianni lived with his mother appeared blocked, but Cara and Fernando managed to step around a fallen barrier, realising that it had not been placed there intentionally.

'Marcella's house is up here, opposite the church of San Giuseppe.' said Fernando. 'But the street is long. Are you tired?'

Cara had begun to drag her heels. She wasn't sure whether she should appear at the house and possibly meet Marcella when Gianni had made it clear he didn't want her there.

'No, not tired. A bit nervous perhaps ...'

'Why nervous?'

'I'm not sure Gianni has told Marcella about me.'

Fernando laughed. '*Ma no!* No need to be nervous. She is a good woman ...'

'What is she like?'

They were walking slowly through the mud, passing more people cleaning up.

'She has had a difficult life. She lost her husband during the war – he left her with a little girl already and Gianni in her womb. Then ten years ago she fell badly and broke her hip. It did not mend properly ...'

'Yes, Gianni told me, that is why she is in the wheelchair. But what is she like, you know, as a person?'

'Very religious. But that is good. She accepts her suffering as being God's will. She would like Gianni to marry and settle down ...'

'I know that,' Cara murmured uneasily.

'But he is young! And he must finish his studies. He has ambition. He is a good son though.'

'Yes, yes of course.'

They had reached the church. Fernando stopped. 'There is the house.'

He was pointing at a one-storey house on the other side of the road. It was long rather than high, with two windows breaking up the exterior wall, a lantern in between, and a door to the right that led to a courtyard. Each window had tall metal grilles that almost reached the gutter under the pitched roof. There was a *carabiniere* standing outside. A male figure came out of the shadowy courtyard and began talking to the uniformed policeman.

'Stefano!' Fernando called out his name as they crossed the road. 'I thought you were away. Have you come to check on your aunt? How is she?'

Stefano turned towards them. He looked shattered, with black rings around his hollow eyes. 'You have not heard?'

'Heard what?' Cara and Fernando said in unison.

Stefano's eyes narrowed and he gave Cara a look she would never forget. The weight of every emotion seemed to be contained there: fear, grief, regret, despair. But mostly there was angry reproach.

Fernando gently laid a hand on Stefano's arm. '*Ma cos'è successo*?'

'I tell you what has happened. *Zia Marcella é morta*.'

He said it flatly. Marcella is dead.

'*Morta*?' Cara repeated, softly.

'*Si, morta*.' The ice in his eyes froze Cara.

'But … how?'

'Gianni was not here, was he?' Stefano continued to speak only to Fernando. 'When the floodwaters began coming through her windows, she had no one to help her. They think she was asleep and woke with water in her room.' He paused and turned to Cara. 'Can you imagine what that would be like? To be infirm, waking up cold and alone, with no lights working and strange noises coming from outside, having to lever yourself out of bed into the wheelchair, knowing there is no point in calling out because your son is – apparently …' his voice was laden with sarcasm, 'staying overnight with your nephew. That is, staying with me …' He said the word 'me' very loudly, like an accusation and then repeated the phrase. '*Con me.*'

Fernando glanced at Cara. She was skewered by the bitterness in Stefano's voice. Fernando's hand remained on Stefano's arm as he tried to interrupt. 'Stefano, this is a tragedy. It is shocking. *Povera Marcella*. I'm so very sorry, but please, it is not fair on Cara …'

'You asked me what happened, didn't you?' Stefano shouted, shrugging off Fernando's hand. 'Well, I am telling you, that is if you really want to hear?' He let out a deep sigh. 'So. Somehow Marcella got herself into the wheelchair and managed to open the window and, clinging on to the metal grill, she called for help.'

'And did someone come? Why could they not help her?' Fernando asked.

'The prior of the church opposite heard her screams and called out to a neighbour to alert the *carabinieri*. With a rope tied to his waist, he lowered himself from his window and swam across the street to her house, but he couldn't get to her because of the iron-work grilles across the window. Meanwhile, the water was rising, and the prior was fearful for his own life …

'And the *carabinieri*?' Fernando looked horrified.

'Yes,' continued Stefano. 'Several arrived in a dinghy. But the water had risen against the door inside the courtyard, so it was impossible to open it, and they couldn't pull her through the windows …' The words were coming out fast, as if he wanted to get the story over quickly.

'That is terrible,' Fernando repeated, 'a real tragedy.'

Cara stood fixed to the spot, speechless.

'That's not the end of it,' continued Stefano. 'By this time another neighbour tried to help by throwing a sheet down to one of the rescuers who somehow managed to pass it through the window to Marcella. She looped it around herself and they were able to hoist the poor woman up above the level of the water that was filling her room; they tied her to the metal grill of one of the windows, thinking they could come back once the water had receded but, …' He swallowed hard. 'As you know, Fernando, she was not strong. She tried to hold on but … ' He covered his face with his hands.

'I'm so sorry …' Cara finally said, softly. She was, of course, desperate to ask where Gianni was now, how was he coping, where could she find him?

'You know,' Stefano said to Fernando. 'The priest told me that he stayed with her as long as he could, although the water was almost over his head. He gave her a rosary. How idiotic is that? All that praying didn't save her, did it?'

'And Gianni?' Cara blurted it out.

'Yes, where was Gianni? What was he doing? Gianni was busy making love to a stupid English girl, while pretending to be with me.'

Hearing Stefano's words, the policeman who had been standing nearby raised his eyebrows and then looked away.

Fernando shook his head. 'Now, come on Stefano, naturally you are upset, but that is unfair.'

Cara fixed her eyes on the ground. 'You have every right to be angry, but look, it's not my fault … or his fault. Is he all right?'

Stefano looked furious. 'I haven't finished! Eventually a wall of water crashed in through her window and Marcella disappeared under it. When they got to her she was still clutching the rosary. Do you understand, Cara?'

It was the first time he had said her name, and it jolted her.

'Yes,' she said quietly. '*Si, capisco*. I understand.'

'I don't think you do. Can you imagine what Zia Marcella went through? The poor woman, gulping for air, swallowing stinking, fetid brown water, the noise of the river in her ears. Trapped, frightened, alone. I hope you will think about that liquid grave for the rest of your life, and when you do, you will feel …'

'That's enough,' interrupted Fernando. 'Your anger is completely understandable, but it's not Cara's fault. Or Gianni's for that matter. It's an act of God.'

'Ha! God?' His eyes bulged as he snorted. 'What sort of God is this? Zia Marcella never hurt a fly …'

'I'm sorry,' Cara mumbled.

'Think about it, *Cara mia*!' Stefano's voice followed her as she turned away, back towards the square of Santa Croce.

From a safe distance she looked behind her. Stefano, Fernando and the policemen were deep in conversation. She was convinced Stefano would turn Fernando – her one ally in this city – against her too. But where had Gianni gone? A son so close to his mother would be devastated. Perhaps, now that the water had subsided, Marcella was laid out on her bed in that house with Gianni grieving by her side. Perhaps the sister Cara had never met would also be there. Would she be blaming her too?

She longed to speak to Mary, to Geoffrey, to Tony. She craved familiarity, home, England. She didn't want to get sealed into this hostile, grieving city, the outsider forever trapped inside.

She must leave this place. She must get back to London.

7

Clerkenwell

MAY 1947

The fact that their affair blossomed in late spring as the weather turned warmer and ended in autumn as it started getting cold felt significant to Mary when she looked back at those six months of madness. It could only have happened at that time of year, for the long days and balmy weather allowed them to meet outside. Mary acquired a secondhand bicycle, having convinced Geoffrey that bicycling would be good for her health. At the same time Pippo explained to his mother that the fine weather meant longer hours on building sites and that a bicycle would save time in getting home.

They saw each other whenever they could, arranging the next assignation before they parted, with the understanding that if either of them didn't show up, it was due to circumstances beyond their control. They met mainly in parks or on Hampstead Heath, turning a blind eye to other couples doing the same. Unlike those engaged in illegal homosexual couplings, they tended to choose places more in view – by a pond or under a tree – rather than hidden by bushes, but if they wanted to be truly private, there were plenty of secluded woodland clearings to be found. When it was raining, they would rendezvous at an afternoon film-showing, taking their seats in the back row, oblivious to what was happening on the screen, grateful for the friendly darkness that left them undisturbed. Always, whatever the arrangement, they arrived and returned separately in order to avoid being seen together.

'You seem so much better,' Geoffrey observed on a sunny morning in July. 'At last you have colour in your cheeks. I'm so glad you are getting out and about more.'

She flashed him a broad smile. The irritation and impatience she had experienced at being condemned to a tedious marriage had been replaced by delight in everything, even Geoffrey. This surprised her. Perhaps the emotion was motivated by guilt, but she began to show him far more affection. A sense of joy and largesse had entered her being, and she brought her renewed energy to the marital bed as well as to her lover.

'My goodness,' Geoffrey had remarked one night, after she had enthusiastically instigated some vigorous lovemaking. 'What has come over you?'

'Are you complaining?' she answered coquettishly.

'Oh, by no means …'

It was then she felt the tug of remorse. She had no wish to hurt or humiliate him. There was even love in her desire to give as well as receive pleasure. She hesitated.

'I'm sorry,' said Geoffrey. 'I didn't mean to upset you. I'm glad you feel so much better. Do you remember, on our honeymoon, I said that I hoped you would grow to love me?'

Mary nodded.

'Well, I feel loved now. And that's made me a happy man. Despite everything that the war destroyed, it gave me you. That VE night when I was sitting on the pile of rubble that had been my sister's house, and you turned up …' He paused. 'You were my angel, coming to save me.'

As the summer advanced, Pippo became less accommodating. It was to be expected, reasoned Mary, after three months rushing about from one place to another and making arrangements that could not always be followed through. This was becoming a strain for her too.

Her lover began appearing late, or not at all, as if the urgency for their meetings had lessened. His excuses were valid and believable. His mother had asked him to take the children somewhere, or his foreman had made him finish a job that went on longer than usual; he had needed to change out of his working clothes and invent a reason to go out again, or he was exhausted after long hours on site, and so on. Mary knew she had no right to complain. But when he disappeared for a week on yet another trip to collect provisions in his truck, she missed him terribly.

They had their first serious argument. The day had begun well. She was in a good mood as she bicycled to the Heath and parked her bicycle behind a tree near the ponds. She had arrived half an hour later than intended and realised that he, unusually, was already there, pacing up and down. For a minute it amused her to watch him, knowing she could look at him unobserved. She intended to spring out from behind a tree and surprise him. In her mind he would laugh and sweep her into his arms.

But when she did it, he was not amused. He jumped in fear rather than surprise. 'What you do that for?'

'I thought you would find it funny.'

'Funny? Why is this funny?'

'Pippo, I'm sorry, there's no need …'

'You are late,' he said sulkily.

'But you are late too, sometimes …'

'It is more difficult for me!' He said it angrily and began kicking the gravel on the path.

'Why are you so cross?' She had never seen him like this before. 'Has something happened?'

'What do you think has happened? But of course, nothing bad happens to you. You have no work; you have no children. You have me, and then you return to your husband.' He paused. 'Why does he not know what you are doing? Is he stupid?'

'No ...'

Pippo came right up to her, too close, and took both her shoulders roughly in his hands. He was looking directly into her eyes. 'And, with this nice English husband, you share his bed, don't you?'

Mary stared at him in shock.

'You are too ashamed to answer. Do you know what we would call you, in Italy?' He paused. 'No, you don't? I tell you. We would call you *puttana*.' He spat out the word. 'That is what you are ...'

Tears stinging behind the eyes, she pulled away from his grasp. That was all she was to him then, a common whore? She turned and walked purposefully back to her bicycle.

'Mary! Mary, please, stop!'

She guided the bike on to the path ahead and had just mounted when she felt him grab her wheel from behind.

'I am sorry, please, you must listen to me.'

'Go away!' she cried, but he was holding firm.

'Listen, please. Listen to me,' he said, from behind her. 'Of course, you are not a *puttana*. You are a lovely girl. I say this because I am upset. I had to leave my mother today, she was crying, and she would not stop.'

Mary turned round slowly. 'Nanella?'

'Yes, today is the anniversary of the day she heard about the *Andorra Star* and that my father and the others had drowned. Seven years ago today. For her, the anniversary of his death is when she heard this news, because "that is when hope ended", as she say.'

Mary climbed off her bicycle as he kept it steady in his hands.

'I'm so sorry, I ...'

'You see, I have been angry – not just today – with English people.' He leaned Mary's bicycle back against the tree. 'The English did not treat my father well. We had made our home here, we were grateful. My father was not a fascist, none of them were, but they were not believed. They were treated badly ... And then put on that ship, as if it were a matter of clearing a house of rats ...'

'I know – it was not right.'

'My mother lost her father and her brother-in-law as well as her husband. My grandfather, my uncle ... It is too much ... And all the others too ... They should never have put them on that ship ...'

'No ...'

'They were good people. They worked hard, they loved their families, they loved this stupid country ...'

'I know,' she repeated. She wanted to say, *but I am not at fault, and I can't make it better.* Instead, she placed a hand gently on his arm. 'Pippo, you should go home now. Nanella needs you there today, and Rosa and Carlino do too. Please, go.'

He took his right hand away from his forehead and kissed her on her cheek. 'Thank you. It is true, I must go home.'

But the tensions and misunderstandings continued, and with Pippo's increasing detachment, Mary fell into heart-sinking insecurity. He was losing interest; she had given it all away too soon. Her dread of his withdrawal made her anticipate the worst.

'When are we meeting again?' she would ask mid-encounter, trying to fix the next time and place before their present assignation had come to its natural end. The confidence she had gained from the romance of the affair, the lightness and excitement it had lent to every day, gave way to fearful instability. She knew her tone of plaintive distress irritated him, but the more she tried to replace it with light-hearted jollity the more she sounded unnatural and forced, even to herself.

And then, when she was close to despairing that all was lost, there would be a good meeting – a synchronicity of good moods, balmy weather, harmony, passion even. She would convince herself that the incompatibility had been imagined; that he wanted her as much as she needed him.

One early morning in mid-August, she was woken by a summer storm. The weather had been sultry and warm for a week and for a few days there had been thunder in the air. Now, as the sun rose, down came the torrential rain. The lovers' arrangement had been Hampstead ponds if dry, the picture house if wet.

'Once I've got my jobs done,' Mary announced, 'I thought I might go to the pictures.'

'That's a grand idea.' Geoffrey reached for his hat. 'The weather does look pretty beastly.' He arranged the fedora on his head and picked the black umbrella out of the stand. 'Well, I'll be off then. See you this evening.'

Geoffrey seemed to be completely lacking in suspicion. That it didn't enter his mind that she might be having an affair was almost insulting. If she had more sex appeal, she wondered, if she was more alluring, would he be alerted to the possibility of other men finding her attractive, of her straying? Because she was angry with Pippo for not loving her enough, she was tempted to pretend to him that Geoffrey *was* suspicious. She wanted to inject some spirit into a relationship that had become stagnant. For a short time, both her marriage and her love affair had been stimulating; it was depressing to think of both relationships sinking into similar dullness.

As she walked into the cinema, she smiled to herself, imagining Geoffrey asserting his rightful claim over her, and Pippo responding with masterful virility. How wonderful to be fought over, to stimulate possessiveness and competition between these two men, to be at the centre of it all. She was replaying her romantic fantasy as she went up to the ticket booth.

'One shilling and five pence,' responded the woman. Then she added, 'Your friend is already here.'

Mary looked up from her purse, confused. How did this woman know her? She didn't recognise her. And how was she aware of the connection to Pippo? Whenever they went to the cinema they always arrived and left separately.

'I think you've mistaken me for someone else,' she said quickly.

'It was definitely her, but it's none of my business.'

'Her?' Mary was about to reply but checked herself just in time.

'Oh, well, thank you.' She hurriedly took her ticket, pulled her hat down, and went into the auditorium.

The lights were still up, and the seats sparsely occupied: a mix of couples, a few female friends in pairs, and the odd single person. She glanced around in the half-light and found their usual place in the middle of the back row. Pippo always turned up late, as the lights had gone down, and the credits were rolling. He had little interest in the plots of the films and never cared whether he missed the beginning. Mary, on the other hand, took more notice these days. She had always loved stories, and although she and Pippo were ultimately there for the same reason, his pawing would distract her, sometimes even annoy her, when she was trying to follow the plot. Today, however, she would be grateful for his attention. She needed reassurance.

When he finally joined her and had settled down, he seemed more ardent than in recent times, and she responded readily. 'I am happy that it was boring,' he whispered as the film was reaching its conclusion, and Mary smiled, her confidence restored. 'You are a bad man,' she whispered back, as she rearranged her clothes.

The lights came on, and Pippo stood up in order to leave first. 'Next week, if warm, the ponds,' he mouthed, before walking out through the curtain and into the foyer. Mary, as arranged, remained behind, leaning down to collect the handbag at her feet. Taking out her compact and opening it with one hand she applied some fresh lipstick with the other.

By the time she got up a minute or two later, the auditorium was empty. As she crossed the foyer, the woman inside the ticket booth called, 'There she is!' Initially Mary didn't think she was being addressed, but as she opened the door on to the street she heard the same voice say, 'There, your friend!'

In a split second Mary realised that this woman had occasionally sold her and Elsie tickets when they used to come to the pictures together, but the change of hairstyle had made her unrecognisable.

It was too late.

'Mary! Hello! Fancy us all being here!'

'Elsie ...'

'Look, I've bumped into Mrs Baldoni's son.' She smiled widely at Pippo. 'Filippo says he was walking past, but I'm sure I saw him sneaking out of the picture! Horrible day, I don't blame him. I was doing the same. Lucky it's stopped raining now.'

'Yes, hello ...' Pippo was offering Mary his hand to shake as if they were virtual strangers. She took it and let it go again as quickly as if she had been burnt.

'I was telling Filippo ...' Elsie was saying.

'Call me Pippo, please ...'

'Oh, Pippo then, as you wish ...' Elsie giggled. 'Well, I was telling Pippo that he should come to the café, it's near where he is working.' Then, turning to Pippo, 'It's run by Neldo and his wife, Anna. Do you know it?'

Pippo pressed his lips together and frowned as if in thought.

'You'd like it. A lot of Italians come and the coffee is good and …'

'I have been there in fact,' Pippo interrupted. 'You did not notice me?' He smiled. 'But I noticed you.'

Mary's eyes widened. She felt the urge to shout out loud, 'How dare you? You're shamelessly flirting with my friend!' *And how dare you look so pretty*, she thought enviously, taking in Elsie's full lips, peachy skin and auburn curls, and the way her eyes crinkled when she laughed, which she was doing now in response to Pippo.

'Charmed, I'm sure …'

'Well, this is cosy but I must be getting back before Geoffrey gets home. I hope you both enjoyed the picture. I personally found it rather boring.'

Elsie darted a look at Pippo and smirked. 'Ooh, Mary, you're sounding like Geoffrey!'

Mary flinched. 'Goodbye, Filippo, regards to your mother.'

Pippo nodded, repressing a smile. 'And regards to Mr Williams.'

'Thank you.' Mary replied stiffly. 'Goodbye, Elsie.'

''Bye, darling,' Elsie replied lightly. 'Come and see me soon!'

Mary looked away, her jaw clenched. She was aware of them behind her, but she was the one to feel left behind. 'Bloody cheek,' she muttered to herself as she walked away as briskly as she could.

'What are you doing?' Pippo said breathlessly, catching up with her.

'What are *you* doing? "I noticed you,"' she mimicked in a sing-song voice with a fake Italian accent. 'You are unbelieveable. Acting all gallant with my friend …'

'I did not want her to be suspicious … wait, are you jealous?'

'Jealous? Why would I be jealous?'

'Ha, you are jealous! Come on …' He nudged her playfully, but Mary pushed him away.

It wasn't really that she was envious of Elsie. Mary didn't consider herself a jealous person. As an only child she had never had to fight for her mother's attention. Yes, there had been different kinds of envy – as a child she had coveted the books she had seen in the bookshop, but otherwise she had never understood this need exclusively to possess something or someone. She was simply upset that her relationship with Pippo was not perfect and that she had no power to control it and make it so. It had changed, she knew that, and the knowledge that it was inevitably coming to an end made her feel desperate.

When, that evening, Geoffrey asked whether she had enjoyed the film, she answered, 'Yes, it was rather good. And I bumped into Elsie.'

'Elsie?'

'Yes, she was there too. She had the afternoon off from the Italian café where she works.'

'Oh, how nice for you. It must have been like old times, the two of you going to the pictures.'

'Yes, just like old times,' responded Mary sadly.

A week later she was sitting on a bench by the ponds on Hampstead Heath with Pippo when he made an announcement.

'I am driving Salvatore's truck next week to take a delivery to Fausto.'

'Fausto?'

'Yes, you know, my father's cousin, with the café in Broadstairs.'

'Oh yes, of course. When will you be back?'

'I will be away for a few days. This time …' He hesitated, then blurted out, 'Mary, I would like you to come with me.'

The longing, the knowing it was impossible. 'How can I possibly come with you? How would I explain that to Geoffrey?'

'You could say you were visiting a relative.'

'I don't have any relatives in Broadstairs. Anyway, what if Geoffrey bumped into your mother and they realised we were both away at the same time? And how would you explain me to Fausto?'

Pippo looked glumly at the pond. A little boy was trying to sail his toy boat with the help of his father.

'You do not want to come with me.'

'Of course I want to come with you, but can't you see that it isn't possible?'

'I do not know ...' He flicked a cigarette out of the packet, put it to his mouth and lit it. 'I think if you wanted to come you would find a way.'

'Pippo, don't say that ... please ...' The plaintive whine was breaking out again. If only she could supress that vulnerable, pleading voice. If only everything was different, like it was in books and films.

He was getting to his feet. He threw the cigarette to the ground and stamped it out. 'I must get back,' he said coldly.

'But ... you haven't finished ... your sandwich ... don't go ...'

'*Mamma mia*, you sound like a wife!' He brushed himself down and began walking away.

Resisting the urge to jump up and run after him, she continued sitting on the bench, looking straight ahead at the little boy whose boat kept capsizing.

That's us, she thought. *Capsizing. There is never going to be a fairy-tale ending.*

Mary avoided Pippo before he left for Broadstairs, but two weeks later she saw the familiar truck at the top of the street. Why had he parked so far from his mother's house? Why should she care, she thought, but was aware that she did. She decided to walk past it, nonchalantly, for what purpose she knew not – perhaps that would become clear to her. And so instead of going into her house she carried on walking. As she approached, the driver's door swung open, and there was Pippo waving at her. After glancing around he said under his breath, 'Get in …'

'Are you crazy?' she said, finding herself being pushed into the back of the truck, surrounded by jars and tins and sacks of food. A packet of something was digging into one thigh.

He put his fingers to her lips. 'Shush …' With a sweep of his hand he cleared a space around them and then took the back of her neck with his other hand and brought her towards him. She felt the cold metal floor of the truck underneath her as he lowered her on to it and made love to her roughly and hurriedly. After an initial play at putting up a fight, she gave in, responding with enthusiasm. There was relief in losing herself to the moment, in silencing the judgements she tended to make about him and herself and their situation. She needed to stifle the melancholy at the core of her being.

But the second he finished and rolled off her, the loneliness returned, only worse than before. She was already missing his need for her; she knew it had gone, and with that awareness she realised that she had to get out of that truck, and as quickly as possible. Pippo was lying next to her on his back, his eyes closed.

She nudged him in the ribs. 'Pippo, quick, let me out …'

He grunted. 'Oi! What you doing?'

'Let me out!' Her voice had urgency.

'You are a funny woman. You want to see me then you don't want to be with me. But OK, I let you out. Wait a minute.' He pulled his trousers back up and climbed into the passenger seat, opening the door on that side.

'*Eh, come stai?*' An unfamiliar Italian voice came from the street outside the van.

'Ah, ciao! Si, bene, tu?'

Oh no, now they'll have a conversation and I'll be stuck here, thought Mary, as she began arranging her clothes. Would she ever get out? The man who had made the greeting kept talking, despite Pippo's monosyllabic replies.

After a long five minutes she heard the man move away, but Pippo still wasn't letting her out. Finally, after another few minutes, he threw open the door.

'What took you so long?' she said irritably. 'I've got cramp stuck in here!'

'Some people were walking past, what would they think of a woman crawling out of a truck?' He paused. 'Why you looking at me like that? What is the matter now?'

'Just let me out.'

She stumbled along the pavement back to her house as if drunk, or at that tipping point in drunkenness when the fun of lost inhibitions turns sour. Whenever they met, the intoxication of lust ended in this hung-over flatness. All that was left was a sickness of the mind and the heart: she was weary of the duplicity, the secrecy, the dishonesty. She longed to talk to someone about her situation, to release some of the anxiety and insecurity. But the people in her orbit – Pippo, Elsie, Nanella, Geoffrey, her mother Nora – were clearly the last people she could possibly turn to. Briefly she considered the Catholic priest at St Peters. He might hear her confession, but could he be trusted? In any case he would say her behaviour was sinful and that she must stop. But for Mary the sin had been not in taking a lover, but in marrying a man she did not love.

Pippo's attempt at loosening their ties made Mary want to cling on more tightly, even as she could see the affair unravelling. She knew it would be in her interests to try and conceal her frustrations, at least to pretend she was unconcerned about the change in their relationship. But every light-hearted comment she attempted came weighted with neediness until she became so self-conscious about saying anything at all that most of their time together was spent in uncomfortable silence. When she was alone, she tortured herself by running through the stupidity – in her eyes – of the things she had said, until she felt the panic of losing him.

He was bored, that was clear, and his withdrawal of affection was becoming impossible to ignore. Even his once passionate love-making had become half-hearted. Whereas before he would win her round after a moody encounter or an outburst of anger, now he seemed to be constantly distracted, as if wishing the meeting over so that he could be somewhere else. It was painful to realise that when they were apart she was no longer as present in his thoughts as he was still in hers.

With the prospect of their trysts coming to an end, her future was beginning to look meaningless again. She had a stock of encounters to replay in her mind when she felt lonely, but she knew these would become stale and eventually begin to fade. Memories need to be replenished with new experiences, but it was looking extremely unlikely that there was any future to be had with him. That was the saddest thing: the sense of years stretching ahead marked by routine and boredom. The cycle of housewifely duties was relentless, and yes, she could take as much pride in a clean doorstep or a good meal set out on the table as much as the next woman, but she could only manage it with Pippo in the background, unlocking the light and energy inside her, encouraging her to laugh and to love.

She searched for reasons to explain his cooling off. Perhaps it had been her rejection of his invitation to Broadstairs? Now, in the unlikely event that he asked her again, would she say yes?

She could not do that to Geoffrey, who had done nothing wrong. And it would mean cutting herself off from her family, from her neighbours. What would Nanella say? It was no good. The shame and guilt would destroy her.

Perhaps, she wondered, it was something about her appearance that had altered and become less attractive to him? The mirror showed her that, apart from the more pronounced shadows under the eyes, she still looked the same. Her hair framed her face in the same way; the lips he had admired were still full and red. The only change she noticed was a greater appetite, an underlying hunger: perhaps a sign that anxiety was using up her energy, or the indication of a need to fill an emotional hole. Rationing was still in force, but more food was becoming available in the shops. She was eating well compared to previous years and her body had become more curvaceous. A month ago, Pippo had said he liked women that way. Why was he not celebrating her newly formed curves? Perhaps if she could become more beautiful to him, the distance between them would be gone. Might he be tempted back?

She scrutinised her face for signs of ageing. There was only one fine line between her eyebrows, and even that was barely noticeable – she was still only in her mid-twenties, after all. She resolved not to frown, to relax her jaw and shoulders, to push out her breasts, to cinch in her belt. And next time she would keep a check on the plaintive questions about when they could next meet.

But the uncertainty was hard to dispel. One evening as she was getting ready for bed, she asked Geoffrey, 'Do you think I'm still pretty?'

'Don't be silly, of course you are,' he said, not looking up from his book.

Anxiety over Pippo was causing physical symptoms. When she wasn't hungry, she was nauseous. She was suffering from dizzy spells again. One morning at the corner of the street, she had to stop and lean against a wall to steady herself. Many times, she had replayed the memory of Pippo rescuing her from the pavement under the viaduct when she had felt faint. Occasionally she became dizzy when she had not eaten. But this time her breakfast had been recent and the porridge plentiful. Why was she so light-headed?

She waited a minute before walking slowly back towards her house, pausing in front of Pippo's home, longing for him to be there, to support her, to tell her that all her concerns were unfounded, to persuade her that he loved her and would take care of her. In a moment of recklessness and longing she found herself knocking on his door. But it was his mother who opened it, beaming.

'Mary!'

'Oh yes, Nanella, hello,' she said, trying not to look or sound disappointed. 'I'm so sorry to bother you but I am feeling light-headed, I didn't want to worry Geoffrey until I …'

'Come here.' Nanella pulled her into her house. 'You must sit down. I get you water. When you feel better, I take you to the doctor.'

'No, it is nothing really, but yes, I will sit down just for a moment.' She let herself be led to a chair. 'Are the children here?'

'Carlino and Rosa are upstairs. But Pippo …' She shook her head. 'He is always out at the moment. He must have a new girlfriend!'

Mary tried to laugh lightly but felt on the verge of collapse. 'Oh yes, new girlfriend! Well there you are, of course, he must be with her!'

Nanella was looking serious. 'You are pale. You are not strong. When you have drunk water, we go to Dr Gould.'

'No really, I shall be fine,' she said, feeling anything but fine.

Mary liked Dr Gould. He conducted his consultations in a wood panelled room, sitting in his captain's chair at a desk covered in red leather, and would ask questions like, 'How are you keeping? How can I help you today?' It made his patients feel cared for, less alone.

'Dr Gould will help you,' Nanella was repeating. 'He will know what is wrong.' And Mary, repressing the urge to answer, 'Can he give me a potion to make your son love me,' said instead, 'Really, I'm perfectly well. I must get home. Geoffrey will wonder where I am.'

Nanella would have none of it. 'Dr Gould will know what is wrong.'

'All right, I give in,' Mary said with a rigid smile. 'But I shall go by myself.'

'And then you tell me what he say?'

'Yes, I shall tell you what he says.'

Before the war Dr Gould senior would have been called to visit at home, but now that he was retired his son, also a doctor, had established a surgery on the ground floor of his parents' home. Those who were able to walk in could come for their consultations – the home calls being restricted to late afternoon. A middle-aged woman worked as receptionist and Mrs Gould, who had originally trained as a midwife, was the nurse.

The last time Mary had sat in Dr Gould's chair had been a year before, when Nora had encouraged her to visit the surgery to ask why, after a year of marriage, she wasn't getting pregnant. 'Have patience,' Dr Gould had pronounced after examining her. 'There seems to be nothing obviously wrong with you. Come back with your husband in another year if nothing has happened, and we shall investigate.'

She had not been back but the moment she sat down the memory of this conversation came to her as if it had happened only the day before.

Dr Gould looked at the notes in front of him. 'So how are we feeling?'

'We?'

'A figure of speech, Mrs Williams.' He smiled, looking up. 'Would you like to tell me what seems to be the matter?'

'I … I have these dizzy spells. And when I'm not ravenous, I'm feeling sick …'

'Hmmm. Do your breasts feel tender?'

'Well, now you mention it …'

'And your last menstrual period was …?'

'I don't know … I've been busy, I haven't given it a thought … perhaps a month and a half, two …' She couldn't remember at all, but was beginning to feel a fluttering sensation in her chest.

'Let me check you over. Please remove your underwear behind the screen and get on the examination table. And then I think Mrs Gould should see you.'

Mary walked back to her street in a daze. The world felt different, changed. She walked carefully, as if protecting herself from falling. As she came close to Nanella's house, she ignored the promise she had made. She didn't want to repeat what Dr Gould had said, for fear it would get passed on to Pippo. She had to let him know herself, or not at all. Would he be angry? She had always maintained that she was possibly infertile, that, as her mother had always said, some women have great trouble conceiving. Her biggest worry, now that they were getting on so badly, was would Pippo think she had tricked him? It must be his, surely? But then it could also be Geoffrey's …

The doctor's words rang in her ears. 'Based on the size of your uterus I would judge you to be about eight weeks pregnant.

You must be very pleased. Please offer my congratulations to Mr Williams.'

Nanella was standing by the ground-floor window looking out, and as soon as she spotted Mary, she opened her front door, preventing her from walking past.

'So, tell me, what he say?'

'It's only blood pressure … low blood pressure.'

'No baby?'

'No, absolutely not,' Mary answered firmly. 'No baby.'

'Oh.' Nanella looked disappointed. 'You no worry, it will happen. I keep praying for you.'

'Thank you, you are kind. Now please excuse me, I must rest.'

'Cook some liver …'

'Yes … thank you …'

Mary closed the front door of her empty house quietly, as if to avoid disturbing someone inside. Her mouth was dry, and her hands were slightly shaking as she turned the tap on in the kitchen to pour herself a glass of water. She continued standing by the sink, even after the glass was empty, trying to think clearly, not knowing yet how she felt about the pregnancy. This was all she had hoped for, what she had almost given up longing for. Having a child would give her purpose, status and, most of all, a little person to love and be loved by. She wasn't barren after all! It made her 'normal', like other women. Her husband, her mother, would be overjoyed. Shopkeepers would congratulate her. Elsie and Nanella would embrace her.

Despite all this she felt a creeping unease. Could this be attributed to apprehension at the impending responsibility of bringing up a child, or was it guilt? How could she look Geoffrey in the eye and tell him he was going to be a father, without feeling any shame?

And whom should she tell first? Instinctively she knew it should be her husband, then her mother. But here was a weapon she had been given, something she could use to gain her lover's attention. When they had last been together Pippo had been so distant that she had not dared pin him down to their next meeting. Nothing had been set. Now she had an excuse to see him.

But first she wanted to discuss it with a person who would not judge her too badly. She needed to unburden, to confess. Not to her husband, not to her mother – that would be foolish. She needed to talk it over with a friend.

It was a risk, but Elsie was the obvious choice. Elsie, who had never been too bothered about monogamy, who during the war had strung along various young men, leading each to believe they were her 'special' sweetheart. 'They need to think a girl is waiting for them at home,' had been her justification. 'Think of what they are going off to do.' As far as Elsie was concerned you could never know what might happen next, so it was silly to become too attached to one or another. In the end, she had been proved right, as several had come back changed, or not at all.

As Mary made her way towards the café where her friend worked, she began to have misgivings. She had not met up with Elsie since that awkward encounter outside the pictures. In fact, they hadn't seen much of each other at all in the two years since Mary had got married. Might it be possible that Elsie would envy Mary's settled position with husband and forthcoming baby? Would it be insensitive to confide in her? Maybe she would resent hearing that her friend had both the security of marriage *and* a lover.

The walk to the café gave her more time to think. Yes, she didn't want to upset Elsie, who never seemed to hold down a stable relationship. She would be sensitive about telling her she was expecting. And then she would drop the bombshell: 'It may not be Geoffrey's.'

She imagined Elsie's shocked expression and realised that this was partly what she wanted: to subvert her friend's presumption that she was a good, faithful housewife. Elsie had to know she wasn't dull, that she too had experienced passion with a lover.

But even as she approached the café door, she wasn't entirely sure what she would say.

It was unusually quiet inside, just a man on his own drinking tea in the corner. There was no sign of Elsie anywhere, only Anna, cleaning the display shelves. Mary walked straight up to her.

'Hello, is Elsie working here today?'

'Yes, and her friend was here.' Anna's expression was half-knowing, half-disapproving.

'Her friend?'

'Yes. Elsie wanted a cigarette. We're not busy so I told her she could take five minutes. I think her friend is still with her, so if you go out the back ... you can come through the kitchen if you like.'

'It's all right. I'll nip out and around. Thank you.'

'Tell her not to stay there too long, her five minutes is already up!'

Mary knew there was a narrow alley at the side of the café that led to the back of the kitchen. It was a dank corridor between two buildings, home to metal dustbins and scavenging vermin. The sort of place that remained dark and damp even on a sunny day like this one.

She turned into the passageway and saw two figures halfway down, a man and a woman. Elsie, cigarette in hand, was leaning against the wall; the man was standing very close, his back to Mary. She watched him snatch the cigarette from Elsie's hand and throw it on the ground before taking her into his arms.

Instinctively Mary stepped back around the corner, into the light. She didn't want to intrude; this was clearly a lover leaning in for a kiss. She would wait a moment, then go back into the café when

Elsie had finished her break. Two women walked past, giving a sideways look at her loitering outside the café door. She pretended to study the cheery 'Open' sign with great attention, as if deciding whether to go in. Through the window she could see Anna wiping a plate. There was still no sign of Elsie. She would turn back into the passage and cough or something to remind her friend that she should go back to work before Anna came looking for her.

Peering back into the darkness again, Mary could see the couple's limbs, tangled in a deep embrace. She sensed she should not watch, but knew that even if she were spotted, her silhouette against the light-filled street behind would obscure her identity. The idea of walking closer to them and pretending to cough seemed awkward: the couple would separate, and Elsie would have to introduce her to the man. Perhaps best to leave it and come back another time. But she was rooted to the spot, compelled to watch, as if by watching them she was reliving the intimacy she had lost with Pippo.

Finally, they came apart. Elsie tittered. He tried to kiss her again, but she playfully pushed him away before walking back through the door into the kitchen. And then the man called after her with familiar, operatic fervour, '*Tu sei bellissima*,' and Mary felt her heart would stop. For a minute she stayed rooted to the spot, biting the corner of her lower lip until it hurt. The blood, when she tasted it, felt good. She gave her head a quick, impatient shake. She must get home. Only when she heard her front door close behind her would she feel safe.

Mary waited another week before telling Geoffrey about the pregnancy, and when she did, she announced it as if it were the most ordinary thing. They were sitting opposite each other in silence over breakfast. Suddenly she said, 'I'm expecting a baby.'

'What?' he spluttered, sending crumbs everywhere.

'Yes, Dr Gould has confirmed it. It's due in March.'

'But ... but that's wonderful! But when did he tell you this? I can't believe it, I thought perhaps you weren't able ...'

'Well, it seems we were ...' She used the word 'we' self-consciously.

'You're so calm, darling! But how long ... when did you think ...? Have you told your mother yet?'

'No, but I shall, of course. You know, I wanted to make sure. And obviously I wanted to tell you first.'

'This is marvellous! We must celebrate! Who can we tell?'

'Yes, who can we tell,' Mary echoed sadly.

'And how are you feeling? You do look peaky. Can I get you something? A brandy perhaps? No, possibly that isn't a good idea at this time of day.'

'Please don't make a fuss. You're always telling me I look weak or pallid or something. I really am perfectly well.'

His eyes were boring into her.

'Really, I'm perfectly well,' she repeated, forcing a smile.

Later that morning she stood waiting her turn in the grocery shop, imagining conversations to come. She needed to tell her mother about the pregnancy but how would she keep her quiet? Within a few days all the neighbouring streets would hear the news, and what was the first thing Nanella Baldoni would do when she got to hear of it? Tell Pippo. Mary tried to imagine how he would react, but every time he came into her mind she would get no further than replaying the scene she had witnessed in the alleyway. The image of the two of them conjoined was searing. No wonder they called it heartache; it hurt like a physical pain.

'Madam?'

She looked at the grocer in a daze. 'Hmm?'

'Can I help you?'

'Oh yes,' she said, pulling herself together. 'I needed some tea, and, let me think …'

A few minutes later, as the groceries sat on the counter and she was counting the right money to hand over, she thought of what she might say to the friendly shopkeeper. *I'm distracted because I've found out I'm expecting*, or *Excuse me, but I have just had some good news*. Once the wickerwork basket was full, she lifted it off the counter and said only, 'Oh, that *is* heavy!'

'They are, aren't they, even when empty,' commented a woman with curlers sticking out of her headscarf. 'It's Mrs Williams, isn't it?'

'Um, yes …'

'I seen you at Dr Gould's …'

'Oh yes, possibly. Well, good day!'

Busybody, Mary thought, leaving the shop. Everyone around here is a busybody.

She had two weeks. That was what she had said to Geoffrey when he had asked her that evening how Nora had taken the news. 'I have to wait at least another two weeks,' she had said. 'It wouldn't be fair to tell her now and lift her hopes, considering how many losses she suffered herself in the first two or three months. At least after three months a miscarriage is less likely, and when she knows she can be happy for me.'

Geoffrey looked concerned. 'And you *are* happy about it, aren't you? You have seemed quite preoccupied lately …'

'I … I don't know …' She wondered for an instant whether to confess everything. 'It's only,' she explained, 'that Ma spoke so often about her sadness at her miscarriages … I can't be happy until I'm quite sure.'

'Of course, I understand. I'm so pleased, that's all. A son! What about "Nicholas", after my nephew? He can follow me into the book business.'

Mary frowned. 'How can you be sure it won't be a girl?'

'Boys often come first, don't they? Perhaps a daughter for the next one.'

'There may not be a next one.'

Oh, the nausea. Mary put a hand to her mouth. 'I don't feel very well … I'm sorry …' She pushed her chair back and ran out of the room.

Elsie appeared on the doorstep ten days later, bright and irrepressible as ever. Her hair had been styled in the manner of a Hollywood starlet: parted at the side and curled into waves that fell prettily around her face. A fringe almost covered one of her eyes and her lips were luscious and red. Mary swallowed the impulse to ask how she found the time and money for such grooming, what with a lover and her job as a waitress …

'Haven't seen you for ages.' Elsie grinned. 'Get the kettle on …'

Mary was doing everything she could to act naturally but couldn't hide her reluctance to welcome her friend into the house.

'You going to invite me in then? Is Geoffrey at home or something?' She pushed past her, and Mary followed.

'What's up with you,' Elsie was saying. 'Come on, smile. You've not said a word. 'Ere, I got some news to tell.'

So had she, so had she.

'Well don't you want to hear it then?'

'Yes, yes of course.' Mary concentrated hard on pouring water into the kettle and putting it on the stove.

'Your hand is shaking. Let me …'

Mary stepped back, letting Elsie take over. She suppressed the need to cry, to shout, to scream.

'You all right, love?'

'I'm just tired.' She pretended to stifle a yawn as she reached for the brown teapot. 'So, go on then, what's the news?'

'Well …' Elsie's face brightened. 'I wanted you to be the first to know.' She leant forward, conspiratorially. 'He hasn't even told his precious mamma yet.'

'He?'

'Your neighbour. I been seeing Mrs Baldoni's son, Pippo.'

'Really? Pippo Baldoni?' She tried to sound nonchalant, but her voice was too high. The effort of feigning surprise was almost too much.

'Yes, that's Filippo's nickname.'

'I know that's his nickname. He said so when we all met up outside the pictures that time.'

'Oh, that's right, he did.' Elsie had a look of anticipation, clearly eager for Mary to ask a lot of questions. 'Well, what do you think?'

'Erm … how long has this been going on?' She asked it so quietly she could hardly be heard.

'For a while, from that time we all bumped into each other, actually. He started coming into the café a lot after that and then, you know …' Elsie crinkled her nose in that way Mary had once found so endearing. 'He's so romantic. Eyeties are, ain't they?'

'Sorry, I forgot the sugar.'

Alone in the pantry Mary tried to slow her breathing. It was shallow and fast. A solid obstruction in her throat seemed to be blocking the pathway to her lungs. She wanted to die. Mostly she wanted Pippo to die. To be accountable, at least. Should she tell Elsie?

She took another juddering breath, picked up the sugar and returned to the kitchen.

'He's funny about his mamma, though,' Elsie resumed. 'He still hasn't brought me to his house. And you being right next door, you must tell me what Mrs Baldoni is like. But … oh Mary! I can't keep it to myself any longer! He's even asked me to marry him!'

Mary stood motionless, sugar in hand. 'He's what?'

'Ain't you pleased for me? You look like you've seen a bleedin' ghost.'

The kettle was boiling and the small kitchen was filling with steam.

''Ere, that kettle is going to boil dry.'

Mary grabbed the handle and yanked it off the stove. 'Move!' she said, pushing Elsie out of the way.

'What's up with you? It's me, your old chum. Why you being so cold?' Her top lip curled down, like that of a sulky child.

'When you going to get married then?' Mary said it to the kettle, not daring to meet Elsie's eyes.

'We're going to do it quietly, in Broadstairs.'

'Broadstairs? Won't Nanella … um, Mrs Baldoni, want a big Catholic wedding at St Peter's?'

'What, like yours?'

Mary was trying not to cry.

'You all right love?'

'Yes … yes I'm pleased for you. That's wonderful, Elsie.'

'We'll both be married women now.'

Mary smiled, grimly.

'Well, don't look so happy about it,' she said petulantly, and then brightening, as if something had just occurred to her, 'Oh, is it because you don't want me to go?'

'Go where?'

'I didn't tell you, did I? Silly me. Pippo calls me *sbandata*!'

'*Sbandata?*'

'It means scatty. He's teaching me some more words in Italian.' She pronounced it *Eyetalian*. 'Oh, come on, Mary, cheer up, please. I'll come back to London and see you …'

'You haven't told me where you're going,' Mary said coldly.

'Oh yes! *Sbandata* me! We're going to open a café in Broadstairs. Pippo has a cousin there … He's called Fausto, helped us find a place and everything. There are rooms above the café so we can live there. Well, until it gets too small, if we have a family, that is!'

A family.

'I know it's a funny time to open a café, but it'll probably take a while to get it ready and then we'll open at Easter. Luckily Pippo can do building work, and Fausto knows lots of people. He can do other jobs as well as getting the café ready, and then I'll be the manager.' Elsie lifted up her shoulders and grinned. 'Me, the manager, how does that sound? It's a scream, isn't it? Mrs Baldoni, the manager … that sounds good, don't ya think?'

Elsie's voice was becoming meaningless noise. Like having the wireless on when you're not really listening. Or the sound of birds, that was more like it, birds twittering in the background.

Don't come near my nest …

'Mary, why are you so sad? You look like you're about to cry! It's so sweet that you'll miss me, but it's not forever. You can come on the train and visit us. It'll be a laugh. Broadstairs is lovely. We can go paddling in the sea. Do you think we're too big for donkey rides?'

'It will be cold, in the winter.'

'Come in the spring, when the café is open, and I'll make you my best eggs and bacon …'

I'm having a baby in the spring, Elsie.

'… Or Pippo's lasagne, 'cos it will be an Eyetalian–English café.'

'Pippo's lasagne?'

'His mamma teaches him … Though he hasn't told her our plans yet. She don't even know about me. Not sure she will approve, what do you think?'

Mary had her own questions. When exactly had he asked her to marry him? But she said nothing.

'Look at you, it's like being in a bleedin' funeral parlour. You're becoming like Geoffrey. Giving me the silent treatment.' She rolled her eyes.

Mary's chest was becoming hot, anger rising. 'How dare you say that? That's my husband you're talking about.'

'Blimey, hold your horses. What's up with you today? Time of the month, is it? I thought you'd be excited for me … I was only coming to say goodbye.'

'Well, goodbye then …'

'Come on, love. Please tell me what's wrong? It's me, Elsie. Not someone you hardly know. You been a right misery for a while …' She tried to take her by the hand, but Mary pulled it away. 'Let's sit down. You haven't even made the tea.'

'I've changed my mind. We're not going to have tea. I've got things to do, if you don't mind. So, if you've finished …' She had to get her out of the house before she told her everything. Her voice took on a pleading tone. 'Please, Elise, you have to go. I'm not very well. But look, I'm pleased for you … and everything. I hope it all works out …'

On the doorstep Elsie turned. 'We'll be here another couple of weeks. Pippo's mamma will have our address. If you want it, that is …'

Mary nodded. 'Yes, your address, good.'

'You will come and see us?'

Mary summoned up all the energy she could muster to nod one more time. Slowly she closed the front door and, finally alone, she sank, disconsolate, to the floor and sobbed.

For days, the impulse to weep would not leave her. She woke with her eyes already moist and swollen as if there had been no break in the crying, even in her sleep. She told Geoffrey that Dr Gould had warned her of this; it was a side effect of pregnancy, along with the nausea and tiredness. Perhaps, Geoffrey suggested, he should call on Dr Gould for advice? And wasn't it about time to tell her mother? Or Nanella Baldoni? They would know how to help.

'Absolutely not!' Mary rejected all these suggestions, especially the last. 'I just need to rest.'

And so, Geoffrey was persuaded to go to the bookshop and leave her to crawl back into bed for a few hours. She lay, feverish with fantasies of revenge, torturing herself with images of Pippo and Elsie together, until exhaustion meant she could no longer think or feel anything at all.

She hated Pippo with as much intensity as she'd loved him. She should never have trusted that he would keep the promises he had made. All the passion, the declarations – how could he have transferred his love to another woman in such a short space of time? And not just anyone, but her closest friend. He had done more than let her down. He had ruined everything, like her father had when she was a child. How had she deserved any of this?

To keep herself sane, she plotted. She would choose her moment and confront him. Or better still she would unmask his duplicity by finding Elsie and, apologising for their last meeting and lulling her into a sense of security, tell her everything. Ha! That would wipe the smile off her face. She would sabotage their happy-ever-after plans. Even if Elsie forgave Pippo – he had that charming Italian way of winning people round – it would plant seeds of doubt in her mind about his future reliability. It would make her suspicious and their marriage insecure.

The potential to spoil their happy future was there. But Mary was frightened as well as angry. She knew she was close to destroying herself as well as others. It would be hard to contain the information, once it was out. The gossips would have a field day. Nanella would be upset. Nora mortified. Geoffrey was blameless, as was her unborn child. It would not be fair on them.

After a week of tears, rage, despair and despondency, Mary's sense of duty took over. There were chores to catch up on, provisions to be bought. These furies inside her were bad for the baby. And the baby was the important thing.

'I'm so happy to see you're feeling better,' Geoffrey said as she produced his favourite supper. 'Shepherd's pie. How delicious.'

Pippo never came to say goodbye before he and Elsie left for Broadstairs a few weeks later. The sense of not being given an ending disturbed Mary for a long time. She had the right to an explanation. Perhaps he was ashamed. Perhaps Elsie had reported her strange behaviour, and he couldn't face the tears and recriminations.

It was Nanella who tearfully told her that they had gone, in between apologies for not having checked to see how she was. 'I knew you were not well, but you said Dr Gould order you to rest. I no want you to worry about me but … I miss him.' She sniffed. 'And now he will be married. She has taken him away from me. They not even having wedding here.'

They were standing close together at the corner of their street. Nanella was wearing a black dress, and her normally cheerful face looked drained. Mary put her shopping basket on the ground and placed a hand on her shoulder. She was tempted – just for a moment – to tell her the truth. That she, too, had lost him. That it was probably his child she was carrying. That they must both be strong.

'I'm sorry,' she said instead. 'But you will go to the wedding? They will be back to see you, won't they?'

'Oh, Mary.' Nanella's tears spilled over. 'They said they will marry quickly, in Broadstairs. Why you think they no want to marry in St Peter's Church?' She wiped her nose. 'And why so fast? I did not know Elsie was his *fidanzata* until last week! Why he no tell me?'

'Perhaps …' she trailed off, not finding an excuse for them.

'Oh, no.' Nanella clutched Mary's arm, as if something had just occurred to her. 'You think she is pregnant?'

'I … I don't know … but … *I* am pregnant,' she blurted out.

'*Ma no! Grazie a Dio!*' She took Mary's face in both hands and kissed both cheeks. 'Why you not say? I knew it to be this! Oh, Mary! Your mother will be so 'appy to become a grandmother.'

'Thank you, yes she will. But keep it to yourself for now. I haven't even told her yet.'

Since her marriage, Mary had hardly visited her childhood home. It was less than half a mile from where she lived with Geoffrey, but far enough away for her to avoid it easily. The atmosphere there felt heavy and unhealthy, as if the house itself had a hangover. Liam O'Neill's drinking had begun earlier and earlier every day, so he seemed to escape hangovers entirely. Sometimes he got into fights and came staggering home with a bleeding nose and a black eye that would last weeks. It was frustrating and painful to witness her mother covering up for him, keeping up the pretence that everything was normal and respectable.

The three-months point in her pregnancy had passed when Mary went to visit her mother and finally made the announcement. Nora was telling her about one of the women she cleaned for, and how she was expecting again, and Mary interrupted with, 'Ma, I'm going to have a baby at the end of March.'

Nora's eyes widened. 'Holy Mother of God! But that's the most wonderful thing! In March you say? But why didn't you tell me before?'

'I wanted to wait to be sure ... you know, because of all the miscarriages you had, I didn't want my hopes – or anyone else's – raised.'

'Oh, this is a miracle.' She clapped her hands like a child. 'I didn't think Geoffrey had it in him.'

Mary laughed.

'I'm sorry, but you know what I mean,' Nora carried on. 'It's taken so long ... I did wonder, I thought you'd put on weight. Oh my, I'm going to be a grandmother! At last! Wait till I tell Pa. He'll be delighted.' She ran out of the room and began shouting up the stairs. 'Liam! Liam!' When he didn't respond, she went up the stairs to wake him up.

'Ma, look I've got to go ...' She hesitated before opening the door to leave, and called out, 'Tell Pa I'll be back soon.'

But Mary never saw her father again. She half expected him to come round to congratulate her and Geoffrey, but when he did not appear, she decided not to go to him. Nora made the usual excuses, 'He's not well, he'll see you when he's better,' but Mary had hardened her heart. She certainly wasn't going to go back to find him stumbling and swearing around the house, bottle in hand.

At night, sleepless and trying to get comfortable, she thought of her unborn child. The two (potential) paternal grandfathers of the child she was carrying had been victims of the war: James Williams bombed, Mr Baldoni drowned. And the maternal grandfather was an insensible old drunk. She would keep him away from the baby when the time came.

In the end, these worries were unnecessary. One wintery morning, still inebriated from the evening before, Liam O'Neill lost his footing and stumbled, falling head-first down the stairs in the narrow terraced house where Mary had been brought up. He banged his head at the bottom and never regained consciousness. 'Dead as a doornail' was the phrase he would have used about himself.

The news left Mary cold. The handsome father she had loved as a small child had died long before. He had become an embarrassment, but worse than that – and for this she could not forgive him – he had taken away all the joy and security of family life they had enjoyed in those early years. His drunken rages had made her anxious and fearful. His brutish behaviour had pushed her into marrying quiet, stable, well-spoken Geoffrey, who never swore or raised his voice. It had shackled her to a life of domesticity she had not been ready for.

The only sadness she felt was for her mother. When she visited her at home over the following weeks, she found her inconsolable. Nora O'Neill's grief was such that it even surprised the neighbours she had tried so hard to protect from knowing the truth. Of course, they had known all along. Well, that's what Mary imagined anyway. As she left her mother's house, she saw a small cluster of them huddled, arms folded, watching her.

'How is your ma doing, Mary?' one of them called out.

'As well as can be expected.' What else could she say? That Nora had said her life was made meaningless without her husband to care for? That she missed all those little babies Liam had fathered, the ones who had never been given the chance to be born? At that point Mary had wanted to interrupt her mother and say, 'Well what about my baby? Can't you be happy for that?' But she had remained silent.

No one ever divulged anything real and true. There were conventions in place. If you were asked how you were keeping, you answered that you were well, even if a few months ago you had thought of killing yourself.

Reveal nothing. Maintain respectability. Whenever Mary walked past Nora's neighbours she imagined them making all the gossipy comments her mother had done everything to avoid eliciting.

The funeral at St Peter's was a quiet one. A few of Liam's cronies from the Coach and Horses came as a mark of respect, but none of the extended family made the journey from Ireland. As the priest urged them to pray, Nora O'Neill wept copiously. Mary sat beside her, holding her hand, with Geoffrey on her other side, looking solemn.

'He wasn't a bad man,' Nora said to her dry-eyed daughter and son-in-law after the service. Neither of them concurred.

'Will you both promise me something,' she continued. 'If it's a boy, you will call him Liam, won't you?'

Geoffrey nodded half-heartedly. Mary knew he had set his heart on his son being named after his dead nephew. She looked her mother straight in the eye.

'Certainly, Ma. He'll be Liam Nicholas,' she said, praying with all her might that the baby growing inside her was a girl.

The baby was not yet beautiful. The midwife had sponged her but streaks of a cheesy substance still marked the little body. And she was hairy, not just on her head. A fine down covered her shoulders and back. There was even some on her forehead.

The labour had been long and painful and lasted most of the night. By the time both mother and newborn had been cleaned up and made presentable, Mary felt exhausted. She peered into her daughter's crumpled face like an archaeologist studying a find. Two eyes, a flat nose, a cupid's bow mouth. All as it should be. And then the shock of wild black hair, the sallow tinge under the reddish-purple blotches of the baby's skin.

Mary had not imagined her baby like this, or really like anything. All she had been instinctively sure of was the child's gender. The midwife's announcement that it was a girl had come as no surprise, in fact she had been close to replying, 'I know,' because for months she had been addressing the bump as 'Cara' in whispered conversations with her belly. And once she was holding the baby in her arms, she missed having her sheltered and concealed inside her. Now that her daughter was out in the world, she would have to share her with others. The world was such a dangerous place; how would she manage to protect her?

'I'll go downstairs and call Mr Williams,' the midwife was saying. 'You can be alone together while I fill in some papers. Then you must rest.'

Their bedroom had been cleared of towels and blood, the evidence of all Mary had been through. Nora had warned her. 'It's agony,' she'd said, but by the time you have the baby in your arms you'll have forgotten all about it. But the memory of the experience was still with her, the violence of it, the sense of her guts being ripped out, the moments she could not catch her breath from the intensity of it all. The pain of each contraction seemed meted out by Guilt, whip in hand, taunting, 'There, suffer!' During the pregnancy, when she could not feel any movement and feared the foetus had died, she imagined this terrifying possibility as being appropriate punishment for her adultery.

A noise distracted her. It was the bedroom doorknob turning and Geoffrey was coming in slowly, sheepishly, as if fearful of intruding.

'How are you?'

'Rather tired.'

'Of course, you must be. But isn't it marvellous? We have our own little girl!'

'Yes,' she said, wanly. She maneuvered the bundle in her arms so that he could take a look. 'You're not upset it isn't a boy?'

'Of course not. The most important thing is that she's healthy.' He peered at the face peeping out of the swaddling shawl. 'She's beautiful, isn't she? Look how dark she is! She takes after you ...'

Mary looked at her husband's pale skin and hair and felt the pangs of guilt again. Perhaps he should take the baby away. Replace her with the right one.

'It's funny isn't it, I never dared hope I would become a father.'

Not the right baby. Not the right wife. Not the right mother. Mary fixed her eyes on the infant's head.

'Was it frightening?' Geoffrey ventured. 'I heard you screaming. I hadn't expected it to last so long.'

'I know. The pain was awful.' She looked up at him. 'Did I keep you awake? I haven't slept at all ...'

'Well, it's over now. You poor thing, I was so worried about you.'

Mary tried to stifle the desperate longing for it to be Pippo saying those words. She did not return her husband's squeeze of the hand. All she said was, 'Has the midwife left?'

As if on cue, there was a knock on the door and the woman appeared: short, plump, middle-aged, briskly competent. 'How are you feeling now Mrs Williams?' She didn't wait for an answer. 'Try and sleep. Let me ...' Ignoring Geoffrey, she took the baby from Mary's arms, pausing before placing her gently into the cot. 'My,' she commented as she studied her features. 'She's a funny little thing, isn't she? All that hair! So dark, like her mummy.'

'That's just what I said,' Geoffrey interjected. 'But her skin ... it's a bit sallow, don't you think?'

Mary closed her eyes. She had given birth to the wrong baby.

'Hmm, we'll keep an eye on that,' the midwife said. 'It's possibly a touch of jaundice and will pass after a few days.' She tucked the newborn up in the cot. 'Dr Gould will come shortly to stitch you up. Might you be able to eat some breakfast before having a sleep, Mrs Williams?'

'I'm not very hungry ...' Mary felt curiously detached. She turned to Geoffrey. 'Have you told Ma the news?'

'Yes, she's on her way.'

Mary woke to find Geoffrey and Nora hovering over the cot.

'What's the time?' She was sore, worn out, tearful.

'You're awake! It's ten o'clock. How are you feeling? We have been admiring the new arrival.' Nora turned. 'Oh Mary! Just look at the little mite.'

'She's perfect, isn't she?' Geoffrey beamed proudly.

Mary glanced at him. 'Really? You're sure you're not upset it isn't a boy?'

'I've already told you, of course not!'

'And you, Ma? I know you were hoping I'd name the baby after Pa.'

'No, I promise you. I'm so happy. She's a little miracle.'

'She is, Ma. A miracle. Geoffrey, as we have a daughter, can I choose her name?'

'Why, what were you thinking?'

'A nice Irish name. It would give you pleasure, wouldn't it, Ma?'

Nora nodded.

'What about Cara?'

Mia cara. My beloved.

'That's beautiful, Mary. Oh, it is a miracle,' Nora said for the umpteenth time.

'That is a nice name,' Geoffrey concurred. 'And your ma is right, she *is* a miracle.'

Little Cara's temperament was easy going. She fed well, slept for hours and hardly cried. She was what women called 'a good baby'. It was Mary who could not stop crying. A few days after giving birth, Nora O'Neill found her daughter trying to smother her sobs into the pillow, not wishing to wake the baby.

'It will pass. It's what happens,' she reassured.

But Mary was inconsolable. 'I'm no good, Ma,' she cried.

'Don't be silly. Of course you're good. Look at your lovely baby. You'll be a wonderful mother.'

No, Ma. Anxiety gripped her throat. She was bad. She had sinned.

She wanted to confess all, to unburden herself from the weight of this terrible guilt. When her repressed sob finally came out, it had a strange, strangled sound. The baby scrunched her face up in response and started mewling, until both were bawling in unison.

'You'll be all right,' Nora said above the noise, picking up the baby and jigging her up and down. 'It's your milk coming in and the like. Give it a few days and you'll be back to normal. When I leave, I'll get your neighbour to pop in; what's her name?'

'NO!' Mary shouted, in sheer panic at the thought.

'All-right, don't be getting yourself so upset. Geoffrey can come home early.'

'No, please …'

At least the baby had ceased crying.

'Well, look, I think you should try and sleep before little Cara needs feeding again. I promise you it will all feel better soon. It's always hard at first.'

'What do you mean, "always"? You've only had one child. How would you know?'

'That was not my choice,' her mother answered quietly, and Mary felt guilty again. So much guilt.

But Nora shrugged it off. 'Rest,' she said. 'Dr Gould will be here soon. He'll tell you. What you're experiencing is normal.'

It took a while. At first Mary went through the motions of motherhood without fully engaging. She responded to her baby's needs but did not experience the surges of love she had imagined. Was she emotionally cold she wondered, was there something wrong with her? It was as if she were being pursued by the shadow of a second self: the bad mother, the adulterous wife; and that persona was taking over. There was no escape from this punitive voice in her head, repeatedly worming its way in. Telling her she was bad.

During her broken sleep, the nightmares came. Punishments of a hell created by her own doing: scenarios in which her secret was discovered, and she was exiled from everything familiar, her baby taken away by a grim-faced Geoffrey. In one awful dream Elsie was laughing at her and Pippo was spitting with contempt; in another Liam had come back to life and was drunkenly shouting that she was a whore.

The shame took hold. She decided she must be punished, to free herself from this torture. She must confess to Geoffrey; she must confess to Nanella Baldoni. She must confess to her mother, and to her daughter as soon as the girl could understand. But then logic kicked in: what purpose would that serve apart from destroying her relationship with everyone who mattered? Then she would decide that that was exactly what she wanted, to destroy herself, Pippo and Elsie – and Geoffrey for not being the right husband. To punish those who had not served her well, whether intentionally or not.

After the dream of being yelled at by her drunken father, Mary decided that the fault was his. It was because of him that she had accepted the first proposal that came her way. It wasn't Geoffrey she had been accepting, but security and peace. And if she hadn't married Geoffrey, she might never have met Pippo, and then she wouldn't be experiencing this unbearable longing for what she could not have. She would gaze at Cara's little face and see Pippo there. She wanted to take her baby to Broadstairs and say to him, 'This is your daughter and I have to live with the lie for the rest of my life.'

Eventually Mary realised she had to face the world. She wrapped Cara up in wool against the cold spring day, added a little bonnet over the wild baby hair and placed her into the old pram she herself had been wheeled around in twenty-five years before.

She returned home an hour or two later and acknowledged to herself that the outing had made her feel better. The ice in her heart was thawing. It had been as she had imagined when she had first married and looked forward to having a child. She felt proud and protective. Women on the way to the shops stopped to coo; shopkeepers congratulated her. She was like the others, she felt connected. No longer marked as different. No longer barren.

Over the next weeks, months, years, the bond grew stronger to the point of symbiosis. Decades later a therapist might have suggested that Mary was looking for the emotional closeness lacking in her marital relationship and that having a daughter provided her with purpose and love. But no one spoke in those terms back then. If Mary had been asked about it, she would have said she was doing no more than fulfilling her maternal role.

Mary's identity became so fused with Cara's that she would refer to her daughter as 'we'. 'We had our first solid food today,' or, 'We must get our first shoes.' Once Geoffrey commented, 'It is as if you are one person.'

When she didn't reply Geoffrey continued, 'Don't look so worried. It isn't a criticism. I am proud of you being such a good mother.'

She hated Geoffrey using that expression. It seemed like all the women around her were judged by this yardstick. She even caught herself frowning at exasperated mothers sometimes, those who occasionally shouted or lightly slapped their children. Who was she to determine who was worthy or not, she asked herself.

On her daily rounds of the shops she was polite but tended to keep her distance from the women of the neighbourhood. 'Good morning, how are you;' 'Very well thank you;' 'Yes, she has grown,' were the limits of her conversation. She also avoided Nanella Baldoni. Nanella had given up bringing food and items for the baby. 'I don't want her fussing,' Mary had told Geoffrey, and finally his aloofness when she knocked on their door meant that Nanella stopped trying.

'I am so busy', Mary would say when they met in the street, 'what with everything there is to do.' To avoid suspicion she would occasionally ask after Rosa and Carlino and, as time wore on, Nanella's grandchildren. She never mentioned Elsie and Pippo by name. Nanella didn't seem to notice, or if she did, she didn't seem to mind. The worst thing for Mary was seeing Nanella peer into the pram, or, when Cara was older, take the little girl's face in her hands, repeating the same familiar phrase, *Che bella bambina, bellissima.* Unspoken words would scream inside Mary's head. *I'm sure this is your granddaughter. Forgive me.*

On several occasions she heard a car stop outside, or Pippo's voice talking deliberately loudly, as if he wanted Mary to know he was there, visiting his mother. *'Don't you dare come near me,'* she would think, fighting the urge to look out of the window, wondering why, if he was with Elsie, would they not knock on her door. And why did Nanella, knowing that Mary and Elsie had been friends, not ask Mary round when they were visiting? Perhaps she had been told that they had fallen out, perhaps she had guessed – Mary would never know.

Every so often she caught Geoffrey studying the child, looking preoccupied. She wondered if he had any suspicions. But she convinced herself it was only her own guilt posing the question. The dark colour and thickness of Cara's hair could be reasonably attributed to a maternal gene. In any case, Geoffrey might well be the father. Mary repeated this many times to herself, although she knew in her heart as she did so that he wasn't, he couldn't be.

For Cara, as a small child, the whole world *was* her mother. The day she joined the Infants at St Peter's School she clung to Mary's leg, bawling as the nuns tried to separate them. The pain was mutual. As Mary walked home, still shaken, hearing the echo of Cara's desperate sobs as the nuns dragged her away, she had little idea how she would manage. It was as if her body had been sliced in two.

Luckily Cara quickly settled down. The tall, narrow building became less threatening, the nuns less alarming, the other children less noisy. Eventually she started looking forward to school every morning, and by that time Mary had grown accustomed to having time on her own.

The school, built in the 1870s for the growing community of Italian and Irish immigrants in Clerkenwell, was a modest affair. The Infants, where Cara began her school life, had only a small yard for a playground, squeezed between a convent and a factory. It was dark and damp even during the summer term and in the winter months it could be icily cold. A row of outside lavatories stood against one wall, and there was an iron fire escape leading to the boys' playground situated on the asphalt roof of the building.

Most of the children were quite poor and wore patched clothes and threadbare coats, but the community was strong, with great loyalty to both church and school. In a hall that had been used as a bomb shelter during the war, the girls and infants danced, performed little plays and prepared for the celebrations that punctuated the year, such as the Christmas Bazaar and First Communion Day.

The highpoint took place in mid-July with the feast in honour of Our Lady of Mount Carmel. Cara and the other children, decked out in white or brightly coloured robes, joined the community to walk through the crowded streets holding banners, wreaths and garlands, following floats arranged with biblical tableaux as they trundled ahead to the sound of a marching band. And, leading the procession – resplendent within a bower of roses and lilies – was borne aloft the statue of 'Our Lady', wearing her crown of stars and swaying on a platform of flowers. For this one day, Clerkenwell was transformed into a vibrant Italian village, celebrating a *festa* with much excitement and gaiety. And it wasn't just for the Italians. The procession drew in the Irish, as well as other Londoners who came to enjoy the atmosphere in streets decked with flags and bunting.

There was so much to hear and see. Musicians, performers, singers; young women dressed like brides in white veils, young boys in white suits, housewives in national costume, older women clad in black clutching rosaries, old soldiers with feathers in their hats. Flowers were everywhere: carried in baskets, draped around banners, strewn on the ground in front of the procession by the flower girls. Houses and shops along the streets had their own little altars and decorations depicting images of saints or the Madonna. Stalls sold wine, snacks and *gelato* to keep the crowd going. This, Cara imagined, was what Italy must be like all the time: noisy, warm, seeped in the ethos of Catholicism. When the statue of Our Lady came to a stop and a flock of doves was released to fly overhead, the denouement seemed to her like an act of God.

It was at St Peter's School that Cara made her first friend. Paola's parents hardly spoke any English and because Cara spent a lot of time in their home, she absorbed the language and culture that Paola's family was eager to maintain. She loved the warmth and exuberance she found with them, and it made Mary happy too. She had none of the prejudice that others of her generation had absorbed. 'You're my little Italian girl, you are,' she would say, giving Cara a hug when her daughter came home and performed a newly learnt Italian rhyme or song.

Geoffrey may as well have not been there. He was not an unkindly presence, just an impassive one. He ate his meals in virtual silence, but this did not bother Mary and Cara. It would have been disturbing if he had suddenly tried to make conversation. His silence suited them. There were no quarrels in the house, no raised voices. Every time Mary craved a bit of excitement, she would remind herself of Liam O'Neill, drunkenly shouting, knocking into things and throwing random punches. Anything had to be better than that.

Even so, Mary would sometimes indulge in a bit of magical thinking. If she overheard Italian voices outside the house she would imagine that Pippo had returned. In her fantasies he had left Elsie and moved back in with his mother. He had come round and recognised his daughter. And then the best bit: he was on his knees imploring Mary to take him back. She would make him earn her forgiveness before she relented and they were reconciled. But then the fantasy would get stuck: what if he laid claim to Cara? And so she would tweak the narrative: Pippo begging her forgiveness and recognising his daughter but expecting nothing back. In time, when she was sure he had suffered enough pain and regret, they would resume their secret affair. She would feel young and desirable again. She would have the upper hand, as he would be desperate to please her.

Her daydreams filled the void of her empty marriage. She knew she had married the wrong man. That she had loved the wrong man. Her child's legacy consisted of half-truths, but Mary would redeem herself. She would give her daughter the stability of a peaceful home, the security of knowing she was loved, and a sense of her heritage, even if the girl didn't know it was her heritage. She was intent on providing Cara with all that was good.

It was Mary who encouraged Cara to draw, paint and explore museums and libraries. The first time she considered taking Cara to the National Gallery she could hear Nora's voice, in that familiar Irish lilt, repeating over and over that such a place was not *for the likes of us*. But she was determined her daughter would never experience the same sense of inferiority she had absorbed as a child, growing up poor in an Irish family where fathers drank and mothers cleaned all hours to make a basic living, where the constant keeping up of appearances was the most important thing, where she was required to be quiet and accommodating at all times. No, her child's life would be different. The National Gallery was free, was it not, and meant for everyone? Why shouldn't they go and enjoy looking at the pictures like anyone else?

On that day in 1955, a strike of London Underground workers forced them into a long queue for a bus at Farringdon, but Mary refused to be discouraged. When they finally arrived in the hallowed halls of this temple to art, she was gratified to see how much more responsive her seven-year-old was than the spoilt, fractious children dragged along by well-dressed parents.

She's artistic, Mary told herself, watching Cara stare in wonder at the Virgins and angels depicted in front of her. *She's curious*. And Mary was filled with a sense of hope.

Cara loved illustrated story books, but her favourite of all was an old translation of *The Adventures of Pinocchio*, with beautiful illustrations of the Fairy with Turquoise Hair and of the wooden puppet who wanted to be a boy and who had a nose that grew longer whenever he lied. Pinocchio's shaming protuberance would grow so long that there was nowhere to hide it. The irony was not lost on Mary. She would be reading out loud to Cara, all the time thinking *lucky my nose doesn't grow when I refer to Geoffrey as 'your father'*.

But no lies had been told. All Mary had ever done was withhold the truth.

It was a cloudy afternoon during the summer of 1958 when Cara, aged ten, called out, 'Ma, there's a funny man outside, staring at the house!'

'What do you mean, "a funny man"?'

'He was staring and then he saw me looking out and made a funny face. He's still there, come and see!'

Mary walked over and immediately shrank back into the shadows. The moment of recognition felt like a sharp pain. She had managed to avoid him all those times he had been visiting his mother, but now there he was, standing in the street in full view. Yes, it was definitely Pippo, in baggy trousers with a well-cut jacket to match, and polished shoes – she sensed the shine even though she couldn't see them. His naturally curly hair was slicked back rather than falling over his forehead, but he was still wearing that fatally charming smile.

'Do you know him? He's making signs at the door. Why don't you let him in? He looks nice.' The little girl turned towards her. 'Ma? You seem frightened.'

'It's nothing, I … No, I don't think I know him.' She put her arm around Cara in an attempt to distract her. 'Come away from the window,' she said, leading her back to the table where the child's book lay abandoned.

What on earth did Pippo think he was doing? It was an invasion, a transgression. How dare he stare at Cara like that, drawing her in, amusing her with his expressions, promising what he would never deliver. Did he realise who Cara was? Had he guessed? He had a cheek.

But the pull back to the window was too hard to resist. As soon as Cara had settled back to her book, she glanced out again and realised that the car he was standing in front of must be his. He was leaning against it, arms folded, dapper and proprietorial. Had he no shame?

Mary positioned herself far enough away from the window so he would not see her, but close enough to observe him. He was clearly waiting for his family to come out of his mother's house. Rooted to the spot, she could not help staring, waiting to see what would happen next. And then she heard them, children's voices, squabbling, laughing. Two boys, aged about eight and six, appeared, neatly dressed in long shorts and jackets, followed by a woman telling them to calm down or the neighbours would be after them.

Pippo opened the car door for the boys to jump in. Then their parents paused, studying Geoffrey's house together, talking and pointing at the window.

You look good, Mary thought with sadness, as she stood peering from the shadows of her home. *Motherhood suits you.*

Elsie appeared more sophisticated than when they had last met that miserable day, over a decade ago. Her prettiness had developed into a mature beauty, enhanced by the well-cut dress with its narrow belt cinching in her waist. Her high heels emphasised the shapeliness of her legs, and a small Juliette cap partly covered a fashionable short hairstyle.

The longing to open the door and embrace her friend was all consuming. How easily Mary might do this, pretending nothing was strange, apologising for her coldness at their last encounter, overwhelming her with warmth and friendliness. She could invent something to explain her past behaviour: she was coming down with flu that day; it had been a long illness and she had meant to get in touch when she got better, she was so sorry. She might even shake Pippo's hand and invite them in, suggest they bring the boys to meet Cara, get the biscuits out, make tea, ask questions about life in Broadstairs.

'Guess who I saw today,' she might say to Geoffrey later that evening, 'Elsie and Pippo Baldoni popped in for tea, a surprise visit. Their two little boys are growing up.' And she knew he would answer in his distracted way, 'That's nice.'

She glanced behind her at the corner of the room where Cara, her head bent, book abandoned, was colouring a drawing with concentration. If Mary did invite them in, would Elsie notice the physical similarities between her daughter and Pippo? Would *he* notice? She felt her anger rising up again, the familiar fury and frustration that needed to be constantly held in check. How could he behave so nonchalantly? How dare he treat her as if she didn't matter, as if nothing they had experienced together had meant anything? How could she even have considered being polite and forgiving?

The noise of a slamming car door and the engine starting made her turn back to the view of the road. They were leaving. They were gone. But for a while she gazed into the space as if they were still there.

8

Florence

NOVEMBER 1966

By the time Cara got back after meeting Stefano, she had no energy left to think. Each step up the stairs felt like a step up a mountain. When she passed the Lotti doorbell she hesitated – should she ring, should she knock? Fernando's wife might be in, offering comfort. The least Cara should do was thank her for the biscuits.

She put her ear to the door and could hear children's voices inside, layered over each other, noisily laughing, squabbling, whining. Their mother was telling them to go and wash their hands before *merenda*, the Italian equivalent of teatime. Sounds of family life continued, whatever dramas were unfolding outside.

The call for *merenda* triggered in Cara a deep melancholy. She remembered a Welsh girl she had befriended a few years before. Bethan had only been at their school briefly, but during that short time she had suffered from a dreadful homesickness. Once, when Cara came across her crying in a quiet corner, Bethan had spoken about *hiraeth*, the longing for home, the missing of something or someone or an era that no longer exited. It was exactly what Cara was experiencing now. Associating Mrs Lotti's call for tea with her own mother calling up the stairs in Clerkenwell, the sound of the kettle whistling, the taste of bread and jam, she felt almost a physical pain. She even missed hearing the old clock on the mantelpiece that had belonged to the grandparents she had never met, its ticking marking the slowness of time passing during every repetitive day. All that had previously seemed claustrophobic and constraining was tinged with nostalgia. She felt very young and – like Bethan had been – very homesick. Since her arrival in Florence she had relied on the kindness of strangers, but herein was the problem. In the end they remained strangers.

Cara moved away from the Lotti door and continued heavily up the stairs. Once in the apartment she methodically checked light switches, taps, cooker and telephone. Nothing was working. In the sitting room the biscuits Fernando had brought her were on the table. She opened the packet and ate a few. That would do as supper. It may have only been late afternoon, but the apartment was dark and cold and damp, and all Cara wanted was to wrap herself in her blankets, close her eyes and slip away.

By the time Fernando had returned to Via Laura, checked on his family and was ringing the bell of her door to invite her to eat with them, she was lying in bed, in that transitional state between wakefulness and sleep. She had been thinking of Gianni, his body tensed against the cold and rain, half wading, half swimming through the windy streets, pushing through dirty, chest-high water, sensing the pressure against his body, desperately, single-mindedly, trying to reach his disabled mother.

Where was he now? Where had he gone? Surely Stefano would have told her if he had drowned too?

Far away, a doorbell was ringing. She hardly had a sense of it. Could it be Gianni? But her legs felt like lead and her eyes were heavy. She turned over, deciding she had imagined it, or that it had been someone else's doorbell or part of a dream.

———

When she finally slipped into unconsciousness, Cara slept for a long time. It was as if her body had needed to catch up on the rest that had eluded her since she and Gianni had spent the night together. Now, woken as usual by the church bells, she was again in the grip of nagging anxiety. Why had he not been in touch with her? Dark morbid thoughts – that he may have died too – alternated with reassuring ones: it was unlikely; Stefano would have included that information in his tirade against her. She recalled the intonation of his voice, his accusing eyes.

She stared up at the ceiling wondering what to do next. Should she ring Fernando Lotti's doorbell and ask whether Stefano had told him anything else after she had walked away from them? Or should she try and forget about Gianni and make her way to Nicoletta's house to see how they were faring. She could ask for help, for advice on how to get back to London. But Gianni was insidiously invading her mind. She knew that unless she returned to Santa Croce and found Stefano, or a priest, or a neighbour – anyone who could explain what had happened to him – she would be running away from what she had to confront.

Despite this, she took her time getting ready. It was hard to get out of a bed warmed by her body and the numerous blankets she had piled on top of herself the night before. That was probably why she had slept so soundly, protected by her cocoon. Every time she thought of leaving its security, she buried herself deeper inside. Out of the bed it was cold and damp, and on the streets it would be worse. It was tempting to remain still, thinking about getting up, running through the motions of dressing, leaving the house, walking to Santa Croce, speaking to people, returning home. She spent so long doing this, she felt she had actually lived the day.

Eventually she pushed the blankets off, wrapped herself in her dressing gown and walked from bathroom – no water for the flush – to kitchen – no gas in the stove – and back to the bedroom. She began to dress, piling on the layers of wool. Vests and tights, crew-necked jumper, the tight tweed skirt she had laughed at her mother for persuading her to pack, the heavy coat – 'you will need all this when the weather gets colder' – all of it had come in useful. The only extra item she needed were the waterproof boots she longed for but did not have, so she slipped on some sturdy shoes instead.

The day felt even brighter than yesterday, with rays of sunshine making more of an effort to break through, but it was very cold. The streets seemed busier; those who had been trapped inside were coming to take stock of the damage outside, which seemed greater than before. More and more rubbish and damaged goods had been piled up in the streets as the clearing of shops and houses continued. The silent shock and desperation seemed to have lessened and there was a greater connection between people. Women were talking to each other across their windowsills or lowering down baskets to street level for others to fill with basic provisions. Friends and relatives from areas less affected by the flood had arrived with bottles of drinking water, cartons of milk, packets of biscuits. What a lot of dried biscuits this city seemed to have stashed away! Cara was relieved to hear a woman mention that bakers in Fiesole had been working through the night to produce bread that would be distributed around Florence by firemen. Where were these firemen? She would have to ask Fernando later.

Cara walked on slowly, deciding not to take the direct route to Santa Croce but to go via the main city square of Piazza della Signoria. She saw more shops and cafés devastated by the flood, with their owners assessing the damage to goods and furniture. But she sensed a slight shift from stunned despair to a determination to get on with restoring normality. In one of the streets she smiled at the sight of a child removing mud with his seaside bucket and spade while his father did the same with an adult pail and shovel. There was hope as well as tenacity in their faces.

Piazza della Signoria was a hive of activity. It had become a liaison centre for aid workers and volunteers. Some were soldiers, some police, some civilians medically trained. Others who were simply there to offer any help they could were being sent in different directions to save those still trapped in buildings.

Cara joined a group of three soldiers standing by a truck and asked, '*Pane, acqua*?' Hunger was making her stomach rumble. Two of the soldiers gave each other a look and the other pointed at the fountain in front of the town hall – the Palazzo Vecchio – where a group of citizens were filling empty wine bottles with water. She opened her hands in a gesture that indicated she had no empty bottles on her, and then put her hand on her stomach with a look of desperation.

'*Ho fame*,' she said.

'*Aspetta*,' said one of the soldiers. He climbed into the truck, retrieved a *panino* and passed it to her with a smile. She took it gratefully, stuffing it into her mouth hungrily as she walked away. '*Aspetta!*' he called again, and when she turned, she saw he was offering her a flagon of water. 'Come back later,' he said, 'more supplies are coming.'

Hunger and thirst dealt with, she stopped at the corner of the piazza and hesitated again about what she should do. Continue towards the river and Nicoletta's house, or take the road to Santa Croce and attempt to find Gianni? She began walking past the Uffizi Galleries towards the Arno. And then paused. What was the point of going to see Nicoletta right now? Right now, she needed to hurry along to Santa Croce.

Objects the floodwaters had seized, dragged, overturned and then randomly deposited on their destructive course through the city a few days earlier had been moved to the sides of the roads, waiting to be cleared away. Piles of rubbish that yesterday had seemed like small mounds were getting taller. When she reached Santa Croce, there appeared to be a lot more people lingering, both around the church and in the square itself, as if waiting for something to happen. The mood was tense.

'Cosa succede?' Cara asked a woman standing near her, pointing to the men loitering around the entrance to the church as if guarding it.

'They're trying to get the Crucifix down. It's taking them forever,' the woman answered, still looking ahead.

In a city full of crosses, Cara knew immediately which Crucifixion it was.

'Il Cimabue?'

'Si. Rovinato. Distrutto.' The woman emphasised every syllable of the words. Ruined. Destroyed.

'Surely it can be restored?'

The woman looked at Cara for the first time. 'There is too much to be restored.'

The sounds of an engine and loud voices were getting closer. A jeep overflowing with men entered the square.

'E il Presidente della Repubblica,' someone called out. Cara recognised him from newspaper photographs. It was indeed Giuseppe Saragat, President of Italy, crushed into the back of the jeep with a lot of official-looking men.

'Ha! He's come to show that Rome cares about us! But we want bread! Not him!'

Others joined in. *'Vogliamo pane!'*

The jeep juddered through the hostile crowd.

'Go back to Rome and bring us bread!'

'Pane!' the people shouted.

'Pane, pane ...' Cara joined in with the chant, feeling slightly

guilty, as she could still taste the sandwich the soldier had given her shortly before.

'*Pane, pane*!' the crowd chanted until the jeep, filled with politicians and local worthies, came to a standstill. 'Ha, he's got stuck!' a man said, and Cara watched as a group of people tried to drag the jeep out of the mud and others closed in, whistling and jeering, venting their frustration.

The air filled with colourful insults. 'And now, we – the victims – are having to save *you* lot, you sons of whores/pigs/the devil …'

Finally, the wheels of the jeep stopped spinning and the President with his embarrassed smile was driven out of the square towards the Biblioteca Nazionale, to shouts of, 'Clear off! Let us get on with the work we need to do …'

As soon as the jeep had gone, Cara was struck by the way the Florentines resumed the behaviour she had witnessed the day before. There was a general pulling up of sleeves, a 'let's get on with it' approach. She watched the woman who had been standing next to her walk towards a shop and pick up the broom she had left leaning against the wall. Gatherings dispersed to resume their various tasks. Those who had been most vocal in their anger had calmed down. It seemed to Cara that they had also lost interest in what was going on in the church. Was she the only person still curious about the Crucifixion's fate? But if you needed food for your family, the fate of a work of art would feel of secondary importance.

The road leading away from the square and towards Gianni's house was a long one. Cara retraced the steps she had made the day before, feeling jittery. She wanted to find Gianni but at the same time was nervous of seeing him. As she walked, she composed what she would say to him. *I was sorry to hear about your mother.* That sounded formal and indifferent. *You must be devastated*. That also sounded detached. Perhaps she would just say what Fernando kept repeating. *É una tragedia.*

She knew Gianni would be grief-stricken. What if he blamed her as Stefano had done? Today there was no Fernando to support her. But if she turned back instead of going to him, wouldn't that seem cold?

As she came closer the road emptied. Marcella's house stood on the corner, showing a dark line on its humble façade, an oily marker of the water's rise. The policeman who had stood guard had gone. Cara paused outside and called out, 'Gianni! Gianni!'

There was no answer. She passed through the arch at the side of the house. The only door in sight looked battered but had not, like many of the others in the street, been pulled off its hinges. She banged the front of it repeatedly with her fist, hoping it would either give way or attract attention. 'Gianni! Gianni!'

No sound came from inside. She pressed her ear to the door and sensed nothing but absolute stillness. Back she went to stand under the window. 'Gianni! Gianni!!'

Minutes passed. Her cries were becoming increasingly determined. She realised she was calling out not just for Gianni but for someone – anyone – to hear, to give her some information, some guidance. Even seeing Stefano and bearing the brunt of his anger again would be preferable to this intolerable waiting in limbo.

But her shouts bounced off the impenetrable walls. She was about to give up, when a woman dressed in a black dress emerged from the house next door.

'Ma signorina cosa vuole? Gianni è all'ospedale.'

'Ospedale?' Cara gave her a startled look.

'Yes,' the woman explained. 'He's in Santa Maria Nuova. He hurt himself quite badly. You heard about his mother?'

Cara nodded.

'Poor woman. Poor son. *Gianni é impazzito.*' The woman added emphasis with her hands. 'He went crazy. He became like a wild animal. They had to restrain him, he was banging his head against the wall and screaming … they ended up taking both mother and son to the hospital, though of course Marcella …' The woman made a praying gesture.

'Yes, it must have been such a shock to him …' Cara said this very slowly, as the information filtered in.

She is dead but he is alive. He is in hospital. Relief mingled with anxiety. *He has hurt himself.*

'*Grazie* … thank you for telling me. *Le sono grata.*'

The woman called after her, '*Ma lei é inglese?*'

Cara was walking away and didn't answer. What difference did it make if she was English or Italian?

She had passed alongside the impressive hospital of Santa Maria Nuova many times, for it was close to the apartment in Via Laura and not far from the Cathedral. During her early meanderings she had stepped into its cloister and read the plaques acknowledging the Florentine noble Falco Portinari, founder of the hospital and father of Dante's beloved Beatrice. Later, she had read about its distinguished history and learnt that even Leonardo da Vinci had performed autopsies here. This time, as she hurried towards it, Cara only had two thoughts in her mind: how would she find exactly where Gianni was? And how would he be?

She walked straight through the cloister and into the building. It was so different from a British hospital. London hospitals had reception areas and signs to lead the way. Here, no one seemed available and it was unclear where she should go, or whom she could ask for information. A few nuns, dressed in white whimples and robes, glided past her. It felt almost medieval to glimpse these ghostly figures disappearing around corners. Uncertain as to whether they were visiting the sick or nursing, Cara was tongue-tied, too shy to ask them for information. She walked on through sparsely furnished rooms, wondering why the hospital looked so empty and abandoned. Where were the patients? And shouldn't there be even more here than usual? Where were the flood victims? The doctors? The nurses?

A woman dressed in a white overall came towards her, carrying some papers under her arm. She looked official.

'*Scusi signora* ...' Cara ventured, '*dove sono i pazienti*?'

At first the woman, possibly a doctor, gave her a suspicious look, but at least she stopped to answer. 'The patients? Many of them have been transferred to Careggi.'

Cara knew that to be the hospital on the outskirts of the city. But Marcella's neighbour had definitely said Santa Maria Nuova. She hesitated.

'Or try the floor above.' The woman looked irritated. '*Ovviamente*,' she added, with a sigh.

'*Ovviamente*?' Why was that obvious? And then Cara remembered Fernando mentioning that patients had been moved to the upper floors of hospitals when flooding into the wards became a real threat. But Gianni was admitted after the water had subsided.

'And the most recent patients?' she called after the woman. Without turning, the woman simply pointed a finger up to the ceiling.

Cara dithered when she got to the floor above. Should she turn left or right? There were stairs and doors in both directions, so it was as unclear as ever where she should go. She decided to open as many doors as she could. Everywhere the wards were crowded with patients, surrounded by family groups. Some visitors seemed to have brought whole meals with them, to feed themselves as well as the patients. Relatives brandishing knives cut through rolls of salami and cheese the way passengers did on Italian trains, filling the air with an all-pervasive smell of meat and feet.

She looked around for someone who might give her information and spotted a nun attending to an old man. They must be nurses after all. Standing self-consciously, not wishing to interrupt, Cara waited for her to finish.

'Scusi …'

The nun looked preoccupied with her task and Cara momentarily wondered whether she should give up asking for help and walk up and down the rows of beds in every ward until she found him.

'Scusi,' she repeated, *'dove posso trovare Gianni Magnelli?'*

'Lei è?'

'Un'amica.' A friend. She supposed that would best describe her.

The nun had finished with the old man. She nodded at Cara, turned her back and began walking away. *'Venga,'* she said over her shoulder. *Come.* Cara followed her out of the ward and into another. The nun stopped and gestured towards a corner of the room, before turning back.

Cara could see two women sitting on either side of a bed where a young man, his forehead wrapped in bandages, lay staring into space.

'Gianni,' she said cautiously as she approached, glancing nervously at the two women. Three pairs of eyes swivelled towards her and narrowed slightly as she came into view.

'Mi chiamo Cara …' she said, introducing herself to the women.

Gianni stirred slightly, more to make himself comfortable than as a response to her. It crossed her mind that he seemed neither pleased nor displeased to see her. She had expected more of a reaction.

'This is my sister Giovanna,' he said, flatly. Cara gave her a tight smile that was not returned and looked towards the other woman.

'Ilaria,' the woman said softly, by way of introduction.

Ah, so here is the married older sister. And beautiful Ilaria, the fidanzata. A Raphael Madonna, innocent and forever blameless.

Both women were dressed soberly in clothes that seemed too old for their years – drab and timeless. Dark hair was pulled off strained faces. They could have been actresses in an old film from thirty years before.

'*Piacere*,' said Cara, thinking no, it isn't a pleasure at all, for any of us. Neither of the women responded.

Cara hoped her face wouldn't register any change of expression. 'I ... I am so sorry ... for your loss,' she stammered.

The women ignored her and looked back towards the figure lying between them.

I know what they are. The Virgin and Mary Magdalene.

Gianni broke the awkward silence. 'Why have you come?' A sharp, frigid voice, like the weather outside.

I have no place here. Though if anyone should play Mary Magdalene ... Cara bit back a bitter smile.

'I wanted to find you, to say ...' She glanced at the two young women, then back at Gianni, '... I heard what happened ... to Marcella. I am so sorry.'

All three of them lowered their eyes. Giovanna looked into her lap. Ilaria fixed her gaze on the floor.

She is so pretty, like an unpicked flower.

Cara stood at the foot of the bed, an English interloper intruding on their grief.

Gianni looked as battered as the streets of Florence. There was bruising on his cheek and the folds of gauze wrapped across his forehead covered a pad of cotton wool. Cara wanted to touch his arms, to caress him better, to encapsulate her guilt and her regret into a compassionate gesture. Instead she simply asked, knowing the answer, 'What happened to you? I mean, the bandage?' She needed to hear it from him, in his words.

But it was Giovanna who answered. 'He was upset. He banged his head repeatedly and punched the wall when he realised our mother was beyond saving. He had pushed his way through many people and arrived at the house just as she was pronounced dead, it was awful … *Si è fatto molto male …*'

Cara was momentarily struck how the phrase 'to hurt oneself' in both languages implies 'causing hurt to oneself', like it was an intentional act, when it is usually an accidental thing. But in his case, it was accurate – the harm was self-inflicted.

'Do you know how long he will stay in hospital?' she asked Giovanna as if Gianni were not present.

Neither woman answered. Cara moved from one foot to the other gracelessly, wanting to sit down on the corner of Gianni's bed. It was too hot in the ward and she was wearing too much wool, but it seemed an inappropriate moment to remove her coat.

'How are you now?' she asked him directly, pulling herself together. Then she noticed his knuckles, deeply grazed and covered with patches of iodine. 'Oh, your poor hand!'

'That is nothing,' he said, more in sorrow than in anger. 'These are scratches and wounds that will heal. But I shall never forgive myself for not being there, with her. It was my duty. I let her down.'

'It was not your fault …' Ilaria said, almost inaudibly, placing her hand protectively over his wrist.

'Nor mine,' Cara wanted to add, feeling excluded and in some way blamed. She wondered how Gianni had explained his absence to Ilaria. Perhaps he had given the same excuse as he had to his mother – that he was with his cousin, making Stefano complicit too.

The bad feelings were rising. It was as if she was stuck behind an invisible wall created by the Madonna and the Magdalene protectively encircling the object of their devotion. She wanted to speak out, to say, 'Your precious Gianni pressured me for weeks into letting him stay the night. Yes, Ilaria, you heard, *to stay the night*. To make love. With me. That is what your perfect *fidanzato* was doing while Marcella drowned.'

Instead she said, '*Devo andare* ... I have to leave.'

'*Vai via, vai* ...' Gianni suddenly burst out.

She stepped back, surprised at the outburst.

'*Vai!*'

He was angry now and raged at her as if she were an unwelcome dog. 'Why are you standing there like an idiot? *Vai via!* Go away, go, go! *E non tornare!* And don't come back!'

Tears of humiliation blurred the objects in her way as she turned and stumbled past the other beds towards the door that led out of the ward.

*

Mary needed someone to talk to. Someone dependable, calm, willing to offer a sympathetic ear. Years ago, Nanella Baldoni had filled that role, but after Pippo married Elsie, Mary had seen less of her and once her neighbour's younger children had left home as well, their paths crossed only at church. They had never agreed to cool their friendship or diagnose what had changed. People didn't, it simply happened. It would be strange to knock on her front door and expect to be invited in like the old days.

There were other neighbours she might go to, of course, as well as the shopkeepers she chatted to on a daily basis. They knew Cara was in Italy and would understand a mother's concerns over a daughter's welfare, given the news of the flood. But she didn't feel like bringing it up again with them. It was as if she had exhausted her share of sympathy for the time being, and she reasoned that they would pass on more information should they hear anything new.

So, she did what she always did when she needed to clear her head – she left the house and walked. In her experience, walking had a way of clarifying her thoughts. By walking, it was as if she was physically shifting the obstacles to a more manageable place.

She turned the corner with no clear plan and found herself going towards King's Cross. She began to feel more positive. The roads were busy, the shops enticing, and as she walked, her thoughts of Cara and the impossibility of communicating with her were interrupted by the occasional distraction of a pair of shoes or a nice overcoat in a window display. She never considered going inside the shops to check them out, for she was still entrenched in Nora's 'make-do-and-mend', 'not for the likes of us', mentality. In any case she couldn't afford these things. But it was enough briefly to imagine owning them, and then to move along.

Before getting very far she came to a halt in front of a large window display. She was looking at rows of television sets with shiny knobs to the sides of the screens, switched off but promising access to worlds of entertainment and information. Above, a sign read: 'Rent a brand new black and white television with Radio Rentals.'

She thought back to two days ago. A woman in the delicatessen had overheard a conversation between Mary and Pasquale about the flood in Florence and mentioned that she had seen a film of the city under siege broadcast on the news. 'It was like the end of the world, the water was so violent, it is hard to imagine anything or anyone surviving …' the woman had said, and then checked herself as she took in Mary's horrified face.

Mary peered into the shop window. Here was exactly what was needed. Newspaper reports were all very well, but she wanted to see moving pictures, like those the woman had described. Reports with commentary would better explain the situation.

But Geoffrey was adamant. 'I have already told you,' he said that evening, as Mary sat in the tartan armchair, darning, 'we are not going to get a television set. Didn't we have this conversation in the summer when Cara wanted to watch the World Cup? You and I have no interest in football, and to be frank I was surprised that she had. Perhaps the idea had come from Tony. As for the news, we can hear that on the wireless. Or we can read the newspaper. Or see the newsreels at the cinema. We do *not* need a television.'

'But there's hardly anything in the British newspapers about Florence …'

'Look, I know you are worried about Cara,' he said, as he picked up the book he had left on a side table. 'We both are. But I am sure we'll hear something from her soon. The Italian authorities will be working hard to get the services up and running again and soon the telephone and the post will be back in order. Have you been to see Mrs Baldoni?'

'No, not yet. But I don't think she knows any more that we do.' Mary sighed. 'It was just a thought about the rental …'

'Do try not to worry …' He opened his book, indicating that he wished to end the conversation.

Everyone was always telling her not to worry. She wouldn't worry, but she needed to do something, to take action. The darned cardigan lay limply across her lap and, as she gazed at the web of grey thread she had woven together to cover the moth hole, she had an idea.

A Funny Thing Happened on the Way to the Forum had been playing for half an hour and the small audience was laughing uproariously at the broad slapstick, but Mary's expression was deadpan. She may as well have been watching a Russian tragedy for the absence of amusement in her face. All she could think about was her daughter and her lack of news. Everything came back to that.

In the flickering gloom of the shabby cinema, she indulged in dark fantasies. Italian men were pulling up a young woman coated in mud from the banks of the river. Blue lips, closed eyes, white skin. It was Cara's face, her body dressed in familiar knits bought last winter in Clerkenwell shops. But, Mary reasoned, the flood happened at night so what would Cara have been doing on the banks of the Arno at 4 o'clock in the morning? She felt momentarily reassured by her own logic. But what if she had become trapped in her apartment, or fallen, or been crushed by masonry or a tree, or stuck in someone's car, or something equally unbearable to contemplate …

A loud splutter of laughter from a young couple in the row behind brought her back to the present. She looked around. Even the usherette, standing at the end of the aisle, was finding the jokes hilarious. Was there something wrong with her? She felt the same sense of isolation she had experienced at other times in her life when everyone else seemed to know how to enjoy themselves. Why couldn't she forget about Cara for an hour or two and let herself be distracted?

Admittedly that hadn't been the point of coming. It had seemed a good idea to go to the cinema and check whether there was any coverage of the flood in the newsreels before the main picture. One of the serendipitous moments in the summer had been when she had brought Cara here to celebrate her agreeing to go to Italy. Before the picture began, they had been shown a Pathé news item about designer Emilio Pucci's Autumn–Winter Collection. Models with extraordinary hairstyles and boldly patterned outfits struck poses around the interior of a beautiful Florentine palazzo. As two of the models appeared in glamorous after-ski wear Mary had joked *sotto voce* to her daughter, 'Perhaps you'll be wearing something like that when you come back to us at Christmas?'

But no, there was no news from Florence. The newsreel this time was a grey and grainy film featuring the King of Morocco in the Soviet Union, placing a wreath at the Lenin mausoleum. And then the main picture began, with no relevance to anything. She stared vacantly ahead while around her the audience continued to laugh. She hated tawdry romantic comedies, she decided, that was all there was to it.

When she was younger, she had loved the pictures. Rita Hayworth in *Cover Girl*, Judy Garland in *Meet Me in St Louis*. The excitement of waiting for the film to begin, sitting with Elsie as the lights went down or, even better, lingering in the dark, Pippo beside her.

*

Cara was cold and hungry and upset. This time her night had been sleepless. By dawn she knew that she must find a way out of Florence as soon as possible. She was certain Nicoletta would have no difficulty in employing another English speaker to have conversations with once normal life in the city had resumed. She couldn't help feeling sad about leaving them – she'd come to enjoy the lunchtime chats over Teresa's tasty spreads – but Gianni had made it clear he didn't want her, so why torture herself with worry about the possibility of bumping into him? It was time to get back home. Perhaps Geoffrey had been right, she thought, feeling her spirits sink. A safe secretarial job might provide the security and stability she needed. She would go and speak with Nicoletta about making arrangements for her departure.

Once outside, she noted with relief that the weather was dry at last; no liquid skies. There was however still so much sludge to be swept out of buildings. Pumps had been set up to remove water from cellars and basements, but they were clearly not sufficient to deal with the scale of the problem. Everyone seemed to be obsessing either about how to rid themselves of water or how to obtain it. The irony was not lost on her. As she crossed the piazza Cara heard a woman tell another that water was being delivered in trucks and some had come from as far away as Naples. 'There is a big red truck in San Lorenzo,' the woman was saying, 'by the market. But it's *non potabile*, you can't drink the stuff, you have to boil it first. But how to boil it, with no gas or electricity?'

Cara walked along the Via dei Servi, saddened by the state of the shops belonging to those she had befriended during the last two months. Some were closed up, but she noticed Beppe's metal grille half opened, and stopped to see if he was inside.

'Beppe?' she called, and from the dark interior he emerged on to the street holding a broom. Thick mud encased the bristles and had stained his trousers, his jacket, and even his hair. Everything was caked with muck. He stood in the spot where only a few days previously he had picked out vegetables for Cara to cook for Gianni while they exchanged words about the constant rain and the approaching *festa*. It seemed so long ago.

All he said to Cara now was one word. *Fango*, Mud.

'*Fango, fango, fango*,' he repeated with desperation in his voice, lifting up the broom like a trophy.

'*Mi dispiace*, I'm sorry,' Cara said as if in some way she was culpable.

'*Aspetta*.' He ducked back into the shop and re-emerged with some bottled water and a couple of carrots. He passed her the bottle and wiped the carrots with his hand.

'Breakfast,' she said as she drank some of the water and put the carrots in her bag. *'Grazie!'*

As she got closer to the river, the stench of sewage and oil became almost unbearable. Rubbish piled high beside the road spilt across narrow pavements, as if tumbled from a landslide. And people added more and more as they continued clearing clothes, furniture and perishable goods. Cara paused to finish drinking her water and added the empty bottle to one of the piles. For a moment, the clean green glass stood out from the filthy mass beneath it and seemed to sparkle, ignited by a ray of winter sun.

She turned the corner on to the Lungarno and took in the scene. Most of the floodwall bordering the river had collapsed, reduced to a mass of crumbled stone. The trunk of a huge, uprooted tree had fallen across the bridge of Santa Trinita, and the path to Nicoletta's house appeared closer to a wetland than a road. Cara picked her way through this urban swamp as best she could, and when she reached Nicoletta's front door, she banged it with her fist in a kind of frenzy.

After a few seconds the shutters of a window on the first floor were thrown open and Teresa's head appeared.

'Ah, *signorina!* Signora Nicoletta is not at home but wait!' The shutters were pulled closed again and shortly after Teresa reappeared opening the front door. Cara felt the relief that comes of being cared for, as the housekeeper took her coat and began asking her questions: how was it in Via Laura, did she have water, gas, electricity, supplies yet, was she hungry, was she cold; they were lucky, *grazie a Dio*, as relatives had been able to bring cooked chickens and eggs as well as vegetables from the hills outside Florence.

Chicken and fresh vegetables! Just hearing these words made Cara's mouth water.

'You look hungry,' Teresa said, reading her thoughts. '*La signora* will be back soon. She will want you to stay for lunch.'

'That's kind but it isn't the right day. I just wanted to know how you all were. Where are the boys?'

As if on cue, Raffaele burst into the room. 'Cara! Mamma went to the post office to try and send some telegrams, but she will be back soon. She was planning to visit you this afternoon, it has been difficult getting about or she would have come sooner.'

The door opened again, and Sandro came towards her to kiss her on both cheeks. 'You are here! We were wondering how you were.'

Cara was taken aback by the warmth of her welcome. They seemed genuinely pleased to see her, and for her part she realised she felt the same about them. It may have been gratitude for human contact and the offer of a nourishing meal – but no, she hoped it went deeper than that.

Teresa left to prepare lunch and, as she watched her leave the room Cara realised she knew virtually nothing about her. She asked Raffaele and Sandro, what was her situation? The boys took turns in filling her in, with information spoken partly in English, when they could, and using Italian words when they were unable to find the right one in English. Teresa was unmarried. She lived with her married older sister and family in central Florence. After the flood, her sister had become very anxious about her *epilettico* brother-in-law Paolo running out of medicine (Sandro didn't know how to say epileptic so he acted out having a seizure). Teresa had been upset and so Nicoletta had agreed to accompany her across to the Oltrano ('beyond the Arno'), an area that had been less affected by the flooding, to reach a friend of Paolo's who was a pharmacist.

'Everyone seems to know everyone else in Florence,' Cara observed, unsettled by Sandro's brief seizure performance but pretending it hadn't bothered her. 'Why did Paolo's wife not go with Teresa, rather than Nicoletta?'

'Because she has little children,' answered Raffaele, as if the answer was obvious.

A door slammed. 'Mamma!' Sandro called out, 'Look who is here!' The fact that he said this in English warmed Cara's heart.

Nicoletta walked into the room, smiling. 'Cara, I am so pleased to see you. I wanted to hear your news but haven't been able to–'

Sandro cut in. 'You have been so long, Mamma.'

'I know, the queues at the post office went on forever. It is a nightmare not having the telephone working.' She said this looking at Cara. 'I am trying to reach my husband in Switzerland, but it is impossible to send telegrams out of the country. We will have to think of a way to help you contact your mother …'

'Sandro was telling me about Teresa's brother-in-law,' answered Cara, changing the subject. 'It must have been difficult to get across the river.'

'Yes, the Ponte Vecchio was guarded to prevent people stealing precious objects that had been flooded out of the jewellery shops, but I persuaded the *carabiniere* to let us pass. It was quite dangerous, holes had appeared through which we could see the river. One way or another we got across the bridge but in Borgo San Jacopo I missed seeing a manhole under all the mud and I almost broke my leg.'

'Oh no!'

'Luckily I only bruised it. Anyway, we did get to the pharmacy and thank goodness it was open, so we stocked up on medicine for Paolo. There were such long queues in front of the bakery; there are queues everywhere …'

'How do they manage to make bread if there is no electricity or gas?' The question came from her rumbling stomach.

'Wood-fired ovens, of course.' A flash of Nicoletta's chilliness had returned, and it made Cara feel stupid. Her way of suddenly sounding impatient could be disconcerting. But then Nicoletta's voice softened. 'In fact, many of the old houses still have them, and Teresa has begun using ours again. Lucky for us! This is what has saved us – that's right, isn't it?' she directed the last question to Teresa who had come in to announce lunch was ready. 'I was describing our adventure in trying to get Paolo his medicine.'

'*Ah, sì!*' Teresa beamed. 'Did you tell them about how you persuaded the policeman to let us cross the bridge on the way back?'

'Yes, that was difficult. It was dark by then, and the guard on that side wouldn't let us pass …'

'The Signora is clever! She said that we had to reach her daughter who was having a baby, and that I was the midwife. Fortunately, he did not see that the bag I was carrying only had the medicine inside it. In the end he got so tired of our pleading that he not only let us go through but accompanied us to the other side.'

'That was because you told him that the baby might die.'

'Well, I know, but in the moment I couldn't think of anything else to say that would have an impact.' A serious look crossed Teresa's face before her smile returned. 'Anyway, I have come to tell you that lunch is ready – it's pizza today.'

Only a week had passed since the flood, but something in the city had changed. The most obvious sign of recovery were the roads becoming clear of debris and some of the shops reopening, albeit with limited stock. But the most significant change was the arrival of young people hoping to help.

It began with the boys on National Service. Young men – who, as a rule, aimlessly roamed the streets looking for girls to whistle at, driving Cara mad by following her everywhere like packs of lost dogs, now had more serious things to do. They were joined by large groups of students. It may have been the coverage in the papers, or the dramatic photographs and scenes shown on television, but the city began filling up with volunteers.

Every time Cara went out, she noticed more young people splattered with dirt, handing mud-soaked objects to one another in human chains: sorting, cleaning, shovelling mounds of muddy mess, doing the jobs that in the first few days only families and shopkeepers had done. This army had an energy lacking in the defeated home and business owners Cara had seen on her way to Santa Croce. In their solidarity with each other these young people were determined to make a difference.

At first, they were mostly Tuscan, or from adjoining Emilia Romagna. Students came from the big universities of Pisa and Bologna. Very quickly, the net extended farther. The streets filled with accents from all over Italy. Then the Americans arrived, the Canadians, the northern Europeans, the Israelis. It was like a student movement or a large demonstration, as if they had all dropped what they were doing in order to rush over and make their mark, to lend a hand. How had they managed to get here in such a short time? Cara wondered. Where were they sleeping, what were they eating? Thoughts of getting back to London had receded. If help was so clearly needed here, why leave? She wanted to help too but did not quite know how. She would ask Nicoletta.

The twice-weekly lunch arrangement had loosened. Cara was going there almost every day, to eat and catch up on news. It may have been that Nicoletta was concerned about Cara being far from home, but she had become less abrasive, almost motherly towards her. And on her part Cara had grown fond of the boys and of Teresa, and less afraid of making a bad impression. The boys' spoken English had improved, as had Cara's Italian, so conversation flowed more freely. She felt confident enough to tease and be teased, and the routine of jokes and repartee they had built up had allowed them to become more natural with each other. And the family was helpful too – Nicoletta had given her an old camping stove to warm food, and Teresa produced some spare buckets to collect drinking water from the distribution points. Water had come back through the taps but it was still only fit for washing and flushing.

It was at the end of one of their lunches, when Raffaele and Sandro had been excused, that Nicoletta asked Cara about her mother. 'Have you written to her, told her what is happening here?'

'I have written,' she answered, looking down at her plate, empty but for a twirl of mandarin peel. 'But I haven't been able to send the letter. The post boxes I've seen are all taped up.'

'Oh, I hadn't thought of that. Some must be still be full of mud and water.'

'Yes, so I didn't think the post was working, or the telephone exchange.'

'I'm not sure about the telephone … but I think that letters are getting through now if you can find somewhere to post them.' Nicoletta paused. 'You mother will be wondering what is happening to you, mothers worry you know …' She said it gently, and the kindness triggered a response in Cara. She felt homesick all over again, but didn't want Nicoletta to see the tears that sprang to her eyes. 'Yes, I will try the post office,' she mumbled.

'You know, if you need to go to home to London …'

'No, I …'

That word. Home. Brown furniture and the eiderdown with rosebuds on her bed. Her mother's teas, Geoffrey coming through the door with a book wrapped in brown paper for her. And Tony. She felt a squeeze of pain. This was all going wrong. She had decided to ask Nicoletta about volunteering to help with the flood, not about leaving Florence. An unruly tear trickled from the corner of her eye.

'Mia cara.' Nicoletta reached over to squeeze her hand. 'I'll get Teresa to bring us some coffee, and then we shall talk.'

*

For two days, Mary had been trying to obtain more information about the situation in Florence but the only related item in *The Times* the day before had been a blurry photograph of abandoned cars under the headline *Florence: The Havoc of the Floods.*

She tried to distract herself with housework but couldn't help repeatedly checking with the telephone operator whether Cara's line was working yet. Every time she was told no, she felt angry, robbed of her right to communicate with her daughter. The frustration of not knowing what to do was compounded by Geoffrey's inability to discuss the situation. After his initial outburst on the day he heard the news, he had become infuriatingly detached. 'Wait and see,' he kept saying, 'we are bound to hear something soon.'

'Morning,' the postman greeted her as she opened the front door to go to the shops.

'Good morning. Is there anything for me?' she asked hopefully, knowing he would say no.

'Not today, I'm afraid, ma'am.'

She made her way towards the newsagent, remembering those years during the war when every mother dreaded the postman in case the news was bad. Or worse: the boy with a telegram coming to a stop at the door like the Angel of Death. In her mind she played back that day twenty-five years ago when, still living at home, she heard wailing next door, and recalled her mother Nora saying in her soft Irish voice, 'Poor woman. I should thank the Lord for not giving me another child.' The neighbour had opened the telegram on her doorstep and let out such a long, deep, agonising cry that Mary had never forgotten the sound of it. What would that be like, to lose your child? How would any mother manage to survive such a loss?

Newspaper in hand, Mary took her change from the newsagent. At the door of the shop, unable to wait, she opened the paper and skipped through the pages until her eye caught sight of 'Overseas News' in a top left-hand corner. The boldly typeset headline announced:

> *600 Paintings and 1,000 Rare Books Damaged in Florence Floods*
>
> *From our Correspondent in Rome*
>
> *The Government met today to study emergency measures for aid to the one-third of Italy that was stricken by what Signor Taviani, the Minister of the Interior, told Parliament were the worst floods in history. The Government is expected to announce special measures to raise funds for immediate relief. The floods that submerged Florence, Trento, Grosseto, Venice and much of the Po and Arno valleys, dealt the national economy a heavy blow. The second day of sunshine today, however, helped 120,000 soldiers, policemen, carabinieri and volunteers in their rescue operations.*

Mary scanned the newsprint, skipping the estimates of the damage to land, economy and artistic heritage, looking for the human stories. What had been the effect on the people of Florence? What of the fatalities? Why wouldn't the correspondent report on that? The article kept talking about the rescue operations relating only to masterpieces of art. Perhaps there was no other information to be had?

> *… The restorers' work suffered a setback today when a microscope used for studying canvases was stolen from the Uffizi Gallery.*

A microscope! Mary sighed impatiently. Who cares about a microscope?

> *... It was the only microscope of its kind to be salvaged from the flood, and the Uffizi's director appealed for it to be returned ... the Pitti Palace, which was relatively untouched, will be the centre for restoration of the damaged art ... more than a hundred art restorers have already arrived in Florence to start work ...*

The article went on to describe the works of art that had been saved and those that were beyond repair. A museum director was quoted as saying that the damage done to the many priceless treasures was 'a national tragedy'.

What of human loss? Mary's eye continued to scan the page until it caught a passage that chilled her.

> *The Queen has sent the following message to the President of Italy: 'I and my husband were shocked to hear of the tragic loss of life and damage caused by the floods in northern Italy. Our sympathy goes out to all who have suffered, and particularly to the inhabitants of Florence and Venice, cities of which we have such happy memories.'*

Tragic loss of life. The words shouted out at her, taunting and tormenting. She stood, reading the paragraph over and over again, until someone trying to get past her coughed, saying, 'Excuse me.' Frowning, she stepped aside before carefully closing the paper and leaving the shop, holding it rolled up in one hand. As she walked home, she wondered what Geoffrey would say. He would be no use at all. Admittedly, he had wasted two mornings trying to glean particulars from the Foreign Office and then the Italian embassy, but without success. They didn't yet have the figures of British nationals who had been affected, they said, 'We are waiting for information.' That was Geoffrey's attitude, wait and see, wait and see. Mary was good at waiting. She had spent much of her life doing just that. But she could no longer wait, not this time.

Geoffrey was normally punctual in his habits, rising at eight o'clock every morning, even on a Sunday.

'It's half past eight,' exclaimed Mary, finding him still lying in bed on her return from the bathroom. 'Has that cold got worse?' Since Cara had gone, he had suffered endless colds that went to his chest, but this one was particularly difficult to shift. A groan emanated from under the eiderdown.

'I'll bring you breakfast in bed.'

As she prepared the objects on the tray – the brown teapot, the three slices of lightly buttered toast in the rack, the freshly boiled egg under its little cosy hat – she decided that today she must achieve something. It was as if she had taken Geoffrey's share of energy for the day and felt twice as purposeful. He could stay in bed, but she had things to do.

Balancing the tray with one hand, she turned the doorknob of their bedroom, and placed it carefully on the bedside table.

'You must rest, today,' she said to the immoveable shape in the bed. 'I have to go out.'

The house in which Tony Herrin lived with his parents was nearby, but in a smarter street. The road was wider and the buildings taller, and they did not attach themselves one to the other like strings of beads. They gave each other space. These were the households that had cleaners like Nora O'Neill. Cars rather than carts were parked outside.

Cara had described the Herrin house as having a bright yellow door. Mary could spot it already. She also knew that Cara never much liked going there because Mrs Herrin was snobbish and Tony tense when his mother was around.

The doorbell rang and Mary smiled to herself. She didn't have a doorbell at home, just an old doorknocker, but hardly anyone used it, apart from the postman occasionally or the milkman wanting payment. Mrs Herrin probably had dinner parties, Mary thought, and wondered why they chose to send their boy to the Italian school rather than somewhere more aspirational. They must be Catholics.

Mary almost expected a maid to open the door, but it was Tony himself.

'Tony! I'm so pleased to see you.'

He looked wary.

'I'm sorry ... I was abrupt when we last met, wasn't I? It's just that I was upset on Cara's behalf, you know ...'

His expression relaxed slightly. 'Please, it isn't your fault, you had every reason.'

'I wanted to talk to you about Cara in fact.'

A voice shouted from inside the house. 'Who is it, Tony? For goodness' sake, close the door, you're letting in the cold.'

And then Mrs Herrin appeared, taking the door from her son. 'Oh, Mrs Williams, how nice to see you,' she said in her falsely friendly voice. 'Tony, why have you not invited Mrs Williams in?' She opened the door wide. She was wearing a green dress that to Mary looked too short. 'Do come in ... you can tell me all about Cara. I understand there has been the most ghastly flood ...'

'Yes, well, that's why ...'

'Come this way.' Mary followed her into a sitting room that was so different from her own. It was fashionably modern and spacious. The walls were painted white and all the hard-edged furniture matched.

Mrs Herrin gestured at an uncomfortable-looking sofa. 'Do sit down.'

Mary hated the way this woman always said, 'Do this … do that …' as if imparting orders, but she gingerly obeyed and levered herself down on to the edge of the sofa. She kept her arm hooked through her handbag's strap.

'I'm so sorry,' said Mrs Herrin, as Tony looked on from the doorway. 'I'm forgetting myself. May I take your coat? Tea?'

'Thank you, that is very kind, but it won't be necessary, I shan't be long.' Mary had never really liked Mrs Herrin. There was something self-regarding about her, and her friendliness was patronising. It could be switched off as quickly as on.

'Tony why don't you sit down too,' Mrs Herrin was saying. 'You can talk to Mrs Williams about your mad idea.' She smiled stiffly at Mary. 'Tony has this fantasy that he will save the entire artistic heritage of Florence.'

'Mother …' Tony glared, remaining standing. And then, addressing Mary, he said with a smile, 'I don't know about "the entire artistic heritage", but yes, Mrs Williams, I'm going to Florence.'

*

Cara gave a sigh of relief. A lamp had come on. It felt almost biblical, being delivered from the darkness to the light. It couldn't have come too soon – she had been eking out her last candle and was getting constant headaches from the squinting. And now the electric heaters would provide her with enough warmth to remove at least one of the many layers of clothing she had been living in, inside the flat and out.

Thanks to the cold weather, she had been using the stairs up to the terrace to keep her provisions cool. The steps had become shelves and were arranged as such: winter vegetables on one, butter and eggs on the next, dry foods on the one above and so on. She had grown up watching Mary tidying and organising the pantry, and here she was doing the same. There was something satisfying in leaving the kitchen to collect food from another space, but now that electricity had returned, it would go back into the refrigerator like before.

Once the food was transferred, she tested the telephone again. Still not working. She replaced the receiver with a sigh. Beside it lay the letter addressed to her mother, stamped but unsealed, that she had not been able to post. She opened it up to read what she had written ten days earlier.

Dear Ma,

You will have read about Florence and this terrible flood. I am fine.

I can't write much at the moment because it's cold and dark. There is no electricity so I'm writing by the light of a candle. It feels like I'm back in Victorian times! I just wanted to let you know I am all right. The telephone lines aren't working but when they are I shall try and call you.

The Lotti family who live downstairs have been very kind. Today I am planning to walk to Nicoletta's house. I'm sure she will be helpful too.

I shall write again as soon as I have more news.

On rereading, she worried that her tone sounded clipped, as if she were hiding information rather than giving it. This was true. What point had there been in telling her mother that the city smelt like an open sewer, that she had to hold her nose to block the stench of dead cats and rotting food and God knows what else; that (like

Nicoletta) she had almost put one foot in an open manhole on the way home that afternoon, regaining her balance just in time; and that on top of it all her Florentine boyfriend's mother had died, and that he blamed it on the night they had spent together and never wanted to see her again.

Of course, she hadn't written any of this. Ma would have worried even more.

She quickly added in the space under her signature, *I haven't been able to post this yet, but I'm hoping it will get to you soon. Please don't worry. Lots of love, Cara*

The envelope went into her bag, her feet into the rubber boots Nicoletta had found for her, and she set off to find a post box that wasn't sealed up.

The streets were still clogged with mud, and everyone seemed to be washing damaged possessions. The day before, walking home past so many housewives and shopkeepers patiently cleaning items or stock, she had been awed by the sense of stoicism present in the city. One little sign on a tobacconist's door read APERTO – SI RICOMINCIA. She needed to contribute to the general renewal, to begin again. She wanted to get her hands dirty, in order to make things clean.

But where to start? Nicoletta had suggested she might go to one of the badly hit museums or libraries. The newspapers had been full of reports about the damage to the contents of the Biblioteca Nazionale, the National Library, near Santa Croce. But she wanted to avoid anywhere near Santa Croce and Marcella's house if possible. There was a university library at the top of her street, and over the past few days she had noticed a group of young people congregating there. She would check that out.

She approached with trepidation. Would they want her? What would she be able to contribute? She had no training in restoration or paper conservation, her Italian was adequate, but she wouldn't be able to understand any technical terms. Her concern was that she would simply get in the way and be more of a hindrance than a help.

'*Cerchi qualcuno?* Looking for someone?' A young woman in her early twenties, seeing Cara hovering, called out to her in Italian.

'*Vorrei aiutare* ... I'd like to help ...'

'*Brava! Vieni,*' she beckoned with her rubber-gloved hand. '*Sono Lucia.*' She had an open, friendly face, and Cara smiled back, before following her into the building and across a lobby.

The smell of mildew got worse as they went down some stairs and into a basement where volunteers were at work. It was like an underground factory, with groups of men and women, mainly young, positioned at different points in the room, sifting through piles of books, passing them on to the next person and the next – chain-gang style – until they reached the back room and were then passed up another staircase.

'They are being taken to the courtyard. The truck is coming back soon,' Lucia said.

'Truck?'

'To take the books to the Forte del Belvedere, where they will be assessed.'

'And then?'

'They will work out which ones need the most urgent attention and they will be processed accordingly. And then they will be restored, as much as is possible. So, you said you wanted to help? Let's get going.'

Cara nodded, bewildered, not fully aware of how her contribution would make inroads into such a mountain of damaged books. And she knew that what was in front of her was only a fraction of all the ruined volumes held in the National Library.

'Hey, you won't help by just standing there!' Lucia laughed, and handed her a small pile of heavy, mud-filled publications. 'Could you put these over on the table, then we'll join in the chain by the stairs.'

When Cara came up for air, she leant against the wall and drank the water Lucia handed to her. 'Have you been doing this for a while?' she asked her.

'Well, I spent a few days sweeping mud out of the church near Via Maggio, cleaning the pews. But I wanted to do more. I came to see what had happened here, because this is where I study.'

'Architecture?' Gianni came back in mind.

'No. Law. Those are all boring law books, but we've still got to save them! I'm going to see if I can try and get placed in the restoration laboratory next. My friend is there, and she told me they all work in a room where the books are put to dry. They have electric heaters going and you sit there separating every page, putting blotting paper between the sheets, and then replacing it when the moisture had been drawn out ...'

'That must take forever! How are they going to get through all those volumes?'

'They mean to but they'll probably still be there in fifty years' time. Once everything is washed and disinfected and dried, the restoration will begin. Some books have been taken to places outside Florence because there aren't enough clean spaces in the city.'

'But how do they keep track of everything?'

'At the moment they have a system of symbols that they attach to each book. It gets over the language problem because everyone can understand. Then they'll have to catalogue them again to see what's missing or un-restorable, because so much has been lost or ruined. And then think of all the bookbinding that will have to be done after that! Some time we should go and see the work they are doing.' Lucia paused. '*Sei inglese, vero*? You're English, aren't you?

You might like it, apparently everyone sits in concentrated silence and someone distributes warm tea …'

Tea sounded good.

'Come on, *inglesina*, back to work. What is your name, by the way?'

By the end of the day Cara was shattered, but happier than she had been for a while. This was what she had been missing: a sense of camaraderie, of working with others towards a common goal. The atmosphere in the basement was fetid and cold, and the dampness was seeping into her bones. But she had made a connection with other young people, and that filled her with renewed energy. Now she could direct her attention away from Gianni and his rejection; she could forget Stefano shouting; she could distract herself from missing her mother. And most of all, she could bury memories of Tony, and obliterate the imagined girlfriend he loved instead of her.

For the rest of the week and into the next she met Lucia in the morning at the entrance to the university library. They worked in two four-hour shifts with a break for lunch, taken in a refectory nearby which was owned by the university. Pasta mainly, washed down with red wine, and it all tasted delicious because the combination of dampness and cold in the storeroom made her hungry.

Lucia introduced her to some of her student friends – il Filosofo, the 'Philosopher' as he was known, who looked like a melancholy nineteenth-century poet and quoted lines from Dostoevsky; her girl-friends, Francesca, Marina, Daniela; a fellow law student whose name she didn't catch. In just a few days she felt she'd become part of something, and all the sadness about Gianni and Tony, might finally be consigned to the past.

Of course, it wasn't going to be that easy. After her new group of friends had finished for the day and knowing they had Sunday off, Lucia made a suggestion: '*Un aperitivo!*' She pointed at the bar on the corner of the street where Stefano worked.

'I'm not sure, I think I had better go home first. I'm cold and dirty.'

'We are all cold and dirty,' the others said. 'Come on, you can change after the drink …'

They had almost reached the bar when Cara stopped, unable to face the risk of being pierced by Stefano's reproachful stare.

'I think I'll say goodbye here,' she said.

Undeterred, Lucia and one of the other girls took her by the arms and marched her forward. 'You're coming with us. You've earned a glass of wine!'

Oh, why not, Cara told herself. He would have gone home by now. Anyway, he was probably not working as his aunt had so recently died …

But Stefano had not gone home. As the group came into the bar, he was there, and he fixed her with those cold accusatory eyes.

'*Ciao, Stefano, come va?*' Lucia asked cheerfully.

Stefano said nothing but continued glaring at Cara.

'Oh, you know each other?' Lucia looked from one to the other.

'I shall see you on Monday. I'm sorry, I have to go …' Cara muttered, pushing herself free of her friends and leaving the bar.

'*Ma, dove vai?*' Lucia called after her, but the back of Cara's stooped neck made it clear. She needed to get home.

The front door of Via Laura seemed particularly heavy this time as she pushed it open. What was the point, remaining here, when there was the risk of coming face to face with such hostility at every turn? Why bother to help? It was not her city … why should she care?

She trudged up the stairs, the rubber boots leaving their mark on every step. Circling one of the landings, she heard a voice.

'*Come stai*? Look at you, all covered in dirt.'

'Ah, Fernando.' She stared down at her splattered trousers and muddy boots. '*Sono stanca*. I'm tired.'

'It looks like you've been working hard. But it is good of you to help. We need young people like you in this poor place. Thank you.'

'But no, I have done nothing ...'

'You must have been doing something, to get so dirty.'

She began trying to explain, and when her Italian stumbled over words 'basement', 'chain of people', 'restoration', she used gestures to replace the words: pointing at the ground, opening and closing her hands, making fists, sweeping, scrubbing imaginary objects.

'*Ma allora sei un Angelo del Fango!*'

'*Un Angelo del Fango?*'

'That's what we are calling the volunteers now. I shall show you something ...'

'Oh ... But aren't you going out?'

'If I were, I would have my coat on, wouldn't I?' He smiled. 'No, I was only going down to the cellar to get more bottled water. I'll bring some up for you in a minute. I wouldn't trust the stuff coming out of the taps. And then I'll show you something else.'

Ten minutes later he was ringing her bell, a bottle of water in each hand. 'I won't stay, I only want to give you these.'

'Oh, thank you, that's very kind,' she said, taking them from him. 'Well, if you're sure you won't come in, I was going to run a bath.'

'*Certo*. Although the water is probably as brown as you are. Wait, I want to give you this too. It was in the *Corriere della Sera* a few days ago. I hadn't got around to throwing it away.' He reached into his back pocket and handed her an envelope on which he had written: *Al nostro Angelo del Fango*. To our own Angel of Mud.

A few hours later, after she had bathed in brown water, she opened the envelope and translated the headline as she read.

THEY SINK INTO THE DARKNESS OF THE MUD
FOR THE LOVE OF BOOKS AND OF FLORENCE.

Whoever comes, even the most cynical, even the most apathetic, will understand immediately ... that from now on no one will be allowed to be disparaging about the Beat Generation.

Cara made a face. The Beat Generation! Was she part of that? For some reason it made her think of Tony, but not of herself. She continued translating, stumbling over a few phrases but understanding the general meaning.

Because this same youth ... today has given us a wonderful example, driven by the joy of being useful, of lending one's strength and enthusiasm for the salvation of a common good.

Honour the Beats, honour the Angels of Mud.

She liked the phrase 'Angels of Mud', repeating it to herself out loud, first in Italian – *Angeli del Fango* – then in English. She knew she was not a celestial being – more of a fallen, flawed one – but she had good intentions, and could identify with the phrase. She had dived into the earth, into something wet and clammy like clay, something messy, something difficult to pull out of, and had emerged cleansed. Whatever Stefano or Gianni might imply about her personally, 'the whore', 'the temptress', 'the outsider', these were archetypes familiar to Italians and she would not let their prejudices drive her away. For now, she belonged; she had not finished her work here.

Despite this return of confidence, her resolutions had an edge of resentment. She was like her mother in this way, she easily felt wronged, and railed at the injustice of it all. A 'whore' for goodness sake! Less than three weeks ago she had still been a virgin. How dare Stefano accuse her of leading his cousin astray. How dare Gianni make her feel guilty and responsible in any way for Marcella's death. Let *them* feel guilty and responsible, let *them* punish themselves with the shame. She would not be accused of wrongdoing.

Two days later she heard ringing and realised it was the doorbell – not the church bell – that was waking her. Had she got so used to that peeling sound that it no longer bothered her? Her watch announced it to be almost ten o'clock. How could she have slept so long? And who was ringing the doorbell so insistently?

She staggered up and crossed the corridor to the bedroom that overlooked the street. When she put head out of the window, she saw Lucia with her friends on the pavement calling up. '*Vieni, andiamo alla Biblioteca!*'

The National Library? Why there? She wasn't keen on going to that area, but shouted back, '*Un momento!*' She banged the window shut, threw on more clothes, pulled up the rubber boots and ran down the stairs without bothering to brush teeth or hair.

'Come on, we'll be late,' said Lucia, and they began walking quickly through streets still slimy with muddy sludge.

'Why are we rushing?' asked Cara, noticing a sign in a bar window offering 'Free coffee to Angels of Mud' and regretting the absence of breakfast.

'There is a meeting for volunteers. I think Mayor Bargellini is going to speak.'

It was chaotic when they arrived. Young people dressed in their uniform of mud-splattered trousers and rubber boots were everywhere, milling around trying to make themselves useful, or – Cara thought – actually looking a bit lost. No one seemed to know anything about the mayor or anyone else giving a talk.

'Typical. These rumours start and they mean nothing,' grumbled Lucia's friend, the one who liked Dostoevsky. 'It's always the same ...'

'I'm going to ask them over there,' Lucia said, pointing at a group standing by the entrance of the Library, and strode towards them. '*Scusi*,' she said to the back of a young man's head, 'do you know what is going on?'

He turned around. '*Non lo so, mio amico inglese é andato a chiedere*.'

'I asked that guy, his friend has gone to find out,' Lucia explained, rejoining her friends. 'Oh, and the friend is English,' she added, looking at Cara. 'Perhaps you can ask him more?'

'Of course.'

Cara walked the few yards towards where the young man stood.

'*Ciao*,' she said, and asked him what was happening.

'My friend heard some Americans talking inside ... he has gone to ask.' He smiled. '*E tu? Inglese*?'

'*Si, di Londra*.'

'Ah, my friend is from London too. I have come from the North.' He pointed upwards, as if he had come from the sky.

They were speaking both English and Italian. 'It is flooded there too, yes?' Cara answered, in the way an Italian would, speaking faltering English. It was catching.

'Yes, but not so bad as here. This is terrible. Terrible.'

Soon they were chatting easily in a mix of the two languages. He was telling her how he had only arrived the day before. He had picked up the English boy who was hitch-hiking and they had slept in the car. But they needed to find a hostel or somewhere else later.

'I hear that volunteers are being allowed to sleep in disused carriages at the railway station,' Cara said, relaying what Lucia had told her.

'Yes, thank you. We could try that. I have sleeping bag in the car.'

She liked his soft Venetian accent. He was taller than the average Italian man, with longer hair, and an attentive expression that was very attractive. In fact, it occurred to her that he looked rather like Gianni. There was something passionate, fiery almost, in his eyes, an invitation to engage.

A voice interrupted her reverie. 'What is happening?' Behind her, Lucia was pushing in.

'I shall go and find my new friend,' said the young man, and turning to face Cara directly, he introduced himself. 'But before I go inside, I tell you – my name is Angelo.'

'Angelo? How perfect!' She smiled. 'And I am Cara.'

'That is perfect too.' He made a theatrical bow. 'Don't go away Cara, I shall be back in a minute.'

She was feeling the cold. In her rush to get dressed she hadn't put enough layers on, and the chill was exacerbated by the fact that she was hungry.

'I have to find something to eat,' she said to Lucia. 'I'm starving.'

'You can't wait until lunchtime? We can get a *panino* later.'

'Look, I've had no breakfast. I'll be very quick and rush right back.'

She walked purposefully, pulling her coat around her for warmth. A side street off Piazza Croce would have a bar where she could grab a *cappuccino* with a *cornetto* and consume them quickly at the counter. She would be less than five minutes, by then Angelo and Lucia should have worked out where the meeting was taking place, or whether, like some had guessed, it was just one of those rumours that circulated without foundation.

Warmed by the coffee and croissant, she turned the corner back towards the National Library. There was Lucia and her Dostoevsky-loving friend talking with Angelo. They were circled around someone else, a tall young man wearing a buff-coloured duffle coat.

His fair hair stood out against all those dark heads. They listened attentively as he held forth …

Cara stood, immobile, as the blood drained from her face. All the energy she had recovered from the caffeine and sugar were gone in an instant. She stared at the gesturing, duffle-coated figure. She felt both shocked and broken. It couldn't be. It was. He'd come.

*

Mary lay on her daughter's bed, thinking. She wondered whether Cara had forgiven Tony. How would she take his arrival? She might be upset, angry. Or perhaps he had not been to see her yet. He had promised to send a telegram as soon as they met up, but so far nothing had arrived, and it had been days and days since he left. Perhaps she might telephone his mother to find out if she had heard anything? Mother to mother – although she had always felt that Mrs Herrin slightly looked down on her.

She had taken to spending more time in Cara's bedroom. It made her feel connected: her daughter's absence less stark. One night after Cara left for Italy, she had crept out of the marital bed to sleep there, waking early to climb back into bed with Geoffrey, hoping he wouldn't notice. This went on for a while until he *did* notice, having woken earlier than usual to find himself alone.

She made excuses. 'I was restless. I didn't want to wake you.'

'You mustn't worry,' he answered, his usual phrase. 'We don't need to share a bed every night. In fact, you talk in your sleep, and that sometimes disturbs me, so it's probably for the best.'

'What?' She felt sick to her stomach at the thought of having no control over her unconscious thoughts. 'What have I been saying? Why have you never mentioned it?'

'It seemed unnecessary. Mostly you mumble, a bit of groaning and moaning.'

'How long have I been doing this?'

'For some time.'

'And you never thought to tell me?' She was mortified. What might she have revealed?

'It's quite normal to sleep badly or make noises as one gets older,' said Geoffrey in his matter-of-fact way, rubbing the bridge of his nose. 'Mother used to complain about Father's snoring ...'

This was her chance to grab the moment. 'Would you mind if I moved into Cara's room, then? You know, so that you can sleep better?'

He looked at her sadly, and she wondered whether he was regretting the lack of intimacy between them over the last few years.

'No of course,' he said rather too quickly for her liking, as if it was a relief. 'And then you can return to our bed when Cara comes home at Christmas.'

'Of course,' she echoed, thinking how the word 'return' sounded as if he were referring to a long journey.

She loved the sanctuary the room offered, and looked forward to the nights ahead, when she would be able to stretch out, to feel both corners of the single bed with her feet, and turn the light on whenever she liked to read. If she wanted to she could sigh or cry or reveal secrets without anyone to hear or see.

The first night she spent there with Geoffrey's consent was liberating, as if she had been freed of the need to censor her thoughts. She always felt guilty and tense when indulging her memories of Pippo while sleeping next to her husband, as if Geoffrey might suddenly be able to mind-read and find her out. There was guilt and shame but, if she was honest, she regretted none of that affair. It had even made her feel closer to Geoffrey for a time.

And now, lying on the single bed, Cara's absence seemed less hard to bear. But it still felt like a gaping hole in her life. The worst thing was not knowing what was going on, how her daughter was coping. Mary thought hard and decided to try one more time to put in a call to Florence. She went downstairs and picked up the receiver. But after a few minutes the operator was saying, 'I am sorry, the number is unobtainable.'

9

Florence

NOVEMBER 1966

'Hey, Cara, I like you even though I don't know you very well, but I have to ask you something. What is all this running off the whole time?' Lucia had caught up with Cara who was striding away as quickly as she could. 'I saw you standing there, and then you turn around and start walking off, just as we are all going to the meeting …' She gulped in some air to catch her breath.

Cara didn't lessen her pace. 'It was someone I knew … someone I knew well …'

'Who? The blond English boy? The friend of Angelo?'

'Yes.' She walked faster, looking straight ahead.

'So why did you not come back and say hello to him? He seemed nice. And what about Stefano? You run from him too?' Lucia was finding it hard to keep up.

Cara stopped suddenly and swung round to face her new friend. 'I can't tell you now. Perhaps I shall be able to, sometime. Now I need to go back to Via Laura. I am sorry. Please … let me …'

'I can see you are upset,' Lucia was saying. 'Maybe I can help?' But Cara turned her head to face the wide street in front of her and continued walking away as quickly as possible. She was both relieved and disappointed when she realised Lucia was no longer following her.

The churning questions began. How long had Tony been here? She remembered Angelo saying he had picked him up hitch-hiking and that they had arrived in Florence the day before. How could he think of turning up in Florence like that? She was the one who lived here, who had more right to be a volunteer. Who did he think he was, butting in, going off into the National Library as if he knew it all? She felt hurt, invaded, humiliated all over again.

When she got back to the apartment, she was unable to settle. The inventory was virtually finished so there was little work to do, and in any case, Nicoletta had supported her decision to volunteer as an Angel of Mud. It was important, a priority, she had said. Cara was due to go to lunch there in a couple of days, but the English conversation arrangement had become looser. Nicoletta, the boys, Teresa, were more like family now. 'Just turn up again when you wish,' Nicoletta had said. 'I am so proud of your decision to help clean up this poor city. We need you all here.'

Cara sat down heavily in one of the armchairs. How strange it was to be eighteen, living on her own in a dead woman's apartment. It hadn't been the first time this had struck her. Both Nicoletta and her mother were so trusting. Wouldn't it have been more natural for her to stay as a guest of Nicoletta and come to the apartment on certain days to work on the inventory, rather than the other way round? For all anyone knew, she might be bringing a different man home every night.

As an only child, Cara was used to being in her own company. Silence did not bother her. In fact, she preferred it to the distraction of noise. She also liked knowing that she could eat, sleep, bathe and go out when she chose to; that she wasn't answerable to anyone. Mary had encouraged this self-sufficiency, and Cara had recognised it in Tony. Part of her admired the fact that he had been picked up hitch-hiking by Angelo. It showed his independence of spirit. She supposed he had hitch-hiked all the way from London. Secretly she longed to hear about his adventures. But spotting him at the National Library had been – as Tony himself would say –'discombobulating'.

He showed up later, as Cara was opening the front door on to the street, about to go out to buy provisions. She heard voices and came face to face with the boys looking at the brass plaque with all the names and doorbells.

'Car!' Tony leapt forward and embraced her. He wouldn't let go, and she, torn between the excitement of being in his arms, and the wish to punish him, stood motionless, accepting the hug but not quite knowing how to respond.

'Let me look at you.' He released her, studying her at arms' length. 'There's something different about you. You look more Italian. Do you *feel* more Italian?'

What was he doing, acting as if everything was normal? She wanted to shout her question at him. But she was checking him out too, noticing how his hair had grown, how he looked leaner, older, scruffier. At least he didn't look ill. She wanted to speak but had become mute.

Tony turned to Angelo who was standing, hands in pockets, to one side. 'Cara and I were very good friends.' He looked back at her. 'I hope we can still be?'

This was too hard. She must not show how upset she was. She would not humiliate herself. She must answer calmly, say anything, however banal.

'Your hair has grown.'

'I know.' He grinned, glancing at Angelo. 'In London I've heard girls shout, "Look, a blond Beatle!"'

'It suits you,' she said wistfully, longing to feel the gold strands between her hands.

They stood on the doorstep in the damp cold, until Tony mumbled, 'Um, any chance we might come in?'

'Oh, yes, sorry ... come ...' She led the way in and up the stairs, with the two boys' steps echoing behind her. 'I'm right at the top, you get used to it after a while.'

The boys followed her up past the three landings until they reached the door of the apartment and entered the tiny hall, looking curious but indecisive, as if they didn't quite know how to behave. It felt strange to Cara too, as if she was doing something wrong, letting them trespass in the dead woman's house. There had been similar moments with Gianni, when she had sensed Signora Nomellini's ghostly presence watching them with disapproval. But perhaps because Gianni was Florentine, his difference, his 'otherness,' had not felt quite so pronounced. Tony, on the other hand, didn't fit here at all. He belonged in London. The hall was too small to contain him, too fussy and old fashioned. But then he spotted the wallpaper through the open cloakroom door and exclaimed, 'That's the same as my parents used to have in their lavatory! Mother has changed it, it's a bright swirly pattern now.'

'Sounds groovy. How is she by the way? And your father?' What was she doing, enquiring politely after his parents? This was Tony, for goodness' sake. She was acting as if he were a stranger.

He made a face and Angelo, who had squeezed into the hall behind them, changed the subject. *'Potremmo avere un caffè?'*

Cara was pleased he had asked her in Italian. 'Si, *certo*.' She pointed at the sitting-room door. 'Go in there, I'll bring it in.'

The smell of coffee filled the kitchen. Three espresso cups and a bowl of sugar were on the tray. She felt so sad, torn between relief at seeing Tony again and a mix of anger and pique. Why had he not come to her straight away? They had exchanged friendly letters having broken the non-communication of the summer. She felt a surge of envy for Angelo, who had known Tony less than a week, whereas she …

'You should know by now that I don't even like coffee. Don't suppose you've got any good ol' tea, have you?' Tony was saying. He had come in so quietly that she jerked back in surprise and wasn't quick enough to prevent her watery eyes from expelling two swollen tears.

'Come here, you,' he said and embraced her again.

He had removed his duffle coat and his jumper smelt of the damp and mud of the streets. She wanted to sob into the musty wool, to wash it clean with all the tears she had cried over him. But she knew that if she gave in, she would never stop. So, she pulled away and said curtly, 'I don't have much tea left, it's expensive here.'

'Don't be cold, Car. Look, Angelo has been so kind. I couldn't come to see you immediately, much as I wanted to. We only arrived yesterday. He's nice, isn't he,' he added as an afterthought.

What do you mean 'he's nice', I don't care if he's nice, I haven't seen you for over four months, when we used to see each other virtually every day.

'*Tutto bene?*' Now Angelo had come in to check that everything was all right.

She sniffed. '*Scusami, é emozionante vedere il mio amico …*' She knew that, by voicing the hierarchical claim on friendship, she was warning Angelo not to intrude. 'It makes me emotional to see my old friend.'

'*Ma certo*. Of course,' acknowledged Angelo.

'Come,' said Cara, forgiving them both. 'Let's sit here. And I'll make Tony some of my precious tea.'

They sat around the kitchen table and Tony described his travels, the early train from London to Folkestone, the ferry to Ostend, hitch-hiking to Bruges, then Brussels, the night in a hostel in Nancy. He had been lucky with his lifts that day. 'Perhaps because you are so good-looking,' Cara was thinking. A businessman had gone out of his way to take him to Nancy and bought him dinner, telling Tony he had a son the same age from whom he was estranged. But the next day had been harder. Bad weather had made 'the drivers less willing to have a bedraggled rat in the car'. By the time he'd found a *locanda* in Como he was exhausted, but the following morning was sunny, and he managed to see the lake, 'so beautiful against the Alps', before setting off again.

'And then, just outside Milan, an Angel stopped to pick me up.' He grinned at Angelo and Cara felt herself tensing up.

'Yes,' continued Angelo in faltering English. 'I had been in Milan and was on my way to stay with my sister in Bologna. She invited Tony in ...'

'I think she could see that I needed a bath!'

'... and we persuaded him to stay overnight.'

'Why are you in Florence?' Cara asked Angelo, with an edge to her voice. Tony was staring at him with adoration, like one of the Magi worshipping the Christ Child. It was annoying.

'I finished my medical studies, and in a few weeks I have to do my – how you say – military ...?'

'National Service,' said Tony. 'In Italy you can put it off if you are a medical student, but then you have to do it when you have got your degree.'

'Since when have you become such an expert?'

'Yes,' continued Angelo, ignoring her sarcasm. 'And when Tony said he was coming to Florence, I tell him, "I come too!"' He grinned.

'Yes, so Angelo drove me here ...'

'Oh, you can drive in?' Cara said, interested now. 'I thought we were cordoned off. I heard that the police had been stopping people entering the city because of the looting.'

'No, we come in. And we stop the car ...'

'Parked,' interrupted Tony.

'Ha! He is always correcting me! We spent the night in the car, he in the back,' Angelo gestured at Tony, 'and me in front.'

'It was bloody uncomfortable I can tell you. Freezing.' Tony shivered at the memory.

'And then in the morning, a *soldato* ...'

'Oh yes! The soldier!' Tony grinned, and Cara bristled again. They were telling this anecdote like a couple would, interrupting and finishing each other's sentences.

'We think it was police knocking on the window, telling us we could not stop the car ...'

'Park,' corrected Tony again.

'We think they come to tell us we could not be there, but no, it was soldier knocking on the window to give us a *panino*.'

'That was nice of him.' Cara responded with a sniff.

'Yes, and then this morning we decide to go to the Biblioteca to see what is happening.' Angelo grinned. 'And we met you. But you not stay.'

'No, I couldn't stay. There was supposed to be a meeting for volunteers, wasn't there?'

'It was a bit chaotic, no one really seemed to know what was going on,' Tony said.

'That's Italy for you,' observed Cara.

'Well, they have to manage all these volunteers, it cannot be easy,' Angelo put in defensively.

'Anyway, they want more help in carrying transportable works of art to this place in the Pitti Palace ...'

'The Limonaia ...'

Cara turned to Angelo. 'Do you know Florence well?' She asked this coldly, annoyed by all these interruptions.

She caught a look between the boys. Perhaps her tone was too frosty, she was beginning to sound like Tony's mother. She changed tack.

'Where are you intending to stay tonight?'

Another glance passed between the young men and it suddenly dawned on her. 'No, I'm sorry ... Look I can't let you stay here. I'm working for Nicoletta and this is her dead aunt's flat, she wouldn't like it ... I'd have to ask.'

Angelo seemed embarrassed. 'No, it no matter, we are going to the station.'

'Yes, one of the volunteers told me there are some disused carriages we can sleep in,' Tony said.

Angelo looked pleased with himself. 'And I bring sleeping bag in car.'

'Just one?' Cara looked confused.

'No! It is my bad English. Two sleeping bags! My sister give another one for Tony.'

Cara was about to say, 'No, your English is good,' but stopped herself. Why did she always use that phrase? She didn't feel like complimenting him.

'Angelo, I think we should go and check it out. We shouldn't leave it too late,' Tony said, in the awkward silence that followed.

Go – don't go – Cara was full of confusion, wanting them to stay, wanting them to leave.

'Car, we need to send a telegram to your mother first. I promised. She's worried about you.'

'Yes, we shall do that. And you must tell me how things are in London. But aren't you hungry?'

'We've eaten. Angelo made me try the tripe from a truck ...'

'*Trippa alla Fiorentina*,' laughed Angelo.

'Oh, that's disgusting!' Cara made a face.

'Yes, as my mother would say, "It's an acquired taste." That's what she said about olives too, but the tripe was ...' Tony cringed.

'I know what you mean.' She felt herself again.

It had been a long day. There had been the excitement of seeing Tony, the fluctuating emotions. She had found Angelo attractive but perhaps only because of his resemblance to Gianni. And she had been thrown by seeing him with Tony. She indulged in a fantasy of the three of them working together as volunteers and becoming friends, going to bars, discovering more of Florence. There was so much she wanted to show Tony, despite the flood damage. The galleries and museums would reopen eventually. And then there were the walks on the edges of the city: San Miniato, Bellosguardo. Now that the buses and trains were working again, they could venture farther afield: Lucca, Siena, San Gimigniano. Then she remembered – Angelo had a car, even better, he could drive them around. She had forgotten to ask him when he had to begin his military service, or how long he intended to stay. She couldn't wait to tell Nicoletta that her friend from London had arrived.

Occasionally thoughts of Gianni interrupted the fantasies she was inventing. She tried to edit him out, but he kept coming back: images of him in hospital, his expression dismissive and cruel. She presumed he had been discharged by now, and was getting on with his life, planning his wedding to Ilaria. What was the point in doing that? He was punishing Ilaria as well as himself. Cara knew he didn't love his wife-to-be. Or maybe he did, and everyone was lying to everybody else. What a mess. Her thoughts were agitating: hope followed by regret, anticipation followed by anxiety, and so it went on until she fell into a restless sleep.

The doorbell was ringing again. She woke confused. Was she imagining it? Was she still dreaming? It was so dark and still. Reaching for the light switch and her watch, she saw it was just past two in the morning. She sat up in bed, her arms feeling cold out from under the blankets. And still that insistent ringing noise. It was probably a prankster walking by, but she had better check.

She shuffled to the kitchen window and opened it, swung the shutter wide then leant out to look down. Far below a figure stepped back from the front door and she immediately recognised it, wrapped in the familiar duffle coat. She ran to the intercom and pressed it to let him in, keeping her finger on the buzzer well after he had pushed the front door open and was coming up the stairs.

'What on earth is the matter?' She was shivering on the threshold when he appeared on the landing and stumbled towards her, shoulders slumped, breathing heavily. As he got closer, she saw.

'My God, Tony! What's happened to you?'

His hair was matted with blood and his face was bruised. Cara pulled him into the flat and to the kitchen where she sat him down at the table. 'I'll get some cotton wool,' she said, not waiting for an explanation. She needed to clean him up first.

She gently swabbed the dried blood with concentration. They were both silent until she had finished and then she said, like a nurse, 'You're lucky, it's nothing serious. You must have had a bad nosebleed and wiped your hand from your nose into your hair. It doesn't seem to be coming from a cut on your head. But your cheek looks bruised. Did you walk into something? Somebody hit you? At the station?'

Tony nodded but couldn't speak.

'All right, you can tell me later.' She sighed. 'If we were in England,

I'd suggest a cup of tea. But we're in Italy and you've already had some of my precious tea, so let's finish the wine instead. I think you need a drink. I do, at any rate.'

She picked up a half-consumed bottle and filled two glasses, pushing one in front of him. 'Come on, drink.'

He sat, staring at the table, not touching the wine.

'Can't you tell me what happened?' She felt maternal for the second time that day. She wanted to envelop him with love, to make him safe. 'Who could have done this to you?'

He still didn't speak.

She tried a different tack. 'Where is Angelo? Did he help you?'

He looked up at her and shook his head. His eyes were watery.

'Your hands are shaking.' She stood up and came round to his side. Kneeling down she tried to embrace him, but he pushed her away.

'I can't tell you. I can't tell anyone ...' He put his face – his poor bruised face – into his hands. 'You'll hate me ...'

She remained kneeling next to him. What could be worse than what had been done to him?

'You can tell me anything, Tony. I won't hate you. You know I couldn't ever hate you.' She wanted to tell him she had always loved him and always would, but restrained the impulse. She had to protect her heart from being trampled on again.

He looked at her like a lost child. 'Are you sure?'

'I truly am.'

'Promise that whatever I tell you now, you won't hate me?'

'I promise.'

His cracked lips moved into the semblance of a smile. 'Well, you've been warned!'

Cara got up from her knees and sat down opposite him. 'All right, I've been warned. I want to hear what you have to say.'

Silence.

'Come on, I'm listening.'

Tony began speaking into his hands, looking up periodically to see how she was reacting. 'You remember London, that last time,' he began, in a quiet sort of voice. 'When I got home that night after we had been to the cinema? When I got home, I wrote to you, explaining everything.'

It was the first time either of them had mentioned that evening and it made her feel cold.

'So, the first letter you wrote wasn't the one you sent to Florence?'

'No. I never sent my first letter. I couldn't. The thing is, that night in the summer, you know, when you seemed to expect …' He hesitated and she sensed the beginning of a blush. 'I … I realised you wanted something I could never give you.'

A strange misgiving came into her mind. Perhaps she didn't want to have this conversation after all. It was her turn to look down at her hands.

'There you were, the beautiful girl whom I love, offering yourself. And all I knew …' He hesitated again. 'All I knew … was that I didn't feel what a normal boy should feel. That I never have done. And then when I realised what I *did* feel, I thought that if being honest would mean shocking you and making you not want to see me, that would be unbearable. Or perhaps you would want to see me again, but you might confide in someone else. So, I definitely couldn't tell you what I needed to tell you.'

She was wounded by his words. He didn't want her, not like that. He never would. She must be brave. She had to confront this.

'Tony, it's not your fault. If friends are all we can be, then let's be friends. There's no point in either of us getting so upset. It's just one of those things.' She laughed nervously, even though the last thing she felt like doing was laugh. 'I'll try not to be jealous of the girls you will fall in love with, you know, in that way …'

'No, silly, you don't understand. The thing is, I *am* in love with someone already.' He paused.

'Oh.' She felt assailed by a stabbing pain in her chest. He does love someone else. *I can't bear it*.

His words came tumbling out. 'He's called Robin. I fell in love with him instantly. There, I have said it. Are you shocked?' He looked up, defiantly.

She met his eye, absorbing his words.

He continued. 'My dream is to move out of my parents' house and share digs with him. I think he feels the same, but I haven't summoned the courage to find out. I didn't even dare ask if he'd come to Florence with me.'

'You mean ...?'

'What upsets me is why this precious, pure – well, not completely pure ...' He grinned lopsidedly. '... Why this genuine feeling should be considered at best shameful, at worst criminal. I feel so strongly about him that I would happily risk going to prison if he returned my love. It's not some fleeting attraction and, believe me, I've had some of those. Can you understand that? I love him, Car. I'm bursting with love. Bursting! There, I've said it.' He shrugged, suddenly looking defeated. 'Take it as you will.'

What a mix of feelings. Partly envious and upset at being excluded from the intensity of that love, and from something so central to his make-up, his sexuality. Partly she was curious. She had never considered that Tony might be homosexual. In her experience homosexuals were unfortunate, unhappy men, the subject of people's whispers, of scandals. Yes, she was shocked. And if she was honest there was an element of disgust too.

'Please say something?' he begged. 'I don't like the look on your face. I won't bear it if you're ashamed of me ...'

'Of course I'm not ashamed of you, I'm just taking it in.' She sounded colder than she had intended. 'Do your parents know?'

'No, they don't.' He looked panic stricken. 'You won't say anything, will you? Promise me! If they found out … it doesn't bear thinking about. Before I know it, my mother will have me locked up in hospital being forced into some horrible treatment, or I'll be relegated to terminal hellfire, which would probably come to the same thing.'

'I would never say anything. You must realise that. But, Tony, you must be careful, you really could be sent to prison.'

'Yes, I know I could. It's crazy … But sometimes it feels like I'm already in a kind of prison. Constantly having to look over my shoulder, treated like a bloody criminal …'

'But have you …? Have you ever been with … have you been caught, you know?'

He looked at her and snorted. 'You're such an innocent!'

'No, I'm not an innocent, if you must know.' She felt her anger rising. 'You know nothing about my life …'

'All right, your turn then. Tell me about your life.'

And so she did. She recounted the affair with Gianni, and sleeping with him on the night of the flood …

'Oh, Car,' he interrupted, 'I can see my innocent friend hasn't been quite so innocent!' They both laughed, and there was relief in that. She would save the drama of Marcella's drowning and the news of Gianni's going back to his childhood sweetheart Ilaria for another time.

'But I haven't finished with you yet,' she said, back to her nurse-like voice. 'You still haven't told me what happened to your …' She pointed at his battered face. 'And why didn't Angelo help you? He seemed so nice.'

'I thought he was nice too.' Tony hung his head. 'We got along well. I misunderstood, that's all.'

'Will you just tell me what happened?'

'Well … after we sent your ma the telegram and you went home, we got back to the car and parked near the station. And there we met up with other volunteers who were looking for places for the night. We were given a train carriage that we could sleep in. There are lots of young people doing this, coming and going, it's quite busy …'

'Keep to the point!'

'We were talking with the Americans we'd met in the afternoon at the Library, and we stayed up late drinking their beer. They were telling us that Ted Kennedy was here last week, did you know that?'

Cara nodded, yes, she had heard, but she didn't want to talk about Ted Kennedy right now …

'And then Angelo and I settled down in our carriage, and we carried on chatting. Angelo was on one side of the compartment, me on the other, each in a sleeping bag. But I couldn't get to sleep, it was so cold, and I realised he was awake too, and I made this suggestion that if we both lay under two sleeping bags instead of having one each, we would be warmer.'

'I see.'

'He thought it was a good idea, but of course the seats on each side were quite narrow.'

'So how would you both fit on the same side?'

'That's the point. I was on the edge and he turned to face away from me, but I was almost falling off, so I put my arms around his waist so that I wouldn't fall, and he didn't seem to mind that. But then …'

'Oh …' She could tell where this was going.

'Well, don't you agree he's handsome?'

'Yes, most Italian boys are.' Cara paused. 'But I thought you said you were in love with the boy in London – Robin?'

'I am. But sometimes it's hard to be in control of …' he shook his head theatrically … 'lustful feelings.'

'Oh Tony! So, he didn't take kindly to your nighttime cuddling? I'm sorry to laugh, but …'

'Well, at first I wasn't sure. It's not as if he pushed me off or told me to piss off. He lay there – quite rigidly, I have to say – but I thought that meant he didn't mind, or even that he liked it.'

Cara resisted the urge to ask exactly what it was Angelo might have liked.

'So, I got a bit more confident, and I sort of … nuzzled … a bit more …'

'Nuzzled?'

'Yes. That's when he completely overreacted. He did push me off and I lost my balance and fell to the floor of the carriage on my back – it hurt, and I told him there was no need to be so aggressive, but I also kind of laughed …'

'Laughed?'

'It was just a nervous reaction, but he thought I was laughing at him. He was shouting stuff in Italian that I didn't understand, and he slapped me really hard across the face. Then he grabbed hold of my hair and it was as if he had gone mad, punching and kicking me … Perhaps he had drunk too much. I kept trying to calm him down, but he wouldn't listen. I mean he had only needed to tell me to stop, I wasn't going to bloody rape him.' Tony looked at her with helpless, pleading eyes.

'I'm sorry,' was all she could think of saying, but it was heartfelt. She had never seen him like this. It was unbearable to witness his hurt, both mentally and physically, and at some level she felt Angelo had hurt her too.

Tony sighed. 'I suppose I had it coming …'

'No … don't say that … you didn't deserve that …'

'Anyway, I managed to grab my knapsack and find my way here. Took me a while, I kept getting lost.'

'Didn't anyone help you?'

'It was cold and two o'clock in the morning. No one was around.'

'So where is your knapsack?'

'Left it downstairs. Didn't have the energy to bring it up. I'm feeling better now so I'll go …'

'I'll come with you. Then I'm going to make the other bed for you, and we'll think about what to do once we've slept.'

She was taking control. That was good. But once she was back in her own bed her mind began wandering again to unpleasant memories of Gianni joking about '*finocchi*', dancing around her with limp wrists.

It was past noon when she woke, but the door of the second bedroom remained resolutely closed. She would let him rest. On the kitchen table she left a scrap of paper on which she had written, *I hope you feel better. Sleep as long as you can and help yourself to anything to eat. I'm expected at Nicoletta's house for lunch, so see you later.*

The city was slowly coming back to life. There was much still left to do, but the sweeping, clearing and hosing during the last two weeks had paid off. The mud was thinner, and the streets easier to walk through. Shopkeepers had rediscovered their sense of humour and some had hung ironic signs in their windows. One near Santa Croce announced, 'Sufferers from rheumatism / For the best cure / Mud from the Via dell'Anguillara / Our mud deposits are open / Modest prices.' Other shop-owners stood patiently behind stalls piled high with damaged linen and household goods. On one there was a mountain of odd shoes. What hope did they have of selling? Cara couldn't imagine any Florentine housewife wanting to buy any of it. But hope was the thing everyone clung on to. They shared the memory of war, of German occupation. Recovery was possible, and it would get better again. It had to.

Teresa, as always, had prepared a good lunch. Today it was one of Cara's favourites, chicken with winter vegetables, simple but delicious. Yet she felt distracted, picking at the food on her plate, making little effort at conversation with Sandro and Raffaele. All she could think about was Tony.

Nicoletta noticed. 'Are you unwell, my dear?'

'Hmmm? Oh, I am sorry, it is nothing.'

The lunch lurched on. It reminded Cara of the early days, when she felt so out of place eating with strangers in this elegant Italian dining room, served by a maid, missing home, missing Tony. And now he was across the city, lying alone in their aunt's flat. Where would he go?

'You look – how you say … that word you tell me. Grumpy.'

'Yes, Sandro.' She smiled sadly. 'It is a good word. But "grumpy" can mean cross, and I am not cross. There is an English word, glum. Or even better, the expression "out of sorts". That is how I feel today. Glum and out of sorts.'

'Out-of-sorts,' Sandro repeated slowly. 'Glum?'

'You know what "sad" means?'

'*Triste.*' Raffaele joined in.

Yes, she was *triste*. Here she was giving an English lesson, but the word alluded to real emotion. All she wanted to do was break down and cry.

'Boys, why don't we leave it for today? You can get down from the table. I think we are all rather tired. Cara, I'll tell Teresa to bring us coffee next door. Come.'

Cara knocked back the espresso in two gulps and sat upright as if the caffeine had given her an immediate jolt.

'You are not yourself today.' Nicoletta was concerned. 'Are you still worried about your mother?'

Cara looked back at her employer. She had felt daunted by this sophisticated woman, and it struck her that at first she had reminded her of Tony's mother, Mrs Herrin. Nicoletta was a dark Italian version: slim, polite, self-possessed, slightly distant. There was something unreadable in the demeanour of both these women, as if they were concealing their true personalities.

'Well?' The coldness Cara imagined had gone. Nicoletta's expression was gentle. 'If there is something troubling you …'

It was the kindness in Nicoletta's eyes that disarmed her. Within a few minutes she had unburdened herself of everything: Gianni and Marcella, her love for Tony, his arrival in Florence, the events of the day before, his fight with Angelo, the confession. Nicoletta listened calmly and unemotionally. 'And where is Tony now?'

Cara felt like a schoolgirl about to be reprimanded. She could easily lie but couldn't think quickly enough.

'Is he still in my aunt's apartment?' Nicoletta sounded curious, not angry.

'Yes, I'm sorry, he will leave, it's only that it was so late, and he was hurt, there was nowhere else for him to go …'

'Shush … He must stay. And when he feels better, I should like you to bring him to lunch here. Teresa and the boys will think he is your boyfriend!' Her brown eyes twinkled.

'But … you are not angry with me? You are not shocked?'

'My dear girl, why would I be shocked?' She lowered her voice conspiratorially. 'Why do you think my husband hardly comes home? He has his own life in Milan. We have an agreement.'

'An agreement?'

She came even closer and breathed into Cara's ear, 'He likes young men.'

'Really?' Cara felt slightly uncomfortable. 'And you don't mind?'

'The marriage works that way,' she answered with a dismissive gesture. 'Our sons know he has to work in Milan because of his business.' She smiled. 'And I have my own arrangement.'

'Your own arrangement?' Cara seemed to be repeating everything, as she had done that first day she and Nicoletta met.

'You are so sweet, my dear! You will understand one day. Now, you must get back to Tony and check how he is.'

Cara hurried back. The route from Nicoletta's house to the apartment had seemed so long and complicated the first time she had made it, but she weaved her way through the familiar streets instinctively now, hardly noticing a thing. She was not distracted by the Renaissance architecture as she had been two months ago, and she had become used to the scenes of recovery in the flood-damaged streets. People went about their business, and she was going about hers.

Once in Via Laura and through the front door, she ran up the stairs two at a time, eager to tell Tony what Nicoletta had said. The ringing sound began as she reached the top-floor landing. Pushing open the apartment door, left unlocked to prevent him being trapped inside, she called out, 'Hey, Tony! The telephone is back,' dropping her bag on the chest in the hall and grabbing the receiver as quickly as she could. '*Pronto*? *Pronto*? Hello?'

'Hello, this is the operator, you have a telephone call from London.'

Cara's heart fluttered. 'Ma? Ma? Are you there?'

The operator responded in clipped British vowels. 'Just a moment, please. I am trying to connect you.'

Various mechanical sounds buzzed and clicked, and then Mary's voice. 'Cara?'

'Ma! The telephone is working at last.'

'Cara, it really is you? I've been trying and trying to get you, but the operator couldn't ever put me through. I needed to speak to you.' Her voice was wavering. Cara could sense her mother holding back her tears. 'I got your telegram, thank you, it was such a relief ...'

'I'm sorry, Ma, I'm really sorry ... I couldn't send you one before, the post office was closed. It's been such a mess here but I'm fine.'

'I was so worried. I was imagining all sorts ...'

'The apartment is on the top floor, I'm quite safe.'

Mary pulled herself together. 'So, Tony arrived and is well? I promised I would let Mrs Herrin know. I bumped into her in Gazzano's this morning. She was telling me about a report she had seen on the television, with Richard Burton talking about the flood. She said it looked very dramatic. There's been more in the newspapers here, but at first there was hardly any information. Now Florence is famous.'

'It *was* dramatic, yes. It still is really ...'

'But oh, my goodness, I'm so relieved you're safe, so relieved.'

'And Tony is well,' Cara lied.

'That's good. Well, I hope that's good.'

'Why wouldn't it be good? Anyway, I've been volunteering ...'

'I meant I wasn't sure whether you would be happy about seeing him again.' Mary left a short silence Cara did not fill, so she continued. 'What kind of volunteering have you been doing?'

'Helping out where I can. There is so much to be done to clean the works of art, and there are mountains of books and papers in the libraries that need drying out. Mud and oil have got into everything ...'

'Yes, Tony mentioned that.'

'You saw him before he left London, didn't you?' Cara lowered her voice because she didn't want Tony to overhear her. He might appear at any moment.

'I did see him. He said young people were coming into Florence from all over the world in order to help.'

'Yes, they are, even from America. But mainly they've come from all over Italy. Some of them are very nice.' She thought with regret of how she had pushed Lucia away yesterday after seeing Tony. 'There is a girl, Lucia, and her friends, and I owe them so much because ...'

Mary interrupted. 'It's wonderful to hear your voice.'

'And yours too.' She realised how much she missed her mother. There was still too much to catch upon, too much to ask. 'How's Geoffrey?'

'He's about to return from the bookshop,' Mary said quickly. 'I'd better go. He won't like me being on the telephone. International calls are expensive. I think that's him coming in now. You will write to me, won't you?'

'Yes, there's a letter on the way. Goodbye then.'

'Keep warm my love. Goodbye.'

Cara put the receiver down gently, as if otherwise it might break, and then she stood, still dressed in coat and boots, staring at the telephone for a bit longer, nostalgic for home. Finally, she lifted her head and began removing her coat and boots as she called out, 'Tony?'

No response. Perhaps he was still asleep. But no, he wasn't in the bedroom where she had left him. Nor in the kitchen. Nor the sitting room. It was as if he had never been in the apartment and she had imagined the whole thing. His bed was tidy, and the kitchen was cleared of the wine bottle they had finished during the night. There was no sign anywhere of his knapsack. The last room to check was her bedroom.

On the pillow was a note, filled with his inky scrawl.

I'm sorry to have been a nuisance. I'm going to try and find a hostel. For obvious reasons I don't want to go back to the station. Thank you for your help. I'll get in touch as soon as I've found somewhere.

She felt her spirits sink. There was more loneliness in the vacuum left by his departure than in the time before he had arrived. He must come back. She needed him to know that Nicoletta was happy for him to stay in the apartment with her. He didn't say when he had left. Her mind darted around the possibility of where he could be. Lucia would know where the hostels were. But Cara had no idea where she lived, apart from a sense of it being outside the city centre. It was already dark, and she had probably finished for the day and gone home.

She sat on her bed, defeated.

Propped on the writing desk in front of her was the red chalk *Daniel in the Lions' Den* she had come across months before, while looking through Signora Nomellini's possessions. She had placed it within one of the gilt frames found stored in another drawer, and although the frame was slightly too big, the glass served to protect the drawing. It enabled her to look at it without holding it in her hands. The bedroom was not large, and if the lid of the desk was open and she turned her head away from the wall she could see it when lying on her bed.

She had encountered so many extraordinary works of art in Florence. The Pontormo in Santa Felicitá, the Fra Angelico in San Marco, the Masaccio frescoes in the Carmine and this little jewel, right here in her bedroom, was one of her favourites. Every time she studied it she spotted new things within it – a ghostly face to the right, a decorative swirl to the left, a barely indicated head of a lion at the bottom of the page. The whole was drawn as if by the wind, with such an ethereal lightness of touch that it looked as if the red chalk had hardly touched the paper.

The figure of Daniel reminded her of Tony. A lithe and muscular physique was conveyed by his limbs and torso, but his head was turned away, the features blurred. He was like a person seen in a dream, a vaporous being, there but not there. She realised then that she would never be able to pin Tony down, and this was part of his appeal. He refused to be predictable or reliable. Every time she had him, he would slip away or confound her expectations. So why rush to catch him if he didn't want to be caught?

The letter Giovanna Nomellini's lover had signed 'Daniele' was stored in the writing-desk drawer.

You are the angel who will protect me in the lions' den.

She wanted to protect Tony. From situations like the one he had found himself in with Angelo. From potential rejection by his friend Robin back in London. From family misunderstandings and cruelty from the police; from older, predatory men. And at the core of this was the knowledge and sadness that of course she couldn't protect him, that it was none of her business, that she was simply an old friend who had no jurisdiction over him. Yet once they had been so close.

Perhaps it was a good thing that Tony was homosexual. During the summer his rejection and disappearance had felt like bereavement. But in different circumstances, in a different era, they might have ended up married and bored with each other by the time they were twenty. At least he had propelled her to make the break from Clerkenwell and discover Florence. And in some ways this city had been an awakening, a rebirth, a literal Renaissance. Death and Resurrection. She smiled at the power of a Catholic education. She carried it deep within her.

Later, as Cara distractedly chased little pasta stars around the broth with her spoon, the doorbell went yet again. She almost did not answer. Levering herself up, she felt as if her seized-up bones had absorbed all the dampness outside. My God, she was tired. By the time she had moved from the kitchen chair towards the door, the bell was ringing again, this time more insistently. She answered the intercom, but a voice came from the other side of the apartment door. 'It's me.'

Duffle-coated Tony was on the threshold, looking even more exhausted than she felt. A bruise had settled under his right eye, and his nose looked swollen.

'How did you get through the front door downstairs?'

'Some geezer was coming out as I arrived on the step. I told him I was your friend.'

'A geezer?'

'He had a felt hat and one of those coats a lot of Italian men wear.'

'It's called a *loden*, it's an Austrian coat. That must be Fernando Lotti. He lives in one of the apartments downstairs.' She noticed he was carrying his knapsack. 'I'm glad you've come back. Have you found a hostel?'

He didn't answer, throwing the knapsack down and following her into the kitchen.

'Soup?' she offered. 'I've made too much.'

He nodded. 'The thing is, if I could stay one more night … the hostel told me to come back tomorrow. Seems there are so many people needing a bed. With these bruises, maybe they thought I was a troublemaker, and didn't like the look of me. I'm so sore, it sorta threw me, that business with Angelo yesterday, and …'

'Of course, you can stay here tonight, in fact …'

'Thank you!' His face lit up. 'But I promise I'll be out of the way tomorrow. I was talking to a girl from London and she said there was a rich English woman who has offered a whole wing of her servants' quarters to British student volunteers, how about that?'

'If you'd let me finish ... you can stay here. For as long as you like.'

'Really? Are you sure?' Tony looked startled.

'Yes, I saw Nicoletta today, and she said you could.'

'But that's fantastic!' He pushed his chair back and jumped up to hug her as she was using the ladle to pour soup into his bowl.

'Hang on, you're making me spill everything! Let's celebrate tomorrow. I'm so tired I can't wait to lie down.'

'Me too.' He peered into the bowl she had handed over. 'Strange soup ...'

They spent the next two days in their respective bedrooms, occasionally bumping into each other in the corridor on the way to the bathroom or the kitchen. He seemed exhausted and Cara was happy to leave him to recover. She didn't feel well herself. For a while she had been feeling queasy, a general sense of nausea that was hard to ignore.

All she wanted to eat were the dry biscuits Fernando's wife had given her when no bread had been available. Occasionally even these would not stay down, and she took to keeping a washing-up bowl by her bed in case she needed to retch into it. On the third day, Tony knocked on her bedroom door and walked in with a steaming cup he placed on her bedside table. 'It's my turn to look after you. I've brought you some of your precious tea, but there's no milk. Are you any better?'

'It must be something I ate,' she said. 'It's not hard to get an upset stomach here. But you look brighter!' She peered into his face. 'And the bruising is hardly noticeable. Thanks for the tea.'

'I thought – if you feel better – that we might go out later. I'm hungry. And to see how we can lend a hand?'

'Yes, that's a good idea. I'll show you around. On the way back we can stop by the university canteen. And I need to find Lucia.'

They were approaching the vegetable shop in Via dei Servi when she felt ill again. She stood still to catch her balance and Tony, seeing her swaying, took her arm to steady her.

'I'm sorry, I feel faint, I must sit down. Let's ask Beppe …' she said, pointing towards his shop. A few minutes later Beppe had found an old wooden chair for her and given them both a banana.

'The colour has come back to your cheeks, Car. You needed food. I did too, I think! *Grazie*,' Tony grinned, turning to Beppe to pass the empty banana skin.

'Mio amico inglese,' Cara said, realising she hadn't made the introduction. It seemed an inadequate explanation, Tony was so much more than simply, 'my English friend', but how else to explain him? And after they left Beppe – thanking him profusely when he refused to accept any payment – this question would come back to her with a forceful blow.

They walked on, arms linked, as had been their habit in London, and Cara talked. As they passed the outside of the Uffizi, she pointed out that it had looked like a murky swimming pool was running alongside it. Now that the water had drained away outside, and been pumped out of the inside, the covered portico was being used as storage for piles of damaged papers, in boxes stacked all along the length of the outside corridor. Generally, she said, the sights were not as dramatic as they had been two weeks before because so much had been cleared, or at least piled to the side of the roads, but she described the eerie visions she had seen: mannequins swept out of shop windows and lying like corpses around the Cathedral;

cars piled on top of each other as if thrown around like toys. She told him where the water had reached, from basements and sub basements to second floor windows. Tony listened to it all, riveted.

Cara had begun to list some of the famous buildings that had been most badly affected and was explaining about the damage inflicted on the Baptistry doors, when abruptly, she stopped.

'*Buongiorno*,' a young man said, blocking the path in front of them. The voice was familiar, but cold, formal even. Cara hadn't noticed him walking towards them because she was so busy talking to Tony, but there, standing on the narrow pavement, wrapped in a black coat and scarf, was Gianni.

'*Ciao!* You are out of hospital,' she observed, unhooking her arm from Tony. '*Mio amico inglese. Di Londra*,' she explained, slightly uneasily. Tony and Gianni acknowledged each other with a brief nod. 'And how is Ilaria?' she continued. 'And your sister?'

Gianni did not respond. Upright and very still, he was staring at her as if she were not a sentient being but a work of art, a sculpture that needed examining. He was scanning her body with his eyes – this body that a few weeks ago he had caressed – as if she was a museum exhibit that he was not allowed to touch. At any moment she felt he might walk behind her to check her out in the round.

'Where are you going?' she asked, trying to sound bright, untroubled.

'*Da Stefano*. We are arranging my mother's funeral. Her body is still in the morgue.'

'I see …' She gulped and turned to Tony to explain. 'Gianni's mother died – tragically,' she stammered, 'in the – that is – in the flood …'

'Oh no, I am so sorry,' said Tony, but Gianni flinched before the arm outstretched in sympathy could reach him. Tony slowly drew it back.

'Yes, it is a tragedy,' Gianni said coolly. 'Now, I must get to Stefano, I'm late. *Arrivederci.*' He nodded like a soldier, clicking his heels, and stepped off the pavement to pass them by.

Tony turned to watch him walk away. 'Poor man. Losing his mother like that. But you'd think they would have had the funeral by now, wouldn't you? It's been three weeks since the flood. I suppose everything has got delayed ...'

Cara frowned. All she could think about was the chilling, appraising stare which Gianni had given her, and then Tony. He had looked at her as if she was a stranger, or an acquaintance he was trying to place. There was no warmth left in his eyes.

'Car.' Tony was threading his arm back through hers. 'You look so upset ... I think you need to tell me who that man is. Hang on, is that your lover ...?'

They decided against lunch in the university canteen that day. It was where many of the volunteers congregated, and they wanted to be left alone. Instead they went into a nearby *cantina* and sat at a wooden table eating cheese and salami stuffed between thick slices of Tuscan bread. Over small glasses of red wine, Cara told Tony more about Gianni and what had happened to Marcella during the night they had spent together. And the aftermath.

Tony waited until she had finished. 'You are not responsible. Gianni isn't either. Neither of you were to know what would happen. It is not his fault that his mother died. And it's certainly not yours.'

'Well I am at fault, in a way. I kept him away from his mother that night, and if he had been with her, he might have saved her. I feel I should be punished. And now he's going to marry Ilaria ...'

'That marriage is happening only to punish himself and fulfil his mother's wish. Can't you see he wants to stop feeling guilty?

To be pardoned in some way. And to lessen that guilt he's also punishing you.'

'I don't know. Now even his cousin hates me ...' And Cara told him how angry Stefano had been when they had met outside Marcella's house, and when, with Lucia, she had entered his bar. 'I haven't had much luck with men so far, have I?' she said, finally.

'No, you haven't. But you're only eighteen. And I still care about you.'

'Yes, but not in that way ...' It felt good to be able to say anything to Tony, including a reference to their loving but unromantic bond.

'Don't despair, there's always Beppe!' Tony lifted his eyebrows in jest, and they laughed together for the first time in days.

Lucia looked concerned. 'I'm glad you're back,' she said to Cara, after a quick nod to Tony. 'But you look tired. Are you sure you're better?'

'I think it was a stomach thing,' Cara replied, not admitting that she was still nauseous.

'I'm sorry. Do you think you'll be able to come with us to the Teatro Comunale on Sunday? They are putting on the first performance since the flood.'

'That's special. What is it?'

'Monteverdi's *L'incorazione di Poppea.*'

'Great.' Cara looked unenthusiastic, knowing little of opera. But when they discussed it later, Tony was keen. ('I've never been to an opera before,' he said.) And the tickets were cheap, so two days later they went along.

In the foyer, she spotted Nicoletta, who, together with Raffaele, was talking to a man in his forties with receding hair and a hooked nose. For a second, Cara wondered if this was the man with whom Nicoletta had her 'arrangement'. Just as she decided this was unlikely – there was an air of formality between them – Nicoletta turned around. 'Cara!' She went to kiss her on both cheeks. 'And this must be …'

'Yes, this is Tony. Tony, this is Nicoletta.'

Nicoletta kissed him on both cheeks too and introduced Raffaele. 'I'm afraid Sandro did not want to come, but you will meet him next week over lunch at our house. I'm sorry …' She looked around but the man she had been talking to had gone. 'I wanted you to meet Remigio Paone, he is the director of music. He is truly remarkable. He has worked tirelessly to make the winter programme begin on time. We still do not have drinking water and there are still problems …'

'And yet,' Tony finished her sentence for her, 'we have music!'

Nicoletta smiled sadly. 'Yes, but look at all the damage …'

Hanging on the walls around them were photographs of the wrecked interior they were standing in, taken immediately after the flood, showing a tangle of damaged furniture, costumes and musical instruments in pools of water and mud. Still present and propped around the foyer was a ruined orchestra made up of disfigured instruments, from warped pianos to broken string and wind instruments. It was a mess of splintered wood and twisted metal.

But in the auditorium the atmosphere was celebratory. The audience was composed mostly of young people like Tony, who had arrived in the city to volunteer. Many were still wearing their rubber boots, as the streets were still '*fangosi*', wet and slippery from the mud, and the floors of the theatre itself were damp.

Before the performance began, Signor Paone stood in front of the curtain and made a welcome speech, informing the audience that only one of the basement areas had so far been pumped out. 'We are the only theatre in the world to have our own downstairs swimming pool,' he said.

Tony whispered into Cara's ear. 'Look at the curtain.' Far above the floor a dark line clearly marked the level the Arno had reached.

'These long lines are all over the city streets,' Cara answered, 'like markers. Reminders.'

The heating plant had been replaced so it was not cold, but Cara still shivered. She felt comforted by Tony's proximity, and couldn't quite believe he was sitting next to her. She wanted to huddle close and hold his hand in the way she used to do during those trips to the cinema in London. How ironic – now that the situation was clear between them – that she could not bring herself to touch him. She must just enjoy his presence in Florence, and at this moment, focus on the performance.

It was far better than she had expected. The costumes had been sent from La Scala in Milan, and the seats for the orchestra had been rented from a nearby cinema. There was no scenery. But the 'making do' aspect did not affect the performances or dent the audience's enthusiasm. Cara understood nothing of the sounds the singers were making, and yet she was moved. It was not stuffy and boring as she had feared, and the audience was engaged and responsive.

The end of the opera was met with a standing ovation. The calls for an encore filled the space with a collective roar and Cara stole a glance at Tony who was joining in with gusto. Later, after they had said their goodbyes to Nicoletta, Raffaele, Lucia and friends, and were on their walk home, he seemed lost for words.

'That was fabulous,' was all he managed. 'I've never seen anything like it.'

'You know,' Cara said the next morning over breakfast, 'it's all very well to go to concerts and worry about the art treasures, but perhaps we should be helping with more urgent things, like getting people's essential living conditions in order. Look at Beppe. He hasn't stopped working in order to put his shop back together. Think of the families with nowhere to sleep or cook or …'

'You've got a kind heart, Car, but those families are getting help. You can't move across a piazza without bumping into trucks bringing in provisions and there are people cleaning and polishing everywhere. Even the shops and restaurants are reopening. The thing is, I've come here because of the art and …'

Cara grinned, 'Not because of me?' It was so easy to slip back into flirtatious banter.

'Well, yes, of course, and obviously because of you. But seriously, aren't there a few pert marble bottoms I can get my hands on?'

'That's you being serious?' Cara laughed. 'You're right. To be honest I'm bored with passing books along human chains and sweeping mud out of doors. Let's see if we can find something more interesting. Wouldn't mind some pert marble bottoms myself.'

Over the next few days Tony threw himself into researching what was going on in the city. Cara was impressed by his ability to chat to anyone, either in English or in the broken Italian he had picked up in Clerkenwell. What he didn't know how to say he conveyed with hand gestures and facial expressions. Nicoletta, Raffaele and Sandro took to him immediately, as did Fernando. '*Un Angelo del Fango biondo*,' Fernando said when Cara formally introduced them. Within a few minutes an invitation to supper had been issued so that the blond angel might meet the whole Lotti family.

Lucia took them to a small eaterie in Via delle Belle Donne. Just the road name made Tony laugh. '"Street of Beautiful Women" – that sounds more glamorous than "Farringdon Road", doesn't it?'

The tavern was run by a short and hairy Communist whose name they never learnt. There were just seven tables in two tiny rooms, but they usually had no problem in finding a space. The meal rarely varied from a plate of pasta, followed by a cutlet of meat or fish, and the whole meal, with a small carafe of red wine, could be got for less than 600 Lire.

Even cheaper was the university canteen, also frequented by volunteers. It was here that a friend of Lucia's talked them through the problems faced by conservationists: how the priming layer of glue and gesso on many masterpieces had been dissolved by the floodwaters and the colours had run. Sections swelled and buckled; others cracked. Like a patient developing symptoms days after diagnosis, works of art that at first had seemed undamaged later developed blisters. As for the frescoes, those entrancing Bible stories Cara had studied in churches all over the city had been badly affected. Even if the water hadn't reached the images themselves the humidity had seeped into the walls and left salt deposits on the surface of the paintings.

Many of the works that could be lifted had been taken to the Limonaia in the Boboli Gardens, where special atmospheric conditions were created. Cara and Tony, together with Lucia and other volunteers, continued to help transport hundreds of panels to this 'hospital', laying them down gently under sheets of rice paper to wait for assessment and restoration. Recuperating amongst these was Donatello's gaunt *Penitent Magdalene*, a wooden sculpture rescued from the Baptistry. She had been laid on a foam mattress and driven very gingerly – they learnt later – by an English 'Mud Angel', with the *Magdalene*'s delicate bare feet sticking out from the boot of his borrowed Land Rover.

Tony was keen to work in the Bargello, the museum that housed the most important collection of Florentine Renaissance sculpture. That, in terms of restoration, had been given a lower priority than the panel paintings and frescoes.

'I'm going to find out what's going on,' Tony announced one day as they ate lunch at Nicoletta's house.

'That is a good idea,' said Nicoletta. 'I know the *soprintendente* – how you say – the director, Luciano Berti. He has an English young man working with other volunteers in the basement. A lot of important sculpture was affected and …'

Tony interrupted. 'Michelangelo's *Bacchus*?'

'Yes, and his *Brutus*. And his terracotta models. And there are so many other masterpieces there. Donatello, Verrocchio. At least most were submerged rather than smashed up. But the *naphta* – the dark heating oil – is so destructive.' Nicoletta seemed lost for further words.

Tony shook his head in dismay. 'And the oil won't wipe off from the marble, will it?'

Nicoletta shook her head. 'There is Greek marble and there is Carrara marble. Some marble is more like stone, but Carrara is – how you say …'

'Porous?'

'Yes, as porous as blotting paper. It is not just a matter of removing the oil from the surface. It sinks inside leaving ugly shadows.'

Normally Cara would have been as interested in this information as Tony, but she heard hardly a word of what was being said. In fact, since Tony had joined Nicoletta's lunches, she barely spoke, leaving it to him to make 'English conversation'. During the last month Nicoletta and the boys had become much more fluent, it seemed hardly necessary to guide them. But the truth was, she had lost her energy. She was constantly below par.

It was Teresa who commented on her looking sickly that day. She had come around the table to replace the dishes and noticed that Cara had scarcely touched her food. And that she hadn't moved her arm to make space for Teresa to remove the plate in front of her.

'*Stai male*?' Teresa asked quietly.

Nicoletta overheard. 'Yes, my dear, you have hardly eaten. Are you unwell?'

Cara forced a smile. 'Oh, I'm sorry …' Everyone's eyes were boring into her. 'I'm just tired. Probably too much wine last night!'

Tony looked concerned. 'But you barely drank last night. It's true, you do look peaky.'

'Please, I'm all right. Really. Tony, let's stop at the Bargello on the way home.'

Soprintendente Berti was leaving as they arrived. A short man, cigarette in mouth, trilby pushed to the back of his head, he replied to Tony's query by saying, 'Patrick is in charge, speak to him. You will find him in there,' pointing to the room on their right. It turned out that Berti had been so impressed by the gallant rescuer of Donatello's *Magdalene* that he had given him the ground floor of the Bargello to set up a workshop.

'I already have a team of seven volunteers,' Patrick said when Tony began pleading with him to take him on.

'Please, I'm a conservation apprentice, and my boss Mr Lengyel says I'm a quick learner and a hard worker. And sculpture is my special interest.' He flashed his most endearing smile.

How will he resist that look, Cara thought.

Patrick looked at them both. He was only in his early twenties himself. 'But there are two of you,' he pointed out.

'Don't worry about me,' Cara said weakly. The thick smell of solvents that had hit her when she walked into the room was beginning to make her feel woozy. She wiped her hand over her face, trying to compose herself, to be in control of the sensation. But the nausea was rising, and in a moment of panic she couldn't tell what would happen first: would she faint or be sick? She must not be sick, she had to tell them that she felt unwell, that she needed air, that Tony would be perfect for the team, that Patrick didn't have to take her on as well, that she would find something else, but that right now she needed to lie down. She bit her lip. Then there was ringing in her ears, getting louder, and then the tingling in her hands had turned into no feeling at all.

'It's not humiliating,' Tony said later. 'You fainted, that's all. It happens.'

'Well it doesn't happen to me. I've never fainted before in my life. You can't believe how embarrassing it was to wake up with you and Patrick peering at me from above. I don't know what the hell is wrong with me.'

And yet really, she did.

Cara knew she had to pretend for one more day before she did or said anything about it. It was Tony's nineteenth birthday and, as it fell on a Sunday, they had decided to pack a bag with salami and bread for a picnic on the move – too cold to stop – and walk to Bellosguardo in the hills just outside Florence. Gianni had taken her to the area when the weather had been warm and she still liked going there when she wanted to escape the city.

Less than one hour's walk from the apartment, climbing steeply uphill, the city turned into a maze of narrow, high-walled lanes dotted with villas, whose boundaries were occasionally broken by vistas of olive groves and cypresses below. Slowly Cara and Tony made their way, occasionally stopping to catch their breath or look at a view. Lads on Vespas circled past them as Tony explained the properties talcum powder had in removing stains from marble.

'You know what people do in Italy when you get spaghetti sauce on your clothes,' he was saying. 'The waiter comes to your rescue with talcum powder and throws it all over you.'

Cara nodded distractedly but was thinking about something else.

'You know, the one that comes in a green flask called *Borotalco 'Roberts'*? You have to let it dry before brushing it off. Anyway, it works because the primary component of talc is a dolomitic mineral, it's used in stain removers you can buy in England like ...' He stopped mid-sentence. 'You've disappeared. You're not listening to a word I'm saying.'

'What? Oh, sorry. Miles away.'

She felt queasy again. Her legs felt full of lead and her breasts were tender and heavy.

'Shall we stop and eat our sandwiches?'

The thought of eating anything made her feel worse. The unpleasant mix of hunger and nausea wouldn't leave her.

'Car, I really think you should ask Nicoletta for the name of a doctor. You haven't seemed very well since I arrived. Perhaps you're doing too much with Lucia?'

It was true. While Tony was occupied in the Bargello, Cara had continued to work shovelling mud and clearing debris out of various university faculties. She was fed up with it, and suddenly felt overcome with resentment.

'It's all right for you and your marble bottoms,' she said. '*I'm* not restoring anything. I don't even get close to any works of art. I'm just a glorified Mrs Mop ...'

Tony put his arm around her. 'What is it, Car? You've also become very moody. Something is bothering you. You can't hide it. I know you too well.'

'No, you don't. You don't know me at all. No one knows me. Oh, Christ. And now it's starting to rain. I'm so sick of this ... I never thought it would rain so much in this bloody place.' She was on the verge of tears, and Tony could see it.

'Come on. Let's go back, downhill. Forget the views, the sandwiches … my birthday.'

'I'm sorry, it's just … Well, as I seem to be swearing a lot today, here we go–'

'Here we go?'

'Yes, here we go. I think I'm bloody pregnant.'

'I know it seems crazy. It was only that one night.'

They were sitting next to each other on the sofa back in the apartment, hands around the last of the tea, but Cara was hardly drinking.

'Grandma Nora is always going on about me being a miracle because she only had Ma. And Ma took so long getting pregnant and had no other children after me. And now this is happening, the first and only time …' She snorted with outrage. 'It's like a punishment for losing my virginity! I'm going to end up going to some witch in a back street and I'll bleed to death, while that bastard has his perfect wedding in San Miniato with the beautiful Ilaria and lives happily ever after. I don't even care about him, but it's not fair …'

Tony squeezed her arm. 'The first thing you need to do is to have it confirmed. Then you have to decide what to do. Let's be calm …'

'It's not your bloody baby, is it?'

'Yeah, but I feel I'm in this with you.' Tony's expression changed as if something had struck him. 'It's really sad. I won't ever get the chance to have a child, will I?'

'You don't even like babies.'

'How do you know? I'd love to be a father.'

'Well, I'd love to be a mother, but not right now, I'm too young. How will it look, me coming back to London pregnant. Ma will be ashamed, Geoffrey disappointed …'

'You don't know that. Anyway, you may not be pregnant. You'll have to ask Nicoletta or Lucia what to do. I wonder what the word for pregnancy is, in Italian? Let's see.'

'But I don't want to ask for more help from either Lucia or Nicoletta. They've helped enough already.'

The dictionary said the word was *gravidanza*.

After Tony left for the Bargello the following morning, Cara walked straight to the hospital of Santa Maria Nuova, through the courtyard and into the building. She stopped a middle-aged woman walking along the corridor.

'Per l'esame di gravidanza?'

The unsmiling woman pointed to the right.

'Grazie.'

Cara cringed. There was something cold and unwelcoming about this hospital. Memories of visiting Gianni the month before weren't helping her nerves. Turning the corner, she glanced through an open door and saw a nurse standing at a table, dispensing pills.

'Scusi, esame di gravidanza?'

This nurse looked friendlier. *'Per lei?'*

'Si.'

The nurse reached for something on a low shelf and brought out a tiny container. After asking her questions about dates, the nurse explained she had to produce a urine sample, leave it with her, and return the following day.

'Well, who did you talk to? Did you see Lucia?' Tony asked that evening as they ate supper.

'I didn't see her. I went to the hospital this morning and have to go back tomorrow for the result.'

'Shall I come with you?'

'No, don't worry, that won't be necessary.'

Tony looked concerned. 'Have you thought about what you will do?'

'There's no point in planning anything until I know for sure, is there?'

'Will you tell Gianni?'

'As I said, I don't want to think about it until I'm sure.'

'Well, I've been thinking about it, Car. I haven't thought about anything else.'

Cara put her fork down and looked at him with a sense of utter despair. In that moment she loved him more than she had ever done before. He cared about her. He wanted the best for her. The awareness of this, combined with the knowledge that there was a part of him she had no access to, was almost unbearable. She wanted to tell him what she had been thinking all day: that she wished that he was the father of the life growing inside her, and that if this little being was real, she knew that she couldn't bear to let go of it. She had to tell him these two things, and after she had pushed away her food, between sobs, she did.

'I'm coming with you tomorrow,' was all Tony said.

They had left Via Laura and were walking to the hospital when Tony broke the silence. 'Thank God it's not raining again.'

Cara gave him a sidelong glance and smiled. 'I know what you mean.'

They carried on walking in silence for a couple of minutes.

'I didn't sleep last night, thinking.' Tony was looking straight ahead, occasionally stepping aside to let someone walk past on the narrow pavement.

'I didn't sleep either, trying not to think.'

'We're going to get married.' He said it bluntly, as a statement rather than a suggestion.

Cara stopped in her tracks and stared at him, stunned. 'Are you mad?'

'Probably. But look, if you are pregnant, I would like to be the father.'

She continued to stare at him, speechless. Finally, he turned towards her. 'We'll tell everyone we got engaged as soon as I arrived in Florence. Or even that we got carried away with the romance of Florence and married here. Isn't that what everyone expected anyway – I mean, that we would eventually marry? The pregnancy can be explained by our … um … celebrating the engagement?'

'You are definitely mad!' A huge smile had spread across her face.

'Definitely. A few unexplained weeks may raise a few eyebrows … but births can come early … Can't they? I don't really know about these things.'

She giggled. 'Don't you? You surprise me.'

'And if I ever marry anyone, it has to be you.'

Joy, Cara thought. *This is what joy feels like.*

Tony smiled. 'There's one condition though. We might need the occasional lodger.'

'I see!' Cara gave him a playful jab in the ribs. 'Perhaps we can start with a handsome young man called Robin?'

'You've understood me perfectly.'

They had reached the hospital. Cara gave her name to a receptionist in the out-patients clinic. She stood, with Tony holding her hand, looking around at the men and women waiting to be called in for blood tests and vaccinations. Middle-aged women accompanying elderly parents, a few mothers with children. A young woman about Cara's age glanced up and smiled before turning back to her magazine. Was she putting them together, Cara wondered, did she presume Tony was her husband? Instinctively she covered the lack of a wedding ring on her finger with her right hand.

The receptionist walked briskly out from behind the counter, her heels echoing in the cold, clinical room, and gave Cara an envelope. She took it in her hands, feeling the urge to rip out the contents but holding back until they were outside. Tony put his arm around her as she opened it.

Her palms were sweating, despite the cold day. Silently she passed Tony the piece of paper after reading the words,

Esame di Gravidanza
Positivo.

LAURA'S DIARY

Clerkenwell

1 NOVEMBER 2016

Funny how we are all only children: Grandma Mary, Ma, me, Helen.

Only girls.

Sometimes, when I was younger, I missed having a sister or a brother and thought that, when the time came, I would break the mould and have a large family. But it has not happened. I followed suit and produced a daughter, and my age suggests it's unlikely I shall ever change the pattern.

That's no bad thing. I don't agree with the common perception that an only child is a spoiled and lonely creature, over protected by their mother from an early age. My mother Cara was never like that with me, and I've certainly never been like that with Helen. In fact, the opposite – if anything – is the case. Cara spent much of my childhood doing her own thing, and I was busy working when Helen was young, so I don't think we can be accused of anxious, fussing, over-present parenting.

The men have all left. First to go was my grandfather. We always called him Geoffrey – in our family fathers go by their first name. He died of pneumonia one cold winter when I was twenty-one. His health was never very good, gammy leg and all, so it's amazing he lasted even that long. My father Tony separated from my mother when I was very young, and lives as a gay man in France. I go and stay with him and his partner Robin and we all get on well, but I don't see them often enough. Then there is my 'ex', Richard, who has reconstituted our shared intimacy with someone else half my age. To be honest I feel no antagonism or outrage towards the woman who replaced me. The relationship had run its course and he's been a good father to Helen, which is the main thing.

Grandma Mary is dying. I'm sure of it. She had her fall a few months ago, and since she has been living in the care home she seems different somehow. Tired, depleted, resigned, as if she has given up on life. Every time I visit, I find her more faded. This is painful for me as we have always been so close. During the upheavals of my childhood she offered more security than my mother did, that's for sure.

I need to begin to distance myself, to record, to document. Perhaps, when she is older Helen will be ready to read this and by doing so will understand more about the tribe of women she comes from.

When I was a child, Grandma Mary listened to me and offered a sense of stability when it was in short supply. She spent her whole married life in the same house – the one Grandpa Geoffrey inherited from his parents during the war. The biscuits I loved as a little girl – chocolate Bourbons and Custard Creams – were kept in a big rusty tin with a picture of a robin on the front that she told me had been given to Geoffrey's mother one Christmas. It seems sad that she stepped into her inlaws' house without ever creating one of her own, but she has never complained about this, or about anything else. She is of that generation, stoically resigned to what life has thrown at her.

Mary's care home is a good one. It doesn't have that institutional smell of urine and cabbage, like some. But it's dispiriting to notice how her health is failing, how her arthritis-riddled fingers bend in strange ways, how the skin on her face has become so thin, stretched over bone. I wish I could press a pause button to keep her from diminishing further.

Ma is trying to sell Mary's house to raise more funds for the care-home fees. I understand why, but it pains me to think of some young professional couple coming in and ripping the whole place apart. Clerkenwell is desirable now, but Mary's brown furniture and pokey kitchen certainly don't fit with a fashionable lifestyle. And secretly I fear that Mary will be gone well before any sale goes through.

I visit her more often than Ma does. I like going there because she always seems pleased to see me, and most of the nurses are friendly. 'Look who is here, Mary!' they shout, leaning into her good ear, and she protests, 'I'm not that deaf, you know.'

After we have said hello, I take Mary's arm and help her hobble into a side room, away from the loud, repetitive moaning made by some of the other more demented residents. Once we are settled in the plastic-covered armchairs, I pull a treat from my bag: always the day's newspaper because she still likes reading. I add the occasional box of soft-centred chocolates, or some new soap or hand cream. The other day I brought in a hand-knitted shawl I had found in a charity shop to put round her shoulders. She is constantly complaining of the cold and the tips of her fingers are permanently white, despite the centrally heated stuffiness she lives in.

'You're like Mary Poppins, with that big bag, you are,' she says with the gentle London-Irish lilt she's never quite lost.

Today Grandma was wearing her usual grey cardigan that – like her – has seen better days. I must get her a new one for Christmas. It looks bobbly and baggy, the way it hangs on her thin, depleted body. There's nothing of her, but I suppose it's hard to eat much when you've only got one tooth. At one point today she turned to me and said, 'Never get old,' and I had to agree with the sentiment.

She is ninety-four years old. If I live that long it means I'm over halfway through already. I'll be celebrating half a century next birthday. Nine months to go.

5 NOVEMBER 2016

I went to visit Grandma Mary together with Helen, who is on 'reading week' from university (although it has to be said she doesn't seem to be doing much reading). Grandma was a bit confused at first but didn't look too bad. She has been given a new haircut, a kind of bob, the silvery hair kept in place with two hair slides on either side such as a little girl might wear.

We helped Mary transfer from her 'walker' – a kind of zimmer-frame with basket attached – into the armchair in a corner of the room, as far as possible from the blaring television. We drew two other chairs beside her. Ma arrived unexpectedly, so we pulled up a fourth chair and composed ourselves into a curious, circular huddle comprised of me, leather-jacketed Helen, grey-cardiganed Mary, and Ma in black ankle boots and Puffa coat. She looks good for sixty-eight, no wonder people often ask if we are sisters.

Flanked by this small female clan, I was filled with melancholy. It was as if all four generations were lost in some way, brought together in this moment, but remaining separate. Grandma slightly away with the fairies, Ma distant, Helen distracted by her mobile phone. And me? God knows. I don't know how I feel half the time, just that I'm going nowhere. But enough of that.

My mother's face was tense. She had unzipped the coat but kept it on, as if she were briefly stopping on her way to somewhere else. Instinctively, I experienced an irritated 'why do you bother to come at all if you don't want to be here?' moment but brushed it away and turned to Grandma.

'I brought you the newspaper,' I said, reaching for my bag, 'but I see you haven't finished the last one.' Grandma Mary has a tendency to stockpile the newspaper cuttings she wants more time to peruse, tearing the pages out and preventing the nurses from throwing them away, even when we all know she will never get around to reading them. She piles them up in a neat stack in the basket of the walker and every so often the nurses throw some away when she isn't looking.

'Yes, did you see?' She pointed at the top of the pile, suddenly appearing full of brightness and energy. 'It was the fiftieth anniversary of that flood in Florence yesterday, the paper had an article about it.'

I could just read the headline: *Florence Flood 50 Years On: The world felt this city had to be saved.*

I turned towards Ma, who was frowning. 'Of course! That's when you and Tony were there, wasn't it? Being volunteers?'

Tony has sometimes alluded to this time but whenever Florence or that period in her life is mentioned, Ma tends to change the subject. This time she ignored me. This wouldn't have bothered me, but for what happened next. Out of nowhere she pushed the chair away with such force that it fell over and knocked a little side table to the floor. I jumped up, righting the furniture as she stormed out of the room.

'That was a bit random. What's up with her?' Helen said, looking up from her phone. 'She only just got here. Shouldn't you go after her, Mum?'

Grandma shook her head. 'Let her be.' There was something in her expression that I hadn't seen before.

16 NOVEMBER 2016

Just got back from seeing Grandma. I'm reeling.

We were sitting side by side in silence when she suddenly said, out of the blue, 'You know, Geoffrey was not your real grandpa.'

I looked at her, wondering if what she had just said was a symptom of her disordered mind.

'Are you feeling all right, Grandma?'

She bristled. 'People have been asking me if I'm all right my whole blinking life. Yes, I'm absolutely all right. You heard what I said, didn't you? *I'm* supposed to be the deaf one, not you!'

So, I asked her about the photograph of her wedding day, the one of her and Geoffrey standing outside the Italian church in Clerkenwell in 1945. The one I remembered as a child that sat on her mantelpiece and is now on her bedside table.

'Your ma brought that one in.' She said it dismissively. 'Thought I'd like to have something from home. To be honest, I never much liked it. I put it in a drawer after Geoffrey died but Cara fished it out again.'

I was speechless. Then, as if amused by my expression, Grandma giggled like a girl. 'You look shocked! Oh, Laura. Being married doesn't mean my husband had to be your ma's father, you know …'

A pause while I took this in. 'What are you saying?'

She just smiled, enjoying my reaction.

I insisted. 'Grandma! If it wasn't Geoffrey, who was it?'

But it seemed like she had said enough for the time being. When I asked her whether Cara knew 'who on earth was her real father', she just shrugged. 'Your ma has her own secrets, you can be sure of that.' She fixed me with her watery eyes, crunching up her collar with her bony left hand, and said, 'We all had our secrets then. It's different now. But in times past, you had to hide the shame.'

She blinked, and added as an afterthought, 'You couldn't let anyone see.'

18 NOVEMBER 2016

Yesterday I went to see Ma. But I can't get anything out of her either. She didn't seem interested in Grandma's statement about Geoffrey. She only said, 'Hmm.'

'Hmm?'

How could she just say 'Hmm' about something so momentous? And when I asked what Grandma could have meant by her comment about Cara 'having her own secrets', all she answered was, 'Every family has their secrets. Only boring ones haven't.' Which, to be honest, was quite hurtful, as I haven't got any secrets. Or nothing significant.

Ma can be brittle sometimes. Since retiring a few years ago she seems by turn either depressed or angry. I thought she would be pleased to have more time to devote to her painting, but the studio room at the top of her house only gathers dust. She says, 'What's the point,' when I try to encourage her to paint. 'I've been nothing but an amateur, an art teacher, not even an art-college tutor.'

I hate that she thinks of herself as second rate, as not a 'true artist'. And I hate her saying it because it makes me feel the same about myself. I've not inherited her artistic talent, but I like to write. And I am a good administrator. I know I should stretch myself in order to have more job satisfaction but I hesitate at putting myself forward. Grandma was the same. Housewife and mother. Never putting herself first. Or perhaps she did put herself first, if Grandpa Geoffrey wasn't my real Grandpa?

Ma was more selfish. After she and Tony separated, she never settled down or had more children, though she had many lovers, both men and women. She wanted what she termed 'a feminist life', unshackled to the kitchen sink, as she perceived Mary had been. I can't blame her for wanting to be free, but I'm not sure her rootlessness made her any happier than Grandma had been.

1 DECEMBER 2016

I'm trying to lead Grandma into disclosing more. This project has become an obsession, I want to know everything. Helen suggested I record our conversations. Grandma seemed to be fine with that but I'm not entirely sure she understands that my phone lying on the table between us is recording what she has to say. I make written notes as well. When I get home, I transcribe our sessions and piece it all together.

She's been speaking quite candidly about her parents, about the war, about marrying Geoffrey. There are moments when she elaborates and then tries to rein it back as if sensing she has gone too far. But I believe that recounting her life to a sympathetic ear gives her a sense of release. She often reiterates that, in her day, women like her had to accept their fate, that there was nowhere to go to and no one to talk to, that she was powerless, in a way I wouldn't understand.

'But I am listening now, and I do understand,' I say.

10 DECEMBER 2016

I've been reading about that period of post-war austerity. It helps, because when I make a reference to rationing or cold winters, it can spark a memory. In those moments Grandma can describe a conversation as vividly as if she were reliving the moment again.

It's not easy. She gets confused and meanders, and I don't want to push her too hard. But she can be remarkably lucid when she gets into her stride. Today her face lit up when describing moments of happiness. It's as if we are painting a picture together.

I take care not to tire her out, but I get so wrapped up in her story that I want it to go on and on. This evening a nurse took me to one side and asked me to be careful because Grandma has been getting tearful after I leave. I must be more considerate.

22 DECEMBER 2016

The care home is full of tacky Christmas decorations. It's a bit depressing. We sit surrounded by tinsel and bright lights, but the decorations look as tired as the residents. I don't know why they bother.

Grandma's narrative is so poignant. When she spoke about her friend marrying her lover, I felt for her. It is made worse somehow that Elsie was innocent of the betrayal. Mary couldn't even be angry with her. All that holding in of guilt, and not being able to tell anyone. How difficult. No therapists in those days.

I've taken to referring to my notebook when she loses the thread, to get her back on track. And I'm trying to be sensitive to her moods, to sit with her in silence when she is quiet, allowing her to gather her thoughts or stay present with difficult emotions. Today, talking about her friend Elsie, her eyes filled with tears. Then she tried 'to pull herself together', as she would say.

'It wasn't all bad you know,' she said. 'I had my moments.'

27 DECEMBER 2016

Another Christmas is over. Grandma was going to stay with Ma, but when we went to collect her on Christmas Eve, she couldn't get out of bed. She looked even older, the wrinkles seeming deeper, the wisps of unruly grey hair framing her caved-in face. The nurses were of the opinion ('of the opinion'! I'm beginning to write like Grandma speaks) that she was too frail to leave the care home. So, we cancelled the taxi and left her there, returning after lunch the next day. This is the first Christmas she has not spent with us and it felt strange. All the stuff on the telly about families coming together, you can't get away from it, it just makes things worse.

Christmas lunch was a bit of a trial. Ma was irritable and Helen was constantly checking her phone – I think there is some boy lurking in the background with romantic intentions. Or maybe it's a girl. I have no idea. Anyway, the turkey was too big and none of us had room for the Christmas pudding. After coffee we opened our presents. Ma gave me a couple of exhibition catalogues that looked as if she'd already thumbed them, and from Helen I got the pen I'm writing with now, which actually is both useful and thoughtful.

And then we went to visit Grandma, but she was tired, so we didn't stay long. That was Christmas. It's never as good as you hope it will be. Sometimes you just want to sprout wings and fly away.

30 DECEMBER 2016

I want to engage Ma with my project, but I don't think she is very happy about it. Perhaps my deepening closeness to Grandma makes her feel left out. Or she's envious of this intimacy. It is a closeness that has been lost in their relationship.

I gave her more details about Grandma's revelations, but instead of saying 'Hmm' again, she said, 'I know. She explained everything when Tony and I separated.'

When I asked her why I was never told, she answered, 'We were afraid you would say something to Geoffrey.' Then she added, 'He never knew. Though I wonder whether he guessed. Things he said about me not resembling him …' She looked wistful, as if she was about to say more. But then she came back to the present and her tone changed. 'Anyway, you'd better ask *her* that question, hadn't you? You're the one doing the oral history …'

It was hurtful.

At least Helen, when she can tear herself away from her phone, does show some interest. Perhaps it's something to do with us being only children – we need to know where we come from.

4 JANUARY 2017

I've been to see Grandma every day to take advantage of the Christmas break, but I'll have to go back to work soon. I've decided I'm going to negotiate early retirement. I think I can do that. We shall see.

Grandma rallied a bit after Christmas, but I'm still worried about her. She's happy when she is lying down but complains about having to get up. I asked the nurse today why she couldn't just stay in bed, but they tell me she'll get bedsores unless she moves around.

I've got most of her story down and she is beginning to repeat herself, I should probably stop pressing her for details. Yet there are times when she can depict a scene so clearly: she and Elsie, the end of the war, Geoffrey. I can see it all unfolding in front of me like in a film.

16 FEBRUARY 2017

Grandma died on 6 February.

It feels so raw, even though it wasn't unexpected. A few days before she died, she virtually stopped eating and absolutely refused to leave her bed. We took turns, Ma and I, to sit beside her, but I'm not sure by the end she even knew we were there. I gently massaged her hands, trying to warm them, for they were so cold.

Neither Ma nor I were at her side when she finally went. The nurse persuaded me to go and rest, promising to telephone if there were any 'developments'. And a few hours later she did. Gone, peacefully, that's all one could hope for.

We gave her a good funeral at St Peter's, the Italian church where she was married. Tony and Robin travelled from France to join us. Rosa and Carlino, Pippo's siblings, who still live in Clerkenwell, came to pay their respects. I wanted to ask them about their brother and Elsie, but when the moment came, I lost my nerve.

After the funeral we invited everyone to Grandma's for tea and cake. The house was full of the neighbours and shopkeepers Mary had known for years. It was when they had left and we were clearing up that I found Ma in the kitchen, weeping into the remains of one of the cakes. Helen and I led her, as if she were a child, up to her old bedroom, laid her down on her childhood bed, and waited for the sobs to subside.

'I'm sorry,' she said to us both. 'I just couldn't bear for her to go. And the cake, it reminded me of her …'

'I know …' I said, feeling tearful.

'Me too …' said Helen, sniffing.

'You know, Laura …' Her eyes were pleading. 'I'm glad you got Mary's story down.'

'She seemed to need to tell it …'

'She did. There comes a time when we all do. One day I'd like to tell you the reason you are called Laura.'

What?

She gave a wobbly smile, taking a hanky out of her pocket to blow her nose. I offered her some water. She shook her head. 'Come on, let's get back downstairs and open some of that wine Tony brought from France.'

24 FEBRUARY 2017

I'm going to start recording with Ma this weekend. To mark the occasion, she has given me the most beautiful, delicate, red chalk drawing. A boy rests his arm on the head of a lion, with a mess of shapes behind, as if the artist is working on different poses, different faces, all on the same sheet. Nothing is easily discerned. So much like life.

'My God sent his angel, and he shut the mouths of the lions,' Ma says cryptically, when I ask her about it. I'm guessing the Bible. She tells me she was given the drawing by Nicoletta, the woman who employed her in Italy, as a wedding present for her and Tony when they left Florence. She has kept it in a drawer like a hidden treasure, to protect it from the light.

She wants me to have it now.

We've decided to conduct our conversations in Grandma's old parlour before the house is sold. I'm rather nervous about what Ma will say. Who knows where it will lead? I suppose memories, like rivers, find their own turn.